QUEEN OF THE EAST

Queen of the East

BY ALEXANDER BARON

IVES WASHBURN, INC.

New York

Edgell

NEN

✳
CI

TG

CONTENTS

1. THE FIRST MEETING: A PROLOGUE — 3
2. THE CENTURION — 16
3. THE CENTURION FORGES A NEW WEAPON — 22
4. "THAT WOMAN" — 36
5. THE SECOND MEETING — 63
6. RUFINUS — 80
7. AURELIAN ENTERS ROME — 94
8. THE BANQUET OF STATIANUS — 109
9. THE BATTLE OF THE MINT — 136
10. ROME KISSES AURELIAN'S FOOT — 157
11. PHILOMENE — 168
12. THE THIRD MEETING — 189
13. A WOMAN FIGHTS — 198
14. THE CHESSBOARD — 208
15. THE POISON WIND — 224
16. TWO PENNIES A DAY — 231
17. WHAT NOW? — 247
18. AT BAY — 249
19. THE FOURTH MEETING — 263
20. THE ACCOMPLICES — 277
21. WHOSE TRIUMPH? — 293
22. CONVERSATION ON A SPRING MORNING: AN EPILOGUE — 307

AUTHOR'S NOTE — 313

QUEEN OF THE EAST

CHAPTER ONE

THE FIRST MEETING: A PROLOGUE

ON AN April morning in the year two hundred and fifty-eight, a soldier rode eastward across the Syrian Desert.

He was tall, great-shouldered, massive of thigh, long-legged, so that beneath him his Spanish horse seemed small as a merchant's donkey. His head was held up arrogantly against the sun's glare. His profile, stamped dark against the painful brilliance, was fierce: lips clamped tight, thick eyebrows hunched, eyes cruelly intent upon the distance. He wore a modelled cuirass of brass upon which sunlight flared, a crested helmet, a sword, and the short scarlet cloak of a general fastened upon his left shoulder with a gold clasp. Despite the weight of his armour the sweat did not run off his skin but made a soft sheen that gave his face, burned and creased by the weather, the hue and smooth hardness of bronze. His name was Lucius Domitius Aurelianus. He was inspector-general of the armies of Rome, and he was riding towards the Euphrates on a mission for his emperor.

Half a mile ahead rode two scouts. Behind him marched a cohort of infantry, men of the Third Gallican Legion, which he had commanded until a few months ago. The baggage column followed, a bobbing line of camels. In the rear, a troop of cavalry moved in close column. Aurelian rode as if unaware that his troops were with him. The infantry marched in silence. Their throats were furred with dust. The heat made a burning weight of their gear, and itself lay upon them in an immense weight. Loneliness oppressed them. The desert was an empty floor beneath a vast sky. They had trudged across it for three days. Twice they had seen nomad horsemen, tiny figures on distant dunes, watching them. Once a caravan had passed, a black frieze on a distant skyline. Otherwise they had been alone in this furnace-heated world. Heat waves shimmered over red sand. Miles of dried mud glittered white in the sunlight, making swords of light to hurt their eyes. The soft, furnace-like breaths of wind from the northwest licked at the skin with a cat's-tongue roughness. Nothing grew but sparse grey patches of desert grass and thornbush. Sometimes a tiny jerboa darted away from them, as if obeying some spell of loneliness that lay upon them. Once, for hours, a solitary griffon vulture followed them high in the sky. Ranges to the north and south converged slowly as the soldiers marched. The shelved limestone changed in colour as the day's light waxed and waned—yellow, then red, then pale violet. By evening the weary column had crawled deep into the funnel of a shallow valley between the hills.

Aurelian rode like a dreamer, his mind busy with its calculations. He was almost halfway to the wide Euphrates, the frontier of Persia. Ostensibly he was going on a good-will mission. In fact he was conducting a reconnaissance. Next year there would be a war against the Persians. That was why Rome's emperor, Valerian, had sent the most hammer-blunt of his generals to play at being a diplomat. In three days—four, for tomorrow would be spent at a resting place—the comedy would begin.

The scouts were poised upon a hillock. One of them flung up his arm. A second later his faint, glassy cry floated back. Man and horse bunched up and shot down the hillside, raising a wake of dust.

Aurelian took the scout's salute and spoke with him. Then he rode on, and the scout cantered away. Soon after, the column mounted a slight saddle in the valley. At the crest, Aurelian reined aside. The leading files of infantry came abreast of him. He saw their faces, dust masks runnelled scarlet by sweat, come alive with surprise. Hoarse shouts burst from their throats. They swung on with unchecked pace, revived, jubilant. One of them yelled, "Good old Hand-on-Hilt!" That was for their general. He never let them down. In the snap of a finger he had produced a city for them out of the empty desert. There it was below them; their general's halfway house on the way to Persia; the desert city; the caravan city; the city of palms; Palmyra.

*

Its background was a deep crescent of hills. Its oasis made a nest of green, in the midst of which rose the city, a filigree outline of towers and slender columns dazzling white in the sunlight. It was an ivory cluster set in emeralds and bathed in white radiance. Beyond it, to the east, accentuating its solitude, the floor of desert stretched away to meet the sky.

Of course, the men had known that they were going to stop here. They had heard veterans' tales, vague legends of a mysterious city hidden in the desert, of wealth and white buildings and beautiful women. On the march, the news must have passed down, from colonel to captain, from captain to N.C.O., to the men in the ranks. Aurelian had been a common soldier himself. He knew that even when soldiers were told nothing they smelled out almost everything. Yet the sight of the city had smitten their senses like a lightning flash. The mystery awed them, of the city standing in its vast circle of desert, of skyline, of silence. The compact white beauty of it awed them.

Aurelian was not awed. To him it was a garrison, an outpost, a name bandied about in staff discussions. His eyes saw no beauty in it. Power he could apprehend, and bigness; not beauty. When he thought of Rome he thought of a million and a half people, the greatest urban mass on earth, and there, to him, was majesty, stirring his senses. This place? Fifty thousand inhabitants—in terms of power, a village.

For all that, he felt pleasure in looking at Palmyra. It was a Roman city. Rome ruled all but the fringes of the earth. The sea was its province. Its legions trod the continents. The earth-shaking legionary tread was in Aurelian's blood. It was the tempo of his consciousness. It was the source of his deepest satisfactions. That slow, deep tread throbbed in his mind as the words law, discipline, commerce, unity. Rome was power to Aurelian, a male force whose touch could impregnate any place with Romanness. The Emperor Hadrian had conquered this Arab city and it now stood, a free city within the Empire, as a Roman outpost. The Arab merchants who ruled it bore Roman family names. Their Senate ruled by Roman law. Their soldiers served in the imperial armies. They sought and earned Roman titles. They were proud, they commanded fantastic wealth, for their city stood at the crossroads of the desert cara-van trails, and they levied taxes on a tide of riches; but they still bowed to Rome, and ruled in the desert on its behalf. And Rome, which was tolerant in the knowledge of its power, let them give themselves Oriental airs, let them call themselves princes, in the manner of Asia. What did it matter if their pres-ent leader, this Odenathus, called himself prince? To Rome he was no monarch, but *vir consularis*, Rome's placeman, the Roman consul for Arabia.

His horse was quivering between his thighs, joyfully mad-dened by the smell of water. There was the secret of Palmyra's being, its wealth. That smell of water drew the caravans from south and east and west across the desert. Water for wealth. Water for an army. Guided by the scouts, he led his men past fields of feathery grass where asphodels grew, past villages where aged herdsmen huddled by their flocks, beneath the foli-age of palms, down the long groves which were blessed with cool and shade. All the time, ignoring the white walls of the city that glimmered through the palms, he was making his calculations, about water, pasturage, camp areas, communications, defence lines, for the army that might come this way.

The air was sweet with the presence of water. Butterflies danced across his path. There were more and more people, coming in crowds to the roadside, herdsmen and camel drivers dressed in skins or shabby cloaks, and merchants in headcloths and gowns of dazzling white. He heard the cohort commander at his back give the word to march to attention. The stir of interest and pleasure vanished from the ranks, and the cohort became a Roman fighting machine cleaving through the crowds, every soldier marching eyes to his front, erect and grimly silent.

Here, to the south of the city, the grassy plain was peopled like an enormous market. There were tented camps and booths and shouting vendors and sounds of music from under the trees. Water, still and sunlight-dappled, gleamed in scores of huge stone tanks, connected one with another, the wells of Efca. The herds grew larger. The lines of picketed camels seemed to stretch for miles.

Ahead, the scouts had reined in before a white stone fort. A group of people was assembled outside the fort. Some of them were talking with the scouts. Aurelian saw soldiers among them, a troop of the heavy cavalry of Palmyra, men and horses made monstrous by scale armour from head to foot. And there was a squad of archers, with massive bows, steel acorn helmets and huge, square-sectioned quivers slung behind their red and green fringed tunics. A welcoming escort? But those men and girls in richly coloured robes? And that chariot, in which an elderly woman sat with a baby on her lap? What made Aurelian curious was that few of them were looking in his direction. Most of the group were gazing towards the south, and he saw one of his scouts pointing in that direction.

Far away, on the dun floor of the plain that fronted the southern hills, he saw a cloud writhing and whirling, speeding towards him like a dust storm. Two horsemen shot out of the dust cloud and galloped away to the right. Two more outriders appeared on the left. Now, at the heart of the dust cloud, he saw what he had been looking for, the speeding chariot.

*

"It is their prince, sir, the consul Odenathus. They are waiting to escort him back to the city."

Aurelian watched the chariot while he heard the scout's report. Two of the horsemen were swerving inward from the east. Something shot away from them, a black blur streaking across the plain in front of the chariot.

He could see two people in the chariot, a Greek-style rig built for daredevils, with two yoked horses and two small wheels whose rim and spokes were so light that the touch of a rock at high speed would shiver them to pieces. A tall man was driving, poised against the knee-board, with the reins in his right hand and a whip raised high in his left. A small figure, childish-seeming from this distance, clung close to the driver. The horses flew over the plain, wild-maned. Aurelian could hear the mad thudding of their hoofs. The chariot swerved towards the flying black streak. Then it appeared to drop back. It had not lost speed, but its quarry had shot away like a catapulted stone.

The hunt was close enough now for Aurelian to discern the black leopard flying for its life. The two outriders on the opposite flank were lying on the necks of their horses, lashing them on, to head the leopard off. He changed direction again. Aurelian could hear the rattle of the chariot wheels and the faint cries of the hunters. The leopard, stretched flat out, went over the ground in a long, sinuous flicker, crossing twenty yards in front of the chariot's horses. The chariot tilted steeply over on one wheel, swerving at a hairpin angle to keep up with the leopard. Dust boiled up around it, and Aurelian waited for the crash of its overturning, but it shot out of the dust, closing in sideways on the leopard. What a charioteer! Aurelian had never seen such skill and daring, even among the professionals of the Circus Maximus.

Aurelian had handed his helmet down to an orderly. He sat his horse upright, drinking a cup of the sulphur-sharp well water, and munching the round, golden Palmyra dates from his left hand. His face was impassive, yet in his stillness, the intentness of his eyes, the force with which he spat the date stones from his lips, there was a kind of excitement. The chariot was coming up, up, alongside the leopard. The charioteer's companion had swung out over the side of the vehicle, towards the leopard, javelin poised point downward. How lithe, how small he was, to be hanging by a hand's grasp over the flying ground, strong against the bounce and jolt of the wheels, iron-nerved against the dizziness that might break his neck, steady against the upboiling dust, fearless of the leopard that might turn and leap at him like a projectile!

Now—*now!* Aurelian lowered the cup from his mouth. The leopard leaped with lashing claws, the javelin flashed downward, the chariot swerved away, and there was the leopard thrashing upon the ground with the shaft protruding from its throat. What superb timing it had been! What a pair they were, those two in the chariot, co-ordinated in the flash and fury of that climax like two parts of a single being!

The leopard lay still in the dust, its paws neatly crossed. The chariot stopped nearby. The horsemen cantered to join their master.

A few minutes later the hunting party reached the fort. Aurelian remained at a distance, to give Odenathus time to learn who the newcomers were. The prince had stepped down from the chariot, and was talking with his attendants. He wore a white tunic belted at the waist and a cloak whose purple border indicated his senatorial rank. Aurelian dismounted. His entourage was waiting: the cohort commander, a bodyguard of four tall legionaries, and behind them, still mounted, the two scouts. He started towards the fort.

The charioteer's companion, the leopard-killer, had dropped lightly to the ground. Aurelian glimpsed an abundance of black hair, a small oval face, and strange flamboyant clothing. He stared, a suspicion growing in his puzzled mind. The leopard-killer was running across to the other chariot, and the light fleetness of his stride stirred the awakening suspicion—his stride? By the gods, *her* stride! The woman—the girl—had taken the baby boy from the nurse in the other chariot and was hugging him to her, his cheek against hers.

Aurelian, his eyes blazing with astonishment, did not slow his stride. "Who is she?"

One of the scouts, riding behind, called, "It is the wife of Odenathus, sir. They call her Zenobia."

Some of the girls had clustered around her, one of them brushing her hair from behind, others bathing her skin with water from a sun-flashing silver bowl which one of them held, others arranging her attire. She was small and slender and young. Her face, upturned to the sun, was radiant at the touch of her child's tender flesh against it. Her complexion was dark and flawless, her teeth white, her eyes large and full of light. In contrast with the dark honey colour of her face and her bare arms was her loose white blouse; and there was an odd, carnival swagger in the wide-legged pantaloons that she wore, of flaring vermilion silk, gathered at the ankles by gold clasps above her sandals of soft red leather.

She and Aurelian faced each other, a dozen paces apart. His thoughts were expressed in his burning gaze. Was this the hunter? The wife of a prince? Dressed gaily as a clown, half-naked like a whore? This wild, childlike creature? For a second her eyes held his: the man brooding and intent; the girl bold and hostile. This was the first meeting of Zenobia and Aurelian.

*

Aurelian remained erect behind his soldier's mask while he exchanged greetings and made formal conversation with them. The girl's voice was cool and low. From time to time, as courtesy demanded, he glanced at her, but without showing awareness of her. He could feel, however, her scrutiny upon him, exploring him. An instinctive anger had leaped up in him against this girl who presumed to a man's estate; he regarded women as a lesser species; and within him he felt her knowledge of his anger clashing with his mood like steel upon steel. The little boy was leaning out of her arms, reaching towards Aurelian, beaming and crowing at him excitedly.

Odenathus smiled. "My son likes you, it appears." He was a burnished blade of a man, thirty-five years old, with the hawk profile and hawk-glittering eyes of an Arab chieftain. His black hair was curled close to his skull and an ebony wedge of beard prolonged the line of his chin. His voice was grave and easy; but even in his calm he seemed poised to attack.

Aurelian stood straight-backed. "A fine boy, sir." He watched the girl, standing beneath her husband's shoulder, a child nestling in a safe place yet a woman whose eyes challenged him without fear. They had told him about her in Rome; facts came up from the mind's storeroom. Odenathus had married her three years ago. Hadn't she been—yes—fifteen years old at the time? And she came from the Septimian family (he could not recall their Arab tribe, but they were a sound family, thoroughly Romanized in sympathies as well as name), the same influential merchant clan that her husband came from. There was another son, wasn't there? It came back to him: Herodianus. He would be eight years old now, the heir to his father's wealth and power.

He was the son of an earlier marriage. The mother had died giving birth to him. Aurelian wondered what conflicts impended between Herodianus and the boy whom this girl so joyfully held. He hated diplomatic manners, but it was necessary for him to take notice of her. "What is his name, madam? How old is he?"

Unlike her husband, who spoke Latin fluently but with the harsh intonations and broken rhythms of the Arab, she spoke in the flawless accents of a Roman patrician. "He is two years old. We call him Wahab Al-Lat, the gift of our goddess Al-Lat."

Aurelian said, "Greetings, little soldier." The boy, uncomprehending, beat the air happily with his fists and cried out in a babble of Aramaic. Aurelian said, "You should teach him Latin, madam. He is a Roman citizen."

He had struck sparks from her eyes. "He is first a citizen of Palmyra, general. A Saracen. I have named him in our own tongue, and I am content that it should be the first speech upon his lips."

The masculine firmness of her voice fed his annoyance. The way in which she had said "a Saracen" inflamed his annoyance into anger. To be an Arab—or an African, or a Danubian villager, or to be a Britisher crouching in his wattle hut painted to look like a blue-arsed baboon—that was something to be forgotten, not a boast. What was there to boast of besides being a Roman citizen? What languages deserved to survive except the soldier's Latin and the merchant's Greek? It was people with voices that rang like this girl's who wanted the world to remain a babble of uncouth languages, a madhouse of lousy little tribes all cutting each other's throats. The rhythm of pride sounded in him again. Law. Discipline. Peace. Rome. As if she sensed his anger, Zenobia spoke again: "In any case, general, you may rest assured that one day he will speak Latin no less well than you."

This was a taunt as sharp as a lash across his face. Aurelian was not Roman born. He spoke the vulgar Latin that the armies had carried to the frontiers of the Empire, a speech with a vocabulary as well as an accent of its own. He remained wooden, but a glitter of fury must have showed in his eyes, for Odenathus, still easy and smiling, placed a hand on his wife's shoulder and said, "The lady Zenobia is young, general. Rome is still a faraway place to her. When she is my age, she will know how near to us it is."

Aurelian sensed that this remark was as much a warning to the girl as an emollient to him. There was a pout of denial in her lips, but she became docile under her husband's hand. Aurelian said, "Indeed, I hope so. Rome is great. Rome sees all. Rome rewards, and punishes, without stint."

"Rome is great," Odenathus said. "And we here are thankful for her protection."

The girl's chin came up and there was rebellion in her face, but she restrained herself.

Aurelian inclined his head slightly, and challenged her with a smile. "Madam?"

"My husband is thankful for Rome's protection. Is Rome thankful for ours?"

Aurelian looked down at her with the deliberate arrogance of a man who has marched through hostile lands with a legion behind him. "And for what need Rome be thankful, madam?"

"Are we not Rome's shield in the East?" Incongruously, she broke off to hush the baby. "How long would she hold her frontiers in Asia without our armies? How much wealth does she receive from us each year? I know what we give to Rome, general. What does Rome give us in return?"

He turned to Odenathus. "The lady, sir, is not well instructed in the traditions of her family. It is not my task to teach her. May I, without discourtesy, hope that you will find time to do so?"

Odenathus showed no sign of discomfiture at his wife's outburst or of resentment at Aurelian's rebuke. "My wife is a most learned young lady, general. She speaks five languages. You will find her as skilled in logic and rhetoric as she is with the hunter's spear." The keen smile, all mockery, white teeth and glittering eyes, flashed across his face again. "She may be impetuous, but she cannot be accused of ignorance."

Aurelian stood stolid as an ox under the goad of two wits more subtle than his own. "You must pardon me, sir, I am only a soldier. I learn as I travel. I have seen barbarous lands, strange customs, and strange animals. But I have never seen women who dressed in trousers, like Gaulish warriors, or who intruded themselves into the affairs of men, or who left their babies for the hunter's chariot."

"Travel broadens the mind, general." Her voice remained low, amused. She rocked her baby cheek to cheek with her, and mocked Aurelian with her smile. "And I assure you that I am a good mother."

Aurelian remained silent. She said, "We shall look forward to the pleasure of entertaining you this evening, general. And I hope, when we meet at the table, you will approve of my dress. I am quite womanly at times, you know."

Aurelian bobbed his head and uttered a stiff "Madam!" of acknowledgement.

Unrelenting light points of mockery danced in her eyes. "This has been a most pleasant meeting, general. For you, too, I hope. May I commemorate it with a little gift?" Freeing one hand from her child, she took something from one of her ladies in waiting. She came close to Aurelian. He could feel her female warmth. She put into his hands a gold comb and a gold-backed mirror.

He stood in stolid bewilderment for a moment, the gifts in his hand. One of the girl servants uttered a giggle, hastily smothered. The scrutiny of the Arabs was heavy with amusement. Their eyes were all upon him, and there was laughter hidden behind their eyes. A blade of comprehension thrust into his breast.

He was bareheaded. His chestnut hair, thick and gleaming with sweat, sprang like a disorder of wind-blown sheaves over his forehead. He looked at the nobles, and at Odenathus, and at the palace servants, their hair ringleted and plastered down upon their skulls with spikenard. And he—*curse the girl! how did she know? how could she look so surely into him and strike at his weak spots?*—he did not even have his hair cut close in the Roman style. In twenty years of soldiering, of discipline gladly accepted, of Roman ways eagerly embraced, he had clung to one custom of his native Balkans. He had kept the thick, smooth, wild hair of the mountaineer. To do so had always aroused a strange twist of pride in him. Now it caused him angry shame.

Odenathus had climbed back into his chariot. "My servants will guide you to your quarters, general. I hope you will be comfortable."

Aurelian made some answer, not hearing himself. Big, soldierly, a man in the prime of middle age, he faced the slender chit of eighteen whose eyes had such secret knowledge of him. She sprang into the chariot after her husband. "Until this evening, general."

Aurelian did not move while the chariot and its escort clattered away. In the future he would tell himself that he had felt, at this moment, a premonition about Zenobia. A self-deception this; for the next day, when he left Palmyra, the tide of great events swept him on.

CHAPTER TWO

THE CENTURION

A JEALOUS senator once said of Aurelian, "He is only a jumped-up centurion."

There was some truth in this statement. It showed up the virtues of the man and his limitations. It was to be criticized only in one respect: that it was meant as an insult. For at this moment in Rome's history the centurion, backbone of the legion, was a man who meant more than any senator. Rome without her Senate of profiteers, debauched idlers, and mob politicians would have been a better place. Without her centurions she would have perished.

*

When a society has fulfilled its desires it begins to die. Once Rome had civilized the world. Law, trade, and the arts had travelled along her spear-straight roads to remote places. Now, after centuries of her Roman peace, she had grown soft. Her conquests had given her a torrent of riches to live on, armies of slaves to do her work. Her rich, once leaders, had become sluggish parasites. Her free peasants, once her reservoir of incomparable soldiers, had been driven off the land by slave labour and now rotted in city slums, an idle mob of cadgers.

Beyond her frontiers were multitudes whose desires were unfulfilled, whose destiny was unachieved. The barbarians surged into Europe, herds roaming the earth in the eternal human quest for peace and a good pasture, and brought by their dream into the perpetual human state of strife. Other hosts, migrating from the east, had dislodged them. The smell of plenty, of Roman weakness, drew them on. They rolled against the frontiers, not in the raiding parties of the past, but in invasions of oceanic power.

And at this time Rome had ceased to produce soldiers. Her people wanted only to shut out the distant, disagreeable noises of doom, and to enjoy themselves.

The legions held the walls. In their distant fortresses they kept Rome alive. To the legions passed the Roman power.

But the soldiers of the legions were not Romans. Why should Romans fight when their wealth could buy mercenaries? The legions found their recruits in the far-off countries where they were stationed. By now, three centuries after the first Caesar, the bulk of the Roman troops were from outside Italy, men born on the frontiers, themselves almost barbarians. Rome to them was not a tradition, not "home." It was no more than a distant city which few had seen, the farthest rear of all base towns, a despised place, a paymaster. The soldier knew no loyalty except to his own legion and his own general.

From afar, the alien legions ruled Rome. They chose and imposed the emperors, and the Senate was powerless to do anything but shout "Aye!" Any military adventurer who was strong, cunning, and popular enough could become emperor. While the barbarians crashed against the frontiers, the legions, caring nothing for Rome, followed their favourite generals in a to-and-fro of riot, rebellion, and civil war. In fifty years there had been eighteen emperors and thirty other pretenders to the throne; almost all had perished by the sword. Meanwhile the walls grew weaker. Waves of invasion burst over them and swirled deeper into the Roman provinces. Each wave was driven back with difficulty. Each time the hordes recoiled with the taste of conquest, the possession of booty, and the growing assurance of future success to stir new multitudes into movement against the vast, sluggish, tiring prey.

*

A centurion? It was not to be wondered that, all his life, Aurelian bore himself like one. It was the task of Rome's centurions to make an army of iron soldiers. The men who did this had to be of unequalled toughness. Nothing had done so much to form Aurelian as his centurion's service.

He was born on the Danube—in the loose phrase of the time, an Illyrian. He had gone into the army when he was twenty, a peasant volunteer, the son of a freed slave. The clan name he bore was that of the Aurelians, the great Roman family that had freed his father.

Strong, brave, capable, with a passion for discipline, he had entered at exactly the right time. The ten Danubian legions, a third of the army and the largest concentration of troops within it, were made up of men like himself, the sons of a peasantry that was long-settled, prosperous, and advanced in culture, but which had always had to fight on its own account to hold back the land-hungry tribes from across the Danube. To their fine native qualities, two centuries of Roman settlement had added a strain of Roman blood and culture and the decisive gift of Roman military science. It was inevitable that men of one mind and one tradition, concentrated geographically, should be able to impose their will among the scattered legions; and the Illyrians had become a commanding force in the army. Aurelian, although a peasant, was thus one of a military aristocracy. Also, the Danube was becoming the main front, and the main field of opportunity; and the Emperor Severus Alexander had just thrown the doors open to unlimited promotion from the ranks.

It took him two years to become an infantry squad leader; but then, within six months, he was promoted in the field to centurion, for killing forty-eight Polish invaders in one day.

There were fifty-six centurions in a legion, all of whom commanded companies except one who acted as adjutant at headquarters. The legion was organized in a series of grades. The

first cohort, eleven hundred strong, was the élite battalion. The
other nine battalions, each of five companies, were five hundred
and fifty strong. A man started as junior centurion in the tenth
cohort and rose by fifty-five steps to become First Centurion of
the legion. For most men this was a life's career. Aurelian did
it in five years. When he was twenty-eight he went to the Sixth
Legion as a battalion commander.

For the rest, his was one of those careers about which young
soldiers are lectured. He spent five years as a battalion commander on the Danube front, a man about whom legends
spread. In three weeks of carnage among the Goths he was reputed to have slain nine hundred and fifty by his own hand; a
feat which, together with his drinking capacity, the soldiers
celebrated in a marching song:

> *A thousand, a thousand, a thousand heads he's chopped.*
> *One man alone, a thousand he has lopped.*
> *He'll down a thousand drinks, who left a thousand dead.*
> *We'd like as much wine as the blood our Old Man's shed.*

A soldier like this was needed. The Germans were flooding
into Gaul. Aurelian was rushed there to command the Third
Gallican (known as "The Lucky") Legion. He drove the invasion back.

Amid thunder and chaos his legend spread. He returned to
the Danube as a staff officer, and another Goth invasion was
repelled. He returned to Gaul as a corps commander, and scored
an annihilating victory over the Germans at Mainz. There was
jubilation in Rome. The Senate gave him an ovation. He married a senator's daughter. The Emperor Valerian called him "the
liberator of Illyria, the saviour of the provinces of Gaul." He was
taken on the emperor's staff as inspector-general of camps. So,

in this post, had come his mission to Persia and his visit to Palmyra.

*

Ten years had passed since that mission.

During that time black clouds of calamity gathered over the Empire. Valerian's expedition to Persia had been wiped out. The emperor of Rome, the demigod, the symbol of seven centuries of supreme power, was a prisoner, whose prostrated body was the Persian king's mounting block.

The Empire in Asia had been saved by the Arab Prince Odenathus, whom Aurelian had met. He had rallied an army and driven the Persians back across the Euphrates. *Imperator*, he was now called in reward, and *Leader of the East*. Even in these titles there was a danger. His power in the East was now almost independent of Rome's. At the very least he was a viceroy, with no equal except the emperor.

The pitiable Valerian had shown that Rome could be defeated. Odenathus had proved that Rome could be dependent on a vassal. The barbarian wolf packs raised their muzzles at the smell of weakness, and charged again.

*

The Illyrians decided that it was time to use their power. Their sense of discipline, of military pride, of honour, was outraged. They took command. One of them, Claudius, donned the purple as Claudius II. Aurelian was given command of the ten Danubian legions. To him had passed the main defence of the Empire.

This, then, was "the centurion," the man whom the soldiers knew as "Old Hand-on-Hilt" because his hand flew there if he saw a hint of insolence in a face; who swore by army regulations and the god discipline; who had once had a soldier torn apart between two saplings for raping a woman in a friendly village; who had soothsayers whipped out of his camps because he despised superstitions, but who worshipped the sun-god of his native province with a peasant's quiet fanaticism.

This was the man who, one sunny March day in the first year of the Emperor Claudius's reign, rode into the base town of Sirmium at the head of a column of cavalry.

CHAPTER THREE

THE CENTURION FORGES A
NEW WEAPON

THE MAIN Roman base on the Danube was at Sirmium, some seventy miles west of where Belgrade stands today. A sentry looking down from the ramparts of the camp could see on the bank of the Sava a town typical of those which the legions planted, white and splendid, with a porticoed forum, thronged shopping streets, a governor's palace, and villas nestling in their gardens.

Between the camp and the town lay an immense parade ground. Here, the day after Aurelian's arrival, the troops were assembling.

On two sides of the square were detachments from the front-line legions resting here. They stood in perfect ranks behind their silver eagles. On their standards and shields were the ram of the First Minervia, the boar of the Second Adjutrix, the goat of the Second Italica, and the bull of the Third Gallican, Aurelian's old command. One side of the square was occupied by the recruit regiments from the training depot. On the fourth side, beneath the rampart, assembled the hundreds of specialist and staff officers of the base. In their centre, seated side by side on the traditional earth platform, were Aurelian and Marcus Aurelius Probus, his youthful Illyrian deputy.

Three clear trumpet notes sounded in the silence. An infantry company emerged from the camp gates and marched towards the centre of the parade ground. The soldiers marched in column of fours, in full campaign order. Their two left-hand ranks carried the pilum, the seven-foot spear shod halfway down its haft with the base of its iron barb. The other two ranks carried light lances, a sheaf of five inside each man's shield. They wore iron helmets with the ceremonial plumes removed, leather corselets thickly padded on the shoulders against a downstroke, with strips of iron fastened across breast and back, swords at the right side, and packs on forked poles on the left shoulder.

A single trumpet note, high and quavering, and a troop of horsemen erupted into the other end of the arena. The horsemen wore linen tunics and shaggy skins. They carried long lances and small round shields. They were big men, mostly fairhaired, with heavily boned faces. They were Goths, prisoners of war brought back by Aurelian yesterday. Their leader, who had long, drooping moustaches, threw up his hand and they rallied to him.

They watched the infantry marching across the arena. The leader raised his hand again, and the horses began to trot. The infantry marched on. The Goths gathered speed. The infantry centurion sounded a short blast on his whistle. His column at once broke into a double march, its head wheeling right three times to form a square. In a few seconds the legionaries had faced outwards, the spears of the two outer ranks presented in a defensive hedge. A moment later the Goths burst upon them.

The horsemen flowed away from the fence of spear points and regrouped. The spectators, freed from restraint now, roared approval of the infantry's drill movement. Thus, neatly and rapidly, a whole legion could take up the same formation, the *agmen quadratum*.

The Goths charged again. This time, as they approached, the two rear ranks of infantry hurled a volley of lances. Horses reared, shrilling. Riders toppled. The spectators now were shouting and laughing like a mob at the Circus.

The Goths cantered away. Their dead and slowly writhing wounded littered the ground outside the square. Not a single legionary had fallen. This was understandable, for the weapons of the Goths were made of wood.

Another charge met another volley of lances, whose straight flight and immense velocity came from the spin they had been given by the twisted throwing-thongs which the infantry used. From the crowd came a surf beat of noise, not the blood-hungry howls of a civilian audience but a mingling of comment; to them, this was no fight, but a drill demonstration. The Goths were merely part of the equipment used.

A new trumpet call pierced the crowd's noise. A troop of Roman cavalry rode into the arena. They were thirty-two against the eighty surviving Goths, and like their adversaries they rode without saddle or stirrup; but they wore breastplates and crested helmets, and the sunlight winked upon their weapon-points.

They charged upon the rear of the Goths, and the crowd cheered. They cut through the barbarians and rallied a hundred yards beyond them. The Goths bunched close and rode in desperation at these new enemies. The Roman horse, neat as a Circus troupe, rode into line, wheeled about and met the charge with their lance-points. They rode forward over the dying, sent riderless horses scattering away; the Goths were a rearing, stubborn, backward-surging wave before their lances. Roman swords lopped the hafts of wooden lances. Roman lances drove through wooden Gothic shields. The Goths had nothing but their anger and their flesh and their beasts; and these they hurled upon the Romans with the heartbreaking valour of tormented bulls; while the crowd, not even seeing them, clapped for the skill and precision of their butchers.

The Roman infantry joined in the display. They marched into column, turned like a machine into line of battle, and moved forward, like a machine, across the arena. The Third Gallican, whose insignia they bore on their shields, stamped thunderously in time with their step. To the thunder tread of the crowd they drove the Goths back towards the Roman cavalry, and their swords flashed down upon those dismounted barbarians who staggered, gashed and blood-blinded, in their path.

There were only a few handfuls of Goths left. They galloped to and fro like birds beating at the bars of a cage. Officers, in their enclosure, turned away in conversation. It was scarcely worth watching the manhunt that remained.

A burst of shouts made these bored men turn their heads again. The crowd-roar exploded into a din of excitement. The Goth leader and a dozen of his comrades had faced a Roman charge. Hanging upon the flank of his horse, he had ridden under the Roman lances, risen up against the body of a Roman rider and, horse to horse, was striving with him. The crowd glimpsed a twist of the Goth's great hands and the Roman flying sideways; and now, amid a roar-roar-roar beating up into the sky, the Goth was away, the Roman's lance in his hand, his horse bursting away from the Romans in a drum and flurry of hoofs. He raised the lance. From all parts of the parade ground his comrades galloped towards him.

The voice of the crowd was welded now into one roar. Twenty Goths, compact as a fist, were hurtling down upon the officers' enclosure. They went straight for the general's platform. The Roman cavalry, pursuing, were left behind by the Goths' head-long flight.

The officers, shieldless but armed with swords, rallied to meet the charge. The generals' guard, twelve tall centurions, formed up to protect their commanders and their standards. Aurelian and Probus remained utterly still in their seats. The roar filled the sky. The charge burst through the crowd of officers. Maddened Goths leaped like projectiles, out among the swarming Romans, down upon the sword-points, clubbing with their wooden weapons, clawing for throats with their fingers. The leader and four of his comrades smashed down upon the centurions' guard. The guard commander went backward with the lance-point through his belly. Three of the Goths whirled their horses' rumps among the guard. Men scattered and the cluster of standards flew apart like a broken fence. Two of the Goths, their leader and a boy, leaped for the platform.

Aurelian and Probus were on their feet. Probus thrust his sword at the boy. The boy wriggled like a salmon, grasped the sword-wrist, and fell backward, toppling Probus with him, into the shouting scrimmage below.

Aurelian and the Goth leader were face to face against the empty sky. They were alone, in full view of the legions. Aurelian watched the unarmed man, like one beast waiting for another to spring. His face was hard with calculation. Then he cast his sword away and went to the Goth, his open hands held wide apart and feinting like a wrestler's. The Goth shouted and leapt at him. The two of them went down and rolled, writhing, upon the platform.

· Below, the Gothic suicide had almost accomplished itself. Probus was on his feet, holding the boy from behind. The boy, in spite of the cruel lock that pinned his arms to his back, kicked and squirmed. Officers scrambled up onto the platform. Aurelian was kneeling on the chest of the Goth chief. His hands strove. He shouted "Back!" His faced was flushed darkly, lumpy with muscle. The Goth, heaving from beneath, half rose. Aurelian almost lost his balance. He drove his weight forward and mastered the man again. He had one knee plunged into the groin. His forearms were braced in a terrible effort to pin down the man's arms. His fingers struggled against the corded throat. The Goth's muscles were like iron; but Aurelian, his own muscles quivering with the agony of this contest, felt the first springy yielding, the first minute contraction of his own fingers. The Goth boy, jerking in vain against Probus's grasp, cried out to the chief. His face was uplifted, drawn with the pain of Probus's lock, and with terror. His profile, identical with that of the man weakening with terrible gasps upon the ground, and his horror, betrayed him as the chief's son. Probus held him, so that he must watch. Aurelian's fingers were closing like slow iron bands. The chief's hands, struggling to prise Aurelian's away, weakened, then flopped outward to the ground. The heaving legs slowly slid flat and limp. Aurelian, braced upon him, relaxed, looked wildly and unrecognizingly about him for a moment, then rose. The breath snored from his throat. From the legions there rose a rhythmical, triumphant "Hail!" "Hail!" "Hail!" Behind the roar, a deep tone of song. The Third Gallican were bellowing, *We'd like as much wine as the blood our Old Man's shed.* Aurelian stood, indifferent, turned away from the acclamations, his chest rising and falling powerfully.

Fifteen minutes later there was silence. The legions were now massed, where they had been marched, in front of the platform. Aurelian stood alone, looking down at them. The chief's body was at his feet. He had ordered it to be left where it lay.

"Men! Yesterday I came back here with two cavalry regiments. We had won a battle. Last night there was a riot in this camp. Infantrymen fought cavalrymen. A canteen was destroyed. A centurion was struck. Roman infantry fought Roman cavalry, because the cavalry had won a battle.

"Soldiers, I am going to tell you about that battle. There was a pack of Goths loose, on horseback, right down into Dalmatia. They were going home, with their loot, and with the news that a Roman province can be raided."

His glance passed over the silent legions. "Legionaries! I am a man of the legions. For thirty years I have loved my legions. But if I had taken a legion against those Goths I should never have caught them. You, soldiers, can any one of you run as fast as a horse? Come on, speak up, I'm listening."

Silence. "So I took cavalry. We got to the Danube before the Goths did. And we taught them a lesson. We killed three thousand of them. We brought home prisoners. We let a few of them swim across the river. They took no loot. They took the news that a Roman province *cannot* be raided."

He paused again, lengthily. "Men, there will be punishment for last night. You will see it, and you will remember it. I promise you that. But I have given you something else to see, and to remember.

"This morning you saw a display. You saw a company of the legion. You saw its discipline. You saw its skill. You saw it repel a mounted enemy. But you saw something more. You saw that the infantry, the legion, cannot defeat cavalry alone. That is no disgrace. It is a matter of speed. The man on foot cannot manoeuvre against the man on a horse. He must wait for him.

"Soldiers! Wars are not won by waiting for the enemy. Wars are won by going to the enemy. That army wins which outmoves the enemy, which chooses the ground for the battle and leads the enemy there. Once our legion could do this. Today they cannot do it. Because the enemies who are coming against us now are on horseback, whole nations on horseback.

"But we know now how to defeat them. What we have done with two thousand horsemen, we can do with twenty thousand. We shall raise an army of cavalry. Our cavalry can never equal the barbarians in numbers. But it will possess a weapon the enemy have not got. You saw that weapon in the arena this morning, when our cavalry cut up those Goths. Roman discipline. Roman skill. Roman science. With these, our legions won the Empire. With these, our cavalry shall restore it."

When he spoke again, his voice was softer. "Soldiers, there will be no more riots in my camps. There will be no jealous hearts between foot and horse. If I punish, it will be without mercy. Once more I promise you that. But I will not have to punish. Because you all know, now, that one arm of war needs the other. Our cavalry cannot win ground unless the legions hold it. Our legions cannot fight without a fist." He raised his own clenched fist. "A fist of cavalry to strike. Men! You're no fools. Since when was the right hand the rival of the left? Legions and cavalry, right hand and left, must meet round the throat of the enemy." He tapped the Goth's body with his right foot. "By Hercules, now! This fellow learned what right hand and left can do. Didn't he?"

The legions roared.

*

"Claudius has gone to Milan to establish a cavalry base for the West. The eastern base will be here. You will be in charge." Aurelian was in a good humour as he rode back into camp with Probus. As always on a parade ground, he felt an immense serenity. He loved the music of the barrack square, a hubbub of distant, ringing commands, tramping feet, and muted clash of arms; the vistas of the vast field covered with an ant-like drilling; and the vaster sky. "You'll build quarters, store fodder, and collect mounts. You'll levy recruits, the right kind. Call in officers and recommend soldiers from the legion cavalry. Draw up a training programme. Special emphasis on horse management, quick mounting, deployment, use of bow while in movement, river crossings with and without infantry, and turnout. Splendour in cavalry terrorizes the enemy. In six months I want two regiments. After that, two more regiments every six months plus drafts for those already in the field. Your job will be to produce cavalry, mine to show what it can do."

"By Hercules, now!" Probus repeated Aurelian's pet oath in a mock-deep voice. "You're sure you wouldn't like me to serve the mares in my spare time?"

Aurelian smiled, a grim puckering of the lips and a warmth in the eyes. A squad of first-week recruits in leather skullcaps and jerkins was being drilled nearby, learning to fall in with six feet between ranks and three feet between men. In the young faces, still as carved wood, he saw his own youth; just as in each of the hundred squads marching to and fro there was a frag-

ment of his own life. He was not a sentimental man, but the
savour of the past was in his nostrils; for he, and Probus too, had
been formed as these boys were being formed, drilled to the
habit of machine-like obedience, standing rock-still under the
whack of the centurion's stick, whirling the double-weight training sword until it was no weight at all, learning the killer's art
as minutely as if it were the goldsmith's, changing, changing—
you could see it in the faces here, from squad to squad—until the
strong, innocent young peasant face had become the fierce,
wine-dark, cunning, soldier face. "You'll be too tired for that,
I promise you."

"Never!" Probus raised a hand in salute as they turned in
through the camp gate and the guard turned out to the sound
of the general's salute on the trumpeter's coiled *bucina*. "I could
raise the strength in my grave. Which reminds me—" The main
street, a hundred-foot width of immaculate pavement, lay ahead,
with the headquarters buildings and main square on its left. The
camp was a grid of such streets, laid out to the same precise
pattern as every Roman camp in the world. In its neat rows of
buildings, stone-built and roofed with tiles, the newcomer would
always know where to find barracks, offices, canteen, chapel,
hospital, stables, guardrooms. It was the universal city of the
Roman soldier. To Aurelian and Probus it was home. This—the
camp, everywhere—was their Rome. "I've got a lovely German
girl. Hair like honey. Want her?"

They had dismounted outside the *praetorium*. A groom took
their bridles. The guard, four men and a centurion, came to
attention. A boy crouched at the foot of one of the pillars. His
hands were tied, and the rope was tied to the pillar. It was
the young Goth. The centurion said, "You sent for him, sir."

Aurelian nodded. "Bring him in."

In the centre of Probus's quarters was a small, open courtyard. Here they seated themselves on couches, before a low

table. Two dumpy peasant girls brought food. Aurelian's secretary, a little Greek, stood deferentially behind him. Probus said, "Well? About the girl?"

Aurelian grunted. "Don't trouble. Eros will send me one of these two for a half-hour when I feel like it."

"A half-hour—?" Probus had a round, droll peasant face, and it came alive with merriment.

"Well," Aurelian's tone was defensive, "a man's got to have a woman sometimes, hasn't he?"

Probus uttered a brief yelp of delight. "Ye gods! What a man!" The young Goth caught his eye. "You wanted me to keep this one alive. What are you going to do with him?"

"I don't know yet." The last ten years had left their mark on Aurelian. His forehead was deeply corrugated, his cheeks hollow. The grimness of his face was contradicted only by the turned-up tip of his nose. His hair was grey at the sides and he wore it in the Roman fringe. His comrades had remarked, years ago, that he had gone on the Persian mission an Illyrian and come back a Roman, for it was then that he had cropped his hair. "It came to me, I'd like to tame him if I can."

The boy stood lax. He was in his early teens. His yellow hair was dirty. White skin and ribs were revealed by his rent tunic. His face was brutal in its bone structure, yet touched with pathos by its honesty and by the fragility of adolescence. His eyes watched Aurelian like the narrowed eyes of a cat. Scrofa, the centurion, towered behind him, a glittering contrast, helmet black-crested from ear to ear (the centurion's badge), breastplate golden-gleaming, the centurion's greaves on his calves, tunic pleated and spotless white, white cloak draped from his right shoulder, a silver valour-bracelet on his right wrist and a large bronze medal on his chest.

"They are fighters, these Goths," Aurelian said. "If I could tame one of them. Make a soldier of him. It might prove a useful experiment."

"He saw you kill his father."

"All the better. Let me have him. I'll try. You, boy—" Like all soldiers, Aurelian had a smattering of the enemy's tongue, which he used now. "What's your name?"

The boy remained silent.

A jug of wine and a large joint of roast beef were on the table: all that the two generals wanted in the way of food. Aurelian spiked a hunk of beef on his knife. "Come on, boy. Speak up."

The boy's eyes moved like a wary beast's, from Aurelian to Probus, back to Aurelian.

"Come, boy, shall I let you live?"

Probus grinned. "You won't win his gratitude that way. He's a Goth."

Aurelian spiked a fresh piece of meat and held it out to the boy. "Are you hungry?" The boy's body remained inert, his eyes savage. "Come, now, answer, your name."

"Permission to speak, sir." It was the centurion. "I know his name. It was my guard this morning looked after them before the show. I speak the lingo, I heard his father talking to him. Name of Maxin, sir." The boy's eyes had flickered to him. "There you are, sir. See him start? Maxin."

"Maxin." Aurelian leaned forward across the table. "Maxin, I am your master. I can make life good for you. I can make it bad. Talk and it will be good."

Only the boy's eyes spoke, pinpointed with hatred.

"Take him away, centurion. Feed him, treat him well, but guard him. I shall see him tomorrow." When the centurion and the prisoner had gone, Aurelian turned to Probus. "Now, these rioters. What are you going to do with them?"

"Flog them. A hundred each."

"And the man who struck the centurion?"

"Two hundred."

Aurelian set down his wine cup. "For striking a centurion?

By Hercules, no! No man strikes a centurion and lives, in one of my legions!"

Probus lay relaxed on his right elbow. He was shorter than Aurelian, and he had huge shoulders, so that the squat bulk of him seemed to obliterate the couch on which he reclined. He scratched his head; the black cat's-fur of his hair was too dense and close-cropped to be ruffled. His eyes, large and clear, yet hooded with slyness by the long, Asiatic upper lids, rested mildly on Aurelian. "So?"

"Crucify him."

Probus's eyes remained amused. "That's not a military punishment."

"It's my punishment, Probus."

Probus took up his wine cup. "This is a stupid, silly, excited recruit we're talking about, drunk for the first time in his life, I'll be bound, and egged on by the old ones. I'll warrant he didn't even know whom he was hitting. Two hundred strokes will teach him his lesson."

"Teach the others. Put him on the cross. For the cost of one man, you'll show two thousand recruits something they'll never forget. That's what punishment is for. To teach the others."

"Is this advice, or an order?" Probus was the youngest senior commander in the army. Throughout his career he had been the youngest of his rank, ever since, in defiance of all regulations, he had been given command of the Tenth Gemina Legion at the age of twenty-four. It was the legendary Probus who spoke now: his voice still mild, but the clarity in his eyes like that of a polished blade.

Aurelian met his look, and frowned, and lay back. After a little while he answered, "This is your command. I shan't interfere."

They ate in silence. Then Probus chatted about events in the garrison. Afterward, Aurelian gave his news from the outside world. There seemed to be nothing but bad news. This was one of those times when every fresh report is a blow, multiplying men's fears and forebodings. Tetricus, the Roman governor in Gaul, himself a Gaul, was threatening trouble. Ulcers of Christianity were erupting everywhere in the provinces, and the authorities were too lax to burn out this orgiastic, immoral, atheistical sect. The silver coinage had been debased again in Rome; now it was only a silver wash on copper. The plague had appeared in northern Italy; Nature, as always, apparently, in times of chaos, piling her omens and disasters on those man-made. There had been another slave revolt in the Roman campagna. And in the East, the Roman consul for Palmyra had been murdered. "The Arab, Odenathus. It was three months ago. Some family intrigue, I imagine. They put him and his older son out of the way at the same time."

"I know. I heard. We have a company of Palmyrene archers here, and their drafts bring news from the East."

"I met him once. Years ago. When I was on my way to Persia. Seemed a good man to me. Too good for my liking. You know what he did to the Persians. There's enough trouble brewing in the West, with Tetricus. It's as well that we're rid of this other fellow in the East. He was too strong, and too ambitious, and too independent, and he had an army behind him. Well, I don't know who the new consul is, but I hope he's less of a problem."

Probus grinned. "He's twelve years old."

"Who is?"

"That's one piece of news you hadn't heard. There's a widow, it seems, with a son. She's set the boy up in his father's place, and no one's tried to stop her." Aurelian had sat up, intent. Probus went on, "Why should we provoke her when we've so much trouble elsewhere?"

Aurelian was upright, his eyes lit with an inward groping, his face grim. He said, as if discovering a buried memory, "Zenobia!"

"That's the one. She's declared herself regent for the boy."

Aurelian sat still and tense, leaning slightly forward. Then he exclaimed, harshly, and with a strange, hostile emphasis, "That woman!"

CHAPTER FOUR

"THAT WOMAN"

AT SUNRISE, golden light brimmed over the hills and crept across the floor of the desert until it discovered Palmyra. The cluster of cold white buildings appeared to expand when the light touched it. The whitewashed walls of its hovel suburbs became brilliant and the marble of its palaces was infused with warmth. The Great Avenue lay empty, the vast breadth of its pavement cleaving the city in two. It was lined on both sides with sandstone pillars which, although sixty feet high, looked tiny against its length. Advancing light gave them a rosy flush against the white dazzle of the pavements.

The temples and palaces that lined the avenue were silent against the sky. On the pavements, only the pacing of sentries could be heard.

In the northwest corner of the city the walls jutted out like the prow of a barge. Within this salient, the base of which was formed by a splendid colonnade, lay the Roman camp, housing a token garrison. The only buildings round about were the tombs of the great Palmyrene families, rows of edifices as magnificent as miniature temples. In one of these, in a vault that was lamp-lit and comfortably furnished, two men were talking.

"Your master Rufinus is Roman governor of Arabia. He is supposed to maintain peace and harmony in this country. Yet there has come into my possession a most scandalous letter he has sent to the emperor in Rome." The speaker was Septimius Worod, head of the municipal government of Palmyra. He was a man in his sixties. His putty-coloured face was wrinkled and quite hairless. His eyes were pale and timid. "Scandalous!"

36

There was the edge of a squeak in his voice. "This letter declares that the prince Odenathus and his elder son were murdered by secret order of Zenobia. A disgraceful suggestion!"

The Roman envoy, in cloak and short-skirted military tunic, smiled. "Now, what a coincidence! You see, we, too, have got hold of a letter. It is a copy of a message from Zenobia to the emperor. Her story is that the murder of Odenathus was planned by Rufinus." He mocked Worod's tone. "A disgraceful suggestion!"

Worod's eyes were large with a guileful innocence. "But Rufinus had a motive. Odenathus was becoming too powerful for Rome's safety."

"Zenobia had a motive, too. She wanted her husband and her stepson out of the way, so that her own son could come to power."

"But she loved her husband!" Worod rose, and began agitatedly moving about the room. "Everyone knows that. She grew up with him. She bore him children. He encouraged all her mad, mannish ways where any other husband would have beaten her to ribbons, and she loved him for it. He got teachers for her. He surrounded her with books. He took her hunting with him. Ye gods, man, he even used to consult her on matters of state! What other husband would do that? I tell you, she used to look up into his face as if he were Jupiter in person. The more he extended his power the more she fired up with pride for him."

"Softly, softly!" The Roman's voice was quiet and amused. "What are you so excited about? Because Zenobia wrote this letter behind your back? Because I am telling you about this, when it is your job to tell us? Because we got hold of the letter through someone else? Softly, Worod, there is no need for you to worry—yet."

"But—"

"No buts. Listen to me. Zenobia had a quarrel with her hus-

band. On just the subject you have mentioned—the extent of
his power. You know as well as I do what everlastingly came
between them. He feared Rome. However Rome's troubles multiplied, Odenathus knew that Rome was still strong. Rome is
everlasting, and Odenathus knew it. He would steal from her,
power, rights, territories, but he would never challenge her. But
your Zenobia, your fury, your madwoman, has never feared
Rome. She hates Rome. Morning, noon, and night she told her
husband that Rome's end was near, that the frontiers were
crumbling, that now was the time for a challenge. It was not
enough for your Zenobia that her husband had grown, in ten
years, from a city chief to the ruler of all Syria and Arabia. She
wanted more. She still wants more. Odenathus stood in her way.
Her stepson stood in her son's way. She had them both destroyed."

"But—"

"If 'but' is all you can say to Zenobia, I understand why she
takes no notice of you. Swallow your 'buts' for a minute and
listen. A year has gone by since her husband's death. She has
proclaimed her son a prince. She has declared herself a regent.
She has had coins struck, with the emperor's image on one side
and her son's on the other—a piece of woman's cunning, this,
for she is proclaiming independence and protesting loyalty at
the same time. Yet she has not marched against us. Why? What
are her intentions?"

Worod had seated himself on the end of a divan, timidly. He
looked up from his thoughts. "Tell me," his voice was sly and
wheedling, "which of them *did* put Odenathus out of the way?"

"Who knows? Zenobia had the assassin killed on the spot.
Who will ever know?" Now it was the Roman who rose,
abruptly. "We are wasting time. I did not come here to discuss
your Zenobia's character, but her plans. What are they?"

"How do I know? Who knows a woman's mind? She never
tells me anything."

"I begin to think highly of her. But we are paying you, Worod, and we want value for money. It is dawn already, and you have told me nothing. Now, out with it, what do you think, will she keep the peace?"

"I do not think she has made up her mind yet."

"Then you must help her to. We must have peace. Do not misunderstand me, Worod. We are not afraid of this woman, nor of any of you. If we have to, we will burn your city to the ground. But it suits us better to have Palmyra as an outpost against the Persians than to destroy it. Let it stay so."

Worod's face was crumpled again in entreaty. "But what can I do? She lets me preside at the council, and she play-acts that I am her adviser, because I am the senior of her own family, and it is the first family here. But she will not listen to me."

"Then you must make her. By Apollo's flaming locks, you are a man, aren't you? And she is a woman? Then what's the difficulty?"

"Ha!" Worod's laugh was shrill with derision. "You are new in this country, I see. You do not know Zenobia. I wish you could spend one day with her. One day only. The day I spent with her yesterday, may the gods have mercy on me! She sent for me an hour after sunrise. She was reading Homer when I went in. She put the book down and asked me straight away for the week's return on the camel tax, the water tax, and the pasture tax. From memory she compared them with the figures of the week before, and she made me explain why they were less, as if I were a cheating slave."

"It seems she knows you."

"I shall overlook your insults. She went to the Temple of Bel, and she made me go with her, and she took the knife from the high priest's hand and made the morning offering to the sun. A woman making the temple offering! It is unheard of! She said 'The sacrifice will come better from my hand.' Then she walked in the town, and I had to go with her, and she wanted to know

why the pavements were dirty in the silversmiths' street, and
why there were not enough police in the cloth market, and what
arrangements I had made to receive the next camel caravan.

"In the quarter of the Jews we found a school of rabbis sitting in the street. They just sit there, in the way, as if no one
else existed. I wanted to send the guards ahead to scatter them
and she said, 'Softly, Worod, these are wise men, and the wise
should be listened to.' And she went quietly up to them, and
when she heard their master say—it was obviously for her ears,
and the most colossal piece of impudence I have heard for
months—'It is the way of woman to remain at home, and for
man to go into the market-place,' she answered him, quite
gently, 'Rabbi Gamaliel, is it not also written in your *Niddah*,
"God endowed woman with more intelligence than man"?' And
there she stood, for the rest of the morning, among these lousy
old yellowbeards, giving them text for text from their own holy
writ.

"Wait!" He raised his hand and uttered a frantic laugh. "The
day is young yet. We came back to the palace, and I can tell
you I was thankful, because I wanted to take my shoes off and
bathe my feet and lie down, while she spent an hour with her
children, which she does every day at noon. But she, she calls
for the two children, and she seats them by her, and she sends
for her secretary, and she starts dictating a chapter of this book
she is writing, this history of the Eastern nations, and she says
to me, 'Stay, Worod, stay. Sit here and listen. You are too fond
of Rome. It will do you good to learn how great is the past of
our Eastern lands. That is what I am writing the book for.' You
see how she treats me? And in the afternoon she took me to see
the soldiers training, and she jumped down from her chariot,
and she marched four miles with them, calling out praise and
all sorts of unladylike jokes to them, and she made me march,
too, in the full heat of the sun, a man of my age, and she laughed

at me, and she said, 'You may not like war, Worod, but you must keep fit for it.'

"No, no, you listen to me. You are always shutting me up. There is more yet. I was nearly dead at nightfall, and I wanted to go to bed, and she dragged me off to a banquet, with all the officers from the city regiments, and she sat there for hour after hour, drinking wine with them, flagon for flagon and never turning a hair, and she kept saying to me, 'Stay awake, Worod. You know how my officers love war. You know how they hate Rome. You wouldn't sleep and leave a little woman at their mercy, would you?' And from that accursed banquet I came straight here, and if you want to know what that woman is like, look at me now and pity me."

The Roman walked to the door. He grinned coldly, and threw his cloak about him. "I am telling you. Restrain her. We will give her more rope, if need be. But let her not break that rope. If you fail Rome, Worod, then will be the time to pity you."

*

The sky, now, was pale blue and cool, veiled with transparencies of high cloud. Speckling the blue, a vast circle of birds sailed over the city, a whirling black dust. They were pin-tailed grouse, Palmyra's heralds of dawn and dusk. During the day not one would be visible.

Their high, complaining note came faintly down to the city's streets. It mingled with the tapping of hammers in the goldsmiths' street; with the grumble of voices and crash of shutters as Palmyra's thousand tailors, the city's wealthiest guild, opened to public view the holes-in-the-wall that were their shops; floated in vain around the silent windows behind which the prostitutes, more numerous than the tailors and almost as powerful a guild, slept after the night's labours; came down to the already-busy caravanserai which, at the city's centre, lay to the north of the Great Avenue; and, across the avenue, invaded Zenobia's palace.

Zenobia lay in her bedchamber. The room, on an upper floor, was large and circular, with alcoved walls. The high ceiling sloped up to a central dome. In the dome a ring of bronze lamps burned softly. Beneath, the room was almost dark. The panelled paintings on the walls showed only as a faint glowing of rich colours, dusky woodlands amid which nymphs and fauns sported amorously. In the alcoves was the faint marble gleam of Greek statuary, a Psyche with childlike face and budding breasts, a Venus draped from the hips, a pair of slender, muscular wrestlers, a reclining hermaphrodite. The only natural light came from an arch which opened on to a pillared balcony. Through this doorway a mat of golden sunlight was lengthening towards the bed.

In the night's heat Zenobia had thrown off her coverings. Nested deep in the middle of her huge, square couch, she looked like a gleaming figurine set in the dark velvet of its case. Beneath her the sheets, of petal-soft Chinese silk, were of a purple so intense that in the shadows it seemed black. The damask counterpane across her thighs was rose-coloured. She squirmed in her sleep, and the lamplight made of her body a supple, sensual movement of honey-sheen among the colours of the couch. Her eyes were still closed, but she was aware of the faint crying of the birds. She knew that the day was here, but she was too saturated with the night's delicious languor to let herself awaken. Her senses fed on the comfort of the bed. The deep swansdown moulded itself to her, and it was like flesh as hot and soft as her own. The sheets, cool in the night's heat, were warm now, as tender against her as the skin of a beloved. She groaned in her throat, a slight pigeon's croon of pleasure, and pressed her body down into the bed, and felt the answering, fleshlike elasticity, and heard herself murmuring her dead husband's name.

She opened her eyes. The carpet of sunlight stretched almost to the bedside, and the bright blue in the balcony archway dazzled her. She turned her head. No sound came from the sentry outside the closed, cedar-wood doors; or from the two doors to right and left, one of which led into the room where her personal maid slept, the other to her children's room. She listened to the birds and to the distant, awakening noises of her city. She moved a hand down her body. Within her flesh she could feel the faintest throb, as if a frightened bird lay beneath her hand. She remembered the moment of half-awakening when she had imagined her husband's body in the bed's warmth, and the hot drench of desire that had gone through her insides. She sat up and faced the light, and let the lust drain out of her.

There were hangings behind the bed, rich fabrics, purple and rose and her favourite colour vermilion, to set it off against the room's cool whiteness. Soft Bokhara rugs littered the mosaic floor. There was no furniture except for a round-backed armchair and a low bedside table which, like the bed, were made of terebinth inlaid with silver. On the table were a pitcher, a cup, and a bowl heaped with fruit, all of silver, and a bronze gong to call her slave. Ignoring the gong, she slipped out of bed, stretched to enjoy the lazy ache of muscles, and reached for the rose silk morning-gown that lay across the chair.

With the gown across her shoulders, she stood on the balcony. The heat had not yet killed the dawn breeze, and she lifted her face to let the coolness and the light touch of early sun dispel the fevered weakness that lingered in her. Her head was clear, despite the previous night's drinking, but her limbs were heavy. Her breathing was deep with contentment. It was always with a feeling of personal possession that she looked down from here at the city. In all directions a skyline of palaces and temples enchanted her; a vision of wealth and power. Beyond, the flat dun floor of the desert, stretching to the south in seeming infinitude, emphasized her city's remoteness from the world, its solitary splendour, feeding again her sense of power.

She went into the children's room. It was smaller than her own, and more shadowy, for the balcony was curtained off, and the only lamp was on a small, claw-footed tripod between the two couches.

Julia, her eight-year-old daughter, was fast asleep, demure beneath the coverlet. She was the image of her mother, with a paler skin that gave her face an ivory delicacy. Wahab, at twelve, resembled his dead father, dark, hawk-boned, fierce of face. Yet it was the boy whom the mother favoured. Wahab's eyes were open. He was watching his mother suspiciously. She sat on the edge of his bed and touched his face. "Did you sleep well, my darling?"

He lay back out of her reach and grumbled, "You always ask me that. Why shouldn't I?"

"Your skin is so hot and damp, dear. You mustn't be angry with your mother. You're such a delicate boy."

"I'm not delicate." He sat up. "Look here, Mother, how long have I got to go on sleeping in the same room as her?" A sulky lift of his face indicated Julia.

"I've told you, dear. When you're a man, you'll have apartments of your own and lots of slaves, and everything else you wish for. But you're only a baby still, and I want to keep my eye on you. I do like to have my two darlings close to me, you know."

"Oh!" He pushed his lips out. "You don't understand."

"What don't I understand, my little sweetheart?"

He burst out. "I'm not your—" He sighed exaggeratedly. "Oh, what's the use?" A defiant look at his mother. "Well, I mean, Mother, women. Where am I supposed to go with them? You dress me up in the purple and show me to the troops, and everyone has to call me 'Highness,' but, I—well, if you must know, I still have to sneak down to the slave quarters if I want a girl." His face was screwed up with anger, and tears were bright be-

hind his eyes, for Zenobia was laughing. "I don't see anything
to laugh at!"

Zenobia said through her laughter, "Sh! Sh!" Julia was stirring.
"Oh, my little boy! Women already? You? My baby?" She put
her arms around him. "Your mother's going to lose you soon.
I can see that." Her face was bright with laughter. "And I want
to do so much for you." Julia was awake, watching them with
wide eyes. "Why, my pet, I'm going to give you something more
than slave girls. I'm going to give you kingdoms." She held him
closer, his cheek against hers, and he wriggled in protest. Unheeding of his discontent, or of Julia in the other bed, she
rocked him against her breast, murmuring, "My king, my king,
my little king!"

*

Two hours after noon, when the midday heat and the midday
sleep were over, crowds poured into the streets of Palmyra. In
the dark caverns of their shops the craftsmen toiled once more,
while the human tides surged through the narrow streets in
front of them and a din of chatter rolled up between the walls.
The market-place was a black heaving of movement roaring
with noise. Strollers thronged the Great Avenue, and from time
to time the sun-bleached pavement in the centre emptied to
allow a troop of desert horsemen to gallop past, a caravan escort,
followed out of the caravanserai by a procession of swaying,
laden camels. Caravans were the source of this city's wealth.
The most important of them were housed with honour at the
city's heart. Between the pillars that lined the avenue stood
statues of famous caravan leaders, of marble, bronze and silver.

Beyond Zenobia's palace the avenue reached the City Square,
with the Senate House on its right and the open, semicircular
steps of the theatre on the far side. People were pouring into the
theatre. The steps were already dotted with seated figures. The
crowds in the square had an air of business. Everywhere were

groups of men with low, urgent voices, frowning, nodding, gesticulating. Small boys in dirty loincloths flitted among them, selling the pistachio nuts beloved in Palmyra. A poet in Roman toga read his latest work to a cluster of citizens in the portico of the Senate House.

At the far end of the colonnade a crowd of merchants, in the striped, coloured robes of the town Arab, stroked their beards in thoughtful silence or murmured to each other while the latest prices were read aloud for spices, perfumes, ivory, gold, silver, myrrh, frankincense, cinnamon, silk, slaves, olive oil, cotton, corn, raisins, grapes, wine, figs, cattle, for dried fish from Tiberias, aromatic oils from the Gulf and furs from beyond the Black Sea. A religious procession passed on its way to the Sun Temple, white-robed priests leading a white heifer, and behind them two girl musicians on a camel, in Greek dresses, their hair coiled in braids, one beating a drum, the other playing a double flute. The crowds were a swirl of many colours, a babel of tongues, their costumes Greek and Roman and Syrian and Arab and Persian and Indian.

People streamed constantly into the theatre. The tiers of seats in the theatre were packed now. On the small, semicircular stage to which the banks of seats swept down stood a high, empty pulpit, draped with shining banners of silk on which appeared the complex monogram of the Christian sect. In front of the stage, the first two tiers were occupied by women in white robes.

All at once the buzz of the audience died away. A man walked onto the stage. On each side of him walked a beautiful girl in a long white robe. Two secretaries were at his heels, scribbling on tablets to his dictation. He glanced at the crowd, the movement of his head careless yet arrogant. He was tall, his broad shoulders held back haughtily, his stately walk imbued with command. He wore a white cloak over a long, girdled black gown. His head, held high, was big, dominating, maned with silver hair. He had a broad forehead and burning eyes, dark skin

and pinched cheeks. His lips were a thin red slash of authority
beneath a prominent nose. This was Paul of Samosata, the rebel
bishop of Emesa, who had twice been excommunicated by the
synod of Christian clergy but who still ruled in his diocese by
main force.

His bodyguard, a score of burly hillmen, had ranged themselves in a semicircle beneath the platform. He dismissed his
secretaries and raised his hands, while the two girls gracefully
lifted the cloak from his shoulders. He mounted the pulpit with
a stately tread; and as he did so the white-clad women in the
front tiers rose to their feet and filled the theatre with the high,
thrilling harmonies of a hymn. Paul stood in the pulpit, splendid
as a hero's statue, till they had finished. Then, once more, he
raised his hands in the vibrant silence, and began to preach.

His voice at first was soft, low, warm. Rich women in the audience sat squeezed between sweaty drovers and street sweepers.
Beggars with sores and stumps and milky eyes, roughs in goat-
skins with daggers at their belts, slave girls, prostitutes, pale
rhetoric students, and thickset porters, all sat hunched forward,
with parted lips and glistening eyes, while the warm voice
caressed them. It told them of the grave, to which all must go.
It told them of a life beyond the grave which the rich, with
their private cults and their private temples, could buy, but
which was closed to the poor. The voice rose and slashed, high
as a trumpet call across the arena. "Why are these mysteries for
the rich? Where is the mystery which the poor may enter?"

His arms were raised again. In the sun's white, flooding radi-
ance, all the faces were upturned to him. "Mine is the mystery."
His voice became harsh and clamant. "The mystery of Christ!
The mystery of Paul!"

The silence was agonizing. "I!" His voice tore into a scream.
"I!" The pulpit thundered to the stamp of his foot. "I!" Again
the thunder of the pulpit and, in the silence, the crack of his
open palm smacking on the lectern. "I, Paul, am the keeper of

the gate, the gate that leads to everlasting life!" He sent a long, searching look round the arena. There was a white fleck at the corner of his mouth. Again his long, echoing scream. "Who comes to Christ? Who comes to Paul? Who wishes to cheat death and live forever?"

Thousands leaped to their feet. The theatre echoed with the thunder of their rising and their cries. "I!" "I!" Men and women were weeping, reaching out as if to clutch for a largess that Paul tossed among them. They stood and stamped, and the thunder of their frenzy rose, and the choir was standing once again, weaving into the uproar the high, spellbinding harmonies of another hymn. Paul stood with his arms upraised, his face blind with ecstasy, as if he were drinking in the noise.

A spreading of his fingers quelled them instantly. He spoke in a voice that was low once more. "The bishops condemn me. The bishops of Rome, of Caesarea, of Tarsus, of Alexandria, of Jerusalem! Holy men! Clever men!" Scornful laughter surged from the congregation. "They tell you that Christ is God come down to earth. They tell you he is only a spirit. I say he is no spirit. He is a man like you and me. He is flesh and blood, and he has entered into God, and he is proof that all of flesh and blood can enter into God. To me alone he has shown the way. I alone can show you the way. You—" He was stabbing his forefinger at the audience. "You! You! That is my treason to the Church. I am denounced because I offer you eternal life!"

A fresh outburst of frenzy. "Shame! ... Long live Paul! ... Down with the bishops! ... Paul! ... Paul!" The tramping and the chanting became rhythmic. "Paul! Paul! Paul!"

A single voice, thin but sharp as a sword blade, cut through the acclamations. "Heretic!"

The noise died for a moment, on a note of astonishment, then exploded again in a furious babble. Paul raised his hand. His face was wrathful. His eyes searched the packed tiers. "Who spoke? Silence! Silence, I say! Let him speak again!"

The noise subsided. In the silence, a man rose. "Heretic!"

He was an old man, a bag of bones clad in skins, with dirty grey hair down to his shoulders and a beard that reached to his waist. He leaned on a gnarled stick. His thin voice rose. "The hymns are to Paul. The prayers are to Paul. The glory is Paul's. You do not call these people to worship Christ, but to worship Paul. For your own ambitions you madden the rabble with promises. You—"

A fresh outburst of shouting drowned his words. There was a surge from the tiers of people rushing to mob him. He vanished amid a flurry of fists and a hubbub of angry yells.

"Stop!"

Another voice, a high, clear woman's voice, sounded through the din. The roar of the crowd continued, but Paul, glancing down, turned to the crowd with a changed expression and shouted, "Stop! Stop! Silence!"

The crowd calmed. Thousands of faces turned at once, looking where Paul looked. An astonished silence lay upon them all.

In the broad entrance aisle that led to the pulpit, a woman sat astride a white Numidian horse. She wore loose Persian trousers, a white, sleeveless blouse fringed with purple, and a golden Roman helmet with a vermilion crest. Behind her, four men abreast on Arab horses, sat her mailed escort, armed with shield and lance.

Paul made an obeisance. "Greetings to the Lady Zenobia! I ask your pardon, lady. Sometimes the ecstasy is too intense. People are carried away."

"So I see." Zenobia's voice was resonant and strong. Her gaze was candid. "Bishop Paul, all religions are protected in my city, for it is my belief that all men are seeking a God whom perhaps none of us has yet found. I do not tolerate in order that others may persecute."

Paul turned to his congregation. "Brothers and sisters, hear the words of the Lady Zenobia! Hear and remember, for they were the very words it was in my mind to utter."

Zenobia looked at him quizzically. "You are a wise man, Paul. Now let Nestor the Hermit speak."

The old man rose again, tottering upon his staff. There was blood on his face. "God bless you, Lady Zenobia." His voice was weak. "May the Lord Jesus bring you to His Faith!" He paused to gather strength. "Paul of Samosata, the pastors of our Faith renounce all riches. You amass riches, from the brethren."

"I accept them from the brethren, but I give them to the poor."

"You give to the ruffians, the idlers, who form your body-guard, and who silence those who try to speak against you. Paul of Samosata, the pastors of our Faith renounce women. You live with two fair women at your side."

"I prove my chastity by living virtuously with these two maidens, teaching them their Christian duties."

"You rant and roar, and you raise devils in the multitude."

"The strength of God is in my breast, and it enters into those who hear me."

A murmur of applause swelled among the congregation. The old man shook his head. "You are too clever for me, Paul of Samosata. I am weaker than you, but Christ is stronger, and you will fall." He turned and stumbled down the steps.

Threats were shouted against him. The murmur of anger grew. Men started up from their places towards him. Zenobia spoke again. "Bishop Paul, if one hair of this old man's head is harmed, now or in the future, many will suffer. Have I spoken for you again?"

"You have spoken for me, and for God, too, Lady Zenobia. See, brethren, your bishop is the friend of our lady Zenobia, and she is his protector." He looked down at Zenobia. His air was once more commanding, assured, male. He spoke softly, directly to her. "And while Paul is her friend, all the Christians are her faithful subjects."

Zenobia smiled. "Indeed, Paul, we understand each other." She raised her voice. "Remember, Christians. You are tolerated. Tolerate each other." She turned her horse and rode out of the theatre.

*

"I need your help with Wahab." It was evening. Zenobia was going to a council of state, escorted by her closest friend, Longinus. "I give him tutors and he just boxes their ears. Poor dear, he has no patience. Why don't you teach him?"

"I am a logician, not a miracle worker, Zenobia. That boy of yours is a fool, and he wants thrashing." Longinus was small, fat, and walked fussily, one fist clutching his Greek gown at the waist. His little eyes on each side of a clown's nose gleamed like those of some greedy or concupiscent merchant. A few strands of grey hair were arranged with pathetic vanity on a bald skull. His big beard, and the quiffs over his ears, were carefully combed. Life, however, like an artist, had added touches which revealed him for what he was, the most famous philosopher of his time, the beloved master of the Athenian academies. It had traced deep lines on his domed forehead, shaped his thick lips into a fearless, assured set, and given his grey eyes a gaze that was level and unflinching. Zenobia had long corresponded with him, as she did with many other savants, and two years ago he had come to Palmyra at her invitation.

They were strolling in a portico of immense length which looked on to dusky, scented gardens. The inner wall was lined with slaves in royal livery who knelt and touched their heads to the floor as Zenobia approached. The long line of backs rippled downward as if a current had run through it. Eyes gleamed with fear as heads bowed. Huddled bodies were tense, as if waiting for the whip, while their mistress's footsteps tapped past them. A chamberlain and a soldier emerged from a corridor and at once cast themselves down until Zenobia had gone by. All dreaded the woman whose presence governed the remotest parts of the palace: noticing and punishing the least incorrectness of dress, the slightest want of alacrity in obedience, the tiniest pilfering from a kitchen, the dust left in a corner. Zenobia marked their prostrations with cold, inspecting eyes. Her carriage was that of an autocrat; but to Longinus she spoke with the voice of a disciple, in a wheedling, feminine whine. "Nobody else talks to me like you."

"My dear girl, you can send me back to Athens if you don't like the truth. It's my only stock-in-trade. Without it I am of no use to you." He indicated the bowed backs. "What does an enlightened woman want with all this? You play at being an Athenian but you live like an Oriental."

"These people are of the East. Any other way would be weakness to them."

"Perhaps. But by what right do you rule like a Persian monarch? You are Zenobia, a merchant's daughter."

"I am widow to a man whom Rome gave the name *imperator*. I claim his rights for myself and for my children."

"Your husband did not make men bow to the ground, for all his titles."

"Longinus"—a sharpness entered her voice—"I am a woman among men. That is like being a man among tigers. If I did not keep them in their place I would have been overthrown long ago. I respect you, my friend, but sometimes you are so unworldly. Tell me, though, won't you try with Wahab?"

"I will not. But I will give you some advice. Stop spoiling him. I am worldly enough to see that you are too much of a man at some times and too much of a woman at others. Your husband would have hardened the boy, to fit him for the future. You are softening him with sweets and kisses."

She laughed. "You know best about Plato, but a mother knows best about her child."

Between double doors, which slaves silently opened, they entered a long, lofty chamber whose walls were lined with busts on pedestals. The three other members of Zenobia's council of state bowed. The bishop Paul was one of them. He was a man of subtle mind and he commanded the loyalty of the Christian community, just as Longinus had much influence over the Greek element in the city. Worod was present as a concession to the Septimian family and to the merchants. The army was represented by its general, Zabda.

The magisterial chair in which Zenobia seated herself was on a dais. Its arms were carved to represent the Palmyrene emblem, the flying dragon. The wall behind was hung with a display of weapons. She nodded permission for the men to sit on stools in front of her and said, "Send the slaves away. Slaves have long ears."

She sat upright, her hands resting on the dragon heads, her chin lifted imperiously. Her voice matched her glance; cold and clear. "You are going to hear a report from Zabda. Then I am going to put two questions to you. When you have answered them, you will go."

Zabda rose. He was of medium height, hard and dark as weathered teak, with a martinet's straight back, and a curled Persian beard, and the fierce, beady eyes of a bird of prey. His uniform was in Eastern style, a red tunic and a long tight skirt of olive green. He gave utter loyalty to Zenobia because she was his commander's widow. His was the iron hand that had silenced the plotters and grumblers against her in the first days of her rule. He read from a scroll in a harsh monotone. "Disposition of Roman forces in Asia. Transfers to the Danube continue. Of nine legions in the East, a war strength now remains of three and a half. Only headquarters sections remain of the Fourth, Twelfth, Fifteenth, and Sixteenth in Asia Minor. In Africa the

Third Cyrenaican is under orders to embark for Italy, in transit to the north, the Third Augustan is down to four cohorts, the Second Trajan remains at Alexandria in full strength. In Judea the Sixth keeps three cohorts, the Tenth Fretensis at Jerusalem is complete. Correct to the first day of this month."

"Now—" Zenobia leaned back in her chair. She was aloof and authoritative, yet her attire was a picture of feminine softness: a Greek robe of ivory colour that flowed to her feet, with an underhanging fold beneath her left breast and another fold pinned to her right shoulder by a large medallion of gold; a flat turban with a gold headband, fastened on each side by a huge ruby; beneath the two coiled braids of her hair, massive, gold-looped earrings from which hung clusters of pearls and emeralds; and a long, two-string pearl necklace on her breast. The wildness, the fawn's softness had gone, yet she was no less beautiful at twenty-nine than at eighteen. The firmness of command enhanced the symmetry of her small face. Her eyes, large and dark, with long lashes whose movements were expressive, were the brighter for the intelligence in them. "You have heard the position. Hardly more than three Roman legions remain in the East. You may be sure that more will go soon, for they are hard-pressed on the Danube. In all the years that we have held the Persian frontier for Rome, we have built up a large and valiant army. The provinces of the East are ours by right. Is this the moment to seize them?"

Zabda was on his feet. "My men are ready."

Zenobia raised her hand to silence him. "And here is my second question. If we strike now, shall it be north to the Black Sea or south towards Egypt?"

Zabda had remained on his feet, impatient as a hunting dog. "I can answer that one, lady. Strike south at once. When you've got Egypt you've cut off Rome's corn supply. Then you can go north into Asia Minor whenever you want. When your enemy is weak, hit him hard where it hurts most."

"Weak?" Worod had jumped up, his hands outspread in dismay. "Rome weak? Lady Zenobia, this man may be useful to you on a battlefield, but when he is in your palace put a muzzle on him, for the love of the gods."

Zenobia watched him speculatively. He was often useful, not only for his connections but for the information he brought. Zenobia's power in Palmyra rested in no small measure on a seemingly occult omniscience. Its source was in an informal but effective spy system. She had an understanding with the Prostitutes' Guild. Worod had a swarm of informers among the slaves of the rich. Zenobia thus learned, from the indiscretions of bed and table, secrets which she used sometimes to mystify, sometimes to terrorize, invariably to strengthen her power.

Worod was shouting, "Rome weak? She has twenty-eight legions, the finest troops in the world. She has Claudius, Probus, and this fellow Aurelian with his cavalry army—yes, you've heard of it, a whole army of horsemen that has destroyed four barbarian hordes. Is that weakness? Zabda counted up the legions in the East. He didn't count up the auxiliary troops or the armed colonists."

"The auxiliary troops are our clansmen. We'll win 'em over. Buy 'em if we have to. The colonists we'll massacre." Zabda spoke from his chair, testy and contemptuous.

"Listen to him, Lady Zenobia!" Worod's voice was shrill. "Talk sense to him and he blows a trumpet at you. A loud noise is his substitute for thought. I beg of you, kinswoman, do nothing rash. Wait awhile and watch. Remember your honoured husband. He knew how strong Rome is. He kept the peace with her. All this talk of her difficulties means nothing. She has such wealth and strength that she will stand forever."

Zabda grunted, "With three and a half Eastern legions? Sit down, manikin."

"Zenobia, my lady, I protest! Is an elder of your clan to be insulted? Why have the Romans dared to reduce their garrisons? Not because they are unsuspecting, but because they do not fear us. They hold the sea. They have a great fleet of transports. It would take them less time to bring troops back here than it would take Zabda to add three and three."

Zabda was up again. "Who talked about insults? It is strange, Worod, how you always speak with the voice of Rome."

"And it is strange"—Worod trembled with defiance—"how you always speak with the voice of Persia, which wants to see Palmyra and Rome at each other's throats."

"You dare to—" Zabda's hand was at his sword.

"Enough!" Zenobia smote the arm of her chair. "Silence, both of you! How dare you act like a couple of snarling curs in my presence?"

Worod bobbed down at once. Zabda stood doggedly by his stool. "My lady, I'm sorry. I'm only a soldier. I speak my thoughts. And I speak for the army, which looks for conquests and riches and glory from the princess it has always supported. And I tell you this, Lady Zenobia—the army can bring you kingdoms for your children."

Response dawned, for the first time, in Zenobia's eyes. She murmured, "Kingdoms—"

She sat in thought. Then, "Now you, Paul."

"But—" It was Worod.

"Please, my friend." Paul had risen, gripping the fold of his robe. He checked Worod with a benedictory gesture. "Illustrious lady, between Scylla and Charybdis the crafty may sail. It would be insolence to tell one so great as yourself to be content with her present realms. But it would be folly, or crime, to say that you should challenge Rome. Rome is not to be challenged. Here, then, is my advice. Take all you can from Rome —without war. Snatch when Rome is looking the other way. Increase your power by guile. Multiply the symbols of your independence. Strengthen your influence in the provinces. Quietly, without fuss, build up your army. But do not fight."

"Yes." Worod was radiant with relief. "Yes, that is it, that is just what I say."

"Please!" Paul subdued him again. "For instance, most excellent lady, there are the brethren of my faith. They are already numerous in the land. They obey the Bishop of Rome, who is the first of their pastors. And he, dear lady, speaks not only as a Christian but as a Roman. Would it not strengthen your rule if the Christians of the East bore no allegiance to Rome? Would it not be better if they formed a church of their own, with a man at its head who spoke in one voice with you?"

"Yes, I am sure. This is all very disinterested. All three of you are very disinterested. Longinus, have you nothing to say to me?"

Longinus was slumped on his stool, somnolent, legs sprawled. He looked up. "Nothing you want to hear, my lady."

"Let me be the judge of that."

"Very well. What is all this nonsense about seizing new provinces? Every morning you debate solemnly with me about the way to the good life. Then you come here and waste your time on follies."

"You call my problems follies?"

"What else? Since when were five kingdoms better than one? Since when was a kingdom better than a city? Since when was it better to govern a city than your own house?" There were noises of impatience from the other men. "Do shut these fellows up, Zenobia. Let everyone live in his own house, I say, and be content. If you are going to seek the truth in your library, seek it also in life. Those who embrace power must drive truth out of their houses. Power and the good life are in opposite directions."

Zenobia observed a moment's respectful silence. Then, in a small, cunning voice, "Yes, that is very true. But Longinus, if

—just if—you were of the same mind as Zabda and wanted to make war, which way would you strike?"

" 'Mind' and 'Zabda' are two words I have never before associated."

"Yes, but—" She made an appealing face. "If?"

"In that case I should certainly go north. The Romans have their hands full. There is just a chance they would yield Asia Minor in order not to become embroiled at this moment in an Eastern war. But to threaten Egypt, their granary, would compel them to strike back at once."

He saw Zenobia nodding, and added, "But mark you, I have not said that the time is ripe."

"No." She beat her fist gently on the arm of her chair. Her expression was troubled. "That is the key to it. What is the true state of affairs on the Roman frontiers? What is happening in Rome? These new men there, how capable are they? Would they defend their Eastern provinces?" She looked up, sharp and decisive once more, majestic for all her smallness. "Go, now. All of you."

"Lady—" It was Zabda. "What have you decided?"

"Go, I say. You were called to answer questions, not to ask them." She turned on Worod, who was hovering pitifully by his stool. "You, too!"

As the men moved to the door, she stepped from the dais and laid a hand on Longinus' arm. She spoke softly. "My friend, forgive me if I disappoint you as a pupil. Perhaps when I am older I shall be able to live by philosophy, but not while my passions are alive. In the meantime, I shall heed you in one thing. I shall make no decision yet. I cannot trust any of these others. I shall send someone to Rome, someone who is known to no one but me, who can be my eyes and ears there and help me to a decision."

He made a slight nod of approval. She said more loudly, "In the morning, then? Plato's *Symposium?*"

When Longinus had left, Paul was still in the room. He waited a few paces from Zenobia, watching her, smiling slightly.

"Have you something more to say, Paul?"

He inclined his head. "Dear lady, I wish to serve you. I wish to talk of how I may help you."

"And how may you help me?"

"I wish to offer you a gift. Illustrious lady, I have watched you this last hour. I saw you alone, facing great problems. And I asked myself a question that has often been in my mind. What is it that a woman needs when she is alone, confronting perils?"

"Well, what is it that she needs?"

"A man at her side." His voice was soft.

Zenobia stood still and placid. Paul moved a pace nearer. "Dear lady, hear me, for I wish only to serve. A woman needs the strength of a man and the comfort of a man. That is the gift I wish to make you. Of my mind you can judge. My person you can see."

He laid a hand on her arm. "Many women could tell you—"

He moved back gently. "My lady"—his voice was low and even—"I meant no disrespect."

Her face was like a stone mask of contempt, out of which her eyes flashed anger. She murmured, "If you wish to live, never touch me again."

She took a step towards the door. The slaves in the corridor, four of them opposite the door, saw her and threw themselves down in obeisance. She glanced back at Paul, a command plain in her face. He began to bow from the waist, his hands to his forehead. She stood erect, no relenting in her face. Paul sank down on his knees, in a feline movement. "Lady," he said very softly, "you must forgive. To me you are a goddess. A goddess of rarest marble." His head touched the floor. She turned her back on him and walked out of the room.

*

At night another Palmyra came to life, the pleasure city. Zenobia, weak and hot from her bath, stood on her balcony listening to the distant, muted roar of voices, the bray of music. Her dark face shone in the lamplight. She looked like a woman waiting for a lover.

The town was a carpet of darkness, red-spattered by a thousand tiny torch-flames, each of which pushed back the shadows to reveal the ghostly white walls of a street corner, a dome, minaret, or angle of flat roof—for the streets of Palmyra, unlike those of Rome, were lit at night—revealing a vista of unreal palaces, peeping out of gloom. Far away a festive bonfire in the courtyard of the caravanserai cast a red glare that threw into relief a whole splendid stretch of the Great Avenue, stately pillars marching into a fiery light and vanishing into the darkness. The tiny, turbaned figures of men hurried to and fro in the firelight.

There it was at her feet, the wild Palmyra of the night, swarming with lean men from the desert, traders from across a dozen frontiers, soldiers, city merchants, most of them life-starved after weeks of crossing burning deserts, all with money to scatter. Down there in those shadowy white streets, in the glare-shot darkness, the cookshops were crowded; the Indian women in their dancing-booths writhed obscenely to the sound of kettledrum, cymbal, and castanet and the rough, eager shouting of men; contending tides of people surged through narrow streets where the luxury shops stayed open almost till the dawn; sellers of honeycakes and pistachios breasted the mobs, shouting their tuneful cries; the litters of the rich moved through the crowds, the torches of their escorts making red glowworms in the distance, on their way to banquets, private theatricals, musical competitions; in roped-off rings, scooped out of black human swarms, huge Thracian wrestlers strove and grunted; and everywhere the white houses of the prostitutes had come to life.

Now, in the night, they were the queens of this city, its reason for being, ministers to a horde of hungry men. The shutters and doors were open, light and music streamed out into the streets, soft voices invited to feasts where every lust might be satisfied, where the black, oiled bodies of African girls, the flesh of milk-white, muscular wenches from Britain and Germany, the subtle sexual cunning of Greek, Indian, and Syrian girls were to be hired. They were down there in their thousands, writhing and laughing in their beds, a whole social stratum of this city's life, an industry, toiling with supple limbs and clinging lips to bring a deluge of gold and silver pieces tinkling down, bringing wealth to the treasury through their taxes, and holding thereby a great organized power in the city.

Zenobia was thinking of the prostitutes; of their panting and throaty laughter. She envied them. She envied them their pleasure, and the crowds, the noise that surged around them. In her aloneness, she felt as far away as the stars, up on her balcony.

She envied them, and all the other women of Palmyra, so different from herself. What was a woman in the East? A creature lolling on cushions, eating sweetmeats, busy with cosmetics, her whole life taken up with the minute study of one art alone: the pleasing of men; a creature useless yet treasured, wielding her influence in the bed. Why was she, Zenobia, so different? Why did a man's energy race through her veins? Why did she hunt and march and scheme like a man, with a man's ambitions? Why could she not be just another idle, happy, sensual female?

The heat was in her blood again, a woman's sensuality coursed through her; but she knew that to keep her power over men, men who had been born and bred to despise women, she must, she must, she *must* keep apart from them. Once let a man strike into her with his strength, once let a man look down into her face after love, seeing his own mastery in her happiness and weakness, and she was lost. And all the other men around her, the crafty statesmen, the arrogant soldiers, the merchant chieftains jealous for her position, would sniff the woman's weakness in her, would know that she could be mastered. She saw it in their faces now, in the face of almost every man who approached her, the hungering look, the questioning look, the wariness of the dog sneaking up on a bitch, the fatuous conceit: it was, at times, the one thing that saved her from reaching out for a man, this shabby smallness of men. It had been in Paul's face tonight.

She went into her room. "Of rarest marble." She uttered a soft laugh in her throat. She knew that she would not be able to sleep for a long time.

She lay across her couch and thought of the council meeting. Plan and counterplan, a hundred questions seethed in her mind. Information, that was what she must have. Rome was distant, its mind hidden from her. She must see Rome. She must see the working of Rome's mind.

She touched the bedside gong. When her maid came, she said, "Bring me the prostitute Philomene."

CHAPTER FIVE

THE SECOND MEETING

ON A small hill, against a leaden sky, stood a group of men. The tallest of them was Aurelian. His staff officers surrounded him. On his left hand was his secretary, Eros, with writing tablet ready; on his right was the young Goth, Maxin.

Two years had passed since the boy's capture. He was seventeen years old, tall and sturdy. He wore a slave's tunic but he had a commanding grace of posture. His hair, cut short, was a cap of yellow. Brute wariness was graven in his face; but his eyes were clear and challenging.

All the group wore thick woollen cloaks, for it was mid-January. The plain of southern Thrace, on which they looked down, was a sodden, grey-green quilt all the way to the distant white peaks of the Rhodope Mountains. All last summer Aurelian had been fighting on the shores of the Black Sea. Now, the barbarian hordes had vanished into their steppeland blizzards. Aurelian had established his winter quarters down here; partly because the mild climate, close to the Aegean, would benefit his troops; partly because his training plans called for unfrozen rivers. It did not seem wrong to him to train his men hard after an arduous campaign. He believed it more important to keep them in trim than to curry favour with them.

To the north, the plain was seamed by the river Nestus curving towards the sea. Echelons of cavalry made patterns across the plain. At this moment, however, Aurelian and his escort were not watching the manoeuvres, nor even the horseman who was riding hard, from the west, towards the foot of their hill.

Their attention was occupied by a group of figures that beaded the crest of another hill, about a mile away.

"Twelve of them," Aurelian said. "Horsemen, first yesterday, now today. Who is so interested in us?"

One of the staff officers spoke. "The patrol we sent after them yesterday found nothing, sir. I sent details into Deraea and Abdera this morning to look around." These twin towns were on the coast nearby.

Eros said, "Master, they have vanished again." The distant hilltop was bare.

The officer said, "Probably pilgrims, sir, on their way to the shrine at Deraea. Or some of the local chieftains come to gape at our exercises. It will do them no harm to see that." He indicated the cavalry, scrawled like the handwriting of power upon the plain. Aurelian nodded. There was satisfaction on his face. He turned to Maxin. "You see, lad? Each of those columns has a regiment of mounted engineers. They carry bridging gear on horseback. No one can move, across rivers or across land, as fast as Roman soldiers. I will make them practice like jugglers until they have the business perfect. In the spring they will be ready for new victories. That is the Roman way, lad. In the winter your people sleep like bears. Rome makes ready. Rome never sleeps."

There was no doubt that the boy understood. His expression did not change, but his body was aware, like an animal's. The first column had reached the river, and he watched its scouts swimming across, their horses towing them. An officer said, "Does he never speak, sir?"

"Not since the day we took him. Quite an achievement for a young boy, eh? There's good stuff in him. Look at him. He understands us. You can see his fur bristling. But he keeps his mouth shut tight. Well, the stubbornest beast gives in to his trainer in the end. He'll tire before I do."

"Has he never tried to escape, sir?"

The boy's head was turned away from them but they could see him tensed, listening.

"Not now. The first three months we kept him tied. He flew at his guards every time his hands were freed. I think he wanted to be killed. He'd have run away then, sure enough, if we'd let him loose. But we were patient. We fed him, clothed him, talked to him. You know the way you talk to a beast, quietly, quietly. I've never let his silence worry me. I talk to him. He's a boy. Things interest him. I can see him listening, in spite of himself. And so it was that one day he changed. I felt it at once. The tamer always sees it right away, this surrender. I let him off the rope and he didn't run away. That was the start. Do you know what had happened to him? He was spellbound. I had shown him wonders he had never dreamed of. He knows that while he is with me he will go on seeing wonders. Our men drilling and fighting, our cities, our aqueducts, our roads, our bridges, our manufactures, our baths, our theatres, our games. For all his silence, he drinks it in like wine. He is halfway tamed already. He's like the dog that won't do its tricks yet but stays at the trainer's heels."

The officer said, "To me, sir, he looks more like a leopard stalking you than a dog at your heels. I'd be afraid to leave him at my back if I had the care of him, for fear of being knifed."

"He won't knife me. He's too interested. He doesn't want to grow into our ways, but our ways are growing into him. He'll talk, one of these days. And that will be a new birth for him. There could be a life in front of him like mine. That's what I'm out to make, the finest fighting man in the world, a Goth turned Roman soldier."

The second column, light engineers, reached the river. They dismounted, unslung floats from their horses, lashed their gear to the floats and crossed the river, horses towing men, men towing floats. On the far side they scattered into a purposeful swarm; and a semicircular palisade sprang up at the water's edge. Some way beyond them the scouts had halted, giving them cover.

Maxin was a living illustration of Aurelian's words. He was poised towards the distant bridgehead, his lips parted, his eyes aflame with thought. When the third column, the bridging engineers, reached the river, he nodded slightly, as if gratified to have guessed their actions in advance. Working as rapidly as their predecessors, they unslung from mules the small, one-piece assault boats which were standard equipment in the Roman army, roped them together and launched them successively. The soldiers in the leading boats paddled across and, on the far bank, hauled their boats back against the current into the palisaded bridgehead. At once the advance party, their palisade finished, swarmed from boat to boat, drawing the linked boats together to make a bridge. On the opposite bank the main column continued to launch boats, while planks were unloaded from the mules and stacked to plan.

The main body, an echelon of six columns far-flung across the plain, was coming up. Aurelian was dictating an order to his secretary. It was addressed to newly promoted cavalry officers. "If you wish to be a good officer, restrain the hands of your soldiers. No man shall steal another's fowl or touch his sheep. No man shall carry off grapes, or thresh out grain, or exact oil, salt or firewood, and each shall be content with his own allowance."

The bridge was complete, the planks laid. Aurelian said, "That was the quickest bridging yet. Send my congratulations, and an order for double rations. And time the crossing." He returned to his dictating. "Are you ready, Eros?—Let them get their plunder from the enemy, not from friendly villagers. Their arms shall be kept burnished, their equipment bright, their boots in good repair. Issue new uniforms promptly when the old ones deteriorate. Let the men keep their pay in their pockets and not spend it in the taverns."

He paused to watch the lone rider who was climbing the hill

towards them. White cloak and scarf, bull's-head on shield. Horse at the last gasp. A tribune of the Tenth Gemina. A message from General Headquarters—important, clearly, since a field officer was employed as dispatch rider. The tribune dismounted, saluted, spoke to an officer, who brought him across to Aurelian. The tribune saluted again. He held out a scroll. "For you, sir. My orders were to give it directly into your hands."

The string of the scroll was fastened by a lead seal on which the imperial eagle was stamped. Aurelian opened the letter and glanced down at it. He was silent for a few moments, frowning. Then he resumed his dictation. "Let all soldiers wear their decorations. Let each man groom his own horse and baggage-animal, let no one sell the fodder allowed him for his beast, and let the men take care in common of the mule belonging to each company."

He paused again. This time his scrutiny of the scroll was prolonged. He looked up. His cavalry, having established rearguard and bridgehead, were crossing the bridge. He seemed, however, to be looking far beyond them. He drew a long, deep breath and looked down once more at the message.

At Sirmium, in the nones of January. To my brother Aurelian. Claudius, ill these three weeks with a fever, is going to die. This is known to all here, including Claudius himself. He names you as his successor, and a majority of the Staff are in accord. The troops applaud your victories. If you show yourself among them, they will be yours. The times call for you. Come at once, and you will be emperor. Ever—PROBUS.

Absently, Aurelian continued his order. "Let each man yield obedience as a soldier and no man as a slave." He became aware of the fixity with which the tribune was watching him. "I'll finish this later." He turned to the tribune. "Do you know what is in the letter you brought?"

"Yes, Caesar."

The word "Caesar" acted like a trumpet blast upon the group.

Every face jerked towards Aurelian, startled, enquiring. An officer, exultant understanding bursting out of him, shouted, "Hail Caesar!" The arms shot up in salute. The voices rang, "Hail Caesar!" Eros went down on his knees.

"Silence!" Aurelian's voice cut the excitement short. "You have heard nothing. All of you. Do you understand? No man is Caesar till he wears the purple. You"—he nudged Eros with his foot—"get up."

To the tribune he said, "I will send you back to camp with an orderly. Eat, bathe, and get all the rest you can. We shall start for Sirmium in the morning."

*

The temple of Apollo, which housed one of the most famous oracles in the Empire, stood outside the west gate of Deraea. Aurelian and Maxin rode towards it across the field where the town's auspices were taken. Aurelian was talking. "You will come with me to Sirmium. You will see how an emperor is chosen. First we shall consult the oracle. It is not a 'yes' or 'no' that I want. A man has to do his duty whether the gods are for him or against him. But it is good to know something of what they have in store for us. And it is right to pay them their due respects."

Maxin was looking away, at the sea, which always fascinated him. Far across the sheet of turquoise stained with purple reared a blue hump, the island of Thasos. "The Sun has always taken care of me," Aurelian said. "Here they call him Apollo. My mother used to call him Attis, and she looked after the shrine of his mate Cybele. Every year in March, when the two embraced, I used to carry a lime branch to the altar. When I was born—my mother told me this—a rose grew in our garden with purple leaves and an eagle swooped down as if to take me from my cradle. The purple and the eagle. There can be no mistake about that. The Sun meant me to be emperor. Take my word, lad, the Sun is over us all and we must all bow down to him. Claudius, now, he had no time for these matters, and see how he has ended. I am not going to die of fever for want of a prayer or two."

Maxin gave no sign that he had heard, as they rode into the temple courtyard through a scattering of pilgrims. They halted by a fountain and he dismounted, stroking his horse's ears and wiping the sweat from its forehead with a handful of leaves.

Aurelian sent his orderly to fetch a priest. The soldier took a bag of gold. Aurelian approved of the high fees here. It kept the ragtag and bobtail away. It was only lately, thanks to some remarkable prophecies, that the fame of the oracle had revived under the management of its new high priest, Cleander. In these times of chaos and anxiety, people rushed to the fashionable oracle as they rushed to the fashionable doctor. Aurelian saw no poor pilgrims in the courtyard. There were merchants, officials, army officers, wealthy ladies, awaiting admission with their slaves around them and the sleek beasts they had brought as offerings. The orderly came back. "The priest can see no one else today, sir."

"Take another bag of gold and tell him who I am."

He sat his horse, deep in reverie, while he waited for the orderly to return. A clatter of hoofs aroused him. A carriage, drawn by two horses, rattled into the courtyard and came to a stop on the far side. A dozen men, riding in double file, halted behind it. He frowned at them, memories stirring. Dark, keen faces, acorn helmets, round shields—these were desert Arabs, such as he had seen many years before on his mission to Persia. One of them had consulted with the occupant of the carriage and was striding towards the temple steps. Aurelian could not see into the carriage. The curtains of its high-roofed box were drawn. A surmise formed in his mind. The horsemen who had been sighted during the exercise?

His orderly returned with a priest, who said, "What does the Lord Aurelian desire of Apollo's servants?"

"To make my vows and to consult the oracle."

"You may make your vows, general, but there will be no words from the oracle today. The threshold must be purified at sunrise before anyone may enter, and the high priest is meditating."

Aurelian raised his finger and the orderly produced a third bag of gold. "Ask him to meditate on this. There is more where it comes from."

The priest accepted the gold calmly. "What will you offer to Apollo? We have a fine Sicilian ox here."

"Good. You will be well paid for it."

Aurelian washed himself in the fountain, and joined the priests at the altar on the temple threshold. The priests spoke prayers in Greek. The ox was brought and slaughtered. The threshold was purified with its blood. Aurelian took a flat wheatcake from one of the priests, laid it on the altar, and made his vows silently. He gave thanks for his good fortune and promised to let no future favour pass without a thank offering. He asked for good health, and pledged himself to promote the worship of the Sun wherever his duties took him. When he was emperor, he swore, the Sun would be the Empire's first god and would one day have the finest temple in Rome.

Another priest came out of the temple. He bowed to Aurelian. "The high priest has had a vision. If you are the man who in his vision promised to present a golden statue of Asclepius, son of Apollo, to this temple, then it will be his duty to welcome you at once."

"I am that man."

The priest bowed. "And, sir, there is a favour that you may perhaps be willing to perform. You know, sir, that no woman may cross the threshold of this temple without a man to sponsor her. There is a lady of rank in that carriage over there, and no

one here but you is worthy to escort her. Would you do her that
service, sir?"

"I have no time—" A new train of ideas cut short Aurelian's
words. Curiosity, currents of premonition, were stirring in him.
Here was a chance to satisfy them.

"If it pleases you, sir, the god would look well on such a
service. She is a lady of great influence and can do much for
our cult."

"You mean the high priest has had a vision about her, too?
Another golden statue, eh?" Aurelian was gazing across the
courtyard, thoughtfully. "Very well."

He went across to the carriage. There was only the slightest
movement of the curtains. He said, "Lucius Domitius Aurelianus, at your service, madam."

There was a rap on the panel inside and the coachman, who
was standing by, opened the door. A slave girl parted the curtains and the woman stepped down. She was small and moved
daintily. One hand held up the hem of her pale-blue Greek robe.
The other held a gold-edged headscarf in front of her face as
a veil.

"Whom have I the honour of addressing, madam?"

She answered with a shake of the head and a low, warm laugh
behind her veil. It seemed that he was going to check her, for
his downward glance was fierce and quick; but she turned away,
and he followed her in silence to the temple steps.

They stood side by side in front of the altar: she docile, head
turned away, yet giving the impression of silent amusement;
he glowering down at her. The priests brought a goat and sprinkled it with cold water. The goat trembled violently, a sign that
the oracle might be consulted. The priests hung fresh laurels
over the doorway, drove away the birds that strutted placidly
upon the steps, and sprinkled the threshold with water from the
fountain. Cleander, the high priest, came through the doorway
to lead Aurelian and the woman into the inner courtyard. He

wore plain white robes. His face was waxen and careworn. He greeted the visitors with a tired, impersonal courtesy.

The shrine lay beyond, with a dark doorway. Cleander said, "Let the lady enter first."

In the moment that the woman moved forward Aurelian moved too. His right hand shot out to grasp her shoulder. His iron fingers turned her gently to face him. Gently, powerfully, the fingers of his free hand moved the veil aside from her face and she did not resist.

A flash of suspicion had impelled him; and the suspicion had been so incredible that its confirmation numbed him. She said, "You remember me, then?"

He could not answer. He released her, staring at her.

"After all these years?" Mischievous lights moved in the large eyes; and the anger beat in his temples as if it were a moment since, not twelve years ago, she had last mocked him. She said, "You have had your hair cut, I see."

Anger brought no flush to his cheeks this time. His face went hard. She looked up at him, smiling yet observant, as if noticing change. Then she went with the high priest into the shrine.

How long did Aurelian wait in the courtyard? He was outside time, his mind crowded with theories, questions, and blind, bitter impulses. Twelve years had vanished and a small, mischievous face was sharp and clear before him.

She reappeared, and came past him, not pausing but smiling once more, with friendly mockery. Cleander was speaking to him. He forced himself to hear the high priest's questions, answered them, and followed into the shrine. It was a small, dark room with young laurel trees set up inside the door. In the centre, on a tripod stool, sat a slatternly priestess, a middle-aged woman with the grim, strong-boned face of a peasant. Her gown was dirty and voluminous, hanging in many folds at her bosom. Around her shoulders, loosely coiled, stirred a black snake. She looked at Aurelian with filmed, unblinking eyes. On her right was a golden statue of Apollo; on her left, a stone altar on which the undying fire burned, tended by a young girl. The room smelt of dirt and old fumes.

In a strong melodious voice Cleander intoned Aurelian's request, and chanted an invocation to Apollo. The altar-girl put green twigs upon the fire. The flames crackled and spurted up, sprinkled with sparks of purple, green, and yellow. Black smoke coiled up into the gloom. The priestess lifted a rolled laurel leaf to her mouth with a drugged, heavy movement of her hand, and chewed it slowly. Slowly she rocked her body from side to side. White vapour drifted up from the cracks in the pavement in front of her. The rocking of her body went on. She began to utter soft, lost moans. The white vapour thickened and billowed up in a soft, sinuous curtain. Through the vapour came the fire's flicker and the priest's chanting. The woman, a vague figure behind the white mist, was rocking herself with increasing violence. The snake writhed upon her shoulders. Her right hand gripped it tightly below the head. The glazed vacancy had gone from her eyes. They were wild now, rolled up, the whites enormous. The room was full of the odour of burnt laurel and myrrh.

Aurelian had been occupied, when he entered, with his own thoughts. He had been trying to batten down his anger, to think and to plan. Now the smell and the thickness in his lungs made him dizzy. He resisted, but a feeling of dream pervaded him. The priestess was foaming at the mouth. She cut short the priest's chanting with a shriek. In the silence that followed, she rocked to and fro, panting hoarsely. She squeezed the snake's neck, so that its mouth opened. A croaking like the groan of hinges sounded in the room. Aurelian, his head swimming, the vapour swirling around him, could not tell whether it came from the snake's mouth or the woman's breast. He tried to resist, to keep his thoughts on the small, mocking face he had seen; but his self shrank under the assaults of sound and smell. Memories took hold of him, and he was a small boy again, wonderstruck in front of his mother's altar. He felt sick and oppressed and drowsy. The priestess squeezed again and again with her finger, the snake's jaws opening and the croak sounding through the vaporous gloom.

The priestess sighed. Slowly, like a deflating bladder, she subsided upon her stool, until she was inert and silent. The snake lay still. The vapour thinned. Aurelian felt a strong, cold breeze upon his cheek and had a sense of startled awakening. The priestess was a slattern slumped upon a stool, eyes glazed in a dirty, witless face. He heard Cleander's voice. "The god has spoken. I shall interpret his message and I shall write it down for you. If you will wait outside, my lord, it will be brought to you."

Aurelian made his way back across the inner court with the long, strong strides of a man whose steps are speeded by impatience but who disciplines his haste. He halted in the portico. Yes, she was there, seated in her carriage, at the foot of the steps. He went down to her. "A strange chance, Lady Zenobia, after all this time?"

"Yes." Her scrutiny was appreciative, her smile friendly; but inside him the old strange anger, an anger of a mysterious quality which had sent him flinging out to the steps in pursuit of her, was as strong as ever.

"Was it chance, my lady?"

"To be truthful, no. I have been here for some days."

"To watch my exercises?"

"And to consult the oracle." Her smile quickened. "And to see you. There is no need to make a mystery of it. They told me you had come to the temple, and I came."

"Why should you want to see me?"

"I have not forgotten you. One does not forget men like you. And I have been hearing much about you lately."

"I have been hearing about you, too."

They watched each other; she smiling, he tall, cold, wary. He said, "Why have you come in secret? Honours are due to you. You would have received them if you had come to my camp."

"But would I have seen as much?"

"What is it that you are so keen to see?"

"Everything. Your army. You. It is rewarding to watch Aurelian, unobserved. You once advised me to pay more attention to the ways of Rome. Do you remember? Nowadays I make that my main concern."

"Why?"

"Why? So that I may serve the Empire better. Why else?"

He leaned forward, hard and tense. "My lady, you are playing a dangerous game."

Maxin had come to his side and was examining Zenobia, his face sombre with curiosity. She said, "Who is your watchdog, my lord?"

Aurelian went on: "You enlarge your powers. You enlarge your army. You treat the provinces in your trust as if they were a kingdom."

"I am the widow of the man you called leader of the East, consul, imperator. I am the guardian of your eastern frontiers. The stronger I am, the more I am respected, the more safe your frontiers will be."

"You are a vassal."

"And you are a general, no more. You forget yourself, Aurelian. When I am at fault, let the emperor tell me."

For the first time the bleakness of his eyes was pricked by something like amusement. "Perhaps he will soon. In the meantime I warn you on his behalf—do not go against Rome."

She studied his face for a few moments. Then, "Tell me, Aurelian, why are you so devoted to Rome?"

He gave her a sharp glance of puzzlement. "Because I am a Roman."

"You are no more a Roman than I am."

"What am I then? A frog? An ass? An owl?"

"I am a woman of Palmyra. You are a man of Illyria. Your people, like mine, had their own ways, their own heroes, their own gods, their own tongue, their own chiefs. Why should you accept the ways and the gods and the tongue and the lordship of foreigners?"

"Romans are not foreigners, madam. Foreigners are those who aren't Romans, and that's their bad luck. Anyone can be a Roman, my lady, if he's worthy of it. It doesn't mean a man of this place or that place. It's a rank. That's what it is. Centurion, prefect, tribune—these, too, are ranks. The men who hold them have shown certain degrees of courage, skill, experience that put them above other soldiers. So 'Roman' is a rank. It means that those who hold it have knowledge in their heads that others have not, power behind them that others have not, a better way of life than any other. It's a proud thing to be a Roman. My people weren't conquered when the Romans came. They were promoted."

"They lost their freedom."

"They were made free. From ignorance and dirt and disorder. The world without Rome would be a dunghill. Rome means one world, one law for all, peace under the eye of the legions, trade."

"A dungheap, Aurelian. That is what Rome is, and that is what you are fighting for."

"I know what Rome is, madam, better than you, because I know what Rome has made of me. Without Rome I would have been an unknown herdsman today, dressed in skins, scratching myself over a fire in a sooty den. Instead, I've risen—I, a peasant boy—to a rank that the whole world honours. I have fame and wealth. I command the greatest armies that the world has ever known. I travel like a king, and all the nations of the earth show me their marvels. All this Rome has given to me. What else it has to give me remains to be seen."

The glint in his eyes grew keener. "Rome gives such chances to every man. My chance came when Ulpius Crinitus took me up. I was a boy, he was a Roman commander, a member of the Senate. Yet he took me up, because he saw that I had the makings of a Roman, and he gave me his daughter to wed. He knew, yes, and he told me, that there were rotten things in Rome. But he also told me of all that Rome has done for a thousand years. He told me of the heroes and the just men and the virtuous women of the old days. He taught me the beliefs that had made Rome great, the beliefs in hard work and plain living and justice and courage. He said to me, 'The bad things can be swept away, boy, and Rome can again be what she was.' He said to me, 'All that we need is Romans of the old stamp, and that's what I'm going to make of you.' And that's what I reckon myself to be, Lady Zenobia. Every man is sick in his lifetime, but the ailments pass and he is sound again. That's what is happening to Rome. But Rome will be sound again."

"Every man reaches his time to die, Aurelian. Rome's dying time is near."

"Not yet, madam. You talk as if Rome was mortal. But Rome is divine. *Diva Roma*, we worship her. She is eternal. She will be cleansed. She will find her old virtues and be greater than she ever was. All she needs is leaders. And leaders she will find. Myself for one."

She nodded slowly, her eyes appraising. "Yes." Her voice was soft and free from mockery. "Yes, she has found one in you."

A priest came down the steps. He gave a sealed envelope to each of them.

Aurelian said, "Let me give you some advice, my lady, now that we have met. Be content with what you have. If you seek more you may lose all. Rome will not question what you have done, but do not provoke her further. You have nothing to gain."

Devilry lit her smile. "No? I am of the East, and I despise

Rome, and I hate Rome for treating us like provincials. Yet I have nothing to gain, no? My blood is Cleopatra's and I have the taste for glory, yet I have nothing to gain, you say. I flame to avenge an adored husband and to raise up my children, yet to do so, you say, is not gain. Oh, Aurelian, how little you can know of what consumes me, how little you understand a woman!" Her calm returned. She laughed. "But then, I hear you are not very interested in women."

Aurelian looked down at her, cold and controlled. "You had better pay less attention to my tastes and more to my warning."

Her voice was tranquil once more. "I shall not take it lightly, I promise you. You have made too much of an impression on me for that. You know, you are a rare man, Aurelian. No, I am not mocking. Has this encounter not made you feel something? The clash of yourself against a metal equal to your own?"

Aurelian turned to Maxin. "Fetch my horse, lad."

"It is a pity," Zenobia said gently. "I could wish you well, Aurelian."

His horse was by him. He vaulted onto its back and called to his escort, "Mount!"

"Goodbye, Aurelian. The gods be with you, for true men are few and precious!"

Her coachman's whip cracked. The yoked horses sprang forward. Zenobia waved and drew the curtains. The coach lurched out of the courtyard, the Arab riders clattering after it.

Aurelian sat staring at the gate for some moments after the coach had gone. Then he opened the envelope that the priest had given him. Inside was a piece of papyrus on which was written:

The Sun sees all the world.
The Sun's dominion is all the world.
The Sun's child shall rule the Sun's dominion.
From a high throne the Sun's child shall rule all men.

When it is time, the Sun goes down.
When it is time, the Sun's child shall go down.
Tell no living soul the sacred words
Or what is prophesied shall never be.

"When it is time—" he murmured. "Well, we must all die someday. This is a good prophecy."

He turned, raised his right hand and called, "Close column— forward!"

To Maxin he said, "And now for Sirmium."

CHAPTER SIX

RUFINUS

"THE Sun's child—" Zenobia was lying in her bath. She lifted a small foot and moved it in time with her words. "The Sun's child shall rule the Sun's dominion."

She was delighted with the prophecy she had brought back from Deraea. She knew it by heart.

> *The Sun sees all the world.*
> *The Sun's dominion is all the world.*
> *The Sun's child shall rule the Sun's dominion.*
> *From a high throne the Sun shall see all men.*
> *When it is time, the Sun goes down.*
> *When it is time, the Sun's child shall go down.*
> *Tell no living soul the sacred words*
> *Or what is prophesied shall never be.*

Her foot and her dark, gleaming shoulders sank again into the water. Zenobia liked her evening bath hot. The steam rose around her, powerfully scented with cassia. Two of her bath slaves crouched on the steps of the sunken pool. Two more waited by a massage couch. They were Indian girls, naked like herself in the steam, copper-dark, dainty as gazelles, their eyes bright and eager. She sighed contentedly at the warmth of the water and the memory of the prophecy.

She believed in the prophecy. Longinus taught that there was a Supreme Spirit whom men recognized fragmentarily in many forms which they called gods. Zenobia's practical interpretation of this creed was to keep on the right side of all gods. She had the best of both worlds, for while she was a sceptic and feared none of them, she was always ready to believe in a good omen from any of them.

She believed, especially, in this prophecy because she needed to. It fortified her to pursue her ambitions. It also fortified her against the news she had received on her return from Deraea, that Aurelian had been enthroned as emperor.

Already, thus encouraged, she had published a refusal of obedience to Rome. She was, at this moment, preparing herself to receive a Roman diplomat who had no doubt come to protest. She relaxed in the bath. It gave her pleasure to keep him waiting.

There was a dome of fine transparent glass over the pool. The surrounding ceiling was supported by slender white pillars with Corinthian capitals, which marched in diagonal ranks across a chessboard floor of tiles. The girls moved among the pillars like gleams of polished darkness. Zenobia lay for so long in the water that she might have been asleep. When she rose, lovely and gleaming, she came up the steps and stood while the girls laid napkins of soft wool on her and dried her with a gentle, skilful patting. The floor was warm to her soles; for, like the bath, it was heated from beneath by pipes, in the Roman way.

Naked, she looked a docile, passive creature, soft, sensual, sleek as satin, the breasts large and proudly firm, the small waist accentuated by full haunches, a golden sheen upon the skin. She might have been an odalisque sister to the clothed Zenobia whom the world knew. She lay on the couch and the girls worked on her flesh with firm, cunning fingers, touching her armpits with the depilatory sap of the white vine and anointing her skin with sweet spikenard. They dressed her in loincloth and brassière, white blouse and loose red Persian trousers, and put Persian slippers of soft red leather on her feet. She stood up, soft and small, and went into her dressing room. There were couches here, covered with soft skins, and chairs, and a dressing table at which she seated herself.

Two Syrian tirewomen busied themselves with their tweezers, combs, and flagons. Zenobia surveyed herself with satisfaction in the oval mirror and imagined the effect of her entry upon the envoy. It was twice a pleasure to keep a man waiting when he was a Roman.

The women rubbed aromatic oil into her hair and tamed the glossy torrent into braids. She turned up her face while they reddened her lips with lees of wine and touched her upper eyelids with a blue dust of antimony. This was the only make-up she permitted; austere by the fashions of the time. They slipped bracelets on her wrists and ankles.

She was ready. The nubile little animal that had emerged from the bath was hidden. Looking at her from the mirror was the public Zenobia, a woman, yes, armed with beauty, but bold and haughty as a man. She went out to meet the Roman.

*

Rufinus, the Roman governor of Arabia, was shown in to the council chamber from an anteroom at the far end. To reach the foot of the platform he had to walk the length of the hall under Zenobia's scrutiny, but this in no way upset his poise. He walked elegantly, not strolling but with an easy, deliberate step, pausing halfway, hands thrust behind him under a fold of his toga, to examine a painting which stood on a small table by the wall. He continued on his way, stopped in front of Zenobia, looked calmly at her for two seconds, removed his hands from behind his back and made a short stiff bow without lowering his eyes. Zabda and Longinus, who were seated near him, he ignored.

"Greetings, Lady Zenobia. I trust you are well."

"Well and in good spirits. Greetings, Rufinus." Her tone was friendly. She knew that the polished insolence of his approach

was a diplomatic counter, made to the woman who had kept
Rome's representative waiting. She had no intention of clashing with him over trifles. "Will you not sit down?"

"Before you, my lady, I shall not consider it a disgrace to
stand." Seated, he would have been beneath her. Standing, he
could bid to dominate. There was in his face an ineradicable
look of suspicion, formed by pinched cheeks, a skin ruined and
yellowed by the East, dull pouched eyes, and scanty hair
combed across his forehead in an absent-minded cowlick. He
looked what he was, hard-bitten and efficient, a member of
that corps of versatile executives who for centuries had been
Rome's unique strength. As such, he was a man of only two
guiding principles: the enrichment of himself and the main-
tenance of the Empire. For these ends he could be counted upon
to perform all necessary miracles of statecraft and valour, and
to practise all necessary perfidies. "How are your son and daughter?"

"As dear to me as ever, but more of a problem every day.
Julia at ten is still an utter child. I think she will want to take
her dolls to bed on her wedding night. And Wahab is such a
forward boy."

"Perhaps he chafes at restraint, my lady. A boy does, at fourteen. It would do him good to go out on his own, to Damascus,
say, or even to Rome. We should watch over him well, you
know."

"I know how well you would watch over him, my dear
Rufinus."

Sourly he returned her smile. "My visit, I regret, must be
brief. I am in haste to Antioch on business."

"I am sorry you will not stay to be entertained. Is this brief
call made out of courtesy or for a purpose?"

"Out of neighbourly regard." He showed discoloured teeth in
another grin. "I watch your progress closely, I admire you
greatly. I should hate to see you in trouble. That is why I have

come. I would like to talk with you, informally, about the proclamation you issued on the accession of the Emperor Aurelian."

"The Emperor Aurelian." She intoned the words slowly, as if to herself. "Aurelian—emperor. It sounds well, does it not?" She flashed a smile. "But I issued no proclamation. I sent him a letter of greeting, that is all."

"You published it in all the cities of the East. Therefore, I call it a proclamation. You sent Aurelian your greetings and congratulations, but you also said—shall I quote?—*Palmyra, once bound in obedience to Rome, now sovereign and free from all vassalage, offers you her hand. Know that you have a loyal partner in the East.* That was a manifesto, my lady, and it was not addressed only to the emperor but to the world."

"You may call it what you like. I call it a letter of friendship."

"My Lady Zenobia, I am not a fool and I have not come here to play games with words. Do me the honour of speaking to the point. Palmyra has been Rome's vassal for two hundred years. Its status cannot be casually changed in a letter which I, speaking as the emperor's representative, call insolent. It can only be changed by edict of the emperor and the Senate."

"It was changed, Rufinus, by my husband, when he defeated the Persians after they had wiped out a Roman army. The price has long been owing and the account is now settled." She leaned back, the lights of amusement gone from her eyes. "You remember my husband, no doubt? If you have forgotten his deeds, I am sure you are well acquainted with the manner of his death."

He stared back, as cold and arrogant as she. "Indeed, my lady. I had occasion to enquire into the circumstances."

They confronted each other, unyielding. Zenobia relaxed and smiled again. "Very well. And now, what is Rome going to do?"

"Nothing, my lady."

"This is what you have come to tell me?"

"Precisely that. I have come to tell you, and to make sure that you do not misunderstand why I have told you. The Roman

Senate will accept what you have done. You, if you are wise, will go no further. There is a time to stop, and I have come to tell you that it is now."

"Rome, the mighty, sends no threat? No ultimatum? She sends the governor of Arabia to confess her weakness to me?"

"I am a realist, my Lady Zenobia, and I treat you as one. I never threaten unless I have the means of enforcing my threat. We both know that I have not. Rome, however, has those means, and they could quickly be made available in the East. I have not come to confess weakness—that is the misunderstanding from which I wish to save you—but to remind you of a strength far greater than yours."

"You are wise to be frank, Rufinus, but are you frank enough? I know as well as you that the death of Claudius has been the signal to all the barbarian tribes to attack. Your frontiers are stormed at a dozen places by Goths and Germans. What can Aurelian do against me?"

"He can teach you, as he is teaching the Goths and Germans, that the new emperor is even more to be feared than the old."

"From the latest news it does not seem so." She unrolled a letter in her lap and read. "*A horde of Germans has come down from the Alps. Rome is in a panic. Everyone with an estate in Sicily is going there and everyone else is trying to get invited. You can buy houses very cheaply but jewels cost a fortune. There are mobs in the streets and when each new rumour spreads you would think a thunderbolt had fallen among them. Refugees pour in. They babble like scared children about the men with yellow hair and trousers and battle-axes who come on horseback thick as locust swarms, drinking blood and shouting like thunder. Many cities have fallen to them. All the great plain of the north is theirs. The country houses burn. The slaves join with the Germans and are the worst butchers of all. The citizens are driven off like herds of cattle to be slaves in the German forests.*"

She looked up. "And this is what my informant says about your great new emperor. *Aurelian was their last hope. He came back from the Danube at great speed, bringing his cavalry and letting his infantry follow on. Now the news has come of a terrible Roman defeat. The Germans were cunning. They hid in the forests. They let Aurelian and his cavalry pass. Then the legions came up, tired after days of forced marches, and the Germans ambushed and destroyed them. Everyone says this is the end of Rome. The Germans are on the main road south, only ninety miles away. The rush from the city has become a stampede. Living here is a bad dream. I have packed my valuables and I am leaving tonight.*"

Rufinus said, "Your informant left a little prematurely. You should employ someone with a cooler head. I expect you will hear from him again in a week or two. In the meantime, perhaps I had better bring you up to date. The Germans are not marching on Rome. They are going home. You see, my lady, after the defeat in the forest, Aurelian turned back and attacked with his cavalry. He himself dismounted, rallied the scattered bands of his infantry and fought on foot. They say it was like the old days, with Hand-on-Hilt killing his hundreds and the legions behind him, not to mention the cavalry."

Zenobia was leaning forward, her face alert.

"That is not all, my lady. He beat the Germans again at Fano and again at Pavia, and then they had had enough. Three days' march from Rome they were when they turned back, on the Flaminian Way. Now they are retreating home, and all they want is to put the Alps between themselves and Aurelian."

Zenobia might have been listening to music, so still was she, so bright and remote were her eyes.

"And this, my lady, is all of a piece with what he has done since he donned the purple. The barbarians, as you say, are attacking everywhere. But he is meeting them everywhere. He went straight from his crowning to the Black Sea—you must know this?—and he stopped the Goths. You must know how, all at once, he reappeared nine hundred miles westward, just as eighty thousand Germans were crossing the Danube, and destroyed them there. I have told you how he sped to Italy, and how he fared. Now he is going north, to the Carpathians, and you will soon hear more of him, I guarantee."

She murmured, "Go on."

"The barbarians, I am told, say he has magic powers, and I do not wonder. How could a mortal man spirit an army from place to place as fast as he does? Alone, my lady, he is holding our frontiers by his speed and skill. He bears on his back the weight of all those invading peoples as Atlas with his shoulders bears the heavens."

Hands clasped in her lap, she crouched forward as if afraid to lose a word. "My lady," he said, "this man who is everywhere can be here, too, in the East, if he is needed."

He had spoken too much. The fierce brightness died from her face. She leaned back, wary and cool again. "Your Aurelian has more than the barbarians to cope with before his hands are free. I hear he is none too popular in Rome. He may be their saviour, but he does not appear to be their darling. What the mob thinks of him I do not know, but I am speaking about the people who matter. The Senate has yet to recognize him, and it is tired of being the army's puppet. The public officials are against him. They have heard of his punishments and they know that if he lives, many of them, the embezzlers, will die. The financiers dislike him because he cannot be bought. The aristocrats despise him for a dull peasant. I understand it is the fashion to make jokes about him. The poets read satires against him and the actors mimic his uncouth ways on their stages. A senator is supposed to have said—" she glanced down at the letter— "it was a man named Plautius Silvanus: 'Generals are no better than gladiators, and can be got just as cheaply.' Aurelian is triumphant on the battlefield, but he may yet come to grief in his own city."

Rufinus, when she had finished, sauntered away towards the picture on the side-table. He stood there, half turned away from her, feet planted apart, hands clasped under the tail of his gown. He turned his head towards her. "My lady, he has not been there yet."

He turned his head away to look at the picture. The sunlight gilded it, a portrait of a young man richly dressed in Persian style. The tints were soft—rose, gold, and olive green—the line delicate and ornate. "The king of Persia's heir. Not a good likeness, my lady. I have seen the young man. Their painters are talented but inclined, I fear, to flattery."

"My dear Rufinus, one should always regard gifts with a generous eye."

"A Persian gift, my dear lady, one should always regard with a suspicious eye. It is not likely that you keep this picture here for your delight. Therefore, it has been placed here for my benefit. Will you be so kind as to tell me why?"

"The hint was not meant to be a subtle one, Rufinus. If you frighten me too much with your talk of Aurelian you might drive me to join hands with Persia for my own protection. The king sent me this portrait with the offer of his son's hand. If I am sympathetic, an embassy will follow."

"My lady." The envoy's posture remained negligent. "I know you too well. You could not be so foolish."

"Zabda, here, does not think the idea foolish. Do you?"

The general was on his feet. "Palmyra and Persia together would smash Rome. And let this Roman hear me say it."

Rufinus turned from the portrait to face Zenobia. "The moment you signed the marriage contract Palmyra's independence would be ended."

"They promise me the opposite. They say my son would be the heir to two kingdoms instead of one."

"A stepson? A rival to the princes of the blood? Your marriage would make your son's murder a certainty."

"I can rule a city. Do you not think I can rule a weakling prince? I can guard my frontiers. Do you not think I can guard my son?"

"What could one woman do, alone, with the Persian army on her territory and the whole Persian court around her? With a host of her husband's kinsmen, and court officials, and soldiers against her? With every slave a possible spy or poisoner?"

"Oh, for shame!" Her voice was amused but charged with intensity. She leaned back, gripping the arms of her chair, smiling at him. "I take it for granted that others should underestimate me. But you, the crafty one? Oh, Rufinus! You are all the same, even the clever ones. You say 'a woman,' 'one woman alone,' 'only a woman,' as if a woman must always be less than a man. You are as bad as Zabda. He has been as pressing as you, but in the opposite cause. He, too, is concerned because I am only a woman, but for that very reason he wants me to make the marriage. He says, 'A woman must take a husband. . . . Lady, you cannot rule alone. . . . It is unnatural,' he says. You see, it is unnatural for a woman to keep her freedom and her power, but it is natural for a woman, however high her gifts, to hand herself over to be a slave, any wretch's slave." She stood up suddenly. Scorn made her face harsh, almost coarse. "It comes to this. I must show you all what a woman can be. I must show Persia, and my old Zabda here, and you, Rufinus, and your Aurelian."

She turned, and took down from among the display of weapons on the wall a Parthian bow. From the quiver next to it she selected an arrow. "I shall return a compliment you paid me before, Rufinus. You were frank about Rome's intentions because you knew I could discern them. I shall be equally frank about mine. Why should I try to keep you in doubt as to my decision when you have wit enough to guess it? You will see me answer Persia, and you will tell Aurelian."

She strung the bow. It was massive, thick as a man's wrist at the middle. Zenobia looked superb, a goddess of the hunt, chin high, eyes fierce. "Aurelian could do this, but you, Rufinus—could you?" She sighted. "Between the lips?" The bowstring twanged, the bolt slammed true, the picture clattered to the floor.

She leaned forward slightly, on the bow. "That was my answer, Rufinus. It was not for your reasons that I made it, but for my own, which I have also shown you. Tell Aurelian that I shall answer any threats from Rome as I have answered Persia. Tell him that I am his vassal no longer. Tell him that if he pushes me I may yet turn to Persia. But tell him that if he wants an ally, an equal partner, I wait with outstretched hand."

Rufinus inclined his head. "May I, in turn, recall to you the three words which I brought you. Go no further. And now, my lady, with your permission, I will withdraw."

*

A guffaw from Zabda resounded in the room as the doors closed behind Rufinus. "By the god Shamash, you knew how to talk to that one! Did he think he could frighten us with his Aurelian?"

Zenobia leaned on the bow, looking down on him as if he were something pitiful. "My poor Zabda, you did not understand much of what passed, it seems."

"What do you mean, lady? I heard you. About this Aurelian? Laughingstock of Rome, dull peasant, gladiator, that's what you said, didn't you?"

"That is what the Romans say—"

"And I, too."

"It is not what I say, and if it is what you say, I shall have to find another general, Zabda, for if you underrate a man like that he will beat you."

"Lady, don't be fooled because he wins battles against barbarians. It'll be a different tale when he meets real soldiers."

"My faithful old friend, I know you will kill for me as long as you can raise your arm. But it takes mind as well as brawn to win wars, and the mind of Aurelian is beyond your understanding."

"It takes men to fight men, lady. You leave him to me."

She thumped the butt of the bow on the platform. "Enough, Zabda! Leave chess to those who can play it."

Longinus said quietly, "He has made a great impression on you, this Aurelian."

She glanced down and met his scrutiny. "Why so? The man is in my path. Whenever I plan, whenever I look at my future, there he stands. I must reckon with him. I give him his due, that is all."

"That is a great deal, by the sound of your voice. Do you fear him?"

"I fear no one!"

To the lash of her voice, to the sharp look of anger she gave him, he returned a steady smile. She laid the bow against the wall and sat down. When she spoke she was looking away, as if the words she sought were just beyond her vision. "To deceive one's self is to destroy one's self. That is not how you taught me to think, is it, my master?" She pondered. "Fear? No, fear is not the word. What is it that I feel? I know this. When I only had to think of Rome I was not daunted. But now, when I think of Rome, I see that man in my mind's eye and there is—a chill?—an apprehension?—what? If you had met him you would understand. He is so tall and hard, hard not like a man but like Damascus steel. He lifts his head up as if he is the earth's master. He looks into a far distance. You, in front of him, might be no more than a tree stump in a road builder's path. He has a way of thrusting his lower lip out when he is thinking. There is no doubt in him, only calculation. Never a 'what if I' or 'dare I,' only the cold observation of obstacles before him and the planning of how to remove them. I see him so, and then this apprehension roughens my skin."

"You have thought too much of him, lady," Zabda said. "He preys upon your mind. Rest easy, there are a score as good as him in your domains."

"If there were one—" The words burst out as a cry. She checked herself. She went on softly. "When my husband died, Longinus"—she did not even look at Zabda—"the last man of my metal vanished from the earth. Or so I thought. Now—"

Longinus did not speak for a few seconds. Then, "Your intuition warns you to beware of him. I should respect it."

"My intuition? I do not know what it tells me. To beware? Yes, but there is also with this feeling another, a need to go against him. Sometimes it seems to me that he has been placed in my path so that I shall go against him, and dare him I must. I dreamed one night that the three Fates—Atropos with her scales, Lachesis with her staff, and Clotho with her loom—stood before me. When I went near them, hoping to see in their faces what my future was, all their faces were the face of Aurelian. What does that mean? The Sun's dominion shall be mine. I cannot draw back. What shall I think of myself if I halt for fear of this man?"

"Do not measure yourself against him. He will be too much for you."

"You, too, then think that my better lives? Aurelian thinks that, Longinus. He is like the rest of you. He has no dread of me. I could see it in him. He looks at me, and he sees only a woman. Understand, Longinus, I must show him, I must; the world must see that no man living can best this woman."

She sat back, exalted. "Aurelian says stop. Then it is time to go on. Do not fear, Longinus, it is not passion but judgement that guides me now. I say that we can push Aurelian, and push him again, and if we are careful how far we push, it will not be war. He is too busy elsewhere. He has a campaign in the Carpathians to fight, and then he must go to Rome. The clever Rufinus told us this. Here, then, is my decision."

She paused, smiling. "I shall be cautious. I shall take the advice you gave a while ago, Longinus. Hear me, Zabda. My armies shall march north. Egypt we shall leave for another day. It is not yet time to put the blade to Aurelian's windpipe. Cappadocia, Galatia, Bithynia, and Pontus, all the provinces to the Black Sea, you will occupy them in my name."

*

In a few weeks the troops of Palmyra had overrun all the provinces of Asia Minor. Zenobia's domains were doubled. At first there were clashes with Roman garrisons. Later, the Roman troops withdrew without resisting. It was obvious that orders had reached them not to fight Zenobia.

For a month after the occupation was completed, no reaction from Rome could be detected. Then a letter came from Aurelian. When Zenobia had read it she walked from the council chamber without a word. She shut herself up in her apartment and she did not reappear that day.

Aurelian had written: *Yes, you judge rightly. While greater problems press, the East must wait. As for my judgement, it erred in one respect. I expected a woman's answer. I received that of a jackal.*

Zenobia did not reply to this letter.

Instead, she wrote to her agent in Rome: *From this day you have one task. Find the man who will end Aurelian's life. From all you have written, and from what I have seen, this Goth boy, Maxin, is the one to do it.*

CHAPTER SEVEN

AURELIAN ENTERS ROME

PHILOMENE, Zenobia's agent, looked at Rome and yawned. She lay back in the cushions of her litter, holding the curtains apart with an ivory-handled toy whip. Four African slaves carried the litter. They were huge, polished men of ebony, wearing only skirts of bleached white. Each pair of bearers, front and back, walked out of step. This, and the jungle softness of their tread, enabled them to carry their mistress smoothly. Slavery had its own arts. A houseboy ran in front, a blond, angelic urchin from Germany in a tunic of red and gold, with sandals to match, and a white cloak. He carried an ivory rod, carved with a snake's head, as pompously as if it were a badge of high office.

Rome bored Philomene. The city lay before her as she descended the dusty white road from her villa on the Pincian Hill, a long view framed by the pine trees that lined the road. Philomene knew many cities in the East. She loved them, compact skylines of ivory and dazzling white within their walls. Rome— the mighty Rome, queen of the world—was no such city. It was a wide landscape of hills in a pale sunlight, running away like a sea swell into hazy distances, and the hills were clothed with a packed sprawl of buildings. It was an immense white rash upon the earth. It was vast beyond all imagining; yet it was disappointing, indefinite.

The view, by its sheer extent, was impressive. But Philomene had no eyes for it. She lay in a mindless languor, content to watch the soft sheen of sweat on her bearers' backs, the exciting flexing of muscles in great, black shoulders. She knew this road so well: every rut, with its faintest sway of the litter; past

the Gardens of Lucullus, where the air was cool with scent and
misty spray from the fountains, and the slopes were disciplined
into patterns of white paths and dark cypress ranks, colour-
blazing flowerbeds and clumped shrubberies; through the Clau-
dian Arch, presenting its framed view of the green slopes and
white temples of the Capitol; and down the long, straight Via
Lata to the city's heart.

To pass through the arch was to pass from one world to another. Behind, on the Pincian, was the suburban Rome of the
rich, white villas in high-walled gardens, space, fragrance, ele-
gance. Beyond was the Rome of the multitude, the most congested streets, the most congested slums in the world. The white
sea swell seen from the heights, silent, calm, infinite in the haze,
sleeping beneath the sunlight, was a deception. From the lower
slopes it came astir with movement. The streets could be seen
as a maze of black clefts seething with life. Those innumerable
insect dots, those crowds, Rome's million and a half, swarmed
through their city like a pullulation of maggots.

Philomene's wisdom was mainly confined to the intimate commerce of man and woman. Certainly she had come to Rome
with no grandiose vision, no historical preconception in her
mind. Yet even she, who cared little what lay outside the bedroom window, had been disappointed at the sight of Rome. She
had expected, vaguely, some kind of supreme splendour to
match the city's supremacy. Instead, she had found a vast
builder's yard; waste ground everywhere, weedy and foul with
litter, stacked with building materials; buildings half erected, in
their scaffolding; buildings partly demolished. There was an air
of futile frenzy about it—speculators' frenzy, she learned later,
for the buying and selling, the erecting and overcrowding and
rackrenting of buildings, were a perpetual craze among the
money-hungry. Badly built tenements, six stories high, made
cliffs above narrow streets, propped apart by wooden booms;
and sometimes at night she heard one collapse, like the fall of

a cliff, and saw the mound of rubble next day. Every day, wooden-floored, wooden-staired, waterless tenements caught fire; and everywhere, black, ruined shells scarred the city.

The streets were so narrow that no wheeled traffic was allowed in the city between sunrise and sunset. At nights they were unlit. The blind collision and striving of a horde of speculators, the mania to turn every patch of ground to profit, made a city (apart from the administrative area in the centre) without grace or plan. Even the smart apartment blocks of the wealthy were jammed among warehouses and slum warrens, and their ground floors were let out as squalid, cave-like little shops. What a contrast it was to the city from which she had come, that jewel casket set in the desert, Palmyra!

For Philomene, there was only one thing to be said in Rome's favour. The shops were wonderful. Rome, to her, was one small area: the parade of luxury shops on the south side of the Via Sacra. It was her constant haunt, the source of her only dreams. She loved the cool arcades, and the florists', and the expensive fruit shops, and the displays of silks and Indian muslins, the perfumers', the shops that showed fine carvings and Greek pottery and glittering sets of gold and silver ware. There were no shops to compare with those in the world, for it was to Rome alone that the entire world sent its best. And there were the jewellers. Philomene, like many women who live by sex, dwelt in a spiritual anaesthesia. She was aware of no aim, no ambition in life, no interest outside herself. She let the stream of time carry her from one day to the next, from one warm bed to the next, from one shop or dinner table to the next, and her mind never sought further. Except for one thing: jewels. Jewels hypnotized her.

She had never loved a man but she touched jewels as if they were beloved male flesh. She hoarded jewels, spent hours before her mirror trying them on, letting them run through her hands into their caskets; not in greed, for she was a prodigal girl and poured away her earnings in happy extravagance, but in sensual pleasure. Once she had scattered them upon her bed, rings, necklaces, bangles, brooches, jewelled pins, tiaras, loose stones, and flung herself upon them naked, squirming and trembling with delight as they nudged and scratched and cruelly broke her skin. No man had ever made her feel like that.

There was a strange duality in Philomene's life. Outwardly she was a most shrewd and capable girl, the reason Zenobia had chosen her for this mission. After settling in Rome, she had learned rapidly to make the right contacts, using her trade as the means. She had formed an accurate picture of public affairs, merely by gossiping and by keeping her woman's eyes open. She had soon cultivated the ability to calculate the trend of events. Her reports were concise and intelligent. Yet all this, to her, was a kind of dream. A dream, too, was her professional life, the succession of nights she spent with strange men, the wild lovemaking that to her was only the cold-blooded exercise of a skill. The only reality to her, hard and clear and material, was in that street of shops and in her jewels.

She could outwit the cleverest of men; but she was equipped with no more than feminine guile. She could take part with confidence in political intrigues; they were a game to her, without meaning. Her real mind was a small, closed, childlike thing. It had no awareness that her activities were part of an immense drama. It could not visualize the Roman Empire, or history, or the world's panorama. All it knew was that a night in bed with a man, and an able report sent to Zenobia, brought the same result: more jewels.

She was coming into the crowd now. The Roman crowd. How it stank! How it flocked into the streets, driven by its own boredom, whenever there was a ceremony! It packed the squares, roared in slow, solid tides through the alleyways, down the winding street stairways. Below her, now, it lined the Via Lata in dense black masses, a sea of heads out of which the Baths of

Agrippa and the Temple of Serapis rose like white stone islands.

The crowds were out to welcome the new emperor, Aurelian. Today, at last, he was entering Rome, a year after his soldiers had enthroned him. War had kept him away from the city. Now he was coming to claim his title from the Senate. A crowd-roar, faint but clear, made Philomene look back, to where the Via Lata joined the Flaminian Way, the main highway from northern Italy. A procession was moving along the narrow white ribbon of road, between the black hedges of spectators. The procession was a black thread speckled with the flash of sun on metal. The procession came nearer, and the roar came nearer. Philomene rapped again with her whip and called, "Faster!"

*

Philomene came from Corinth, in Greece. She was twenty years old and she had been at her trade for eight years. She was a frail girl, with auburn hair, pale skin, and large, gentle eyes. Like many girls of avid sensuality she looked timid, patient, and dreamy. Corinth was the world's academy of lust and she had taken it for granted that, since she was a pretty girl, she should become a prostitute. She had not the intellect to become a *hetaira,* a courtesan fit to keep company with men of learning. She was too shrewd to be a *dicteriada,* a common whore. She became one of the *aulatrides,* the dancing girls who were hired for banquets. For her, the life was ideal: laughter, noise, wine, hectic nights, and idle days.

Inevitably, she had migrated to Antioch, the great pleasure city of the East, a whores' paradise; and then, since she was tired of fat Levantine merchants and thought to arouse her jaded flesh with fierce, cruel men from the desert, men with money to burn, she went to Palmyra. In time, the Prostitutes' Guild there had elected her treasurer. She was popular with the other girls, because she seemed quiet and submissive, never

competing with others for the interest of men; and she was
shrewd enough to keep the guild's purse and watch over its
slave bookkeepers. As treasurer, she had made friends with
Zenobia, who liked the companionship of prostitutes, because
they could laugh at men and gave her much in taxes.

She was an excellent choice for the Roman mission. Who else
could have come to know Rome, without any need for explana-
tion of origins, and gained rapid entry into influential circles? A
diplomat would have been suspect; a merchant, from some
quarters, excluded. An expensive prostitute, accomplished,
original, entertaining in the smart villa that Zenobia had enabled
her to rent, attracted men from every important category: politicians, civil servants, diplomats, businessmen, soldiers, writers,
and fashionable gossips. She listened to the talk at their dinners,
when the wine flowed. She questioned and intrigued in bed.
What she could not prise from the men she learned from their
wives, for wealthy women came to like her and made free with
their husbands' secrets.

Her rapid success was due to one thing: her understanding
that in society one must, to be noticed, be a *character*. She had
made herself famous, then, for a placid insolence which smart
Rome found all the more unexpected and diverting because it
came from so slight, quiet, and pallid a girl. Elderly men, and
men in high office, loved to be treated with impudence. In a
complex way it reinforced their vanity, since it was permitted
to only this one person, this celebrated exception. She made it
her business to prick publicly the pomposities of the most emi-
nent, those whom others wanted a chance to laugh at. She did
outrageous things on solemn occasions. Once there had been a
ceremony in the Forum to salute the probity and public service
of Julius Placidianus, a knight and a financier. The ceremony
had been instigated by the army of hangers-on which he, like
every powerful man in Rome, maintained, and was well paid

for in good gold coin, although it was common talk that he had used his tenure of a magistracy to put through several land deals to his own advantage. In the midst of the flowery speeches a litter, borne by the four well-known black slaves, had come through the crowds in the Forum and halted at the foot of the platform. Philomene had stepped out, dressed in the robes of a vestal virgin. She mounted the steps, and when someone asked her, "What is the meaning of this?" she turned to the crowd and answered, "If Placidianus is an honest man, then I'm a vestal virgin."

On another occasion she was visited, to her annoyance, by a senator noted for his impotence. He had kept her awake all night with his attempts, and at last had achieved a feeble success. The next day she sent a procession of slaves through the city in a sham triumph, some on foot with placards, some on asses, and an actor made up as the senator rode in a mule-cart among them, and the placards announced: "ORFITUS HAS DONE IT AT LAST."

This alone would have made everyone talk about her and men flock to her. She had, however, a second trait which appealed. Among the army of Rome's prostitutes, she distinguished herself by the fact that she never made any attempt to please. In the company of a man she always affected an immense indifference. When she went to a banquet she took good care to be excellent company; but in bed, more often than not, she was contemptuously cold. This coldness was genuine, for she had never loved a man, and felt merely numb at a man's touch. A prostitute was supposed to be unhesitatingly compliant with every whim and perversion of her clients. Philomene obeyed no whims but her own. Once she had refused some bodily demand made of her by the consul Claudius Tacitus. He had complained, "After all, woman, I have hired you."

She rang for her maid and said, "Give this man his money back, and a farthing besides. What he really wants is a *quadran-*

taria." (The *quadrantariae* were the farthing whores, the lowest outcasts of the streets.) And, of course, the men flocked even more eagerly to her.

Moreover, it sometimes happened that a man would strike a spark of pleasure off the granite surface of her coldness. Then she would become a mad creature. There was no soft, sensual yielding to be expected from Philomene. She would fling herself upon the man in a battle of lust, a furious fight for the satisfaction she never fully received, challenging him to endure her, to master her. She would tear at him like a bacchante, fist, teeth, and nails. Since this did not often happen, it was taken in fashionable male society as a compliment to the man involved, a badge of his outstanding masculinity. There was scarcely a man of rank who did not hope to swagger into the baths one day and show his scratches, saying with complacent pride, "Look what Philomene did to me!"

The crowds were dense around her. Anticipation surged among them as the roar of welcome swelled, announcing the approach of the procession. The air was stifling. Philomene held to her nostrils the handkerchief she wore beneath a bangle over her right wrist, a wisp of bright yellow silk soaked in perfume. Her houseboy was crying "Make way!" and waving his wand, people were laughing, and the crowd opened continuously in front of her. Hundreds of faces turned towards her, the white, mean faces of the Roman poor. There were shouts for her, and snatches of bawdy song above the parrot-house din and chatter of the street. She was well-known even to the mob.

Her litter, held high, rode now like a small boat over a wide human sea. She was at the city centre, with the Capitol rising in front of her, resplendent with fine buildings, and the white colonnades of the Forum emerging above the expanse of heads on her left. There was a spectacle to be seen: that alone had been enough to suck this multitude of idlers from their dens throughout the city, from the packed hovels of the Suburra and the wretched shantytowns of the outskirts. Banners tossed above the bobbing heads. All the workmen's guilds were out. She saw, close by her, the symbolically decorated banners of the drovers, the dockers, the porters, the masons, and the wreckers. There was a spectacle to be seen. And there was the excitement of five days' games ahead, given by the new emperor, who was reputed to have sent two thousand pounds' weight of bar gold ahead of him to pay for it.

But the size and density of the mob, she knew, were not due to this alone. Nothing had been left to chance. The hero's welcome had been organized. Philomene knew by whom, and why. Political bosses had ordered the workmen's guilds out on to the streets. And the unemployed, the majority of the city poor—those rotting masses who lived on doles, which a whole Empire was squeezed to provide—they had been routed out; and she knew which influential men had sent their "clients," their hangers-on, into the slums to do it. She knew who had decked the buildings on the route with awnings and coloured drapes, and given out wine to the crowd, and posted cheerleaders along the way.

All this had been done by the enemies of Aurelian. It was part of their plan to kill him.

*

Aurelian was to be put off his guard, beguiled, entertained—and slaughtered. The secret of the plot had been closely guarded; but Philomene had learned of it. Some of the biggest men in Rome were in it. More than one of them had let slip a hint in her bed. She had pieced the hints, each in itself meaningless, together, and then herself hinted, probed, provoked, when some man or other was sprawling at her side, all hot and languid and fuddled. She had not got the full story yet, and she had to step carefully. There was a cold and deadly man at the head of this conspiracy, and if he suspected that she knew anything—in the stinking, stifling heat of the crowd she felt a chill of fear and excitement—she might suffer the fate of those who were inconvenient to him, who were usually found strangled in the sewers.

Her bearers turned into the Via Sacra, and the cold clutch of fear seized her heart. There he was. On the lowest slope of the Capitol, fenced off from the crowd, a stand had been built overlooking the route. It was hung with cloth of purple and gold, and thronged with fashionable men and women, who sat in coolness and comfort waiting for the procession, while slaves went among them with refreshments. In the centre sat the man who was the host to the party; the conspirator; the only man of whom she was frightened, and who always frightened her. He was an African, as big as any of her bearers. His skin was the colour of cedar wood and he sat, quite still in his lavish robes, like a polished wooden statue. His name was Felicissimus and he was comptroller of the imperial Mint.

She closed the curtains on the side facing him, although he would recognize the litter if he saw it. He was a freed slave who, like many of his kind, had risen to immense power in the public administration. He had embezzled a fortune from the Mint. He was one of the biggest spenders and entertainers in Rome. Everything he had gained, and his life, too, was menaced by the return of Aurelian. Philomene hated freedmen. There was something malignant about so many of them, a latent hatred of free men because they had once been slaves, a ferocity of purpose to climb and climb and climb, away from their origins, a cunning born in past servility, an obsessive pleasure in humiliating others. Felicissimus was the quintessence of all freedmen. Sometimes he sent for Philomene and she went, without question. He was cruel and gross and beastly in his ways, and she humoured him. She grovelled to him—that was his pleasure with her, as with all others—and was glad to get safely away from him.

Yet she was excited, now, as she passed him. She was excited by her fear, this freezing emotion which was a sensual pleasure in itself. She was excited because Aurelian, she hoped, was soon to be murdered, and that was what Zenobia wanted. She was excited because, in a little while, she had a move of her own to make: one of her acts of audacity, which always played deliciously upon her nerves.

The head of the procession came into sight, past the crowd-packed steps of the Temple of Trajan at the bend of the Via Sacra. Now for it! The moment for her gesture was near. Soon the emperor would pass, on his way to the Palatine Hill, where his palace stood. The policemen of the Urban Cohorts lining the road linked arms to hold the crowds back.

The procession came past without bands or banners. It was not an official triumph. The present visit was only a respite from a continuing war. On foot, in front, was Postimius Varus, the city prefect, wearing his purple-bordered robe of office and preceded by twelve attendants carrying the symbolical bunches of rods. Behind him walked the leader of the Senate, the great monopolist Manlius Statianus.

A cohort of the City Guard followed, glittering expensively in polished, engraved armour, as befitted a militia recruited from the moneyed classes. Beyond, down the sweep of the roadway, Philomene saw a train of ox-wagons crammed with German prisoners. The yelling of the crowd grew wild, for these were the men who would fight to the death at the coming games.

Now!

She tapped her head bearer's back with the whip. The black giants rammed their bodies forward and went through between two policemen like a charge of elephants. One of the policemen yelled, "Get back! Get back! You can see from the pavement!"

Philomene opened the curtains. She spoke loudly enough for the crowd to hear. "Philomene comes to be seen, not to see."

"Get back, I say! At once!"

She called to the crowd. "Look at him! He's dressed up like a toy soldier and he thinks he's a real one." The crowd cheered. The Urban Cohorts were recruited from freedmen, and they were too overbearing to be popular. They wore short cloaks, light ornamental breastplates, and helmets with metal crests. The two policemen shouted down the line for reinforcements, and one of them drew his sword.

"Put that away," Philomene said. "It's too short to wave at a girl like me." The crowd yelled with delight.

She was where she wanted to be now, alone in the roadway, conspicuous. She settled complacently back on her cushions as the city prefect came abreast. Three reserve policemen were running down the road towards her. The prefect was chief of police, among his other duties, and she called to him, "Varus, my friend, call your dogs off, will you?"

Varus looked stiffly ahead of him, pacing like a soldier, holding the hem of his robe.

"Varus, darling!" Her voice was gay and mocking. Varus passed on, his back rigid with anger.

"Oh!" Philomene turned to the crowd again, her face woeful. "And last time he saw me, he called me his little honey-pigeon!"

There was a fresh hubbub of delighted ribaldries from the crowd, then a swell of cheering. The prisoners had passed, and now there were two hundred snow-white bulls for the altars, with gilded horns and coverlets of coloured silk. Then, riding alone, came four horsemen, the emperor and his companions. In the rear was a long, serpentine column blazing with reflected sunlight, the escort of the Praetorian Guard, the crack Household Brigade that was permanently encamped outside the gates of Rome.

The reserve policemen had come up, and were pushing against her bearers, who stood like massive black statues. The crowd was cheering for Philomene, and it was cheering for the emperor, and now the emperor came past.

Philomene could not have been more conspicuous. This was as she had wished. The bearers stood immovable, the policemen leaned up against them like a group of caryatids sprung to life, shoving and shouting. In the litter atop this group, Philomene leaned back in her bright-coloured nest of cushions and gazed boldly at Aurelian.

If she had hoped for some flash of interest, she was disappointed. His glance passed over her as if she were rubbish in the gutter, and he rode on. She decided, in a spurt of feminine resentment, that he was a dull, cold man, and that if this was the great Aurelian he had better go back to his battlefields, because here in Rome he was easy game for the cunning of Felicissimus.

Of the three men who rode in line behind him, she did not know the general on the right. The fair-haired boy in the centre must be this Goth Zenobia had written about: she might have to find a way, someday, to make his acquaintance. On the left was Capito, the commander of the Praetorian Guard, a lean, sun-cured Spaniard. It amused her to see him riding protectively at Aurelian's shoulder. He was solely responsible for the emperor's safety in Rome; for Aurelian's Third Gallicans, the legion that had come south with him, were encamped twenty miles north of the city. And Capito was in the plot.

Her attention was attracted by a cry of alarm from her houseboy. The enraged policemen had drawn their swords. One of them shouted, "Come with us, or we cut your slaves down!"

She cried, "By Venus! I'll have you thrown to the beasts if you do!"

Her high, clear voice attracted the attention of the general at Aurelian's right. He looked over his shoulder. She was leaning out of her litter, her toy whip raised to strike, her robe fallen back to reveal her shoulders. He brought his horse dancing round, and in a moment he was at her side. "Hands off!" The snap of his voice froze the policemen, ridiculously, in postures of menace. "I'll see to this. Away!" The policemen had snapped agonizingly to attention. "Do you hear me?"

He turned to her and his eyes, dark and stern with command, became droll, impudent. The crowd was applauding, but he seemed unembarrassed by their presence. "Well, you're a nice one! So pretty, and so silly!"

She had been looking after the retreating policemen. She turned vague, dilated eyes on him, and spoke faintly. "I was carried away by enthusiasm. I did want to see the emperor."

"You'll see the other world if you break through his guards again. They're supposed to look after him. You know, they should really have cut your throat. Just for safety's sake."

Her eyes were wide and innocent. She put a hand to her throat, emphasizing its bared, slender grace. Her cheeks were still flushed from the encounter with the police. "Not me," she said, her voice fragile; "everyone knows Philomene."

"Philomene." He tasted the name upon his tongue. He spoke with the throaty accents of a frontiersman, and in crude soldier's Latin. She was fascinated by him: by the comic, pudding face with its sly, smiling, hooded eyes; by the barrel breadth of his chest in its dazzling cuirass; by the thick, short legs sticking out over his horse's flanks. His scarlet cloak and brave crested helmet made him look strong and dashing, but his bull neck, massive shoulders, long arms, and round cheeks were those of a peasant wrestler in some street booth. She glimpsed the close fur of his hair beneath his helmet. Yes, he was like a cat, to be stroked and dandled yet crackling with energy in his fur. "I am Marcus Aurelius Probus, and now I, too, know you."

"*The* Probus?" She had guessed his identity by now, but she spoke with practised, eager surprise. "The great Probus?"

"Himself." She sat serene under his sly, smiling scrutiny. He was reading her from her clothes. Everything about her spelled prostitute. Compelled by law to wear a man's toga, she was dressed in a green toga of the gauzy silk known as "vapour," which revealed her white breasts through its transparency. She was not allowed to wear jewels on her hands; she wore a constellation of them in her hair, and plain gold bangles on her wrists. Obliged to dye her hair red or green, she had rinsed it to bring up the natural auburn tints, and let it fall thick and free over the whiteness of her shoulders and the green silk of her robe. She saw a fire of hunger and approval in his eyes; the velvet-dark eyes that stirred her so. "And Probus tells you this. The emperor is a strict man. He likes his guards to do their duty. He notices things. In a parade of two thousand men he notices a tarnished breastplate. I am sure he noticed you. He is a great man for discipline. He will want somebody punished. You, or the guards. Or all of you. Who knows?"

"Oh!" She was not smiling at him; but in her eyes there were deeper signals, a woman's signals of recognition to a desired male. She was stirred by this man. And her brain, working nimbly, reminded her that he might be a means of access to the emperor's presence, to that Goth boy who might be needed in the future, to— She saw the signals of appreciation, of response, in the back of his eyes. "Oh!" she charged her voice with feminine dependence. "Aren't you his friend? Can't you tell him that I only wanted to show my loyalty? Couldn't you take me to him? I'm sure I could explain."

"I'm sure you could." He glanced over his shoulder. The procession had almost passed. "Don't worry. I'll look after you. I'll have to go now. I don't want to get left behind, and ride at the tail like the jester on his donkey, do I?"

She laughed. "No. Will you get into trouble?"

"It's not likely." The sly smile spread into a grin. "Unless I'm confined to barracks. Then you'll have to keep me company."

Her lips parted in pleasure. "At the palace?"

"Where else?" He waved, and rode away.

CHAPTER EIGHT

THE BANQUET OF STATIANUS

IT WAS appropriate that the house of Manlius Statianus, leader of the Senate, should crown the Quirinal Hill; that the habitations of the rich, a scatter of white buildings in a dark wool of treetops, should lie beneath his view; and that Rome's floor of fetid slums, the city of the poor, should be too remote from these pleasant heights even to check his passing glance.

On the night following Aurelian's arrival in Rome, Statianus was waiting on the steps of his house for the new emperor and for Probus, who were dining with him. His house was a group of buildings steeply terraced, so that the third floor of the lower terrace was continuous with the ground floor of the upper. A long white road wound up through the grounds of his estate, rising at intervals in broad flights of steps. The emperor and Probus came riding up this road, with an escort of fifty mounted Praetorians behind them, the rhythm of hoofbeats breaking into a torrent of clatter each time the horsemen swarmed up one of the staircases.

Statianus's first thought as he greeted his guests was: *How small we Romans are!* He, by Roman standards, was counted a tall man; yet he, and all his fellow citizens, seemed puny beside these Illyrian soldiers who came south, these tall, broad, clear-eyed, free-striding semibarbarians of the frontier. He felt it now, a twinge of disquiet, facing Aurelian and Probus.

His second thought was: *This man may be a commander-in-chief, but has it entered his provincial head what it means to be emperor?* For Aurelian, who had ridden up to his front door on a restless Gallic pony instead of travelling in the gilded imperial litter, wore none of the robes or trappings of his office: only the belted, grey woollen tunic of a soldier, with sword but no armour. However, as Statianus escorted his guests across the lofty, domed hall, he felt no big-city superiority towards them. He watched them as they looked up at the circular gallery, forty feet above their heads, and at the splendid main corridor flanked by columns of Oriental alabaster and with vaulted roof, and at the sweep of a broad marble staircase beyond, with its mosaic landings. He saw the easy pride of their carriage, and the lift of their chins, the unabashed, assessing scrutiny in their eyes, and he knew that he must not underestimate these men. He must watch, watch, and reserve judgement.

Certainly this Aurelian, "centurion" or not, was able to appreciate realities. He had thought fit, on his second day in Rome, to accept an invitation from Statianus. Evidently he knew that, for all the armies behind him, there was one power in the Empire that, in its way, matched his own, the money-power; that his future depended on his good relations with that power, which would enable him to pay his armies and finance his campaigns. And money-power, in Rome these days, meant Statianus.

There are some men whose resources are so great that they can profit from anything, even ruin. Statianus had always been a powerful man in Rome, but in the last ten years he had acquired an almost monopolistic hold on some of the Empire's main sources of wealth. These were times of invasion, chaos. Banks had crashed, cities been destroyed, estates laid waste. These were times when thousands of once-wealthy men became bankrupt; and when Statianus and his associates, with their vast resources, could harvest the losses of others at bargain prices.

He had started with a concession, bought ten years ago from the Emperor Gallienus, to run the Spanish silver mines at Cartagena, which employed forty thousand slaves. This had provided him with the capital to buy up the estates of landowners ruined by invasion on the Danube and in northern Italy. This land, in turn, had been utilized for large-scale farming, concentrating on three commodities: olives, sheep, and wheat. The scale on which Statianus produced these products enabled him to wipe out a multitude of smaller competitors; and then to institute a virtual monopoly of them throughout Italy. He had always maintained, on the side, many trading interests, and these he expanded with his new capital, exporting at low prices, which no rival could equal, the luxury products of Italy, always in demand abroad. He imported in return, almost as monopolies by now, cattle, horses, slaves, and skins from Germany, amber, furs, and fish from Scandinavia, corn, hemp, and honey from Russia, silk from China, incense, camels, and spices from Arabia, jewels and cottons from India. Statianus owned fleets of merchant ships as big as the emperor's navies. The web of his power was as wide as the emperor's.

Thus, although there was respect in his bearing as he accompanied his guests to the rest room, where, in luxurious surroundings, they could bathe and perform their toilet before dining, there was also in him a couched, serene arrogance. In these times, when the Senate was a mongrel rabble of new-riches from the four corners of the world, he was one of the few men of the old Roman stock, and he looked it. At seventy, he was still a handsome man. He walked upright, yet with a relaxed grace, and the folds of his robe, their arrangement dictated so strictly by tradition, hung in that easy perfection which, mysteriously, only the true aristocrat could attain. His skin, well-kept for years, was pink and clear, his hair combed in a floss of gleaming silver. Beneath jutting, bushy eyebrows which were still ginger, his frosty blue eyes were penetrating, fearless, yet always ready to be pricked with lights of humour.

He watched the masks that were his guests' faces. He knew that, behind their taciturnity, they were impressed; and he was satisfied. He thought: *I have seen the tokens of Aurelian's power, in his victories. Let him see the tokens of my power, in my house.* He was glad for them to see the army of slaves, moving, soft-footed, everywhere, organized, trained, and disciplined like soldiers. He was glad for them to see the great dining room where the waiting guests were all bowing towards the three men in the doorway: the floor, pillars, arches, and ceiling a symphony of marbles brought from every corner of the world, delicately veined and blushing with soft colours—violet-spotted marble from Phrygia, dazzling-white from Hymettus, yellow from Numidia, the reddish-yellow, green-veined marble from Euboea, the wine-stained stone of Melos; the wainscotings of tropical woods inlaid with silver; the great table of citrus wood with ivory legs, surrounded on three sides by couches, the fourth side left open for the servers; the couches themselves, covered with silver-woven satin cloth, with costly Russian furs scattered as rugs on the floor roundabout; the tableware of rock crystal, the most fashionable and the most fantastically expensive material in the Empire; the sideboards laden with gold and silver plate; and the tall vases of Corinthian agate. Statianus looked on his possessions, and they were good, because they were significant.

In strict truth, not all his home surroundings were to his satisfaction. He was a man of cultivated tastes, and he liked a certain austerity in decoration. His possessions fell into two categories. There were the things he loved, the panelled murals, for instance, around the dining room, the work of a wonderful slave painter he had imported from Greece, a man named Cleon. He could sit in front of them for hours, dreaming in an armchair, all the driving pressures in his mind washed away by those rich olive greens, those ruby reds, by so many harmonies of line and colour, by the invitation into a new world of woodland groves where Pan frolicked and pursued, and beaches where youths and maidens bathed beneath a white sunglare, a world of riotous, titanic battles of the gods. There was the bronze of Silenus, his face like a merry wine bag, sagging in happy drunkenness upon the arms of two satyrs while he urinated shamelessly. There was the marble piece in that far alcove, Amor bending over a swooning Psyche, kissing her mouth, fondling her breast, both of them so lovely. He always felt a special triumph before this piece, a feeling of victory, of his own power, for behind the acquisition of its sculptor-slave there lay a story of contest and victory against rival collectors as grim and ruthless, in its way, as the greatest of his operations. There were these and a host of other beloved works of art.

But then, besides, there were the countless sideboards of gold and silver plate, the gold statues, the gold picture frames, the huge silver urns, the candelabra of precious metal. These bored him. They were so much clutter. But the reason for their presence was marked upon them. Every item of gold and silver had its exact weight engraved upon its base. For Statianus's houses were his banks.

In these times of collapse, when every bank in Rome had crashed and the coinage was worthless, a man like Statianus kept his wealth under his eye. He kept it in his land; in his houses—Statianus had eighteen, in every part of the Empire; in gold and silver ware; and in slaves. Statianus had six hundred slaves in this house. There were five hundred in his seaside mansion at Sorrento. In his provincial houses there were over two thousand. These, of course, were only the household slaves. Those who worked on his farms, in his mines, factories, warehouses, and offices, were enough to duplicate the thirty legions of the regular army. No man could usefully employ so many slaves in a house, even though every task was minutely subdivided to provide employment for as many as possible. But he kept them as a mark of his status—and as living capital.

The slaves were moving around the table now, a flow of human shadows, the bowl-bearers and the towel-boys, for the washing of hands, the cup-bearers, the flagon-bearers, a ballet whose master was the major-domo, majestic in the background. Statianus rose and held aloft his jewelled crystal wine cup, for the opening libation. "To our Emperor Caesar Lord Aurelian Augustus! May the gods watch over him and prosper his reign!"

He surveyed his guests as they rose to make their response, "To the Lord Aurelian!"

He had not been governed by protocol in making his invitations. Statianus was above protocol. A host of dignitaries, hungry for the proper recognition of their degrees of precedence, had been ignored. He had selected his guests to suit certain purposes of his own.

On each side of the table, as he faced it, was a triple couch. The nearest man on the left-hand couch, in the place of honour, was Rufinus, the governor of Arabia who was at present enjoying a long furlough. Next to him lay Plautius Silvanus, a flaccid young man, overdressed by Statianus's standards, whose bald head, puffy cheeks, and glistening, lashless eyelids gave his face the peculiar softness of a shelled egg. He was known as a lover of good living, an æsthete and a practising poet. He had inherited a large fortune and augmented it by marrying an heiress, a misfortune for the girl, since he was a pederast, but one for which she had since amply consoled herself. She was, indeed, known in Rome as "the gladiators' delight," a title which might equally have applied to her husband. Silvanus was active in the Senate, not out of any political talent, but because idleness and the need for nervous excitement made him a fervid intriguer.

On his right, in the lowest place of the whole company, reclined the gross bulk of Flavius Cilo. He was a knight who had bought his way into the Order, which represented the financial element in the city, and a building contractor. He was using both hands to stuff hors d'oeuvres into his mouth, as if he were one of his own slaves shovelling earth under the whip. The hors d'oeuvres had been brought in a revolving dish, four feet in diameter, with twelve compartments each ornamented to

represent a sign of the Zodiac. In the compartments were flamingo tongues, lobster garnished with asparagus, milk-fed snails,
dormice coated with honey and poppy-seeds, stuffed thrushes,
hot truffles, African figs, a fry of small fishes, braised lambs' kid-
neys, peahens' eggs stuffed with anchovies, served on bayleaves
with a white sauce, lamprey, and a stew of oysters and mussels.
He was a man whose appetite for women was as enormous
as his appetite for food. He ran chariots in the Circus, gambled
spectacularly, gave the most lavish and debauched banquets in
Rome, and kept a private stable of gladiators so that he might
enjoy, at his leisure, his favourite diversion of watching limbs
hacked and entrails spilled. His head, on his huge body, was
small, his face veined and florid, his voice hoarse. He was the
son of a freedman from Gaul and, except when his presence was
politically necessary, was not considered eligible to enter the
house of Manlius Statianus.

The head place on the opposite couch was occupied by Aurelian's father-in-law, Ulpius Crinitus. Statianus respected Ulpius,
for he, too, was in many ways a Roman of the old school; but
he could feel no warmth towards the small, severe man with the
pepper-and-salt hair. Ulpius was too stern, too solemn, with no
redeeming sense of irony and no eye for the fine arts. Postimius
Varus, the city prefect, on his right, was a self-important man
and quite insufferable. He bore himself erect as a spearshaft,
although he had never been to war, and his large nose, protruding from his swarthy face, was carried in the air like a symbol
of office. His importance in the city rose because he not only
controlled the *aediles*, or police superintendents, but the political machine of the city—the horde of spies, mob orators, ward
managers, and street captains who herded the slum crowds to
suit their masters' requirements. The Spaniard, Capito, lay next
to him, tense and sombre as if he were at a gambling table.

At the head of the table were two double couches. On the
left-hand couch, Statianus, occupying the outside place so that

Ulpius was his neighbour across the corner of the table, accompanied the emperor and saw to his needs. On the other couch lay Probus and Philomene. Statianus was old-fashioned enough not to like inviting women to his dinners. On this occasion he had been allowed no choice. With a barbarian contempt for good form, Probus had announced that she would be coming; and at a time like the present one did not argue with the emperor's boon companion. In any case, Statianus was not greatly put out. It was not unusual to have a fashionable courtesan to enliven a male party. He liked Philomene; although, being faithful to his young and charming third wife, he had never been among the girl's clients; and he could not help admiring her, for although it was only a day since Probus had arrived, she was already established in his quarters at the royal palace and talked of in the city as his mistress.

There was a chatter of talk about the table. Aurelian lay, oddly dull and heavy in his manner. Statianus's curiosity was aroused. He had not expected this social lameness from a man who could spring so lightly from his horse and stride so boldly up the steps of a great mansion. As he served the emperor with lamprey and called for more of the white Setinum wine, he watched, with a veiled alertness, Aurelian's face, trying to penetrate the mask of sullen embarrassment. Aurelian took his cup with both hands, and drank the wine neat. The chatter went on, with only that faintest lift in pitch that is heard when people pretend they have not seen something, but Statianus saw a glance pass between Silvanus and Varus. In Rome it was considered vulgar to drink wine unwatered.

Silvanus said in a fine, fluting voice, with too-musical inflections: "Statianus, I met an angry man this morning. The master of the Mint. He is so keen to pay his respects to the emperor, and he felt, with his position in the city, that he should have been invited."

"There are a lot of angry people, I am told. In fact, the whole

Civil Service. In any case, I do not have freedmen at my table. Felicissimus can eat with my slaves if he wants to come here."

Let them report that to Felicissimus, Statianus thought. He wondered what game Silvanus was playing, to bring in Felicissimus's name like this; for Silvanus was a member of the plot. Probably only playing with fire. That was the danger of rich neurotics. They craved excitement; they could never be relied on to keep silence, to show cold nerve, to be disciplined.

Cilo had loudly applauded Statianus's words, backing his shout with a thump of his huge fist upon the table. There was a surge of soft laughter around the table, edged with mockery, that Cilo the upstart should hope to obscure his own origins by bellowing against freedmen. There was also, for Statianus, an added touch of humour, for Cilo, too, was in the plot.

Statianus, inevitably, knew about the plot. He was not involved. He was above such things. He had been content to invite Silvanus, who led the plot in the Senate; Cilo, who represented the ruffian-rich, the scared grafters; Varus, also in the scheme, who represented the police and the mob-managers; and Capito, of the Praetorians. It pleased him to bring them face to face with Aurelian, and to watch. He might be amused, and he might learn something.

Statianus could afford to be neutral in the affair. If the plotters won, they would need Statianus and his money, for they would have to buy the loyalty of the legions at once or else face overthrow by the army. If Aurelian stayed in power—well, Statianus wanted to see a good soldier in command, for the fulfilment of certain commercial visions of Statianus involved war. Either way, the important thing was that he, Statianus, must be able to go on pulling the strings. If he could not, he would have to put his own schemes in motion and set his own nominee on the throne—later.

Philomene looked up over Probus's shoulder. "That Felicissimus frightens me. He's a bad man to anger. He's so cunning."

"All freedmen are cunning. And they have altogether too much power these days. First they are allowed to run households, then the affairs of cities, now the affairs of the Empire." Casually, intently, Statianus watched Aurelian's face. The emperor, ignoring the pointed shellfish spoon which lay among the row of untouched cutlery in front of him, took a snail and cracked it between his teeth. The crack resounded through the talk, and there were quick, furtive looks at him, and again a glance by Silvanus, at Varus and at Capito, a shadowed, triumphant smile. Aurelian pulled the meat from the shell and put it in his mouth. Munching stolidly, he let his eyes move, from one speaker to another, following their talk in a silence which seemed to be only half comprehending.

Ulpius spoke. His voice grated. It was a pity that a man with such sound opinions should have such an unlovable voice. "What can you expect? The freedman is powerful because the slave is powerful. I was in a man's house the other day. He had a slave in every room, to announce the time of day. 'My clocks,' he boasted. Placidianus, now, has a library of slaves. One recites Virgil to him, one Homer, one Horace, and so on. 'My books,' he calls them. You are nobody in Rome today unless you have a slave to walk in front of you and tell you when to avoid a crack in the pavement, and slaves to lift you from your bath to your couch, and slaves to wipe your bottom, and a different slave to look after every garment in your wardrobe, and one to shave you, and one with the comb for your hair, and one to put each shoe on, and it will soon be one to breathe for you. The Roman of rank today does nothing, nothing for himself. Everything is done by his slaves. The Roman becomes useless. He becomes helpless, like a queen ant—have you seen one?—that ugly white mass palpitating at the heart of an anthill—and the slave becomes the master. I tell you, we have always been frightened of the field slaves, because they have the brawn, but we should be just as frightened of the house slaves, for they have the cunning."

No, Statianus thought, watching Aurelian, *I never pictured him as this, a dumb barbarian. There is something wrong here.* Probus, with Philomene nuzzling on his shoulder, was saying jovially, "Don't you worry, father. You don't have to worry about the field slaves or the house slaves as long as the army's about. We'll keep them tame for you. We always have, eh?"

Slaves came with perfumed water, to wash the diners' hands, to change the napkins, and to serve the interval cup of honey wine. They brought the entrées to the table, a stewed mullet, a ham, and a goose surrounded with braised wood-pigeons. Statianus kept a plain table, by the standards of the day, although he had an unsurpassable chef. He let his attention stray to his paintings. There they were, his escape, the world of his imagination, away from this chatter of little men.

Silvanus' voice sounded, interminably, it seemed, in the background: "... there is no medicine to compare with wine. A Myndian for the digestion ... prick the truffles so that they are saturated with the juice, add your dressing and serve them hot. They must be piping hot ..." The slaves glided round the table with hot rolls, with red Falernian for the wine cups, with silver dishes of beans, beets, quince, shallots, leek, lettuce, melon, cherries. The paintings. Those lovely terra-cotta reds. The lines of the ideal human figure. He had donated a gallery of paintings to the city, set up in a series of porticoes in the Forum; not to court public favour, but out of a kind of contemptuous munificence. Paintings ... Aurelian's face impressed itself on his vision again. He heard himself talking to the emperor, suavely, about nothings. His mind was protesting, *No, no, no! This is not the man!*

"Tell me, my lord"—it was the thin, impudent voice of Silvanus, addressed to the emperor— "what entertainment can we offer you during your stay in Rome? It would be such an honour to us to please your tastes." There was the briefest flash of complicity in his eyes for his friends, but Statianus saw it, and heard the growing boldness of voice, the sword-edge of mockery being uncovered.

Varus took it up, in his heavy, pompous voice. "Yes, my Lord Emperor, what does it please you to enjoy? The theatre? Poetry? A ballet? To see fine sculptures?"

Statianus looked at the faces, heavy and glowing with their mockery. They were at it now. They were losing their fear of Aurelian. . . By the gods! That was it! Statianus looked again at Aurelian, stolid as a block of wood. This man wanted them to lose their fear of him. There was a subtle game being played here; and not by these men who thought themselves so clever. Aurelian looked up across the table, frowning earnestly, as if to summon reluctant words. "Well, gentlemen, to tell you the truth, what I like most is to see a good eater."

"An eater?" Silvanus fluttered his eyelids in a fatuous imitation of rapt attention.

"Yes." A smile dawned in Aurelian's face. It was a naïve smile, yet keen, the skin crinkled around the eyes as if looking into the distance; the smile of a blunt, uncomplicated soldier. A real admiration began to stir in Statianus. By the gods! There was a man-and-a-half at work here! He was beginning to understand the game. "Yes," Aurelian was saying, "a good guzzling match. We have 'em in camp. Don't you have 'em here? Now, I've got a man, a Thracian, I bought him cheap in a job lot. Phagon's his name. I've won a fortune on him. Do you know what he ate in one night?" He flashed the keen, innocent smile around him again, expectantly.

"We can't wait to know, my lord." Silvanus spoke in a voice of almost comic yearning. The silly little wretch must be carried away by his own boldness. Statianus sensed the conceit of him, the swelling contempt for this brave, brainless soldier-emperor. Varus was smiling, and even Cilo, proud that he had caught on to this game of baiting, was grunting with laughter on his couch.

"He ate"—Aurelian's voice was triumphant, hearty—"a boiled pig, a hen, a hundred eggs, a joint of beef, and then—here, listen to this—he ate the tablecloth, all the beer pots, a bag of hobnails, and a truss of hay. What d'you think of that? A truss of hay!"

The conspirators joined in a sycophantic, mocking chorus of laughter. How could they be such fools? Could they see nothing? Clever men, clever men, and always blinded by the same thing in a conflict: their own pretensions, their contempt for all outside their own breed, their fatal compulsion to underestimate their adversaries; because they really believed that they were lords of the earth, that provincials, aliens, barbarians were of lesser clay. And Aurelian was playing with them. It was gratifying to remember that he, Statianus, had not underrated the man. But what was Aurelian's game? How much did he know? Was he aware that these were conspirators? Or was he only anxious for Rome, all Rome, to underestimate him? Who was he trying to lull, to put off guard, to tempt to action, and why? This was a piquant situation. Statianus settled down to savour it.

"Bravo, my lord!" It was Varus. "You set an example. It is the simple pleasures that we need in Rome. I promise you, sir, the eating match of our generation!"

"Yes," Silvanus cried. He was beside himself now with vainglory. The roasts had been brought in; a side of beef, which was placed before the emperor; and a wild sow, carried on a silver litter by four slaves, stuffed with dates and hot apples, and bathed with sauce from the mouth of a silver nymph. At each of the sow's ten teats there suckled a baby pig of rich pastry. "Look!" he cried. "Wonderful, wonderful, a credit to our host! And a fine Cæcuban, dark and digestive, to drink with it! Magnificent!" He raised himself on his left elbow, cup held aloft. "To our emperor! To the Lord Aurelian, supreme ornament of our culture!"

Ulpius was staring at his son-in-law, his eyebrows hunched questioningly, grooves of indignation around his mouth. Evidently Aurelian's game, whatever it might be, was a lone one. Certainly Ulpius did not know of it. Nor, by all appearance, did Probus, who was eating like four men and drinking like ten, holding Philomene to him in a bear hug, and answering every remark addressed to him with the same wide grin and chesty laugh. There, now, was a real barbarian!

Silvanus was swinging away on a tide of wine. "Reflect, my friends, how much we owe to our emperor! We adore the divinity of our emperors when they are dead. Now I shall hurry to acknowledge the divinity of Aurelian Augustus when he is dead!" He looked around him, his face round and smooth with insolence. Aurelian, calm-eyed, went on cutting a thick slice of roast beef.

Rufinus had eaten and spoken little. It was said that his health had been ruined by too much indulgence in the pleasures of the East. He spoke now, with a tired, ironic smile. "You may not live to see that unfortunate day, Silvanus. I hear you follow dangerous sports."

The impudent moon-face glistened at him. "Bear-baiting? That is not dangerous, my dear Rufinus, for the expert. My Lord Aurelian, we bow to you as our emperor, and we salute you as the strongest of all those strong men who guard our frontiers. Thanks to them, those wild beasts on two legs whom we call barbarians are held in check. Thanks to them, our mode of life, the noblest, the most advanced that the world has ever known, flourishes in peace. Hail to our soldiers, who defend civilization, so that we may hand it on to our heirs!"

Philomene bobbed up on her couch. "You? What heirs could you produce?"

"My dear, I have three children."

"Your wife has three children. You pay a good price for your slaves, dear Silvanus, and they are good breeders."

Ulpius, munching grimly at a leg of goose, said, "Their slaves even make their children for them."

Silvanus' smile was unruffled. "You do not offend me, my friend. I am a modern man. I am broad-minded. Happiness is the only end of life. I am happy and my wife is happy. What more can one want?"

Ulpius, without looking up, muttered, "Decency."

"Decency? You dear, old-fashioned man. Tell me, what wife in Rome is constant? Saving yours, of course, Ulpius, and yours, respected Statianus, and of course"—a bow—"the gracious lady of our emperor. These are enlightened times. People of breeding know that life is short, that we must take our fill of its pleasures while we can. To do otherwise is to starve one's self, to throw away the gift of life, to show one's self base and vulgar. Let the pork butcher guard his wife. Let us, who are cultivated, taste the pleasures of good talk, good wine, good food, of the baths and the beach and the book and the theatre, and of lovely, living flesh. Let us enjoy them, as we will, without restraint. That is civilization. That is what the soldiers are fighting for."

"Your women of breeding, as you call them, parade the streets like prostitutes looking for well-built men. They serve, free of charge, for their sport, in the brothels. I have heard it said that one woman in five in this city is available, for money or without money, to all comers. Is that your civilization?" Ulpius questioned.

Silvanus answered: "That, my friend, is civilization. I am civilization. Look at me. The brute parts of me have died for want of use. That inflammation of the brain they call courage. Those horrible lumps called muscle. The lust to breed upon a woman. That fear of the darkness called piety. I am a free man. I have broken down those prison walls called morals, conventions, ethics, virtues. I am bred, like a prize flower, for one purpose only, to decorate the world. And that is civilization, the highest achievement of the human race. I—my tastes, my demands—

have called into being all the poems, the paintings, the rare silks and fine furnishings that are our glory. What can the barbarians show to equal these? Fools have asked: Why should soldiers die?—why should brute herds from far lands be driven into slavery?—why should the rabble sweat and toil? I will tell you. So that I can flourish. So that I can crown the world with its supreme achievement, my own existence."

"Bravo!" Cilo thumped a thunder of approval upon the table. "That's good, that is! That's very, very good! It ought to be written down and read out to the people. Teach 'em to respect us." He belched. "Show 'em what we're doing for 'em. Make 'em proud of their heritage."

The desserts were on the table: mounds of black grapes in golden bowls, plump pears from Syria, Chios figs, Damascus plums, Sicilian peaches, lemons, pomegranates. The wines, when served with fruit, were cooled with mountain snow. Cilo shouted, "*A commissatio!*"

Statianus murmured to Aurelian, "Perhaps some fresh air, my lord? If I may accompany you to the balcony?" Aurelian rose. Statianus said to the others, "Carry on, my friends. My house is at your disposal." Let them have their *commissatio*. The drinking debauch after a meal was a ritual in most fashionable houses. Statianus detested it. He looked meaningfully at Philomene. "Why don't you dance for these gentlemen?"

She was slumped upon Probus, looking drunk and reckless. Statianus had never seen her look at a man so feverishly or clutch his arm with such hungry fingers. She clung to the burly general as if he were the secret of life discovered. Nevertheless, she made a slight, understanding nod to Statianus. He signed to Rufinus to come with him, and went out to the balcony behind the emperor.

Now, for Statianus, the real business of the evening was at hand. The three men were seated on the balcony, fruit and wine on a low table in front of them, the marble balustrade stamped white against the well of darkness that was Rome-by-night. Statianus made polite conversation for a while. From the room, he heard shouts of laughter, the clapping of hands. He glanced over his shoulder and saw Philomene poised, like a wild statue, upon the table, her feet bare, her green silk gown, held at the waist by a belt of rubies, open to reveal her breasts, her hair dishevelled, wine at the corners of her mouth. He heard his own voice; and the rough laughter of Cilo; and the fluting, endless monologue of Silvanus, "flamingo should be cooked with leeks and coriander, and for your sauce take . . . a wine, like a boy, is just right in its fourteenth year . . . and I read my poem . . . the loveliest house, it looks straight out to Capri . . ." All the time he watched the brooding profile of Aurelian in the darkness. Would the emperor keep up his dull-soldier pose? How to penetrate the guard, to signal, *I know you, Aurelian. Do not pretend with me, for each of us needs the other?* It was time to give a lead to Rufinus.

"I hear you will soon be leaving for the East, Rufinus."

"In ten days' time."

"Have you enjoyed your leave? Is your health better? Are you glad or sorry to go back?"

Rufinus uttered a dry sound that might have been a cough or a laugh. "It is always the same. A man comes back from the East. For the first week every sight and sound of Rome is a pleasure. He feels, 'If I had stayed out there one day longer I should have gone mad. This is the life. This is where I want to be.' And he wonders how he will ever tear himself away from Rome again. Two weeks later he is a little bored, and wondering how things are going on the other side. Another six weeks, and he is thinking, 'The gods be thanked, I will soon be going home again.' 'Home' is out there, and that is where his mind is, even if his body is still in Rome."

"You will be going back to some pretty problems."

Another cough. "Not so. A year ago there were problems. I

was governor then. I had to rule. But now there is precious little left for me to rule. The troops of Palmyra are in control to the Black Sea. I shall go back to Damascus by their leave. I shall entertain, and keep on good terms with all their bigwigs. What else? Nothing. They are the masters now."

Not a sound, not a movement from Aurelian. He looked into the night, into that black bowl from which the nocturnal murmur of Rome arose.

"Still, there will be problems," Statianus insisted.

"Only one. To keep the peace. The emperor's ruling is, 'Let Palmyra guard us from Persia. No war with Palmyra.' The emperor is occupied on the European frontiers. He does not want war on two fronts. My task is to save the weight of the East from falling on his shoulders. Is that not so, sir?"

Aurelian turned his head towards them. He did not speak, but there was a glitter of alertness in his eyes as he nodded. "And if—?" Statianus asked. He had seen that telltale glitter in the eyes. Now was the moment. "If they attack Egypt?"

"It is not for me to speak. Policy is the emperor's prerogative."

Another murmurous silence. Aurelian lifted his head. "This woman." His voice was low, heavy. "You know her well, Rufinus?"

"Zenobia, sir?"

"What do you think of her?"

"She is dangerous, sir. As dangerous to us as Cleopatra, whose descendant she claims to be. She is dangerous because she is clever, as brave and clever as any man. She is dangerous because she is a woman, with a woman's vanity. She postures in front of the world as she might posture in front of a mirror. That is what makes a woman dangerous."

"No woman is dangerous, Rufinus. You are a man. Can you not get rid of her?"

"It is too late to get rid of her, sir. Now it will take armies to do that. Your armies, sir."

Aurelian's eyes, gleaming with thought, were upon Rufinus. "And before? At the beginning? Why did you not get rid of her then?"

"I am a diplomat, my lord. I made a diplomat's mistake. I underrated her. If you hold me responsible, Lord Aurelian, here I am before you to answer for it. But in frankness, sir, it might be considered a pardonable error since you are making the same one now." There was no sign of displeasure from Aurelian. Rufinus went on. "When she came to the throne, sir, I thought as you did. I thought that her husband was the menace, friendly though he was, for he was a strong and capable man. With him out of the way, I assumed Zenobia would be easy to manage, for she appeared to me nothing more than a romantic hoyden."

"With him out of the way? But it was she who put him out of the way."

Statianus watched Rufinus. Rufinus looked steadily at Aurelian. "Yes, sir. From the facts of the case, there can be no doubt about that. Some nephew picked a quarrel with him and slew him, and she had the boy killed on the spot. Before he could reveal who had put him up to it, obviously."

It fascinated Statianus to see the lines of tension deepen in Aurelian's face, and to hear the roughness of his voice when he spoke next. "The bitch! The carrion! A woman killing her husband!"

Here was the crack in the man's armour. Statianus intervened. He spoke lightly, "Come, my lord! It is a commonplace. What does the prince do who wants the throne? He kills his father. What does the brother do who wants to be heir? He kills his brother. What does the ambitious woman do? She kills her husband."

Aurelian turned on him; and now there was a flush of fury beneath the soldier's tan. "Is that how great ones are? No loyalty? No love? By Hercules, the peasants in my village lived better than that! A family was a family, and a wife knew her duty to her husband. You should have punished her, Rufinus. You should have killed her there and then."

Statianus spoke softly. "You shall punish her, my lord. Sooner or later it will have to be war, and then Aurelian shall bring to her the punishment that the gods reserve for the impious."

Aurelian relaxed again, looking out at the night; but Statianus could sense in him the flow of roused anger. He leaned forward. His voice remained soft. "I shall speak openly, my lord, for I believe that I understand you, as others do not. And I wish you to understand me. Between you and me there should be understanding." This was his challenge; and in the lingering exchange of glances that followed, he knew he had made contact with Aurelian. "There must be war, my lord. Let us choose the time, not her. Let us strike her down before she grows too strong. Of the threat to Egypt, and what it means to us, I shall not speak. But there is another threat. The Syrian merchants are growing too powerful. It is not only in the East that they are ousting us, but everywhere. You will find them in every city in the world. Travel the roads in Gaul and Spain, go to the coast of Africa, go even to the shores of far-off Britain, and you will find these smooth, wily, wheedling fellows with their pack trains and their merchant ships taking the trade away from us. All the commerce of the East comes to us through Syria. A few more years and Syria will no longer be the channel, it will be the centre. A military rival, sir, may be tolerated for a time. A trade rival must be destroyed."

He leaned back, leaving the emperor to digest his words. Then he struck again. No matter whether or not the emperor responded. Let the thought be planted in him now. "I know, sir, it is a matter of resources. But I have the resources. Do you want money for a new campaign? I have it. Do you want stores? I shall build you a chain of depots such as no general has enjoyed in our lifetime. Do you want men? I shall raise fresh troops for you. Do you want remounts for your cavalry, ships to transport your troops? I have them. I shall serve you well, sir, and you shall smash her."

Aurelian rose. He stood with his back to the other two men, close to the balustrade. "All this to deal with a woman?" They waited. "No woman is worth this much trouble. What is a woman to a man? A woman is only a woman." He turned. The singing in the room had become a discordant din. "There must be a way to deal with her without war."

Ulpius had come out onto the balcony. Statianus remained silent. He did not wish to press his point further tonight. Ulpius said, "My lord, will you permit me to retire?"

Aurelian glanced into the room. The men around the table had fallen quiet, hugging their cups. Philomene stood on the table, legs astride, head flung back, hair cascading over shoulders from which her robe had fallen, leaving her naked to the waist. She was singing from the throat, a wordless song, hard, high, slow and savage, a woman's cry to Dionysius, a song from the beginnings of Greece, from Asia. Standing there, with one bare leg thrust forward out of the folds of her robe, she accentuated the tune with a slow, spaced stamping of her foot. Her arms were slackly outstretched, shudders of movement travelling along them to snaking fingertips. The wail in her throat became harsher, higher, fiercer. Its tempo quickened. The thud of her foot on the wood quickened with the tune, faster, faster. Her face was flushed. All the muscles of her body were leaping with the tune, a beat in the hollow of her throat, a wild rippling of her arms, a jerking of her breasts. Alone, with no instruments to accompany her, she held the men in the room crouching and panting on their couches, with the wild sustained cry from her throat and the fluid writhing of her body.

There were shouts and laughter from the men on the couches. Cilo, who had been holding a slave girl by the arm, pulled her down to his side. Varus and Capito were drinking again. Silvanus, who had been lolling over the side of his couch, quietly sick, rose, and lifted his cup to drink with the other two men. He saw the group watching from the balcony and cried, "To the good life!"

*

Capito rode down the hill behind Aurelian, with the Guard clattering after him in a double file. He was in that mood, languid yet exhilarated, which follows the drinking of good wine. The air of a winter night chilled like metal upon his cheeks, refreshing him, feeding his vainglory. In the darkness the ordered gardens of Statianus glimmered: flowerbeds shedding faint gleams of colour and touching the air with their scents; the black, ranked shadows of myrtle and laurel groves and shrubberies of box; still fishponds; the patterns of dark cypress trees and white terraces, colonnades and ever-plashing fountains. Down the white road, down the long flights of steps, he rode with a river flow of hoofbeats in his ears, and the wind faintly whispering, and the dark bulk of Aurelian in front of him, silent.

Now, by the gods, now should have been the time to finish the man off! Probus out of the way with that woman. No witnesses except a troop of cavalry who would obey their own commander. A quick stab in the back. But Felicissimus would not have it that way. Oh, no, he was too clever, that damned freedman. He was not going to let a Praetorian do the job. Nor was he going to carry out his stroke with the usual small group of assassins, who could be crushed within a day by the army. No, he preferred a full-scale uprising, mobilizing his own troops, so that he would have a force behind him to keep the army in check while he bargained with its generals.

Down past the gate, and down the open road towards the city centre and the palace. Above them the house reared like a fortress, sheer above the hillside on the cliff of its seventy-foot

retaining wall, dominating the city. The pleasure-fortress of
Statianus. Capito rode in a half-dream, adrift on a warm wash
of wine-fantasies, wine-grudges, wine-ambitions.

"Capito." Aurelian's voice awoke him. "Come here."

He rode up to the emperor's side.

Aurelian was silent for a little while. Then, "Capito, tell me
about the plot."

The conviction of betrayal hit Capito like scalding water in
his face, sluicing away the wine-fuddle. His expression, however, showed nothing but roused concern, and his voice was
steady. He was a Spaniard. "Sir?"

"The plot, Capito." The emperor looked down at the smaller
man, his face creased in a smile. "The plot to kill Aurelian."

"What plot is this, sir? I have heard nothing. I shall alert the
Guard at once."

Aurelian shook his head gently. "No, Capito. I do not want
you to alert the Guard. I want you to tell me about the plot."

"Sir, how can I know anything of a plot? Are you suggesting—"

"I am, Capito. You are in it and you will save yourself by telling me what you know."

Had there been treachery? Was this bluff? What did the man
know? The great thing was—Capito clung to it in the seething
of his mind—not to be trapped. "Sir, I can tell you nothing. I am
the commander of your Guard. I am under oath to be loyal. If
there is a plot, tell me of it and I will crush it. But do not accuse
me, sir."

"I am accusing you, Capito."

"Then what are your proofs, sir? Tell me. Perhaps there is a
plot. Perhaps someone has told you lies about me or put forged
papers into your hands. In justice, confront me with them. Be
mindful, sir, that if someone is really plotting against you, I,
as commander of your Guard, am an obstacle in their path, and

you would be doing their work if you let yourself be instigated to remove me."

Aurelian sighed. "Capito, you waste my time."

They rode on. "Capito, listen carefully. There is not much time. Let us examine the possibilities. First, that you are innocent. I know that this is not true. Second, that you are guilty. In that case, I could do one of two things. I could arrest you, which would bring neither of us profit, for you would die and I would have given the alarm to your colleagues. Or I could let you go.

"If I let you go, you could do one of two things. You could serve me, and help me crush the plot. Or you could warn your colleagues.

"If you warned your colleagues, they could do one of two things. They could remain quiet. This would serve them little, for some would be known to me, others would be suspected, and you, who had informed them, would be lost. Or they could strike at once. But what chance do you think a hasty blow against me would stand? I am not unguarded. I have my own picked men with me at the palace. My best legion is less than a day's march from Rome. And of your own Praetorians, many are my countrymen, and the Illyrians will not go against me. You cannot make use of the whole Praetorian Guard against me—this is your weakest spot. You, personally, have joined the plot for your own profit, but what can you do? You can collect in secrecy a small number of cronies, men not devoted to me, from among your soldiers, to take part in an attempt on my life; they would have to be few, for if the news leaked out the bulk of the Guard would be roused in my defense. Or, more likely, you could guarantee your masters that at the decisive moment you would use your powers to keep the Praetorians in camp, out of action, until your plans had succeeded in the city.

"So you see, none of these possibilities offers you any profit. Let us return, then, to the remaining course. This is that you should serve me, and I warmly recommend it. After all, you have only gone into this business for one end, your own advantage. Consider, and you will see that your advantage lies in serving me. I am not wheedling you. I do not need your help, but you need my forgiveness. For your own sake, however, I say, what can you get from your present masters? Money? Office? And most likely, since rogues always fall out, a knife in the back at some near date. What you can get from me is a different story. You can judge my future from my past deeds, and the men who serve me well shall share my future with me. There is no limit to the ambitions a bold and able man can attain if he stands at the right hand of Aurelian. You may well fear me, but it is not fear that I hold over you. Rather I offer you the chance to join the winning side. See this, and see that your advantage is bound up with mine, and no one will be more fervent in my cause than you. Think well, Capito."

It was a few moments before Capito answered. "Sir, I tell you, you misjudge me. All this talk is a mystery. My head is in a whirl. A plot? What plot? For the love of Jupiter, enlighten me."

"Capito!" The emperor's voice roughened. "Do not play with me."

"Sir, take me now to the chapel of the Guard and I will swear before the sacred eagles that I am innocent."

"Capito." The emperor's voice was soft again. "Listen. I know about the Caelian Hill. I know about the Mint. I know about the gladiators. Now do you think I am bluffing?"

Capito felt the sick thumping of his heart. This was no trick. He was trapped. What to do for the best?

"You are silent? Capito. Listen again. This is your last chance. We are five minutes from the palace. If you have not spoken when we enter the gates, it is the end of you."

Capito remained silent.

"Do not think to ride away now, or to draw your sword against me. I am Hand-on-Hilt, and I can deal with twenty like you. Five minutes, Capito—less now. Your death sentence lies between those gates. I shall be silent now, and you will think."

Hoofbeats marked off the seconds. They rode the length of a silent street.

"Three minutes, Capito."

Another brief silence, then, "Sir, it is a long story to tell in three minutes."

"Your judgement has proved sound, Capito. You will do well with me, I promise. Now, listen. Your story will keep for a little while. You are commander of the Guard, and it will not arouse suspicion if you remain at the palace tonight, so long as you stay in the Guard's quarters. Do not try to leave the palace or to send a messenger out, for whoever goes will be stopped. On the other hand, you must not come to see me. You are certain to be watched, for plotters do not trust each other. If Capito is closeted with the emperor by night, your masters will surely hear of it. And, as you must have gathered, my concern just now is to put them off their guard."

Ahead of them the palace gates were opening. "When you have reached your quarters, Probus will come to join you in your night inspection of the sentries. That is why he left ahead of us. He thinks of other things besides that girl, you know. It will take you about ten minutes to ride round all the posts. In that time you will make your report to him. It will be concise, a soldier's report, and when your round is finished Probus will dismiss you. There must be no lingering, no muttering for spies to see. For the rest of the night you will be watched. In the morning, Probus will return with you to visit the Praetorian camp. There, among your officers, he will meet countrymen, old comrades, and it will be natural for him to talk with some of them. The men with whom he talks, Capito, will be at your shoulder from that moment on, and you had better keep as silent and faithful as they. You see, there is no turning back for you now. Be wholehearted, then, and strive for great rewards."

Capito was still mentally adrift, swept upon the tide of this man's will. "By Jupiter, sir—" He checked himself.

"What is it?"

"Nothing, sir."

"You were going to say, 'Aurelian is not such a fool as he seems.' Well, keep it to yourself. It is not yet time for others to learn this fact."

CHAPTER NINE

THE BATTLE OF THE MINT

"HOW much did you know that night?" The room, part of the emperor's suite in the palace, was dark. Through three open archways could be seen the long, white curve of the emperor's sun-balcony, with the face of the Palatine Hill cut away beneath it to render it inaccessible from below. Probus, the speaker, stood inside one of the archways. Aurelian and his wife Severina sat, half-facing each other, on the balcony. Against the far wall of the room waited Maxin and a slave named Lucipor, who was Aurelian's major-domo. "When you cornered Capito?"

Aurelian was looking out into the darkness, to where the Caelian Hill rose, on the far side of a noisy promenade. On its black and silent bulk the edges of buildings were stamped against the pale night gloom; on its summit the long low cube of the imperial Mint. "Nothing."

"And you made him talk? He's not what I'd call a soft man. How did you do it?"

Aurelian leaned back, relaxed, as if the armchair were his throne and the darkness his kingdom. He did not turn his head. "We shall fight the battle tonight. Do you feel calm, Probus?"

"Do I ever feel calm before a fight? I feel hot, inside me, and time crawls over my skin like a swarm of ants."

"The man who feels impatient before a fight is a good man to lead a charge. But the senior commander must know how to be calm, as calm as a lake. You'll have to learn that, my old bear. You'll be in my shoes one day." Aurelian sank back into his silence. "How did I make him talk? Well, we have to wait. We have nothing to do but wait, till the fight starts. So I might as well tell you." He turned his head. "Maxin, come here. This is for you, too."

When the boy stood behind his chair he spoke again. "This is a lesson, Maxin, in the art of command. That is why I am speaking. One day you, too, will command. Politics and war are one. The means are different but the basis is the same. Mind against mind. The good general sees into the mind of his foe, learns to think with that mind, and can make his own plans because he can see what the enemy is likely to do.

"Before I came to Rome I knew that I must watch out for a plot. I knew how much the Senate must hate to accept yet another emperor from the army. I knew how many others feared my coming. All this was common sense. It was borne out by my Intelligence. My father-in-law, and my Severina—" He looked at his wife. "No army officer could send better reports than you, my dear—they were my eyes and ears in Rome. From them I knew who uttered a sneer against me in the Forum, who imitated my supposed accent at a dinner, which comedian spoke verses against me, and which well-known spectators cheered him. My enemies enjoyed themselves while I was away. They also identified themselves for me.

"I reasoned that a plot against me must either be in Rome or in camp, either sooner or later. Sooner was more likely than later, for later I would be more firmly in power. Rome was more likely than my camp, for in camp I have friends all round me; in Rome, enemies. Nobody knew when I would come to Rome again. This visit, then, might well be the time my enemies chose.

"Then—who? No, I did not think of the Mint officials. I might have, for they are the most guilty. But a man does not see everything. Where to find the first marks in the dust, the beginning of the trail? I looked to the Praetorians.

"No plot in Rome can succeed unless the Praetorians are either friendly or neutral. Five thousand troops, double-pay men picked from every part of the Empire, camped on the doorstep of the capital. No one in Rome, without the legions, can defy them. But I know that many of the Guard are countrymen of mine, and seven of their centurions out of ten swear by Aurelian. It would be hard to turn the Guard against me. No sufficiently influential group of officers could be approached without one of them coming to warn me. Therefore, it could only be a question of keeping the Guard out of the way. And, most likely, that task would have to be entrusted to very few men, to one man, even. If I were in charge of the plot, a large bribe to the commander of the Praetorians, to keep them inactive till the blow was struck, would be my solution. There, then, was the man for me to tackle.

"Well, bear, I tackled him. But I should never have broken him down if I had not known three words: Caelian, Mint, gladiators. I was bluffing when I used these words, for I made him think I knew far more than I did. But it was not all bluff.

"You, Maxin, if you were riding out with a patrol, and you came over the saddle of a pass and looked down on a village, you would expect to see the smoke rising from the huts, the women washing by the stream, the children playing in the dirt. One morning, you ride over the hills, and glance down, and all seems the same. But you have the soldier's eye. All is not the same. There are no children playing. Why?"

An eagerness to speak glowed in Maxin's eyes. But he remained silent. Probus said, "An ambush."

"Yes. The enemy are down there. They have made the villagers carry on as before. The women are by the stream, trembling. The fires are alight. But children cannot be made to play. They are hidden away in the huts. Only the good soldier will notice that, and he will be warned against a trap. That is the eye for detail. Julius Caesar was once marching through the Alps, with the enemy massed on a height ahead. He heard stones fall from high up, and the sound echoed. He sent men up, hidden by the clouds, and when they were high enough, they shouted and clashed their shields. The enemy heard the sound of troops echoing above them, from both sides, and thought they were trapped, and ran away. Thus he avoided a fight on unfavourable ground. You see, his ears gave him the little detail.

"On my first morning here I stood on this balcony and I looked out towards that hill opposite. It is called the Caelian. As you can see in daytime, there is a lot of waste ground on its upper slopes—a big fire cleared it some years ago—and there is a lot of new building going on. There are stacks of material everywhere, scaffolding going up, swarms of workmen, and brown scars all over the face of the hill where they are digging foundations. And I looked. And it was a strange place. A confusion. The eye passes over it without interest. But the soldier's eye should never be without interest, especially in enemy territory, and that is where we are.

"Something caught my eye. I looked, and looked again. It was only a scar in the green, among all the other scars. A trench, just below the Mint. I looked at it, and then I turned away. But in my mind, a voice asked what was wrong. What was it that was wrong? I came back to the balcony and looked for the third time. The trench was a hundred and fifty paces from the Mint, on open ground. It was in a position where the ground stopped sloping steeply and levelled out. The sort of place where soldiers, attacking, find that the uphill trudge is over, and they can re-form and charge. The sort of place where you would dig a ditch to stop them. And my eye went to the Mint, and I saw what a fortress it was. That long, blank wall. That flat roof with its parapet. The one great door, barred and iron-studded. The Mint. I remembered then about the Mint, and the men who ran it. I saw the trench again. It only ran round one end of the Mint, on the most approachable side. A drainage trench? What drainage trench begins and ends nowhere? Foundations? What foundations follow a long curve like that? No. It could more easily be a trench for war than either of these. Then I sent Lucipor over there." He turned to the slave. "You still have the soldier's eye, Lucipor. You saw the things that mattered. Tell them what you saw."

"There were men working, and there were men who did not work." Lucipor was Aurelian's age. He was a Thracian, tall, gaunt of cheek, with a mop of still-black hair falling over his eyes. Twenty years ago, as a field slave, he had taken arms to help drive off a raid of the Scythian steppe-nomads. His conduct had pleased Aurelian; he might have become a soldier and a free man; but in the fighting he lost his right arm at the elbow, and Aurelian had taken him as a personal servant. Now he was in charge of the household. "The men who did not work lounged about in groups, sitting on stacks of timber, keeping to themselves. They were a tough-looking lot, and when they moved they moved like fighters, light and quiet of tread. They had many scars, and below their knees there were the marks of greaves."

"Soldiers do not wear greaves," Aurelian said. "Gladiators do. And I have known, from reports, that for months past agents for unknown principals have been buying up gangs of gladiators, paying the highest prices, at the schools at Ravenna, Capua, and Alexandria. Who buys fighters by the hundred? And why are they hidden among the labour gangs on the Caelian?

"This was all I needed for the attack on Capito. He talked. In the circumstances, it was the intelligent thing for him to do. The plan, of course, followed from my clues. An armed rising, with the Mint as its headquarters. The Praetorians to be bought off, and the armies kept tame with good pay. The power of the Senate to be restored—in other words, the power of the swindlers to be unlimited."

"And a freedman as emperor?" Probus growled.

"No. Felicissimus is too clever for that. Emperors are too

short-lived. He would be content to stay behind the scenes. The new emperor is to be—prepare yourself for a shock, Probus—the pervert, Plautius Silvanus."

"That bit of fluff over the Empire? You're joking!"

"There have been worse. That is what Rome has become. You see, they do not want a strong man. They want a puppet, and the puppet must represent the Senate." He paused. A rumbling came up from the darkness. The wagon trains, barred from the city's choked streets by day, were rolling in, ceaselessly, on all the main roads. "Their forces are considerable. On the Caelian, under the guise of building operations, they have stored arms in the Mint, assembled as so-called labourers seven hundred gladiators, and another fifteen hundred men from their own bodyguards, hooligans from the slums, and so on. From the police, Varus has guaranteed a total of three thousand out of seven thousand. More than half the City Guard will join in—say, twenty-five hundred men. Nearly eight thousand in all.

"Tonight the main force will attack this palace frontally from the Caelian. The police, whose headquarters is down there on the left, next to the Baths of Trajan, will attack us from the rear. All the City Guard has to do is to seize a number of important buildings and junctions in the city, and murder in their beds various citizens who might stay loyal to Aurelian. It's the only sort of job they're fit for."

"My plan has been to draw them out. When I saw the welcome they had organized for me, to put me off my guard, I thought, that is just what I must do to them. I welcome this plot, Probus. I am going to bring back the old Rome. I am going to set up respect for law. This place is a nest of enemies, and I must wipe them out before I leave. But I must wipe them out within the law. Rome has had too many emperors who massacred at their whim. I do not wish to appear as another.

"Let Felicissimus do my work for me. Let my enemies rise, and let the sword of the law wipe them out."

Severina laughed. "And that is why he has been playing the clumsy centurion since he has been in Rome." She was fifteen years younger than Aurelian. With her frank eyes, her strong, straight nose, and her hair plainly braided up, she resembled a statue of a classical matron. When her father had married her to Aurelian she had been a shy, severe girl of fourteen. Ever since the wedding night, there had been a politeness, a respect, between her and Aurelian which had been at once a bond and a barrier. They had never achieved any intimacy of spirit. Neither suffered from their long separations. She knew, though it did not greatly concern her, that Aurelian paid little attention to other women: not out of weakness, but out of a streak in his native character, the chastity of the barbarian. She managed Aurelian's affairs in Rome, looked after her father, had little to do with other women, and was scarcely aware of her own womanhood. In essence, she and Aurelian were no more than good comrades, always fond yet always shy of each other. Now, as they sat together, they seemed united, but upon each of them there sat an unacknowledged loneliness.

"Husband, I tell you, you have even made me blush at times, watching you standing there, all stiff and awkward, while all the grand men and their painted women came to inspect you, and kiss your cheek, and say sarcastic things you were not supposed to understand, and go away laughing at you. Six days of play-acting. There is not a mummer in Rome who could equal such a performance."

"I hope I have not overdone it. Maxin, all this is war, too, though it may not sound like it. For every desperate man who joins a plot there are ten waverers, who stay on the fringe, and twenty cowards who sympathize but keep clear. Those waverers and cowards hate me as much as the desperate men. Let them die, too. That is why I have taught them to despise me, to see Felicissimus as the sure victor, and to rush to join him.

"Another thing. I feared that Felicissimus, who is a cunning man, might not be fooled by my game. I knew how to deal with him when I heard of his anger that Statianus had not invited him. When he came to the palace to pay his respects, I had him turned away. I made insulting remarks about him, and saw that they reached his ear. I hope I have enraged him. I hope I have kept him so impatient for the moment of revenge that he has not seen through me. Maxin, lad, there are two ways of bringing an enemy to battle. You can tempt him, by hiding the strength of your forces. Or you can provoke him, ordering your troops to taunt him until he is goaded to attack. Sometimes you can do both at once."

Maxin raised his head, as a beast raises its muzzle, and looked at Aurelian. His face was sombre, but there was a tension in his poise, a quiver of bunched muscles, that betrayed eagerness.

Aurelian smiled. "Tonight, lad, you shall come with me. Until now you have refused to bear a sword. Tonight, I shall give you a sword. After all, you will only have to kill Romans."

The lights in the boy's eyes were the beginnings of a smile. He nodded.

*

The twelfth hour of night, in Rome, began seventy-five minutes before first light. At this time the city was silent. The rumble of traffic had died down, for the two main roads that flanked the Caelian Hill to north and south were packed with ox-wagons standing still, nose to tail, in traffic jams of unusual stubbornness and size.

Just below the open ground on the summit of the Caelian there stood two blocks of expensive apartments, five-storey buildings of white stucco and steep-pitched red-tiled roofs, with flower-hung balconies, gay, striped window awnings, and gardens all round.

Maxin lay in the thick shadow beneath a laurel bush, peering into the pale gloom. He had been here for an hour. He could not see the trench, for building materials had been dumped in front of it to form an almost-continuous barricade. He lay and listened to the thrumming silence of the night.

A spurt of yellow leaped up into the darkness from the Mint roof. He knew that this was the signal to the rebels at police headquarters to synchronise their attack. He waited. He heard, above him, a padding and a murmur and an occasional clink of metal. The gloom above the barricade thickened suddenly in a wavering, irregular blur of blackness. The blackness seemed to pour over the barricade, like the fall of a roller upon a beach, and to spread into an army of shadows. He felt a hard, happy thudding of his heart. He was a warrior again, and he was looking at the enemy, three thousand of them, rising up out of their trench and coming down the hill.

He raised himself onto hands and knees and moved back, cat-silent. He passed between the two blocks, and flitted down, between more flowerbeds, across the street, and down through the slum area at the foot of the hill.

Hardly a sound, from the rebels in the darkness above, disturbed the silence. He was almost at the promenade that divided the Caelian from the Palatine. In the distance he heard a trumpet. It sounded from the palace, faint, yet clear and exciting in the night. Then, away to the north, another trumpet spoke, answering. To the south, another. He seemed to hear, from high up on the hills where the rebels were, a *burr-burr* of bewilderment, of hesitation, and he laughed aloud, proud of his master's genius. Then, from beyond the Caelian, a new sound: a toppling crash. And another, and another, and the crashing spread all down the Praenestine Way; and to the south, the same, strange river of crashing noises passed down the Appian Way. He could imagine the rebels up there, pausing, listening, mystified, frightened. He turned and faced them, and he shouted, in a harsh strong voice that echoed from the walls, "Come down and die, you Romans!"

Trumpet calls, near now, stabbed the night, brazen and lovely, searing his blood with exultation. Battle, battle! All round the Caelian Hill the trumpets were calling, one to another, legion trumpets, sounding the attack, and the night was full of crashing, and clashing, and shouting, and the sound of men running.

In the covered wagons that had stretched in two long jams from the city gates, one to the Flavian Amphitheatre, one to the Circus Maximus, had been hidden five thousand men of the Third Gallican Legion, brought secretly from their camp in the last two days.

Maxin heard them pouring from the wagons, and overturning the wagons to block all the streets coming down from the Caelian, and forming up, and pouring along the two transverse streets that connected the Appian and Praenestine Ways, surrounding the Caelian on all four sides. They were moving up, now, in companies, along the promenade on which he stood, the main body preparing for the frontal assault. There, in the centre, were the silver eagles, and there, beneath the eagles, stood Aurelian, purple-cloaked, sword in hand. He hurried to his master's side.

He knew the plan. Four thousand legionaries were to attack the hill. A thousand were down in the city to meet the first onslaught of the three thousand rebel policemen. Then the Praetorian Guard would come into action. It could not be alerted earlier, for to have done so would have warned the rebels. Now, the infantry of the Praetorians would be coming at the double, two thousand of them to reinforce the counterattack against the police, fifteen hundred to strengthen the attack on the hill, and fifteen hundred, including all their cavalry, to hunt down the rebellious City Guard detachments throughout Rome.

Staccato trumpet commands. The lines of legionaries moved forward. Through the dawn gloom, past the Temple of Claudius, into the slum area, dark files threading through the steep alleyways, up long, winding flights of steps between high, grimy walls; and there, ahead, were the apartments, and in front of them the street that Maxin had crossed a short while before. the Via Capitis Africae.

Above the apartment blocks the rebels were a black swarm spreading down the hillside in a roar of bravado. Below, the soldiers were silent files moving up to meet them.

The legionaries reached the lateral road that faced the apartment blocks. They were deploying into line of battle when the rebels burst round the buildings like a flood tide. There were no shouts of alarm or panic movements from the legionaries. Swiftly they ran to their places in the last seconds before the onslaught reached them, silent but for the clatter of boots and the sharp, commanding voices of centurions.

The noise of the enemy, the purposeful silence of the soldiers around him, the impending release of battle, fired Maxin with excitement. As the wild wall of bodies and yelling faces bore down on him he drew his sword, let loose a long, harsh howl and plunged forward. A grip of iron held him back. It was Aurelian. "Keep the line, lad."

And Maxin saw for the first time that he was not a man alone among others, but a segment of a *line*, with two more lines behind; and that a Roman soldier did not fight like a leaping beast, but *kept the line*, and it was the line that fought.

Thought blinked to a stop. The enemy were upon him. The heat and smell of their bodies, their angry shouting, their jarring weight assailed him. It was thrust with the sword and up with the shield and strike and parry and jolt of clashing steel in his wristbones. Confusion had lifted from him. There was only one man at a time, the man he had to kill, one face clearly printed against the blur; and there was an instinct which turned him here, or here, or here, to meet each new threat. It was a cold night, but already the sweat rolled down him. The weight of the enemy bore upon him and he was going back. He became aware that all the legion line, sagging and wavering, was being borne back.

Maxin went back, step by step, unfrightened, because he had a sword in his hand and because there was the line on each side of him holding firm, and because next to him, all the time, there was Aurelian, tall and protecting, always there with a grunt of encouragement or a saving thrust of the sword when he was hard-pressed.

He could hear the centurions walking up and down behind him, as if they were supervising recruit drill, calling, "Don't bunch! Open out, men! Keep your arm's-length! Leave room for sword and shield! Up on the left, there! Steady, the centre!" Their voices kept him cool, kept him in his place, kept him aware of *the line*. In all this surging and screaming and clash of iron, the legionaries kept their line. They were two thousand against three thousand, but discipline multiplied their strength like the gears of a machine. The wonder of it swelled in Maxin's breast, exalting him, filling him with love for these men and what they represented.

The legion was standing its ground. Then it was advancing. Maxin was advancing, and with each step the wonder of discipline exalted him. The rebel flood roared slowly back uphill, pouring between the apartment blocks and around them. Maxin felt the soft earth of flowerbeds clogging his feet, stumbled over bodies. The rebels were ebbing away between the buildings. Some of them were running into the doorways. Already, from upper windows, javelins streaked down upon the legion. Maxin dashed for a doorway in pursuit. Once more Aurelian restrained

him. Legion trumpets were calling, and their message penetrated his awareness. "Halt! Halt!"

All along the road, to his right and left, he saw the legionaries re-forming into long, straight lines, each man sinking down
on to his heel to rest, shield before him, sword still ready. Why
were they halting? Why were they letting the enemy get away?
Why did they not storm the apartments and clear out the rebels
who were shooting arrows from above?

Men came up past him with barrels, and flung the barrels
into the doorways of the buildings. He saw the spread of thick
black liquid, caught the pitchy smell in his nostrils, saw the
flaring torches flung through the gloom into the doorways, and
the searing upbursts of flame.

A voice was speaking in his left ear, through his battle-dream.
It was Aurelian. "Some of the best families in Rome live in those
apartments. The people who hate me. Let them burn. The others
will remember better."

Cries and screams, a panic of women and children, came from
the windows. Flames licked up the walls, greedily eating the
buildings; firetraps, these blocks, as much as the meanest tenement, with their wooden floors, stairs, and joisting, and their
few, narrow doorways. The trumpets sounded "Forward!"
Maxin moved forward, the dream upon him again, with the line.
He hardly felt the heat as he moved between the two burning
buildings. Aurelian was speaking again. "Never get held up with
house-to-house fighting. It's slow and you lose too heavily. Burn
them, like rats in their holes."

The line formed up beyond the buildings. There was the
waste ground ahead of them, the rebels swarming back, spilling
over the barricade into the trench. Behind, the heat of the fire,
the scream and thud of falling bodies, and the glare lighting up
the dawn. Again the trumpets. "Charge!"

Small groups of rebels stood and fought on the stacks of
building timber in the trench. The others, beyond, fled before

the legionary charge. The huge doors of the Mint were swallowing up the fugitives. For the second time, Maxin heard the trumpets sounding "Halt!" The legionaries were masters of the trench. They leaned against its forward side, weary. Maxin was drenched in sweat, and the sweat grew cold upon him. His shoulders ached mightily and, now that he was not fighting, there was a pain in his head. All the way down the hillside the humped dead were scattered. The sky was bright with the glare of the burning buildings. Black smoke rolled up. A wall toppled outward and crashed in a billow of flame and saffron dust. Among the dead, the wounded squirmed and crawled. The legion men had lost heavily. The rebels, with no hope of mercy if they lost, had fought well, especially the gladiators.

Maxin, apathetic with weariness, saw the doors of the Mint close. Behind the roof parapet, there was an insect scurry of men. At intervals, the length of the roof, threads of smoke climbed to the sky. He wondered how the grim stone fortress on the hill crest was to be captured. For the sake of secrecy, the legion had left all its siege artillery behind. He knew that Aurelian wanted the battle to be ended swiftly, so that the games might commence on time.

It was not left to the commanders to solve the problem. Like all well-trained soldiers, the rank and file of the Third Gallican were imbued with initiative as well as discipline. While Maxin lay weary against the trench wall, soldiers were climbing up among the stacks of building material, and passing it down into the trench, and clustering in an instinctive, wordless swarm of activity like ants, to collect ladders, long scaffolding poles, and heavy timber joists, or staggering along the trench with great coils of rope over their shoulders. A centurion paused in front of Aurelian. Maxin knew him well. It was Scrofa, the man who had guarded him when he was first captured. "Permission to speak, sir? Plenty of scaling gear here. Are we resting long?"

"No. The men have got their breath back. Bring up the colours. Where are the trumpeters?"

And, to the call of trumpets, the soldiers spilled over the lip of the trench for the last charge. As they drew near to the Mint, the rain of missiles began: arrows, javelins, and stones. Men were falling everywhere, but the attack went on. The ground was covered with storming parties, running forward carrying poles and ladders.

The first men were at the foot of the wall. The first ladders were swinging up. Improvised battering rams thundered at the door. Over the parapet there shot a blur of dazzling white. It descended like a blink of light, and others followed, all along the wall. Ahead of him, Maxin saw the white spurt pour down upon the first ladder that had been erected, and the climbing soldiers scattered out into the air, falling, screaming, flame-fringed. Soldiers writhed upon the ground or lay, charred and blackened; and from the roof there poured down the molten bronze, brought up from the workshops of the Mint, which the defenders had prepared over fires on the roof.

The attackers fell back, out of the range of the molten deluges. Their ranks were thinned. There seemed only a scattering of men left, against this solid fortress. Trumpets sounded behind Maxin. A new wave of legionaries rose up out of the trench. A thousand men had been brought from the detachments covering the other sides of the Mint. The original assaulting force, thirty paces from the walls, crouched on their heels, protected by their shields, panting. The new wave went through them, and up to the walls, and the ladders went up, and the white tongues of blazing metal poured down once more, and the second attack had failed.

Maxin rose. He spoke to some legionaries near him. They did not seem to hear. He shouted. "You! You! Help me! Lift this pole!"

They were staring at him. Then the centurion Scrofa came

towards him. "D'you hear! You men there! Do as the lad says!"

The men were moving, obeying. Six of them seized a long scaffold pole and began to raise it, butt on the ground, like a flagpole. To the upper end clung Maxin, holding on with his legs and right arm, left arm holding his shield above him as the arrows sped at him from the roof. The pole rose, in a slow, wavering arc against the sky. One of the party at its base fell, pierced by a spear, and the pole almost went down with him; but another man rushed to take his place, and others, with their shields, formed a semicircle to protect the working party from missiles.

Maxin saw the roof coming nearer, white sky all round him; and on both sides of him other poles, with other men clinging to them, going up, close enough to the wall to pitch a man on to the roof, too far to be drenched by the flaming metal.

Then the pole fell forward, and Maxin was on the parapet. Two startled rebels were in front of him, holding a pot of molten bronze between them. Beyond, he saw a rush of men coming at him. He drove with his sword, and the man holding one side of the pot fell dead. The bronze spilled, and the other man uttered a hoarse cry of agony as the dazzling white pool spread around his ankles. The heat beat up at Maxin. The pool ran out, driving back the rebels who had been coming towards him. He saw other legionaries fighting on the parapet. He heard the crash of a ladder behind him. Aurelian came over the parapet, then Scrofa, and the soldiers pouring up behind; and more swarming up poles; and ropes flung down by the first stormers, and the ropes knotted with climbers; men seething up the walls like insects and a new wave of reinforcements coming up the hill, fifteen hundred of the Praetorians arrived from camp at last.

It was full daylight. On two pillars of smoke from the burning buildings there rested a flat grey cloud, beneath which Rome lay, silent and terrified, while its masters fought their battle on the hill. On the parapet of the Mint a thickening fringe of sol-

diers fought the desperate rebels. Attackers fell from the para
pet, tumbling against the sky as others swarmed up.

Aurelian was like a giant in the midst of his men. He made
for the thick of the fight again and again. He shouted encourage
ment. He joked. He praised. These were his legionaries, the men
who fought his hardest battles and suffered the worst losses
Now, in battle, he must overcome their discontents, make him
self a legend among them, make them sing of him, for although
the cavalry was the main offensive arm, the legions were still the
basis of political power. Where he went, Maxin went, shouting
wild war cries in the Gothic tongue; and as often as the sword
of Aurelian had saved Maxin on the hill, Maxin's shield now
saved Aurelian.

The fight swarmed all over the roof. The legionaries were
established. Now, in number, they were superior. They drove
forward, around their triumphant standards, and it was the
rebels now who toppled from the roof, into the centre courtyard
From the hillside below came the thunder of battering rams
against the door.

Rising head and shoulders out of a group of combatants across
the roof, the rebel leader stood at bay like a butcher in his
slaughterhouse, with the cloven corpses of his enemies tumbled
about him and the floor slippery with blood. Felicissimus carried no shield, only a battle-axe which he wielded with both
hands, expelling a loud, workman's grunt each time he struck a
blow. His great body, naked but for a slave's skirt, shone with
sweat. White skirt and brown skin were spattered with blood.
His face, uplifted in wrath, was like the head of an African war-
god, with a broad flat nose, snake's eyes, and slab lips. He saw
Aurelian, followed by Maxin, thrusting towards him and he uttered a sound like the boom of an African drum.

Aurelian lunged at him, slipped in the blood and toppled sideways. The axe came down in a swing from above the shoulder
that carried Felicissimus whirling after it. Maxin leaped for-

ward, sinking on one knee in front of Aurelian with shield advanced. The axe sheared into the shield and sent the boy sprawling away, jarred and half stunned. In the second that Felicissimus stood trying to prise the axe free, Aurelian had regained his feet and came in again with the sword. Felicissimus fled, unarmed.

The back of the fight was broken. The Third Gallicans were masters of the roof. The last rebels were swarming down through skylights into the interior of the Mint. Below, the main doors had been burst open and legionaries were pouring into the courtyard.

Aurelian raised Maxin to his feet and helped him across to the parapet, to sit and rest. Gently he wiped blood away from the boy's arm and made sure that the shock of the axe-blow had broken no bones. Only then did he give his attention to the runners who had arrived from the other parts of the city. Their reports showed that the battle had been won everywhere.

From inside the building there still sounded the stampede of feet and the shouts of strife; but on the roof the men of the Third Gallican sprawled like idlers, clustered, in groups which were few and pitifully small, around their standards. They were sweating and filthy, red of face, bone-weary of movement, and brooding with a deep, slow-burning anger, upon the sight of their dead comrades heaped around them.

"Right!" Aurelian was on his feet, calling to the centurion Scrofa. "Get the men on their feet. We'll finish the job."

Scrofa said, "No prisoners, sir? Petition from the men."

"No prisoners. I want Rome to remember my legions."

They descended a dark, winding staircase that was already clogged with corpses. They passed along corridors littered with torn papers and smashed furniture, ignoring the open doorways inside which legionaries trampled and destroyed and killed. Down more stairs, towards the last noise of fighting, to the basement where the great coin workshops were.

They went through a door into a great hall. The air was dry and overheated, pressing upon the face like an invisible pillow. A row of furnaces were built into the far wall, some of their doors open to reveal dazzling interiors of fire. The glare of the furnaces cast an uncertain light throughout the hall. Down the centre of the floor stood the presses, big tables, each composed of an upper and a lower block, the upper with dies set in its underside, the lower with moulds cut into it. A five-foot wooden screw rose from the centre of each table, turned by a capstan bar which could be worked by two slaves.

Men ducked and dashed among the machines like a blur of dancing shadows, faces mad in the firelight, fireglare gleaming on breastplates. Weapons clashed, voices snarled, the heat buffeted. At the far end of the workshop a cluster of legionaries hung upon Felicissimus, trying to pull him down. His bellowing filled the room as he plucked a soldier off him and smashed the man's head on the edge of a table, seized two more by the scruffs of their necks, banged them together and flung them away, shook others off him like a mighty dog, sent bodies flying across the floor. He burst free, seized a long furnace shovel and, clearing a path for himself with it, leaped onto one of the tables. Alone, he towered above the fight, a huge naked creature with the red glare rippling on his skin.

Aurelian jumped onto the table at the other end of the room, and came leaping from table to table towards Felicissimus. The two men came face to face once more, crouching and feinting with sword against shovel, while their men fought at their feet.

The length of the shovel and Felicissimus's great height gave him a reach that was longer than Aurelian's by over two feet. Thus, when he launched himself at the emperor, flailing with the shovel, it seemed that one of his blows must surely find its mark or force Aurelian off the small table. But Aurelian ducked behind the centre bar, and protected himself by dodging so that he kept it between himself and his foe. Felicissimus, his eyes ape-red with anger, seized the haft of the shovel with both hands and drove it like a spear at Aurelian's chest. As the Negro lunged in, Aurelian seized the chance to come to close quarters, ducked under the capstan bar and sprang up with a sword-thrust. But Felicissimus stepped nimbly back and parried the thrust with the shovel handle held between his hands. Then he drove the shovel forward, his weight behind it, and Aurelian toppled backward off the table.

Felicissimus uttered a roar from the depths of his chest and leaped, shovel upraised, so that his immense bulk should fall upon his enemy. Aurelian rolled clear, just as a surge of strug-gling men filled the aisle. Felicissimus smashed men out of the way with his shovel, hurling himself towards Aurelian, but the emperor was on his feet again.

The fight was drawing to a close. Few rebels were still resist-ing. Others were huddled, captive, in corners. Aurelian shouted, "Clear the room! Into the fires with them!"

The maddened legionaries needed no more prompting. Fur-nace doors were flung open. Prisoners were dragged, screaming, across the floor and bundled into the fires. Wounded rebels were tossed in after them. The room resounded with cries and crazy pleadings, and a stench of burning filled it.

Felicissimus had abandoned his attempt to reach Aurelian. He was backing towards the end wall, at bay before three men whom he held off with swings of his shovel. It took Aurelian a second or so to see why the three attackers—Scrofa, Maxin, and a private soldier—were able to drive Felicissimus back instead of being swept away by the shovel. Scrofa had a javelin. He was crouching, weaving as he advanced, waiting for the chance to fling it, and Felicissimus was holding the blade of the shovel in front of him, ready to use it as a shield, ready, too, to use the handle as a club if any of the three came too close.

Felicissimus retreated into the full glare of the furnaces. He was almost up against them. The three men enclosed him. He and they were tensed, watchful for the adversary's false move.

Suddenly, with the astonishing speed of which he was capable, he flung open a furnace door with his left hand, sank
down, as Scrofa's javelin flew, and rammed the shovel into the
furnace. The javelin tore open his shoulder and bounced off the
wall. In the same instant that the three men leaped forward
with their swords he whipped the shovel from the furnace and
flung its load of white-hot charcoal into their faces. Scrofa and
Maxin reeled back, shields up to protect them. The third man
squirmed on the floor clutching at his face.

Aurelian, who had come up quietly from the left, took his
chance in this moment. With all his force he kicked shut the
furnace door. Its glowing-hot inner surface slammed against the
rebel leader's left leg.

Felicissimus jerked his head back and roared with pain. His
body was arched backward, his hands, gripping the shovel,
flung up, in an instantaneous, irresistible reaction to pain.

Aurelian plunged beneath the raised guard of Felicissimus,
and drove the point of his sword upward. It entered beneath
the jaw and went through to the brain. The great body crashed
down as if there had never been life in it. The head fell back
inside the furnace gate and the hair caught fire.

Aurelian took the long shovel, placed its blade in Felicissimus's groin, and rammed the body of his enemy into the furnace.

CHAPTER TEN

ROME KISSES AURELIAN'S FOOT

THE next morning was cool and sunny: the kind of winter day in Rome that made for a quickening of the step, an excitement of the blood.

The people were out early in the streets. From the Suburra, from the slums at the foot of the hills, from the squalid quarters across the river they poured in, converging in swelling, noisy streams towards the Flavian Amphitheatre, where the fights were to take place, and the Circus Maximus, where there was to be a programme of chariot racing.

On the walls that towered over them, on boards outside shops, even on the wayside gravestones in the suburbs, they read announcements in red paint:

TWO THOUSAND PRISONERS WILL FIGHT TO THE DEATH IN THE AMPHITHEATRE

THIRTY PAIRS OF WOMEN WILL FIGHT

ELEPHANTS WILL FIGHT TIGERS

LONG LIVE AURELIAN!

AWNINGS WILL BE PROVIDED

SATURNINUS WILL RACE HIS CHAMPION FOUR-IN-HAND AGAINST ALL COMERS

TODAY AT THE FLAVIAN—ROPEWALKERS, STRONG MEN,
DANCING BEARS, BIRDMEN, ANIMAL PARADE,
CHORUS OF FIVE HUNDRED TRUMPETERS, FREE

LOTTERY FOR SPLENDID PRIZES, JUGGLERS,
DANCERS, REFRESHMENTS FOR ALL
FIREWORKS TONIGHT
LONG LIVE AURELIAN!

Crowds had slept on the pavement all night to get good seats in the topmost galleries where the poor were herded. Tents had been set up in all the squares. The taverns were crowded. On the approaches to the Amphitheatre and the Circus, street-corner astrologers harangued the mobs, hucksters sold cartwheel straw sun hats, cookshops and fruit stalls did a roaring trade, Syrian women danced obscenely in their booths, and the cheap prostitutes lined the walls like a police cordon.

The jostling throngs of the poor came, towing their strings of brats behind them. The walls echoed with the braying of their laughter. Their faces glistened with inane eagerness. In the millionfold clatter of their footsteps, in the parrot-uproar of their cries, there sounded the one refrain. The games! The games! Wonderful spectacle! A good time! Something to gape at! Free food! Free prizes! Free drinks! Come on, children! You'll see Proculus racing at the Circus; he's a man, he leaps from horse to horse, and he picks up his prize from the ground at full gallop! Something to gape at! A good time! Good old Aurelian! There're dwarfs and giants and hermaphrodites and the man with no legs and the little boy with four heads! Free! Free! Remember that German who fought with his guts hanging out? Come on, children! When you see a coward, jeer like your father. Look at that one! Won't fight on just because he's had a hand chopped off! Whip him on! Rip him open! Good old Aurelian! Come on, come on, hurry, children!

On the slope of the Caelian stood the blackened shells of two apartment houses smelling of death, the tombs of three hundred families. The crowds poured past them. On the crest of the hill stood the Mint, silent, and all the way down the hillside, dotted like dung, food for the crows, lay the rebel dead, left there by order of Aurelian for Rome to see. In the yard of police headquarters, for Rome to see, were heaped the slaughtered thousands of the rebel policemen. Slumped in the bloody gutters at a hundred street corners, where the avenging Praetorians had caught them, were clusters of dead rebels, left by order of Aurelian. And the Romans roared past in their tens of thousands, men, women, and children, laughing, staring, poking, stealing the last rags of clothing, trampling and befouling the heaped, naked flesh of eight thousand dead. Good old Aurelian! They say that was some fight yesterday! Look at that one there, hacked through to the breastbone! Who cares? None of our business! The games! The games! Come *on*, children!

On all the street corners stood grim pickets of the Praetorian Guard. Rome was hurrying to its games under the swords of Aurelian, but Rome did not care. The slopes of the Palatine twinkled with the flash of sun on metal. The three thousand survivors of the Third Gallican were camped there, a cordon around the palace, vengeful and alert. They were a thousand fewer than the Praetorians, but Aurelian had taken care to disperse the Praetorians while he concentrated his legionaries, and to make it known in Rome that his cavalry regiments were moving southward from Milan, Rome did not care. It was hurrying to its games.

Towards midday the crowds were thickest around the Senate House. There was another free show here. Here was something else to cheer, something to gape at, something for the children to remember. The emperor was coming, and the Senate was going to bestow its official acknowledgement on him. The crowd buzzed with talk. He's coming. He's not. Who's that senator there? Look at that one, thinks a lot of himself; Aurelian has knocked the wind out of these proud ones! A hail for the emperor, the Provider of Games, the Food Giver, the Man on

Top, Ruler for Today! Who was Yesterday's? Can't remember. Who will be Tomorrow's? Don't care.

The bronze doors of the Senate House, by ancient custom, were wide open, but the packed crowds could come no nearer than the foot of the steps. Only the sons and grandsons of senators might go in to watch.

Inside, Manlius Statianus sat on the platform, in a curule chair. Next to him was an empty chair for Aurelian. Ranged on a lower level were the places, rapidly filling up, of the praetors and tribunes. The body of the hall was filled with senators, sitting on rows of stools facing inward, with a broad aisle of coloured marble down the centre.

Elbow on an arm of his chair, hand over his mouth, Statianus leaned back. They were quiet this morning, the great men of Rome. Odd how expressive, musically, was the murmur of their talk, a low, apprehensive rise and fall. And how they seemed to ignore, by unspoken consent, those empty stools, the single stools, here and there, and the eloquent little rows of unoccupied stools, the places of senators who were now lying in the gutters of Rome. A roar surged up from the crowd outside. If all the beasts in all the menageries in the world roared at the approach of the keepers who provided their food, it would sound like this. A rumble in the hall, and the senators were all on their feet facing the doorway. Statianus, without urgency, rose.

The entrance was a tall rectangle of blue sky. Framed in it were two tall soldiers, in sun-blazing brass and scarlet cloaks. They came down into the hall, and behind them, hands on swords, came the senior officers of the Praetorian Guard and the Third Gallican Legion. So! It was not just the man, it was the army that was coming to receive the submission of the Senate.

Here was the emperor's fire bearer, and now, in the doorway, Aurelian. There was a thunderstruck, fearful quality in the silence of the senators, as he walked down the aisle, with his officers before and behind him. For the first time he had put on the full regalia of the emperor. Statianus, calmly, saw him as a man who had cast off a disguise. The senators gazed as if the gods had magically transformed him from one man into another. Gone was the stiff, clumsy, plainly dressed soldier. He walked in silence, cold, tall, commanding. The imperial toga, of almost-black Tyrian purple, was draped across his chest, four deep folds covering the front of his body, a corner hanging over his left arm. The toga swept the floor, and carried a blaze of gold decorations—crosses, stars, crescents, suns. Beneath it could be glimpsed the long tunic of royal blue, also worked in gold. The golden laurel wreath on his head was surmounted by the spiked emblem of the sun's rays, the *corona radiata.* His slippers were scarlet, and in his left hand he carried a golden mace topped by the imperial eagle.

A new murmur grew out of the silence. A senator stepped into the aisle and shouted, "Hail, Aurelian!" Others pushed forward, and in a moment they were all crowding to the aisle, shoving past each other to be seen and heard. "Hail, Aurelian, Germanicus, Gothicus! . . . Hail, Emperor Aurelian Augustus! . . . Hail, Emperor Caesar Lord Aurelian Augustus!" They were fighting each other to demonstrate their loyalty. Their shouting deafened. "Hail! Hail! Hail!"

Halfway down the aisle, a senator threw himself before Aurelian, face to the floor, and kissed the hem of the imperial toga. And then another, and another. Statianus watched them crawling into the aisle, thrusting their faces forward to kiss the emperor's foot. These were the men who a few days before had kissed Aurelian's cheek so patronizingly, and winked behind his back. Statianus's eyes followed Aurelian appreciatively. Here was a real manager of men. It was at Aurelian's orders that the senators were crawling to kiss his feet. The ritual of the kiss for the emperor was a long-standing one. He had turned it into part of his animal-tamer's act. And the robes of state, too. Statianus knew that Aurelian genuinely hated pomp, cared little for the luxuries of the palace. Yet, since pomp was part of the emperor's estate, he had assumed it, to show all men that the estate was truly his; and Statianus knew that henceforth Aurelian, the austere, would be an emperor surrounded by more panoply and ceremony than any emperor of the past; and this would be because the Romans had called him "centurion," because they had called him "barbarian," because it would be the outward proof that Rome crawled at his feet.

Aurelian mounted the platform. Statianus, who was a man of moderation in all things, bowed, but only to the waist; and he kissed Aurelian's hand. Aurelian said, "Greetings, friend." Statianus, satisfied, looked into the emperor's eyes and saw there the tokens of alliance. The bodyguard formed up behind them.

Statianus and Aurelian sat side by side, while the sacrifice to the gods was made. Then Statianus rose. He spoke without any of the gestures of the rhetoric schools, without the florid imagery of the fashionable orator. There was a calm clarity in his voice. "All thanks to the immortal gods, Conscript Fathers, and above all others, to Jupiter Optimus, for we have been given such an emperor as we have always desired." He let the hint of a smile fall upon Aurelian. "Oh, Jupiter, best and greatest, thou, Juno, our queen, thou, Minerva, patroness of the virtues, thou, concord of the world, and thou, victory of Rome, grant this to the Senate and to the people of Rome, grant this to our soldiers, to our allies, and to foreign nations—may he rule even as he has served."

He made a slight, soft bow towards Aurelian. "Therefore, Conscript Fathers, in accordance with the united wish of us all, I vote him the name of emperor, the name of Caesar, the name of Augustus, and I add thereto the proconsular command, the revered title of Father of his Country, the chief priesthood, the right of three proposals in the Senate, and the tribunician power."

The whole Senate rumbled to its feet. The shout went up: *"Omnes! Omnes! Omnes!"* Then the assembly burst into a new cheering and a new hailing of the emperor.

Aurelian rose. He let the cheering go on for several minutes. Then he raised his hand. The noise died off to silence. *Now,* Statianus thought, *for the orders of the day.* A moment later he was rebuking himself for underestimating this man once again. He had been prepared for the harsh voice of command, ripping through the hall as if across a parade ground. Instead, Aurelian spoke quietly, with a mildness that was deadly.

"The Senator Plautius Silvanus sends apologies for his absence. He was waiting in his house, for some good news. Instead, a messenger arrived with bad news. The messenger was my private surgeon, and he obliged Silvanus by opening his veins for him."

He looked around, almost dreamily, while servile laughter filled the hall. "Conscript Fathers, I am grateful that so distinguished a body, of its own free will, has chosen me for the supreme command. I shall do my best. Two tasks await me. The first is to make the frontiers safe. The second is to bring virtue back to Rome. The first task is a clear one. We have driven back the Germans. The Goths are licking their wounds. In the months to come we must go to Gaul, where the pretender Tetricus is claiming the sovereignty of the West, and we must teach him that there is only one Rome, only one empire, only one emperor. The second task is harder, for it concerns both the public and the private life of all of us. We shall make a start by confiscating the moneys, properties, and lands of all those families that were involved in the recent criminal revolt. We shall use the proceeds to improve the value of our currency, so that trade may proceed in a stable manner, and to pay our armies. Also, we shall have discipline in Rome. Discipline in our camps has saved the frontiers. Discipline in our cities shall restore the Empire. When I have gone to Gaul, my officers shall remain behind, and they will punish seditious talk, the theft of public money, and the hoarding of vital commodities as acts of military treachery. The citizens of Rome, at their own expense, will build a wall and fortifications around the city. This will remind them that they are not idlers on Parnassus but soldiers in the front line."

Statianus listened indulgently. None of this concerned him greatly. He was turning a gold coin between the fingers of his right hand.

"Conscript Fathers, I know that you, in whom the ancient blood of Rome flows, will be with me in my task." Aurelian gazed around the hall, mildly, and Statianus, looking with him at the rabble of profiteers from Greece, Spain, Gaul, Africa, and Asia who were today's aristocracy, thought, *Irony, too?*

"While I am away, you shall not be left alone to face your labours. My Praetorian Guard will be always at your side, and in the depots of Milan my cavalry regiments will stand ready to come south, should their presence be required." He paused, enjoying the silence. "I grant you the right of deciding on appeals from the magistrates, to appoint the proconsuls, to name your legates to the provinces, and to sanction by your decree all the laws that I shall enact." He paused again. "And that is about all." He sat down.

A tumult of acclamation followed, and a succession of eulogies, the senators bobbing up and down like excited children to make known their loyalty. Aurelian looked away over their heads, in a distant, smiling dream.

Statianus leaned towards him. "My lord."

Aurelian turned to him. "My lord," Statianus said softly, "I have news for you, which reached me only as this session began. You must not think badly of me, that it came to my ears before it came to yours. It happens that I have an excellent postal service. Your courier is on his way from Ostia, with news from the East. My courier, who landed from a fast, small boat, arrived an hour ago."

He extended his hand, and let the gold coin fall from his palm into Aurelian's. Aurelian turned it over. On one side was a figure of the goddess Providence emptying a cornucopia upon an altar. On the other side was a woman's head, crowned with a diadem. Around the head was the legend: SEPTIMIA ZENOBIA. QUEEN OF THE EAST.

Statianus said softly, "My lord, her troops have entered Egypt. You will have to fight her now."

*

That night Aurelian walked down the hill from the palace, through the camp of the Third Gallican Legion. Maxin was at his side. Both of them were in soldier's dress.

Soldiers moved to and fro in the glare of campfires. There was pleasure in Aurelian's face. The murmur of voices, the rough bursts of laughter, the clatter of wooden dishes were music to him. Up in that cold, vast palace he was an actor on a stage. Here he was at home.

Shouts came from behind them. "Watch out, men, here's the Old Flogger! . . . Have some wine, Hand-on-Hilt? . . . When do we get a bonus?" A centurion stood in their path, stiffly at attention, with his stick under his arm. It was Scrofa. He grinned as they came by. A soldier, squatting by a fire, shouted, "Where's your cavalry now, Hand-on-Hilt?" and another yelled back, "It's always the legions when there's dying to be done."

Laughter rose in Aurelian's throat. He was among the only men in Rome who did not fear him, and he was glad. These were the legionaries, who made emperors and murdered them. They would follow him to Hades, but if he ever angered them or lost his gift of dominating them, they would tear him to pieces like beasts springing upon their tamer. "You, Scrofa—did they get their double rations today?"

"Yes, sir. They're still pretty restless, though. After a fight like that, half the legion killed or wounded, they want to warm this town up a bit. They'd be as quiet as lambs after that."

"Warm it up, Scrofa? They'd burn it down." Aurelian turned to the men who clustered at the roadside. "I'll give you cities to loot, lads. But not Rome. I know it's bad to be kept in camp, when there're girls and wine down there. But you're on duty. The job's not done yet. Finish it as well as you've started it, and I shan't forget you. There'll be a bonus for every man. Six months' pay."

He and Maxin sauntered on, through the hubbub of pleased voices and cheering. "You see, lad, if you want your men to fight well, you've got to pay them well."

Maxin answered with a cat's glare of contempt and a shake of the head.

"Not your people, you're thinking. Well, it's easy for them. They fight for a bit of land, for their womenfolk and their children. But what has the legionary got to fight for except pay? One year he's frying in Africa. The next he's up to his neck in some German marsh. Later he's climbing mountains in Spain, and the year after he's freezing on the steppes. Pay, lad, pay is the first god of the soldier."

They were standing above the camp palisade, looking down on the promenade at the foot of the hill. A torchlight procession of five thousand slaves was snaking through the dense crowds with a ripple of red flames that cast a bright glare over the whole street. From all directions, in the Roman darkness, came the roar of holiday crowds. The roar was pierced by bursts of rowdy singing, by the warring music of many orchestras, by the amorous screams of women. "There you are, Maxin. Rome!"

They looked down in silence. "Why are they all so ugly, lad? Here's this city, queen of the world, they call it. A thousand years old. All the fine shops, and temples, and theatres, and clever men. Our people on the Danube are savages to them. Yet our people are good to look at. And look at these—did you ever see so many little ones? So many potbellies and slouch backs? Look at those faces. You wouldn't think there was bone beneath them. Bags of lard or pinched little lumps of putty. And the scabs and the pimples and the bald heads. And the stink of them!"

Thousands of gaping faces stared up at them in the torch-light. A voice screamed, "There he is!" And there was cheering.

"Why are they cheering Aurelian? Five days of games, that's why. Figs and plums and cheese and pastries showered from the Circus roof. Free meals in all the squares, meat, wine, mash, and beans. That's what you rule Rome with, Maxin. Mash and beans."

Maxin nodded, and grunted assent.

"When are you going to speak, lad? You shouted to me in the fight, you know. You saved my life. You're wearing a uni-form and you're carrying a sword. I need you, Maxin. I need a lot more like you. Those crowds down there; d'you think I can save the Empire with them? No, it's you, the likes of you, who can do it."

The frenzied roar of the crowds beat up at them. "You like fighting, don't you, Maxin? I'll give you plenty more. There's Tetricus in Gaul. And this damned woman in Syria. I shan't take you to fight against your own people. But there are plenty of others to kill. Will you kill them for me?"

Maxin answered with a lingering, exultant look.

"Good lad!" Aurelian looked down at the carousing mob. "You hate them, don't you?"

Maxin nodded.

"So do I. The Senate and the people of Rome. I hate them all."

CHAPTER ELEVEN

PHILOMENE

THERE was one torture that Maxin was too young to bear: impatience. He had been waiting for an hour in the empty hall of a small villa, called the House of Hermias, in the town of Ratiaria. Maxin was fully informed about the town in which he found himself: it stood on the last bend of the Danube, it was the headquarters of the Fourteenth Gemina Legion and it was the latest base of his master Aurelian. Of the house he knew nothing, except that there were three rooms on the ground floor, which he had explored to kill time, a loft for the slaves, and a small garden whose door he had left open to air the musty hall. He was waiting in this unknown house because a woman had told him to.

Sickened by stale air, driven by impatience, he kicked open the front door and strode into the street. The daylight dazzled him for a moment, and he collided with a passer-by.

"Good morning, Maxin."

It was Eros, his master's secretary. Eros smiled, inclined his head in greeting, and turned down an alley beyond the next house. Maxin stared after him with suspicion. Then he decided that Eros, who had a bundle of scrolls under his arm, must have been passing on some official business. It did not take him more than a few seconds to forget Eros, for impatience, an agony, possessed the whole of him.

That he should be waiting for a woman was a measure of the change that had come over Maxin in the eight months since the battle on the Caelian Hill had uncaged his spirit. He had grown up in the tradition of his people, that he must remain virgin to conserve his warrior's strength until he chose his one life's mate. Yet now he was waiting, tortured by desire, for a woman. There were three agents of this change. The first was Aurelian. The second was the land of Italy. The third was the woman herself.

Aurelian—what an adventure these eight months had been at his side! He had kept Maxin's cup of joy filled with the shock and din of battle. He had given the boy the pride of following a great man, the pride of counting himself a man, the pride of belonging to a feared army, the pride of knowing that he was one of the makers of a legend, the pride of knowledge, the pride of achievement, the pride of endurance. They had gone to Gaul and dispersed the rebels like chaff and brought the pretender Tetricus back in chains to Rome. They had made more of those lightning marches at which the world gasped. Maxin had seen a dozen lands and wonders beyond reckoning. These eight months had flowed past him like the unreal splendours of a dream, with the warm back of his pony jogging beneath him as he rode through the dream, to remind him that it was reality.

True, a dissenting shadow sometimes stirred inside him. But, if his old self was not dead, it was drugged by present excitements, imprisoned within an ever-thicker wall of new experience. Indeed, when an incident had occurred three weeks ago that offered it release, it had remained quiescent.

Aurelian had signed a treaty surrendering Dacia, a whole province beyond the Danube, to a tribe of Eastern Goths. Maxin had been puzzled by this act, for he had not thought that his hero would ever yield an inch to anyone. But Aurelian had inflamed his admiration anew by explaining that a commander who was sure of himself was never afraid to retreat, and that the Goths in Dacia, their land-hunger satisfied, would act as a buffer against fresh invasions from the east by defending their new home. They had been sitting their horses, side by side, watching the Goth wagon columns on the move, when suddenly Aurelian had said, "Do you want to go back to them? I would not stop you."

Maxin had not spoken, and he had not moved, and he had ridden back to camp with Aurelian. There had been no articulate decision in Maxin's mind; he had merely stayed, as a cat stays by the fire.

And Italy—how did Italy work upon a barbarian boy? It entered into him with the sun's benign heat and warmed his blood. It coloured his vision with a golden daylight that made all things appear new and newly wonderful. It excited him with the marvellously bright colours of nature. Unaware of beauty, he was all the more defenceless against it when he saw for the first time, against a background of pale-blue sky, a smoke-blue sheet of sea or a landscape of green startling and intense as flame. A cypress tree, the Tuscan hills, the misty purple bloom on grapes, each cast a spell, He, who had always known nature as the bleak enemy and life as a cold, toilsome affair, was now spellbound by the vision—weakening to the warrior spirit, which must always be kept hungry—of how rich and genial life could be.

As for the woman, she had only reaped in him what Italy had sown. For, in the midst of that vision of Italy's bounty which had so disturbed his spirit, the bounty of her women had tormented him most. He had walked, abstaining, in the midst of a universal feast of the flesh. He had refused the kindness of slave girls and the gifts of rich women. He had hated the women, as he had hated all the sunlight and colour and richness of Italy. But, as the spirit of the land had assailed him, so the women had assailed him, with their laughter, their brilliant eyes, their lovely blend of tenderness and insolence. The more they had tempted him, the more his hate had grown, and the more, in spite of himself, he had become prey to wild, uncomprehended appetites; so that one day, quite simply, this girl, this Philomene, had taken him by the hand and led him to her bed, and the whole nature of life had changed for him.

Maxin and Philomene had met for love only half a dozen times, when her master's back was turned. But those few stolen hours had filled him with a new knowledge of women and of his own powers. All his days and nights were a waiting for Philomene. His mind lingered always upon what had passed between him and her. His body craved her. A furious strength strained within him, crying out for her to set it free. When she did so, she roused him to shouting vanity. When she would not do so, she could make him cringe like a dog. She was the secret centre of his life.

There she was at the street's end, cloaked, her head scarf held in front of her face. The kick of craving in his entrails sent him swiftly to her. Her eyes, over the scarf, were angry. "What are you doing in the street? I told you to keep out of sight." He followed her into the house. She saw the open back door. "Why is that door open? Bolt it." He obeyed.

The bedroom was small, with only a wide couch, a small table and stool, and a ladder to the slave loft. Philomene let her cloak fall, threw herself on the bed, leaned back against the wall and kicked her sandals off. She freed her hair from the green ribbon that bound it and shook the auburn tresses over her shoulders. Only then did she take notice of him, with a quick, radiant smile. Maxin, who had been watching her from the doorway, humbly yet with menace in his tension, came to her.

"You are too rash, my darling," she said. "You must not be seen with me in the street. He would show us no mercy."

Her dress was a gleam of russet silk, the pastel pallor of her skin showing through it. She swung her legs up onto the bed and the skirt fell back from them. Maxin, sitting on the edge of the bed and gripping her shoulders, said, "I am not afraid of him. Why should you fear him?"

"If we are dead, we cannot love. If we want to love, we must stay alive. What a strong little savage you are! Let go of me, you are hurting."

Maxin laughed, and pressed her back. She said sharply, "Let me go!"

The intensity of her displeasure daunted him. He released her and she sat up, rubbing the red marks he had left on her shoulders. "That is better. You must always do as I tell you, Maxin. It is no use trying to master me, or you will lose me. Do you understand that?"

"Yes."

"And you will always do as I tell you?"

"Yes."

"You would do anything for me?"

"Anything."

"Anything is a big word, my lovely savage. It means that to please me you would draw back from nothing, nothing at all. Is that what you mean?"

"That is what I mean." He started forward.

"Stop! Sit still! There, now you understand, now you are obeying me, my pretty boy. You are learning that you cannot have Philomene by grabbing. You must be nice to her. You must please her, and if you please her enough, the fancy will take her to love you."

He sat with his head bowed, his face fierce, flushed with the agony of a child that is being teased. She laid her hand on his. "Sweet Maxin, pretty Maxin, lie back beside me, here, and turn your face to me, and soon I will love you. What would you do to make me love you?"

"I have told you. Anything."

"You would do it without question?"

"Yes."

"Even without reward?"

"Yes."

"Even if it meant your death?"

"Yes."

She sighed contentedly, and stroked his forehead. "How hot

you are! No, stay still. Can you feel how cool my hand is? That is how I am. I am not ready for you. You must wait till I am as you are, you must make me hot like you."

"How?" He leaned over her, and she squirmed away, laughing.

"Not like that. Not like a puppy. But like a man, making me grateful to you, making me admire you."

"I am a man."

"You are a boy, my dearest. In all your ways you are a boy."

"Ask my master how I fight. I fight like a man."

"Your master. Who is that?"

"Aurelian!"

"Ah!" She turned towards him on one elbow, the ghost of a smile in her face. "You call him your master? Yet you call yourself a man."

"Why not? I do not understand."

"Maxin, my pet. You want me to admire you. You want me to think you a man. You want me to love you. Yet I see you trotting after Aurelian like a little boy. Would a man do that?"

Bewilderment furrowed his brow. "Thousands of men do that."

"Thousands, I know—but you? Who are you, Maxin?"

"I am his soldier."

"Whose son are you?"

He sat up on the bed and stared down at her. It was a few moments before he answered. "My father's."

"Where is your father?"

Another pause. Then slowly, "My father is dead."

"How do you know? Did you see him die?"

No answer.

"How did he die?"

No answer.

"Was he killed? Why don't you speak? Who killed him?"

No answer.

"Maxin—who killed your father?"

His head was lowered, his eyes glittering. "You know who killed him."

"Yes, I know who killed him. I want you to tell me. Tell me who killed your father. Maxin, sit there dumb another moment and I will leave here. Who killed your father?"

"*He* killed him."

"*He?* Who is that? Are you frightened of the name?"

"Aurelian killed my father."

"Again?"

"What game is this?" His voice was choked with fury. "Aurelian killed my father."

She subjected him to an acute, silent scrutiny. His chest was still heaving with emotion. She spoke more gently. "Why are you so angry, my darling? Had you forgotten this thing? I had not forgotten it. Nor had others. Maxin, my little one, had you forgotten?"

No answer.

"Had you? Do not be afraid. Tell me!"

A deep flush burned in his cheeks.

She insisted. "Had you forgotten your father? Do you know —people say that you follow Aurelian about as if he were your father. They say you look at him, and speak to him, as if he were your father. But he killed your father. Did he not kill him?"

A muttered "Yes."

She said softly, as if to herself, "This is the thing I do not understand in you." She subjected him once more to her pensive study. "Maxin, what is the law of your people concerning the slaying of a father?"

He lifted up his head as if it were heavy. "Why do you ask me this?"

"What is their law?"

"That the son must kill the slayer."

"But you have not killed your father's slayer."

No answer.

"You have been the servant of your father's slayer. Why? Perhaps you are waiting for someone else to kill him?"

No answer.

"Many hate him. Someone else may kill him soon. If that happens, will the law of your people be satisfied?"

"No. The son must kill the slayer." He stared at her so intently that he might have been spelling out words he saw written in her face. "Shall I kill him?"

She sat up and put her arms loosely about his neck. "Yes."

"Then I shall kill him."

She clasped him to her, straining her mouth against his. She drew back. "You must kill him soon." There was a touch of colour in her cheeks and an urgency, as of rising lust, in her voice. "You must not wait, for if another kills him you will be disgraced. For the rest of your life you would say to yourself, 'Why did I wait too long? Was I a coward? Was I bribed by Aurelian's favour?' And others will say these things of you, too. The task is yours, my darling. Be quick, for me, be quick."

She embraced him again. With his weight upon her she sank back. Her harsh, quick breathing was louder than his. This time it was he who freed himself, prising himself up, as it were, from her arms. He looked down at her, his eyes gleaming with deliberation. "Philomene, why are you so eager for me to kill him?"

"Have I not told you? Oh, my darling, do not talk now, not now."

He leaned over her, unmoving. She said, "I have told you. I want to see you as a man. I am ashamed to see you as a boy, who dotes upon his father's killer. I am ashamed that others sneer at you for this. I want you to make me proud of you. I want you to avenge your father, and show yourself a chief, as he was."

"It is for my sake, then, that you tell me all this?"

"Yes, my darling. Do not talk any more. Come close to me."

"And you will love me when I have killed him?"

"Yes."

"Shall I die or shall I go back to my people?"

"You will escape back to your people. I will help you. You will be a chief among them."

"And you, will you come with me?"

"What else?"

His face, peering at her, was no longer that of a boy but of an old, wary animal. "You will leave Probus?"

"Yes, I will leave him."

"I am the one you want?"

"Only you."

His eyes were cunning. "Then I shall kill Probus, too."

A movement of her lashes gave her eyes a sharp, stricken look for a second. Then she laughed. "Maxin, my little one, will you never learn? When your girl is ready, and the moment you have been waiting for has come, you must not sit and talk of silly things. You must love her."

He sat, a block of stubborn flesh and bone beside her. "Shall I kill Probus?"

"Why should you?" She spoke lightly. "It would only make your task harder, and escape more hazardous. Why risk it, when we want to escape and be happy together? After all, he is not your enemy."

"He is my enemy. Every night he is my enemy, when I lie down alone and think of you with him."

Her gaze lingered on him. "Very well, kill him. But kill Aurelian first. Then we shall see about the other."

"That is a foolish thing to say. I shall not be given two chances. I shall kill them both, and Probus will be first."

It was she, now, who remained silent.

He said, "Philomene, because I am a Goth and because I am young, you think I am a fool."

No answer.

"Because I come to you, and lie with you, and say nothing about Probus, you think I care nothing that you are his woman."

No answer.

"Because I am silent when you tell me you do not love him, you think I believe you."

Still she said nothing.

"I am not such a fool. I see how you look at him. I see how you lean towards him. I see how you hold his arm. I hear your voice when you speak to him. Should I not know what you feel towards him, when I feel thus towards you? Do I not yearn for you more when I see you yearn for him—and rage, and hate, that you should love him so—and dream revenges against him, and want you all the more? I have despised myself for humbly following you, but I have followed all the same. I have said nothing because my need is greater than my pride. But when you tell me that you do not care about him, that I may kill him, it is too much. I know, then, that you are lying. I know that you will not let me kill him. I know that you must have other reasons, which you have not told me, for wanting me to kill Aurelian. I know that if I kill Aurelian you will not come away with me. Perhaps, even, it will serve your purposes if I am caught and executed when I have done your work."

She said haughtily, "And would that stop you? Do you love me so little? You said you would do anything for me, without reward, without question, even if it meant your death. Where are your fine words now?"

"What I have promised I will do. I will kill him, and I will not betray you when they take me. To my shame, I still love you. For my father, and for you, I shall kill Aurelian. But first, for my own honour, I shall kill Probus." He swung off the bed and stood up. "I will go in to them now. They will not suspect me. It will be easy to catch them unawares." He looked down at her. His laugh was harsh and adult. "Probus will be first, my love."

She jumped up after him. "Darling, what madness has seized you? What has caused all this talk between us? Let us forget it. Let us forget it all, for a little while. Oh, my pet, I was so happy when I came here, thinking that soon I would make you happy with me. Let us forget everything, until afterwards, and make up now, and love each other again."

He gripped her wrists and put her away from him.

As he turned, she sped past him and barred his way, pressing her body up to him. "Look at me, my wood pigeon." She ripped her gown open, baring her breasts. "Are these not sweet? You have always found them sweet. You will not refuse them now."

His face was distorted. "I am rotten, that I have let a woman bewitch me. You are witches, all of you, you women of the south."

He put a hand on her shoulder and tried to push her aside. But she, with a force that could not have been suspected in her frail body, rooted herself to the floor, and clung to him. "No, you will not go! You will not leave me!"

His anger broke its last bonds. He was filled with humiliations crying out for revenge, with desire curdled into rage, with hatred of himself no less than of her, with bodily strength demanding an outlet. He groped for her throat. She fought his hands back with hers and screamed. He got his fingers upon her neck. She screamed more shrilly. "Help! Help! He is murdering me!"

He was squeezing now with his fingers, blind, close to ecstasy, the Goth ecstasy of killing. Unheeding, he heard shouts, a banging at the door, a convergence of running footsteps. Her screams were hoarse, stifled, dying away. She was sinking beneath his hands.

The door burst open. A torrent of shouting poured into the room. Bodies stampeded around him, hands clutched at him,

wild white faces pressed close, voices assailed him. He let go of
the girl who, unaccountably, began to claw with her finger-
nails at her own bosom. He struck out with his fists into the
surge of bodies around him. The joy of the fight took hold of
him. He was hitting out, shouting, laughing wildly. He felt
exhilarated, cleansed, a Goth once more. He trampled bodies
underfoot, heaved against the weight of his attackers upon him,
kicked, gouged into yielding flesh with knee and elbow; gasped
for air in a room that had become a furnace, sweat stinging in
his eyes; until he was down, and it was over.

He lay spread-eagled on the floor, four men pinning down
his limbs, one holding his head down by the hair, another holding the point of a sword to his throat. A mass of furious faces
looked down at him. Spittle splashed upon his face. He heard
their taunts. Philomene's plaint came to him through the press
of bodies. "He dragged me in here. He tried to rape me. Thank
you, good people, thank you all. I am the friend of Probus. Kill
this slave and Probus will reward you."

There were shouts in the packed room. "To prison! . . . To the
magistrates! . . . No, kill him! . . . Kill him now!"

Philomene cried, "He is a barbarian slave. He would have
raped and killed me. No woman is safe from these savages!"

"Make an example of him! . . . Tear him to pieces! . . . Barbarian dog! . . . Kill him!"

The voices were like a baying of hounds. The feet were trampling in upon him. A voice from overhead cut through the noise.
"Stop!"

The sword-point was biting into his throat.

"Stop! You with the sword! The emperor's orders—stop, or you
will die."

The man with the sword looked up, and the point came away
from Maxin's throat. The surging of bodies had stopped. All the
crowd were looking up. The trap door of the loft was open, and
at the head of the ladder stood Eros.

Philomene cried, "Never mind that man, kill the slave now. Probus will reward you."

Eros raised his right hand. "In the name of the emperor. I am Caesar's secretary. Heed me or you will regret it." He came down the ladder with a light, oddly jaunty step.

The crowd was silent. Philomene's voice sounded desperately. "Kill him, I say."

Nobody moved. The voice of Eros, thin and sharp as a razor's edge, commanded, "They must go before the emperor. You people down there, do you hear me? Seize them both, and take them before the emperor."

Maxin felt himself being heaved to his feet. He was pushed towards the door. It was hard to tell whether Philomene, in front of him, was being helped along or dragged along; but her face, when he glimpsed it, was terrified.

*

"My lord—" Philomene, half naked in the rags of her gown, stood before Aurelian with clasped hands and piteous eyes. Maxin, battered and bloody, was at her side. Behind them was the centurion Scrofa, with an escort of four soldiers. At one side, like a self-satisfied terrier, Eros waited. "This tale you have heard from Eros makes my head whirl. There is some plot against me. Save me, my lord, I am only a helpless woman."

"Sir, can you doubt that I speak the truth? I live only to serve you." Eros's voice was unctuous. "Why else have I watched these two for so long and noted all their meetings? Why else did I follow the boy today to the house of Hermias?"

"It is a plot, I tell you!" Philomene cried. "This one here," she pointed at Eros, "told me that I was to meet my master at the house, and when I got there the boy was waiting for me, and tried to rape me. Whether he, too, was lured there by Eros, to ruin us both, or whether they were in it together, I do not know, but I am innocent, my lord. Probus, Probus, my master, I implore you, do not believe this story, make Caesar heed me."

Probus, hunched in his chair, did not move. His eyes gleamed at her from beneath their hooded lids. She ran towards him. He raised his head and said harshly to the nearest soldier, "Keep the prisoner in order!"

Philomene hesitated, stricken. The soldier grasped her arm. White-faced, like a betrayed child, she turned to Aurelian. "My lord, I live for Probus, and I know that he lives for you. Why should I wish your death?"

"Torture her, sir," Eros piped, "and find out. She lived in a dozen cities before she came to Rome. Corinth, Athens, Heliopolis, Antioch, Palmyra—"

"Palmyra." Aurelian leaned forward, chin resting on his hand, eyes brooding.

"And she might be in anyone's pay."

Aurelian cut Eros short. "Quiet!"

He pondered, then addressed Maxin. "You, lad, what have you to say?"

The boy stood like an ox.

"Maxin, Eros has accused you of a crime which is punished by death, and so has Philomene. Tell me what happened."

Philomene, looking at the boy with a strange intensity, cried, "He will not speak!"

He turned his head slowly and stared at her up and down.

"Come, lad," Aurelian said. "Don't play the fool. Your life is at stake."

Philomene, still meeting the boy's eyes with a brazen expression, said, "What can he tell you? He is guilty. Let them take him away and kill him."

Eros bobbed forward. "Sir, the boy has loved the woman. Even now he will not speak against her."

Aurelian asked, "Did you try to rape her?"

The boy remained silent.

"Did you say you would kill me?"

Maxin raised his head. "Yes."

"It was nothing to do with me, my lord." Philomene broke away from the soldier and ran close to Aurelian, holding apart the rags of her dress to show her scratched bosom. "He said he would kill you. He spoke like a madman. I could not make him stop. I heard him, yes, I am the witness of his guilt, but I am not implicated. How can I be? Look at what he did to me. He tried to rape me. Can you not see, my lord?"

Eros darted forward, seized her hand and held it up. Aurelian had been staring at Maxin, and only now did he seem to notice the girl before him.

"Master, there is blood and skin under her nails. Whose is it? Not Maxin's. There are no scratches on him. She marked herself to make it appear that she had been attacked."

"Woman," Aurelian said, "you stink of scent. I can smell it from here. Your skin is oiled. Your nipples are painted. You went to that house prepared to meet a man, yet you say it was rape."

"I went to meet my master."

Probus said, "She was not expecting me till evening."

"Eros told me—"

"That your master wanted to see you in some wretched little house?" Aurelian watched her with cold eyes. "And you prepared yourself for love? Is that likely?"

A touch of the old insolence showed in her voice. "Caesar, you should learn more about women. When my master calls for me, I go without thinking."

"You suggest that Eros and Maxin might have plotted together? Yet Eros condemns Maxin?"

"Thieves can fall out."

"Woman, you are guilty."

She showed a change of tack: a small, appealing smile. "My lord, I am all in a muddle. I do not know what is happening. I am innocent, but I do not know how to convince you. All these

people around— You know what we women are like, my lord.
May I not be alone with my master Probus for five minutes?
Only five minutes, gracious Aurelian. Then I will feel more
calm, and I will be able to explain myself better, and help you.
Please, my lord?"

Aurelian glanced at Probus. "Will you talk with her? Or shall
I go on?"

"Go on."

"Philomene"—Aurelian's voice was deep and stern—"look me
in the face, and be careful what you say. You are very close to
death. Zenobia sent you to Rome, did she not?"

She gave him a long, guileless stare, then, with a naïve cunning in her voice, said, "My lord, there are many interesting
things I could tell you. Would you spare me if I did?"

"I make no bargains."

She eyed him for another moment of calculation. "Forgive
me, my lord. Yes, Zenobia sent me. I wrote letters to her about
all that passed in Rome."

"And she ordered that I was to be killed? When was this?"

"Just before you went to Rome, my lord. Gracious Caesar,
please believe me, I did not wish to do this work, but I was helpless. She holds my aged mother as a hostage against my obedience."

Probus did not raise his head. His voice was a sleepy rumble.
"Your aged mother died six years ago. She was thirty-four years
old at the time, and her throat was cut by her pimp in Byblos.
You told me so yourself."

Philomene turned a haughty face to him. "Are you against
me? Then let me die."

Aurelian said, "Guard, take them away."

"My lord!" The jerk of her head towards him was a spasm of
revealed fear. "I have told you what you asked. I can tell you
much more. Let me live, and repent, by telling you all I know."

Probus, slumped in his chair, uttered a grunt of laughter.

She gave him a pallid glance of defiance. "It is for you that I wish to live."

Aurelian said, "You will know my verdict later. Take them away, centurion."

*

"You see," Aurelian said to Probus. "She fears me."

"She—"

"Zenobia," Aurelian cut in impatiently. "She wants me killed. She fears me." He noticed Eros lingering by the door. "What do you want? I told you to clear out with the others."

"Sir, a word before I go, please?"

"What is it?"

"Sir, have I done well?"

"Yes. Is that all?"

"I have always served you well, Lord Caesar. Do I not deserve some reward?"

"You will get gold, do not fear."

"Sir, what is gold to me? I am your secretary, yet I am a slave. May I dare tell you the reward I crave? To be made a freedman. That would be my great happiness. And it would be only fitting that the emperor's secretary should be able to claim respect where he walked."

"Eros, you are a slave by nature, and you will remain a slave. I will not tell you again to get out."

Eros bowed low, a malevolent humility in his eyes, and backed out of the room. When the door had closed, Aurelian said, "This affair bears out what I was saying to you before. If she fears me, then there is a chance that I can bring her to her senses without a war in the East."

"You still fear war?"

"I am a good enough soldier always to fear war."

"But a woman? To draw back, in front of the whole world?

I would sooner go for her throat. We could finish her off in no time."

"I am not so sure of that, old bear. I begin to suspect that this is a very special woman. Facts are facts, and must be swallowed however they taste."

"You will leave Egypt in her hands?"

"No. That I cannot do. For practical reasons, and as a demonstration to the world, we must take Egypt back without delay. You are the one who will do it. I have got plenty of men for you. The troops released from Dacia are pouring back into my depots, ready for a war in the East. That is why I shortened the frontier. You will take three legions at full strength, with auxiliaries. You will assemble and transport them in secrecy. You will strike unexpectedly and strike hard. So much for Egypt. With luck, however, this should not lead to a general war, which would still be a serious matter as long as we are involved in the West. I shall make her a final offer. Our blow in Egypt will have taught her that we are ready to fight if need be. Let her ponder on that, and yield up her gains in the south, and retire to the frontiers that she held eight months ago. I should accept them, and then there would be peace. It is the last chance."

"How will you make this bargain with her?"

"I shall write to her suggesting a meeting. The place and circumstances can be arranged to guarantee the safety of us both. Although, who knows?" His lips smiled. "It would save a lot of trouble if I could seize her by some ruse and bring her back with me. That would be cheaper than a war, and more appropriate in dealing with a woman. Even with this one."

Probus chuckled. "I'll wager you've never thought so much about a woman in all your life." He frowned, in a comic simulation of thought which his next words explained. "Look here—if you are writing to her, why not send the letter with the girl?"

"You don't want her to die?"

Probus said stiffly, "I am only making a practical suggestion."

Aurelian sat with folded arms, his head lowered. "She has done me a bad turn, that girl. Oh, not this stupid plot! It's what she has put into the boy's head again."

"It would be a gesture, to send her back alive."

"In that case," Aurelian said after another pause for thought, "it would not be fair for the boy to die."

Probus grinned.

"After all," Aurelian said doggedly, "what chance did he stand against one like her?"

Probus's grin broadened.

Aurelian permitted himself the beginnings of an answering grin. "Send for them."

*

"If I took you two seriously," Aurelian said, "you would both lose your heads. Luckily for you, I don't. When people like you conspire, you endanger only yourselves, like children playing with sharp knives. I advise you not to try it again. You"—he turned his gaze upon Maxin—"you and I have come a long way together. I'm not going to give up now, just because you've made a fool of yourself. Do you know what I'm going to do with you? You've had it too easy, my lad. You've been loafing in this town too long, getting too soft. Women! I'll sweat that out of you. There's a bridge to be built upriver. A three weeks' job. It'll be tough. There are rapids up there, a tricky current, quicksands, I'm told. You'll go, and you'll work with a sledgehammer to build that bridge, as a common soldier, along with all the others. You'll be shown no favours. I'll see to that. Well? Anything to say?"

Maxin remained silent.

"What's the matter? Still want to try to kill me? You'll get over it. You did once before. You don't fool me, my lad, with your sulking. I know you'll enjoy it up there. Something else to learn. All right, you can go now. Get your gear together and report to Fourteenth Legion headquarters."

Maxin made a move.

Aurelian rapped, "Like a soldier!"

The boy paused. Ferocity glittered in his eyes. Then his arm stabbed up in salute. He turned smartly and strode out of the room.

Aurelian remained for some time in a reverie. Philomene fidgeted, and he looked up at her. "As for you, girl, this is a lucky day for you."

She interrupted joyfully. "I am forgiven, my lord?"

"You are spared, because you can be useful to me. You will take a letter from me to Palmyra, and give it to Zenobia."

"It shall be done."

"And you will not show your face again in Roman territory, under pain of death."

Her stare was incredulous. She looked about her helplessly, and again at Aurelian's unyielding face. She whispered, "But that is impossible. My master—"

"You will stay away or die."

"But—" She was blinking in perplexity. "I must come back. Probus is here. Lord Aurelian, let me come back, please let me come back. I can do so much for you. I will send false information to Zenobia at your dictation. Think how important that could be. Give me the chance. Let me show how useful I can be. I will do anything for you, anything."

She saw no hope for herself in the emperor's countenance. She turned to Probus. "My love, please listen to me." Her words flowed swiftly, her voice soft and intense, with a vibration of panic in it. "You must not let me go. You must tell the emperor. Please, my love, forgive me. Keep me with you. What did the boy matter? I was forced to do it. I did not think it important. He meant nothing to me. No man is alive for me but you." She was haggard. A tear rolled down her cheek. "I can't give you up. You're the first man, the first one in my whole life, I've loved. I shall never find another. Probus, you don't know what it means, all these men, and hating them. You don't know what it means to be without you. I couldn't bear it!" She stared at him, breathing hard. "Speak to me, please, say something. Say something!" She shrieked, "Probus!"

He sat like stone.

She threw herself at his feet. "I won't go! I won't go, I tell you. Kill me, what do I care?" She was screaming at him. "What is the matter with you? Speak to me! Say something! Don't you know me? Are you dumb?"

She lay in a sprawl of red hair, shuddering and sobbing. She glared up at him. He was not looking at her. She clutched at his ankles and began to bang her head on the floor. "No! No! No!" Her screams were deafening. "No! No! No! No! No!"

Aurelian said dryly, "Make up your mind. Will you go, or will you die for your love?"

Her shrieking ceased. No sound came from her except the quick, harsh gasping of her breath.

Probus spoke to her, gently this time. "Go, girl. It is for your own good. As for the future—who knows?"

She rose wearily to her feet. With a quick, oddly proud movement, she shook her hair back.

"Well," Aurelian said, "will you go?"

She was still trembling, but her face was composed. She said, "What swine you all are," and walked out like a betrayed queen.

CHAPTER TWELVE

THE THIRD MEETING

THE meeting between Zenobia and Aurelian took place a month later.

An empty ship had been moored in the Hellespont. This channel, a ditch between Europe and Asia, separated their two empires. A point had been chosen at which it was little more than a mile wide so that the ship, isolated though it was on neutral water, was in full view of the troops encamped on both shores. Joint patrols of Roman and Palmyrene ships had been posted at the two ends of the channel to keep other vessels away.

Aurelian sat in the bow of a fishing boat. The white lateen sail bellied over his head. In the stern, Lucipor, his only permitted escort, held the tiller. Aurelian looked across the deserted expanse of water to the conference ship. Zenobia had provided it, but it was of Roman construction, probably a prize of war. It was forty feet long, low in the bows, with a high stern carved in the shape of a swan's head. There was a long bowsprit and a mast amidships. The spritsail and the square mainsail were furled. The great steering sweeps hung unmanned from the stern.

He did not study the ship with any special vigilance. By agreement, a Roman search party had already been aboard. Scrofa, its leader, had done his job thoroughly and had even dived under the keel. No doubt Zenobia, as a precaution on her side, had watched his search party from the shore, counting to make sure that they had all left the ship.

He climbed aboard, helping Lucipor over the gunwale. A few moments later Zenobia came aboard, accompanied by Longinus.

She said, "Good. You have brought a one-armed slave. I have brought an old man. We can both feel safe. How are you, my old friend?"

"Well enough. And you?"

"Happy to see you again." Her eyes were clear and friendly. "May I offer you some refreshment?"

Aurelian made a slight, soldierly bow. They seated themselves with the length of the table between them. It was simply set: wine in two earthenware pitchers and fruit heaped in silver bowls. Zenobia offered fruit to Aurelian. He said, "Thank you, no."

She took a peach from the bowl and sank her teeth vigorously into it. Her eyes smiled at him over the peach. The juice trickled down her chin. "Here." She held the bitten peach out to him. "It is not poisoned."

He laughed and took another peach. Longinus poured wine, grinning like a tubby satyr. "And you can see there is nothing wrong with this. I pour it all from the one jug."

Zenobia's glossy hair was braided up at the back. To set off her vermilion trousers and sandals she wore a white jacket edged with stiff gold brocade and fastened with ruby buttons. "Aurelian, do you know the history of Antony and Cleopatra? A ship was their meeting place, and she was my ancestor."

Aurelian was still smiling. "He was not mine."

Her laughter was soft. "Aurelian, time has put a polish on you. And you have grown a beard. But of course, it is the mark of the emperor." His beard was the merest pencil line, framing his face. "Do you remember the first time I saw you? Your hair was long, your accent uncouth, and you went red in the face when I spoke to you."

"I remember. I have always remembered." Their eyes met. "Perhaps that is why I am different now."

She held his gaze and spoke without teasing. "That is a confession, Aurelian. Did you mean to say as much? I could say much in reply." He did not respond, and she went on. "But you overrate me. You would have changed if there had been no Zenobia. There was always an emperor in you. Aurelian, the last time we met it was I who sought you out. Now you have sought me. Why have you come?"

"To make an agreement, Zenobia, for your sake and mine. You and I can go no further unless we agree, or unless one of us destroys the other. For us the world is no more than a small room, in which each of us is always in the other's presence. Even when we are a thousand miles apart we are face to face. The world will be too small for us unless we can find a means of living in it together."

"Why should we not fight?" There was nothing challenging or militant in her manner. She spoke mildly, almost with melancholy.

"What is the gain? Others are waiting. The barbarians are out there in the dark, hordes of them, another mankind, like wolves beyond the light of the campfire. We might weaken ourselves, to our common danger. Let us think of civilisation before our own ambitions, and not risk its downfall."

"Why not?" Longinus, sitting between them on a coil of rope, paused in his noisy attack on a peach. "Would it be such a bad thing? If these hordes who press upon our frontiers end our world they will make another. Today's wanderers are tomorrow's builders. Perhaps it is time for us to perish."

"I would sooner defend the Parthenon," Zenobia retorted, "than let it be pulled down by savages who might build another in five centuries' time." She smiled at Aurelian. "I am with you in that. But it is for you, not me, to think of consequences. Do you admit me so formidable that a contest between us would carry so much risk?"

"Why should I conceal it? I am here."

"That is the greatest change of all in you, Aurelian. At last you respect me." She poured wine for herself. "And, to be candid, it was what I hoped to discover. You came here to talk affairs of state. Shall I tell you why I came? To see you."

"The woman speaks to the man. It is your one touch of folly, to confuse the personal with the political."

Longinus cut in again. "If you have any sense, Caesar, you will fear her folly more than her virtues. Silliness is the salt in women. There is no more destructive element in the world. Troy perished because of Helen's silly smile. Folly makes women terrible antagonists. A general must predict his enemy's moves if he is to win. How can he predict the next move of a woman? Her greatest strokes will fly in the face of reason. Impulse, vanity, pique, will drive her to attempt the impossible, and she will succeed because she does not know it is impossible. Tremble, Caesar, at woman's folly."

"Why do you keep this fellow with you, Zenobia? He belongs in your library, writing his great truths in a book. Are all who meet you compelled to undergo his homilies?"

"Once upon a time, Aurelian, I thought it would be a splendid thing if a state could be ruled according to such truths. Alas, I find that statecraft and philosophy are not easily yoked. However, he is my good friend, and I will not let you speak unkindly to him."

Aurelian pushed a jug towards Longinus. "Commune with this, then, philosopher, and I shall respect your wisdom." He leaned on the table, and looked directly at Zenobia. "Why should you want to see me?"

"For my pleasure, perhaps. Are there not people whom it pleases you to see?"

"Not those whose death I have desired."

Her laugh was light. "Oh, that is over and done with! You had insulted me. I can permit no one to insult me. Least of all could I bear it from you. But I am satisfied. I have done better than to kill you. I have compelled you to respect me."

He, too, laughed as he leaned back. "Well, I bear no grudge. As long as you only send prostitutes against me I shall not be frightened. Did you punish the girl?"

"On the contrary. I keep her at my court. With all her faults, she is more useful to me than most of the men there. After all, you were gentle enough with her yourself. And you are the pitiless Aurelian!"

"When policy demands it. Only a weakling is cruel by habit. Fear makes him so. Listen, Zenobia, it is time to talk business. At dawn this morning, as you will know when your messengers arrive, my troops should have landed in Egypt."

They sat at their two ends of the table with Longinus looking from one of them to the other: Aurelian with lips compressed, eyes keen; Zenobia withdrawn, her face heavy with fatality. She raised her head. "You are not without a feeling for drama, Aurelian."

He waited, sitting tensely upright.

She said, "Why did you come here to tell me this?"

"Because I want peace."

It took her a second to comprehend, then her eyes cleared. "You have terms?"

"A peace treaty. You to hold all your conquests in the north. Rome to be given back Egypt and Arabia. These we must have."

"Is this the way to make peace?" She still spoke mildly. "You launch an army and expect me to capitulate?"

"It is the only way to make peace. We have warned and you have not listened. You think you are dealing with weakness. You must be shown that you are dealing with strength. I am prepared to regard your seizure of Egypt as a miscalculation. You knew from your spy that a plot was laid against me. You thought that I would either be killed or be too occupied between the frontiers and a rebellious Rome to deal with you. This, you thought, was the moment that must be seized before it passed. Now I have shown you your mistake. My armies are on the move against you. If need be they will march on until they reach and take Palmyra. Hesitate, try to play at words with me as in the past, and it will be too late to stop them. Today you must decide. Is it to be a fair treaty, which will bring my armies to a halt—or war?"

After a long, troubled silence, she said, "Aurelian, let us send these men away."

They faced each other, along the table, in a colloquy of the eyes. Then he nodded.

When the two small boats had sailed away, each to wait at an equal distance from the ship, Zenobia spoke again. "It was not a miscalculation when I seized Egypt. It was a necessity. When one starts along that road one cannot stop. To go on has become one's reason for being. It is no use expecting me to turn back. Besides, there is no safety for me now in any treaty with you. I am queen of the East. You have been careful in all your talk to avoid that title, neither challenging it nor acknowledging it. Oh, do not look so ready to oblige! It is not just a question of courtesies. I would rather you called me Zenobia than Augusta. But I know this, that Rome cannot allow its Eastern empire to secede and to survive under its own queen. That would be a sign to the world that Rome's authority is failing. Your treaty is only a device to gain time. When you are ready you will turn on me. Since I have to fight, it is better that I do so now. Why should I give up Egypt and Arabia first? Why should I wait till you are ready? After all, to confound you I need not beat you in the field, I need only hold out. If your other enemies see you locked fast in the East, what do you think they will do? You see, Aurelian, you, too, need to avoid war. I have shown that your alternative will not do. I have another." She faced him with clear and earnest gaze. "The world would not be too small for us both if we were allied in marriage."

He stared at her in sombre fascination. "You are truly an ambitious woman, Zenobia."

"It is more than ambition that prompts me. I have put forward reasons of state, because reasons of state will most appeal to you. But I have other reasons, Aurelian." She rose. The movement was sad and graceful, invested with dignity but making no claim to command. "How can I speak of them? I am a woman, but pride dictates that I may only talk to you as a queen."

Her pose, leaning lightly against the table, was an appeal for him to speak. When he did not, she went on. "Aurelian, do you not know loneliness? You are a hard man, and perhaps you never think of it, yet there is a terrible solitude upon you, like a cloak. It is the price we pay for setting ourselves above all others. Aurelian, who else in the world is there for you but me? Who else for me but you?"

She waited, then broke out again. "Must I say more? Must I humble myself, then? Grim and lonely you go through life. Destroy me, and you will go grim and lonely to the grave. And me— what other man could I permit to touch me? If it is not you, then it is no one, and I am never more to be a woman."

"I have a wife."

"I know. A vinegar pot, that was what Philomene called her. Romans divorce easily, don't they? It is not hard to set a wife aside. It has been done often enough, especially by emperors."

"It is done every day, I don't doubt, among the fine gentry in Rome. But, you see, I'm not one of them. I'm only a barbarian, and uncouth enough to cherish an honest wife as long as she lives. Tell me, Zenobia, are you really willing to put yourself into my power? Do you realise the risk you would be taking?"

"We should both have a mighty kingdom at our feet. The two empires would be united in peace. You would have a woman who understands you; I, the only man I can respect. You would have an heir in Wahab and he would inherit the power I dream of for him. A Syrian boy was emperor in Rome once before. Why not my son? Neither of us need fear, for there would be so much to bind us, and, as to treachery, we are both strong and cunning but neither of us is base, and we could trust each other. I have thought about all this, Aurelian. Where is the risk?"

He was leaning forward, his elbows on the table. He might have been a judge weighing his verdict. Decision could be seen in the set of his mouth. "No, Zenobia," he said slowly, "the risk would be all mine. A woman who has murdered one husband may well have no fear of a second. But the man whom she favours might as well bed with a cobra as with her."

Her face was calm but her eyes betrayed the change of mood, the flicker of incredulity, protest, pain, contempt. She murmured, "You can believe that?" She bit her lower lip in perplexity. "All that we have said today, the kindness between us, it means nothing?" She stood stiff, gripping the edge of the table. Energy flared into her voice. "Have you learned nothing about me?"

"I have learned that you are a clever woman. You can beguile. Whenever I begin to forget that you are my enemy, I remind myself, 'This is a husband-killer.' And that is enough, for where I was born a husband-killer is carrion." He paused. "Well? No explanations? No protestations?"

She shook her head slowly, with scorn. After a brief silence she said, "At least you have given me back the power to hate you. I shall need it if we are to fight."

He rose and came along the table towards her. She took notice of him with a kind of weary anger. "Stay still." Her right hand had gone behind her back. "I will not have you near me." Her hand was at her breast again, grasping a blade a few inches long and fine as a bodkin, with a thumb-guard halfway down. It was small enough to have been sheathed in the brocade lining of her jacket. "What is in your mind? To snare me, or to strangle me, since the talking has failed? I have not come unprepared for such a thing."

He stopped. His face relaxed, until it was grinning. Grunts of laughter shook him. "Come, Zenobia, why the tantrums? Your past is your own business. I should not have spoken about it. The future is more important. Let's be sensible, in our own interests. And don't think I'm frightened of that pin you have there."

She, too, had relaxed. "This pin, as you call it, is poisoned, and I should be strong and skilled enough, as you know, to prick you with it before you could overcome me. Go back to your place, Aurelian, and don't behave like a boor." She walked to the ship's side and threw the blade into the sea. "That is not the way for two such as we to settle matters. A war, yes—a brawl, no."

He was seated again, his legs sprawled out across the deck. He watched her wave for her boat. "Woman," still laughing quietly, "whatever you are, there is no one else like you!" His voice sobered. "Is it useless to make one last appeal to your common sense?"

"Common sense does not come into it. Even if it were wisdom to accept your offer, I could not."

"Why?"

"Because you are Aurelian."

"A moment ago you spoke of marriage with Aurelian."

Her slips smiled slightly. "If I cannot marry him I must fight him. Perhaps the satisfaction will be equal."

"That is beyond me. You had better lose no time, Zenobia, on your journey home. I shall be coming after you."

CHAPTER THIRTEEN

A WOMAN FIGHTS

AURELIAN kept his word. He struck at once. He came south from Asia Minor with his Danubian legions, and his advance was like the sweep of a hand across a chessboard. Probus cleared Egypt and marched up through Arabia with Zabda's army scattered in flight before him. In two months the Romans recovered all they had lost in two years.

Zenobia was busy in Palmyra organizing the war. It was only now that she understood what a power she had let loose against herself. All the immense weight of Rome was descending on her. Aurelian, a tall, terrible vision in her mind, was coming to punish her. But she was a woman whom fear made resolute. She sent orders to Zabda, and to her commanders retreating from the north, to meet at Antioch, where she would take command of the army.

Aurelian moved too fast for her. On a spring day in 272 she arrived in Daphne, a wealthy suburb south of Antioch. As her carriage rattled into the streets, horsemen galloped past in the opposite direction. They were wearing her uniform and she knew they were in flight. More horsemen streamed past, and the streets began to fill with tired, panic-stricken foot soldiers. At the governor's palace she learned that Aurelian and Probus had already joined forces and defeated Zabda, and that at this moment the Romans were entering Antioch, the second city of her empire.

She left the tired Longinus at the palace and made Wahab stay with him in spite of the boy's protests. Led by a guide, she went to the heights outside the town where Zabda and his staff awaited her. At her side in the carriage was Philomene. With her were a deputation of chiefs from the desert tribes who had joined her on the way from Palmyra, and her royal guard of two hundred young officers; handsome young men, these, from the great families of Palmyra, Romanized in gymnasium and *auxilia* yet infected now by her with great ambitions and a mighty contempt for the foreigner; and worshipping, every one of them, their young, beautiful, and unattainable queen.

Zabda and his staff were gathered on the brow of a cliff overlooking the road from Antioch. The ribbon of roadway below was crammed with fleeing soldiers. Zabda's face was grimed and haggard, and black, sun-dried blood splashed his dusty armour. He saluted Zenobia. "My lady"—he was hoarse from shouting and from the dust in his throat—"if I had not known you were coming here I would have gone down to meet the enemy and died. Do not think I am a coward. When I have spoken with you I will go back to fight."

Zenobia laid her hand on his arm. "Do not talk of dying. You will serve me yet. The first thing is to stop this rout."

She turned aside. Philomene was at the cliff edge, looking westward, her face dreamy and avid, to where the sun flashed and twinkled on the weapons of the Roman army. Zenobia, too, stared westward.

"My lady," Zabda said, "we have done all we can. How can we stop them? The men have been retreating for weeks without food or sleep. They have been beaten a dozen times. They go crazy with fear when they hear the name of Aurelian. They slay the officers who try to bar their way, or trample them underfoot like stampeding bulls. They will go on running till dark and by then it will be too late."

Zenobia did not seem to hear him. Philomene murmured to her, "He is really there?"

"What is the matter?" Zenobia spoke with irony. "Do you still hanker after your Probus?"

Philomene grimaced. "Bring him to me and I will cut his heart out." With a touch of spite she added, "Aurelian is there, too."

"Yes." Zenobia did not take her eyes from the distant turrets of Antioch.

"My lady—" Zabda began.

She held her hand up to silence him. He waited at her elbow. She remained at the cliff edge, isolated by her thoughts. When she turned, it was not to him but to Philomene. The two women moved away and consulted. Their voices were low. The waiting officers heard the tone of questions from Zenobia, puzzled answers from Philomene, then laughter from both women and the sounds of agreement.

Zenobia turned to Zabda. "Do not fear, we shall stop the rout for you. What are you staring at? Do you doubt me? We two women will give you back your army." She silenced his interruption. "Never mind how. This is what you are to do. Collect all the officers you can find, and assemble them at the governor's palace. I shall need them when it is time to muster the army again. Then, till I come, rest and get some food. You need it, and you will be useless otherwise."

She strode across to her guardsmen, who were drawn up on horseback in five ranks. She spoke to them quietly, in a warm, friendly voice. She told them that on this height, which commanded the main road from Antioch, a rearguard must be left to hold up the Romans. With their long-range Parthian bows they could wreak havoc among any troops who tried to pass below. She asked them to do this for her, and said that if they could give her eight hours she could save the army. Let them do this, she said, and they would be heroes, of whom future poets would sing. She promised them honours, high posts, and her own lifelong affection, and guaranteed that the children or kinsfolk of those who fell would enjoy no less rewards. The young men cheered her, and their commanders swore that they would hold the road.

Less then two hours later, the mobs of fugitive soldiers pouring into Daphne found their way barred by crowds. They heard the sounds of a procession approaching and they were told the incredible news that Aurelian was a prisoner.

They protested that his cavalry had been chasing them all day. More fugitives came pressing behind them, but the crowds made flight impossible. The fleeing army came to a halt, packed in the streets of Daphne.

A clamour of rumour and argument gave way to a roar of cheering. The procession passed by. At its head was Zenobia in her carriage. In its centre, flanked by double files of spearmen, marched a man with bound hands. Only those in the front of the crowds could see him. Yelling for his blood, they were pressed back by the guards. His head was lowered as if in shame or exhaustion. Bloody bandages swathed his head and one side of his face. The rest of his face was smeared with dirt. But there was no mistaking his tall, soldierly build, his fringed imperial beard, his purple cloak and golden breastplate.

The crowds cheered, mad with joy. The news was shouted back by those in front. It was true, Aurelian was a prisoner. A horde of fugitives was transformed into a mob of carousing victors. The army made merry in the streets of Daphne.

Zenobia rode sedately through the town and into the governor's palace. The gates closed behind the last file of her retinue.

The crowds remained in possession of the streets. The citizens, who an hour before had been preparing to welcome the Romans, now hugged Zenobia's soldiers and brought them wine. The soldiers, only too eager to forget their panic, boasted and strutted. They did not know what to do next, but they knew that there was no more need to run away.

Officers came out of the palace and rounded them up. They

were formed into new units and herded away from the town. Marching columns, threads of order, moved through the crowds. They grew until they were an army again.

In the palace the man who had impersonated Aurelian was counting his pay. He was a Greek actor named Dion, an old crony whom Philomene had found for her mistress.

Zenobia, author of the mime in which he had played the lead, had forgotten him. She made ready to join her officers.

*

Several documents awaited her. They had been prepared by Longinus, who, hater of war though he was, had come forward in time of crisis to be her chief of intelligence, a job which he carried out with a skill beyond that of any professional soldier.

Here was an analysis of the latest strength of the Roman army. Here was a summary of the resources, in manpower and materiél, of the Palmyrene empire. Here (she smiled, not greatly caring) was a report that Bishop Paul of Samosata had appeared in the Roman camp, offering his services.

Here was a record of Aurelian's activities, brought by spies. He appeared to be confident, for he was given to entertainments when action was not imminent. For instance, he was greatly taken just now with a giant who had been presented to him. This Kaba, as he was called, came from that tribe of cave-dwelling giants in the hills of Palestine who had once been prominent in the chronicles of the Jews. He appeared to be a great favourite with the emperor. Every night for weeks he had wrestled against all comers, he had been handsomely fed and wined, and more than once important business had been kept waiting while the emperor, in his tent, had apparently found it amusing to converse with the giant through an interpreter.

Here, more significant to her, and not cheerful, was a political report. In the West, no trouble had yet been provoked by the outbreak of war in Asia. In the provinces that he had conquered Aurelian had scored a great success. Instead of subjecting them to the traditional punishments of pillage and slavery, he had returned to them their former privileges, promised religious freedom, even to the Christians whom he hated, and undertaken to bring them stable government, peace, and profitable trade. As a result, the population, far from resisting, welcomed him.

When she had read the papers she went into the courtyard, where her principal officers were assembled. They all straightened up and turned to face her, and she gave them a kindly greeting. Longinus was among them, with Wahab at his side. The boy, wearing the same olive-green tunic and red Persian trousers as the guardsmen on the heights, looked as fresh as a flower among all these tired men. He came forward eagerly. "Mother—"

"A moment, my dear." She called a slave to her and told him to bring a seat for Longinus. Fatigue, which had made the soldiers look gaunt and deadly, had made Longinus look old and sloppy and fatter than ever. All his flesh sagged, pouches hung beneath his eyes and his few grey hairs stuck out in absurd clumps from the side of his head. She said to him, "You are wearing yourself out. Campaigning is too much for you. You must look after yourself, for my sake."

"Mother—" Wahab was tugging at her sleeve. "I heard about the guards. It is wonderful. I should have gone, and then I could have stayed to command them."

"Brave boy! How like your father you are! But you must stay with me and look after me."

"Mother, let me join a regiment, today."

"No, the people must see you at my side. They are fighting for you as well as for me."

She straightened his acorn helmet, maternally blind to his hurt, nonplussed stare, and turned to face her officers. "I have

come to take command of my army. Zabda will remain your
leader. He will carry out my orders in the field. We have suffered
setbacks, but if we learn from them they will show us the way
to victory. I blame no one for what has happened. You are brave
and loyal, my Zabda most of all. You have my love and, when
we have won, you will have kingdoms to rule over in my name.
First we must win, and to do this we must be bold, and ready
to set aside old ways if these no longer serve. We have fought
the Romans in their own fashion and we have lost. Now we shall
fight them in our fashion and win. As long as we fight in their
way we are bound to be at a disadvantage, for although our men
have served with honour in their armies for two centuries, how
can we make legions to stand against the matchless, ancient
legions of Rome? No, we must fight them with our own means—
our archers, whose weapons outrange the Roman bows, our
heavy cavalry and swift desert riders—and, above all, our land
itself. We shall not stand our ground here, where the Romans
are fresh and close to the sea and can slaughter us. We shall fall
back, and let our country defeat them."

"My lady"—consternation had aroused Zabda from his weariness—"we have retreated three hundred miles already. It is
only a hundred miles to Palmyra."

"A hundred miles of desert, Zabda. As we retreat, our numbers will grow. As they advance, theirs will dwindle. They cannot hope for reinforcements. They have stripped their western
frontiers for this war, and they dare not strip them further.
Time, too, will be our weapon. They hope to hurry home victorious before their other enemies have awakened. We must delay
them until those other enemies are roused." She looked around
her. "Shall I tell you when we will give battle to the Romans?
When they have crossed the desert and are reduced in numbers
and exhausted. Shall I tell you what will happen to them when
we have won the battle? Those who are left will have to retreat
across the desert, and not one of them will emerge from that

hundred miles alive. That is my plan." She saw the faces of her officers. They were bright with enthusiasm, and she was satisfied.

Across the courtyard the Bedouin chiefs, in their brown cloaks and striped, belted robes, watched. She walked across to them. "And you, chiefs of the free tribes, will you help us?"

One of the chiefs said, "It is not our war, but a war of cities."

"Palmyra is your city."

"No city is ours. The desert is ours. We are alone and free in it. We are of no one's kingdom, only of the desert. Let the cities make war on each other. It is all the same to us."

"Between my city and Rome, it is not the same to you. You have never bowed to me, but I have never tried to make you do so. Instead, I have paid you to protect my caravans. I have left you as masters in your own place. Do you think the Romans will leave you alone? A desert is something they cannot bear. They will not rest until they have tidied it and brought roads to it, and water, and crops, and then your freedom will be gone. They will tax you and take your young men into their army. If you raid caravans, which is the salt in your life, they will not pay you to desist, as I have, but they will burn your tents and slaughter your families. If you rise up to defend yourselves, they will send armies clad in iron, and you, the free men of sand and stars, will end your lives in far-off lands with chains on your ankles."

The chiefs did not speak. Their eyes gleamed at her from beneath fringed headcloths. She paced up and down, her movements quick and catlike, self-absorbed yet confident in front of the dark, bearded male faces. "Once I was defeated, who would protect you? You would be alone."

A chief spoke. "Bath-Zabbai." He called her by her Arabic name. "What can we do, with only horses and camels and swords, against armies clad in iron?"

"You can destroy them. Listen to me now. I do not want you

to stand against them in battle. I am not mad, nor are you. This is the season of the simoom. The Romans call it the poison wind. When the Romans are crossing the desert, let your riders be a second simoom, destroying them."

In their eyes she saw the same fierce understanding that she had kindled in the eyes of her own officers. "It will take the Romans seven days to cross the desert. When they have crossed it, they will stand before Palmyra, and I tell you that Palmyra will be ready for them. In those seven days they are yours. You will come at them out of the night and out of the sandstorms, you will be silent and invisible, and you will kill them, and kill their animals, and steal their supplies, and make them search and sweat and march and stay awake and keep watch in vain. You will tire them and you will bleed them, and when they come to me, reduced in numbers, I shall fall upon them. More, while I do so, you will raid the convoys sent across the desert to supply them, so that they will fight short of food and armaments. In this way we shall beat them together."

One of the chiefs said, "There would be much loot in this."

"Yes, and more. There will be gold from me, to buy camels and cloth and weapons. You will be rich, and free, and stronger than before."

She stood before them, serenely poised, while they talked among themselves. A chief stepped forward. "Woman, who will command?"

"I. Who else? You will strike, but I will tell you how."

"Since when did Bedouin let a woman tell them how to fight?"

"You saw me today at the pass. The men did not know how to stop the rout. The woman did. Whom would you sooner trust?"

Her words struck a mutter of response from some of them.

"Or perhaps," she went on, sword-sharp, "because you shut your own women up in your tents, you feel bound to despise me.

Let me teach you not to. Bring me your champion archer and I will beat him. Bring me your best swordsman and I will disarm him. Bring me your finest horseman and I will outride him. Well? What do you say?"

There was another conference. The spokesman stepped forward again. "Bath-Zabbai, we have decided. Kill a sheep for us, and we will feast with you and drink to the death of all Romans."

CHAPTER FOURTEEN

THE CHESSBOARD

IT PLEASED Aurelian to receive the Christians in the court-yard of the Sun Temple. He would rather have crucified the lot of them than talk with them. But his policy was: only one enemy at a time. He would deal with them later. Now he must isolate them from Zenobia, whom they had so far regarded as their only friend. In the meantime, it at least emphasized their submission that they should come to him in the courtyard of his own god.

He sat in the long shadows of the portico. Probus was with him, and Rufinus, who was about to return to his post in liber-ated Damascus. The Christians stood twenty paces away, in the full glare of the sun.

Aurelian had come to the temple as soon as the city had fallen, and he had offered thanks. He practised his religion vigorously without ever pondering about it. The thing seemed clear to him. There must be a Supreme Commander. All his army experience had proved that to him. He despised the Greek and Roman gods as a shabby lot, too human by far. He knew, as a peasant, how much power was wielded by the spirits that lurked in woods, caves, springs, and cornfields. But what was over all in the uni-verse? The sun. What was the source of all life? The sun. Could any living thing look into the sun's face? Obviously the sun was the Supreme Authority.

He listened to the disputation of the Christians. His face was attentive, his contempt well hidden. They wanted him to decide who was the lawful bishop of Antioch: the nominee of the Church Synod, Domnus, who was here with his supporters, or

Paul of Samosata, who stood alone, calm, arrogant, and elegantly dressed in the Roman manner.

Domnus was a feeble-looking old man in a dirty white gown. His four backers were all elderly. They looked more like respectable city fathers than the spokesmen of a new faith. They had been lecturing Aurelian for an hour on the merits of their case, going into the most nonsensical and trivial details, earnestly propounding arguments that could mean nothing to an arbitrator outside their cult. What prosy, bigoted bores they were! It seemed to Aurelian typical of their arrogance that they could come in all seriousness and expect him to treat their stupid quibbles as immensely important, while they scarcely deigned to notice the clash of empires around them.

He considered their complaint: that Paul had maintained himself in office by terror, although their Council had three times excommunicated him and nominated Domnus. Good for Paul, Aurelian thought; but he suppressed his inclinations and sought for the political implications of their quarrel. All the while, most of his mind was brooding upon greater problems.

Yesterday his advance troops had reached Daphne expecting to find and destroy a rabble. Instead, they had been checked by a fanatical rearguard who wore the colours of Zenobia's royal escort. Later he had heard of Zenobia's presence in the town and of her ruse. This morning his scouts had reported to him that the enemy was making a disciplined, fighting retreat. The new spirit, the new tactics, the image of her riding through the town, all warned him that he was face to face with her at last, in the decisive contest.

Since his last meeting with her, there had broken free in his mind the unashamed recognition of her as an adversary to be feared. A curious corrosion of his hatred had begun. Like a duellist he had focused his consciousness upon her. From now to the end of the fight he would not dare to take his eyes from her. Every move he made must take her into account. He must think with her mind as well as his own, compel himself to enter, as he had never done before, into her personality. Such a process left no room for hatred. Indeed, it necessarily engendered a fascination, even a kind of sympathy, such as must always exist between adversaries of kindred skill and courage. He had entered into a relationship with her more intimate than if she had been his wife, that of mortal combat. He would have denied any change of feeling towards her, but the searchings of his mind were sufficient evidence to the contrary.

If she stood up to him stoutly, she could bring terrible dangers upon him. He had left the frontiers in Europe thinly guarded. Worse, his own legions might turn on him if the casualties were too heavy, the separation from their homes too prolonged, the profits too scanty. They had come here expecting to loot fat cities. For political reasons, he had spared the cities and denied his men their plunder. The legions were marvellously disciplined in battle, but otherwise they were a pack of wolves. They murdered emperors as casually as they enthroned them. They sang songs about Aurelian now because they thought him infallible and they feared his beast-tamer's punishments. A few reverses would suffice to break his spell upon them.

And here were these damned Christians droning on. . . .

It was not so bad when Paul spoke. He expressed himself with calmness and dignity. He spoke acidly of his enemies' arguments. "What do you, as an outsider, if I may use the term without disrespect to Caesar, think of these men? Has their theological hairsplitting any resemblance to logic? The priests of all religions in the Empire are, in a sense, public functionaries. Would men like those, like Domnus, be a credit to Rome? Have they the Roman mind, the Roman clarity, the Roman care for precision and order? Have they the necessary presence, intelligence, and authority? It is in the interest of the Empire, my lord, that the bishop of Antioch should be a statesman, a man of sense, a Roman in spirit. Look at me, my lord. Who looks more

the Roman, Domnus or I? Have I not proved my attachment to
Rome, by coming to you from Zenobia, at the sacrifice of the
wealth and honours she bestowed on me? These men accuse
me of raising mobs. Let me be blunt, my lord. Would you be
displeased to have a Christian bishop who could raise mobs on
behalf of Rome? Domnus is a nobody. I am famous in this land.
In coming over to you I have set an example. If I am seen at your
side, many others will follow my example."

Rufinus leaned across and spoke in Aurelian's ear. Aurelian
nodded. He said, "Paul, the bishop of Rome is the head of your
cult, is he not? When you were with Zenobia, it was your ambition, I believe, to become head of an independent church in the
East, denying his authority."

"To be against the bishop of Rome is not to be against Rome,
my lord. Christianity is not favoured by the state."

"The bishop of Rome is a Roman. Zenobia challenges Rome
temporally. You challenged Rome spiritually."

"My lord, I shall not waste words denying your charge. The
governor of Arabia"—bowing to Rufinus—"is renowned for the
excellence of his spy system. I shall only say that I have no such
ambitions now."

"Men with ambitions like yours never give them up. They
only set them aside for a while."

"Lord, Lord, great Caesar." Malchion, the rhetorician, whom
the Synod had brought as their first spokesman, was in front of
Aurelian, bowing like a carpet-seller. "God speaks through you.
Your wisdom is infinite. Paul is an enemy of Rome, for the
bishop of Rome has excommunicated him and has ordained
Domnus as bishop of Antioch."

Rufinus said, "That is true."

Paul stepped forward. "My lord"—he spoke softly—"you are
the authority in this matter, not a contemptible bishop in Rome.
Our church in Syria is rich. If I stay in office, half its funds will
be brought to you as a thank offering from the faithful."

Aurelian was leaning back, thinking.

"My lord"—Paul's voice was still quiet, but more urgent—"I was Zenobia's adviser. I know her secrets. I know her mind. You will need me at your side."

Aurelian kept silence for a few moments longer. Then, "Come closer, Paul."

He waited till Paul was at the arm of his chair. "Paul, I like you. I don't deny it. You are a rogue, but a genial one, and a useful one. And at least you look like a Roman. You don't care a grain of birdseed for your religion, but why should that worry me? You deserted Zenobia, but I do not hold that against you. You would desert me if things went badly, but so would many others. You could do a lot for me in Syria. I would like to see you bishop of Antioch."

He paused, stroking his cheek. Paul's face was grave, calm, yet with a glitter of gratification in the eyes, a complacent fatness in the cheeks. "Unfortunately—" He paused again to watch the effect. There was none, except for an alert flicker in Paul's eyes. "The bishop of Rome is against you. And you are not to be trusted, as these fanatics are, to stay faithful to him. The bond with Rome. That is the important thing. I do not like you Christians, but if there are Christians, let them at least turn in the direction of Rome. In times like these, anything is of value that holds the Empire together. So"—he ignored the flash of appeal in Paul's eyes. He raised his hand and called loudly—"I name Domnus as bishop of Antioch."

The bishops embraced each other, shouted their thanks to their god and to Aurelian, threw themselves down in bows to the emperor, remained on their knees to gabble prayers. Paul, as elegant and proud in his posture as before, watched calmly. Aurelian said to him. "You can still be of use to us, you know. Why not come into the army?"

"My lord, I am a man of peace. Perhaps you need a superintendent of taxes in one of the conquered provinces?"

"I think not. I hear your tastes are expensive."

"Then, my lord, since I am not appreciated in my own church, and since all religions are voices of the one God, I shall make a journey through the Empire, studying all religions till I have found the one that is my true home."

Rufinus chuckled. "Start with Greece. Some of the shrines there are extremely prosperous concerns. You could do worse than set up a nice little oracle somewhere."

Paul bowed. "So I was thinking, your Excellencies."

*

Aurelian had guessed that if Zenobia made a stand, it would be at Emesa, where her line of retreat must turn away from the valley of the Orontes into the desert; and here she stood.

He had also guessed how she would dispose her troops. It was early morning, cool and grey, when he watched her army deploy. He could not see her in the pattern of black specks massing upon the battlefield but he felt as immediately in her presence as if he faced her across a table.

Their chessboard was a plain out of which a few small hills swelled. He sat his horse on the forward slope of one of them, above a scattering of dun tents. Maxin was by him, silent and withdrawn, and staff officers clustered around. Far away, a low, wavering rim of mountains framed the plain, upon which the two armies were tracing themselves like black furrows.

Opposite him, behind the enemy army, was another hill, beyond which the white buildings of Emesa could be seen. Aurelian peered at the flash of armour on its forward slope, imagining that he saw a red dot which might be her.

At Antioch, Zabda had faced the Romans with an army set out in Roman style: three lines of infantry backed by archers, with the *clibanarii*, Palmyra's heavy cavalry, in the centre. Aurelian, feinting with his own cavalry, had lured the *clibanarii* into a headlong charge which had tired them and left them useless. In the meantime his legions had made a flank attack across the river at their exposed infantry and won the battle.

Zenobia, as Aurelian had expected, had not repeated Zabda's errors. She had understood that her main weakness lay in her inferior infantry, and that her main assets were her heavy archers in defence and her mailed cavalry in attack. She had formed her infantry into a phalanx, a solid block which would give courage to its individual soldiers and would probably hold fast against a Roman attack. She had put her heavy archers in front of her main force, thus bringing them five hundred yards nearer the Romans and increasing the velocity with which their shafts would hit an assault.

What he had not foreseen was the formation she had designed for her archers. They were in two crescents, whose concave sides faced the Romans, pivoted on the forward corners of the phalanx with the *clibanarii* between them, so that they could cover with their volleys front and flank, infantry and cavalry.

Aurelian's task, as he saw it, was to expose her main force to annihilation by once more enticing her *clibanarii* forward; and this time they, too, must be destroyed. He had a surprise weapon in store for this purpose. To prevent her phalanx from escaping before his main attack, he had a column of troops moving across the plain far out to the left. This consisted of the Third Gallicans, escorted by a regiment of Moorish cavalry. They were to cleave into the enemy's rear and pin him down when the main Roman line moved forward. Their attack, too, would offer a diversionary target to the enemy's archers at the vital moment, so helping the frontal attack. They would lose heavily, but that was their privilege as assault troops. He was not a spendthrift of lives, but he knew that if he could achieve decisive victory today he might avoid the perils and delay of a desert campaign.

He made his first frontal move. Two regiments of horse from

his reserve charged at the Palmyrene center. The *clibanarii,* not
to be tempted again by the feint that had been their undoing
at Antioch, stood firm. Instead, the archers, reserving their volleys to the last moment, massacred the light Roman cavalry, of
whom only a few galloped back.

Aurelian waited. The two armies were still, like diagrams
drawn upon the ground. Silence weighed upon a host of men,
all waiting in the fatigue and apathy that made up most of a
battle. Aurelian was not disturbed by the failure of his attack.
It was a bait, to give Zenobia false confidence. Now, he hoped,
she would send forward her *clibanarii,* that mailed fist which
could crush any infantry. This time they would not charge, but
would advance deliberately, arriving with strength unspent to
break the Roman line. For this, too, he was ready, with his surprise.

Apparently Zenobia had taken the bait. The *clibanarii* began
to move forward. They came on, wall after wall of mailed mon-
sters. They rode beneath a forest of upright lances on which the
dragon pennants of Palmyra fluttered. Horses and men were
completely covered with scale armour of iron and brass, faces
hidden by perforated visors. Infantry could not harm them with
sword or spear. The light arrows of the Roman archers would
rattle off their mail. The Roman cavalry, bareback Dalmatians,
Moorish javelin-men half-naked with small round shields, axe-
throwing, trousered Germans, was no match for them. If they
reached the Roman line unchecked and unwearied, they could
pound it to pieces with their great, studded maces.

Aurelian watched them without anxiety. He searched their
ranks for a sign of Zenobia. She was not among them. In his dis-
appointment there was a grain of approval. His adversary was
proving worthy of him. She had understood that it was more
important to command than to show off.

His skirmishers were scattering in front of the *clibanarii.*
What use were javelins, stones, the lead bullets of his Spanish

slingers, against mail? His Dalmatian horsemen, charging from the flanks, swirled around the mailed, advancing cohorts. He glanced at the tents on the slope beneath him. His weapon was ready.

The *clibanarii* were almost upon his front line. He knew the fear that his legionaries must be feeling, down below in their silent, unflinching ranks. He raised his hand.

Close by, a trumpet sounded. From below, another answered. One of the tents billowed. It was flung back like a cloak, to settle in a deflated heap upon the ground. Out of it stepped a giant.

The giant raised a shaggy head and shouted. All the tents were falling and from them arose a regiment of giants. They advanced down the slope, through the three lines of the Roman infantry, and Aurelian could see the faces of his soldiers turned towards them in relief.

Kaba marched at their head. He was the wrestler who had entertained the emperor in camp. The sight of him had given Aurelian the answer to the *clibanarii*. Recruiting officers had been sent in strict secrecy to the hills of northern Palestine, and they had rounded up three hundred men of Kaba's tribe.

Kaba was nearly eight feet tall, and every one of his men was above six feet. His face peered out of a tangle of hair and skins clothed his body. Like all of his clansmen, he carried no weapon but a five-foot length of oak branch, of which the striking end was as thick as a normal man's thigh.

The giants surged into the cavalry like a herd of great apes. They clubbed at horses and riders. They were massive enough to catch the mightiest sword-strokes on their clubs so that the blades were buried deep in the wood, then to pluck the weapons away from their owners. They were nimble enough to duck the mace-blows of the knights. They pulled the mail-clad men off their mounts and mashed their brains out while they lay, helpless in their iron casings, on the ground. They set their shoulders beneath the bellies of horses and reared the animals up so that their riders toppled. Aurelian watched with a special pleasure. His thoughts were of Zenobia. He wondered if she could see what was happening. She had shown herself cunning at Antioch. Now let her see that his mind could always cap hers in cunning.

The *clibanarii* were riding away. The giants lumbered after them, pulling down stragglers, then came to a stop, leaning on their clubs, the ground around them littered with mailed bodies.

The second move had gone to Aurelian. He had struck Zenobia's one offensive weapon out of her hands. Now he must close his trap. He gave an order. There were more trumpet signals. His main line of infantry began to advance.

The jaws of his trap closed like a diagram upon the plain. In the distance the Third Gallican moved in from the left. Below, three straight lines advanced, made up of four legions that bespoke the marvellous Roman discipline, with cavalry on their flanks and the reserve behind them.

Then he saw that he was not to have his prey. It was slipping out from between the closing jaws. Far away to the right a line of pennants moved, the *clibanarii* leaving the field. Behind them the enemy's phalanx was melting into a black, moving stream.

Red signal pennants were tossing in the Roman attack line. Probus, leading the attack, had ordered a general charge by his five regiments of cavalry to prevent the enemy's escape. Cohorts of infantry went forward at the double behind the horsemen. From the left, the Third Gallican had hurled forward its escorting cavalry regiment.

But Zenobia's two brigades of heavy archers were protecting her retreat. One of them, with a speed and skill that Roman troops might envy, doubled to its flank and poured volleys upon the third Gallican. The other faced the frontal attack.

The two cohorts of infantry sent by Probus deployed rapidly into tortoises, solid rectangles roofed and walled by shields. As the cavalry charge melted away in front of them under the volleys of the archers, they moved forward. The volleys stopped; then, when they were at closest range, began again. Aurelian saw the iron walls break and lose shape, waver and lose shape and collapse again. Shields and their bearers could not stand up against the hundred-fifty-pound velocity of the broad-headed Palmyrene arrows.

Aurelian's cavalry had veered away from the archers and were galloping to intercept the main retreat. But Zenobia had sent to each of her archer brigades a contingent of her light cavalry, unused as yet. These took the archers on their horses and galloped between the Roman cavalry and the general retreat. The archers dismounted in the path of the Romans, stopped and slaughtered them with regular disciplined volleys, and when the Romans rode away to attack at another point, mounted, and rode to block their way again.

Aurelian surveyed the battlefield. The mass of the enemy were moving out of reach. His main infantry had no hope of catching up. His cavalry, beyond recall, were hurling themselves to their deaths in hopeless charges against the mobile defence of the Palmyrene archers.

Some of the enemy infantry had not been able to escape. The Third Gallican was in among them, and was slaughtering mightily in revenge for the men it had lost at the hands of the archers. But what comfort was there in killing these half-trained peasant infantry? Zenobia could get plenty more. Perhaps she had even abandoned them in order to hold up the Gallicans.

The two brigades of archers had broken the power of the Roman cavalry charges. Now they were retiring in bounds, one retreating while the other covered it, then in turn dismounting to give cover while the other fell back. They were a moving shield behind which the enemy escaped. The battle was over.

Beyond the hill the white walls of Emesa gleamed in the sun of full morning. Soon Aurelian would enter the town in triumph.

He had smashed the *clibanarii*. His soldiers were butchering some laggard regiments of enemy infantry. Tonight they would carouse and sing of victory. His clerks would send news of a victory to Rome. But Aurelian knew that he had won no victory. His adversary had given him the slip. She had left him nothing but a couple of pawns and an empty chessboard. In return, she had knocked the breath out of his army on the eve of a great ordeal, the desert crossing. At a time when he dared not send for reinforcements, she had inflicted his first serious casualties on him. Above all—was it by design?—she had destroyed half of his cavalry, his main arm of pursuit.

He could not see her in that distant, retreating host; but he felt as if she were standing in front of him, smiling; with just such a smile as he saw, when he turned, in Maxin's eyes, mocking and challenging.

*

When Aurelian dismounted outside his tent Maxin rode on without looking round. He had gone back, these days, into his world of silence. He followed his master like a threatening shadow. When his duties were finished he vanished into the slave quarters where, of his own choice, he slept. His only talk was with the slaves.

Aurelian was too weary to care what Maxin did. He had done nothing but sit his horse all day, but he ached in his bones as if he had been beaten. His first action was to see that his horse was cared for. His second was to empty in one swallow a pitcher of wine which Lucipor had kept cool in the earth for him. His third was to strip and stand outside his tent, flexing his weary muscles, while Lucipor sluiced cold water over him.

He towelled himself without mercy, slicked his hair back with an iron comb, put on a clean tunic and sandals, told Lucipor to lay bread, meat, and wine on the table, and went to the field hospital.

As befitted a marching community which could build bridges, roads, fleets, and monuments as well as fight, the legion could boast that it was the only military force in the world with good medical services. The legion's baggage train included hospital tents and equipment, and the medical staff was as well-drilled and efficient as the men in the fighting companies.

The tented camp was laid out to the standard Roman pattern. It might have been a miniature reproduction in canvas of Chichester, Narbonne, or Belgrade. The hospital marquees, joined by covered passages, lined the whole of one of its main streets. The wounded filled the tents in neat rows, and the street outside was packed with laden stretchers. The muted talk of the wounded, and their quiet groans, rose in a single, rhythmical murmur.

Aurelian walked down the narrow aisles talking to doctors, stooping to joke with wounded men. He comforted them with the rough, teasing talk they loved. In his eyes was the lucent, unconcerned gaze that hides the soldier's pity. There was calculation, too, in his glances. He did not know the precise figure of his losses, but they were considerable. The helpless men in these tents were so many battalions stolen from him.

A group of officers lay together near the door of the Third Gallican's tent. Among them was the governor of Arabia. Aurelian paused at his side. Rufinus said, his voice weak but clear, "Have we won?"

"Yes."

"Have we killed her?"

"No."

"Then we have not won."

When Rufinus smiled his face moved like the flow of hot wax. His eyes in their sunken sockets were like candle-flames in their melted pits. Aurelian could not see his wounds but he knew that he was looking at a dying man. He lifted the blanket. Rufinus was heavily bandaged from waist to groin. Aurelian said, "Amateurs should keep out of battles. I have officers who know their jobs."

"I assure you I shall not do it again."

Aurelian let the blanket fall. "Of that I am certain."

"Also," the dying man's face creased in a grin, "a certain pride, somewhat futile, I admit, at this moment impels me to remind you that I am no amateur. I was a tribune for three years in the Tenth Fretensis."

"That is very interesting." Aurelian looked restlessly about him. "You should have stayed with them in Jerusalem."

"You are impatient, Aurelian?"

"I have a lot of men to see. Men who've been with me for years."

"I apologize for keeping you. I shall try not to take too long in dying."

"Die? With that? Rubbish! If you can stick it without water for a few days, they'll sew your guts up, you'll see."

"My entrails are cut in two, but that is the least of it. I was also trampled by a horse when I was on the ground, and something has happened to my spine. I am paralysed."

"Then you're lucky. You can't feel anything. Your guts would be driving you mad with pain otherwise."

"Yes, and instead there is only a coldness, a freezing coldness, from my waist down. As you say, I am lucky."

Aurelian, his lips compressed, half turned away. "Is there anything you want to put down in writing? A will? Notes for your successor? I'll send my secretary to you."

"Thank you. He will be someone to talk to. Dying like a Roman is all very well, Aurelian, but dying is a lonely business."

A face across the aisle had caught Aurelian's eye. His smile signalled *I'll-be-with-you-in-a-moment.* He turned brusquely back to Rufinus. "Perhaps you'd like to end it more quickly? It can be done."

Rufinus moved his head in a ghostly negative. His smile flickered like a disturbed flame. "No, I am comfortable, and it is at least something to lie here and think. I am in no hurry. After all"—Aurelian was moving away, and he was speaking to a half-turned back—"there is a justice in this. In a manner of speaking, I brought this war about."

Aurelian glanced back. His look was surprised but only half attentive. "You? How?"

"When I had Odenathus killed."

Aurelian was standing over him again. "*You* had him killed?"

Rufinus' head made the faintest movement of assent, emphasized by a drooping of the eyelids. "A diplomat devoted to his mission does these things. Call it private initiative. My task was to keep peace and the obedience of Palmyra. I thought it would be safer with Zenobia than with her husband. I was wrong. I let loose a war instead."

"And in Rome?" At the house of Statianus? You lied to me?"

"Naturally. You were Aurelian, the new man, the man who might make a clean sweep, the man who punished without pity. How could I admit that I was responsible? I feared you." His eyelids drooped again, adding weariness to his smile. "I do not fear you now, Aurelian."

Aurelian, too, smiled a little. "No."

"Also, it was the aim of Statianus to persuade you to make war on her. I had decided, by then, that only war would curb her. So I said what I thought would make you heed Statianus."

"Who is Statianus that the emperor should heed him and you should help him?"

"Statianus?" The candle-flames of mockery leaped up in the dying man's eyes. "Who is Statianus? Why, Statianus is Rome. If you are wise you will always heed him."

Aurelian looked away, not at the other men in the tent but far beyond them. "So she did not kill her husband." His eyes were glittering. He was speaking to himself.

Mockery flared again in Rufinus' eyes. "What is that to us, Aurelian?"

Aurelian cast a brief, indifferent glance down at him. "I'll send you my secretary."

He strode away.

CHAPTER FIFTEEN

THE POISON WIND

IT TOOK seven days for the Roman army to cross the desert. Those seven days transformed its spirit. At the outset the men swung along, not yet bereft of the holiday feeling that attends the early days of a campaign. To their long-striding step they chanted:

Mille Sarmatas, mille Francos, semel et semel occidimus,
Mille Persas quaerimus.

They had killed thousands in other lands and they had come to look for "Persians"—for so the common soldier termed all Easterners; surging along six-deep behind their silver eagles, felt caps on the backs of their heads, helmets dangling from their belts, canvas covers on their shields; jesting and calling to their commander as he rode down the column. A week later they plodded in silence, strained dark faces glimpsed within a moving wall of dust.

The dust of their own march was an enemy. The heat was an enemy. The sun's glare, hurting their eyes, was an enemy. Thirst was an enemy. Worst of their enemies were the simoom and the raiders who came with the simoom.

The poison wind moaned in the empty desert. Again and again it leaped into a frenzy and smote them for ten, fifteen minutes at a time with furnace gusts. It covered their mouths like hot hands to stop them from breathing. It rasped their skins, fraying their nerves to fury. Its dryness sucked the moisture from them, so that men collapsed and beasts died. Thousands of miles it had come from the depths of Asia to assail the invaders. Veterans of the East had warned of the strange, senseless despair to which it goaded men. Now, as the Romans marched towards battle, it did its work for Asia, filling men's breasts with despair.

Sometimes it brought sandstorms with it and then, while the sand stung and blinded, the Bedouin came, hidden within it. They never stayed longer than the storm. Out of the yellow, whirling fog rode the robed men on racing camels, mouths covered with scarves, swords flashing. They cut a path of dead through the column and when the swirl of sand had gone they, too, had vanished.

Their attacks were cunningly aimed. They did not kill large numbers, for they would not linger to fight, but they set fire to corn, fodder, and the siege engines which the army would need when it reached Palmyra; and they slaughtered the precious draught animals.

Between raids they were never seen, though the army felt that it was always being watched. Patrols were sent over the skyline and, more often than not, were never seen again. Aurelian could not scour the desert for the raiders. The bulk of his troops were infantry, brought for siege battles—and Zenobia had killed half his cavalry.

A continual vigilance had to be imposed on the men, and this was worse than the raids. The tormented soldiers were denied even sleep, for the Bedouin made noisy demonstrations against the camps at night.

The soldiers marched with bowed backs and glaring, sunken eyes. Anger waxed in them. Men who are suffering need someone to blame. Soldiers at war do not hate an enemy army, country, or city. They choose a person, a personification, whom they may hate. Sixty thousand Roman soldiers saw the cause of their suffering in Zenobia. The heat, the dust, the poison wind, the Arab raiders, the misery of stumbling over bad ground, the thirst, the glare, the fear, the sleeplessness, the oppressive silence of the desert—all were named Zenobia in their minds. Because she was a woman they hated her even more.

After the raid a soldier swore that he had seen her among the Bedouin. From that moment, she haunted the army like a spirit strayed from the underworld. Ten, twenty, fifty men were to be found after each attack who shouted that they had glimpsed her, white horse and all; and nervous sentries claimed they had seen her in the night.

Aurelian, who knew how legends spread in an army, doubted that anyone had seen her. He did not imagine that she would waste her time with raiding parties, although he saw her intelligence behind every blow that was struck. It was sufficient token of her quality that the legends should have arisen.

As the men's hatred for her mounted, his diminished. No liking for her took its place. He was aware only of a furious concentration of his wits to defeat her. Victory over her had become the single necessity that dominated his life. Sometimes he recalled, with a touch of wonderment, what he had learned about her in the hospital tent at Emesa. It had not lodged in his consciousness, yet it had purged him of malice. Grim, resolved, confident that he would destroy her, he nevertheless shared none of his men's sick bitterness at the hardships and reverses of the march. To him this desert crossing was only the journey to a rendezvous, on which his eyes were fixed.

It was a tired army that in the first days of May arrived before the walls of Palmyra. Its casualties in the desert had amounted to only a couple of thousand men, but it had lost valuable stores and engines of war; and both its stamina and confidence had been impaired.

During their journey the men, soldier-wise, had not thought of the embattled city that awaited them, but of the cool oases, the rest, the water they would enjoy. When they arrived their dreams were punctured. The shady palm groves had been cut down. The ground had been stripped of foliage. All had been

stored in the city, and the attackers had been deprived of cover
and fodder. The cattle had been driven inside the walls. The
wells, except, unaccountably, one, called the Spring of Efca,
to the south of the city, had been poisoned. Before them reared
the city walls, restored by Zenobia, fifty feet high with many
loopholed bastions. A ravine, twenty feet wide and almost as
deep, formed a natural ditch in front of much of the wall.

There was no oasis; and there was no rest. Aurelian saw less
risk in driving his men than in letting them relax. He ordered
an immediate attack.

He had brought a strong train of artillery; two hundred
ballistae, wheeled, dart-firing crossbows issued one to every infantry company; and forty catapults, one to each battalion, ox-
drawn weapons which could throw a hundred-fifty-pound stone
for four hundred yards. He massed these opposite the south
gate, while during the night he masked his concentration by
sending patrols up to the walls at many points and filling the
darkness with a confused movement, all around the city, of columns of camp followers, some marching in a clatter of borrowed
swords and shields, some mounted on mules, some dragging
dummy siege engines.

He launched his real assault while it was still dark. As the
infantry moved forward, the artillery opened up. Endless dart-
volleys made a roof of whistling black streaks over the attack.
The missiles poured into the black fringe of defenders on the
wall and a faint bird-crying of the stricken could be heard
among them, but no other sound. Volleys of huge stones from
the catapults shook the gate, striking a continuous thunder
against which could be heard the blare of trumpets and the
cheers of the assault troops.

Grey dawn infused the darkness, and through the gloom the
black clusters of attackers moved forward, pioneers with sandbags and brushwood bundles for the ditch, infantry trundling

ladders and battering rams on wheels. There was still no reaction from the walls.

The catapult crews changed their ammunition. Fireballs, made of pitch and tallow, flew in a continuous stream over the heads of the attackers, a myriad of flame-streaks converging with a *whoosh whoosh whoosh* amid their glare, clusters of fiery comets pouring at the wall in an endless cone.

The city awoke.

There was a stir on the walls. Into the embrasures were wheeled hundreds of dart-guns. The first Romans poured into the ditch, a black cascade of bodies that vanished into a vast terrible screaming. Zenobia had filled the ditch with sharpened stakes, which she had covered with a false bottom of canvas hidden by sand. Men laden with their assault gear, horses with their riders, plunged screaming to impalement. The next wave of men halted at the ditch, shouting for planks and sandbags and spades, and while they swarmed there, the dart-guns on the walls sent a sleet of missiles down at them.

The attack surged forward again, over the earth, dead bodies, rocks, sandbags, and timber that had been heaped in rough bridges across the ditch. Company after company plunged into the ditch, through the ceaseless shower of arrows, and each emerged with only a handful left. In the ditch the mounds of bodies grew.

The gate should have been blazing by now. But as the fireballs burst against it they were snuffed out by a torrent of water that sluiced down it, from hundreds of vents which had been let into the top of it. The Roman soldiers, plodding forward from the ditch, head down against the missiles, were mystified at the prodigality with which this besieged city was using its water. Their staff officers knew, however, that Zenobia could easily afford the water, for there were five big wells inside the city.

The first parties of assault troops swirled beneath the walls. Their ladders went up. Their rams began to thunder. The men swarmed up the ladders. From the bastions on each side of them, grapnels were flung out on ropes, and the ladders were pulled over sideways, showering men to earth. More ladders went up. A crossfire of arrows and red-hot clay bullets, from the loopholed walls of the bastions, swept the ladders clear and slaughtered the Romans crowding at the foot of the wall.

A new glare lit the sky. High overhead hung a score of flaming balls. More and more sailed up. They were being fired from inside the city, from engines set up in a cleared zone behind the wall. Instead of being fired on a low trajectory like those of the Romans, they were being shot up almost vertically, and they began to rain from above just as the mass of the Roman legions approached the wall. The fiery bombs burst in dozens among the crowded companies, flinging their ribbons of flame far and wide as they exploded.

This was to be remembered by the legionaries as "the night of fire." The Roman fireballs *whooshed* in their endless cone at the gate. Down through them, trailing vertical lines of fire in the gloom, fell Zenobia's fireballs. On the ground beneath, men swarmed, the wink and spatter and dazzle of bursting fireballs among them, the screams of fear and pain going up from them, the gloom speckled by firefly streams of red-hot bullets from the bastions. The dead lay thick, and the fresh companies rose up out of the ditch as if the underworld were vomiting thousands of its dead back to life; and beyond the ditch the Roman gun crews, as if they were giving a drill display, served their weapons smartly by numbers, while the sleet of missiles riddled their gun shields and mowed them down.

The losses were too high. At daylight Aurelian called off the attack. He stood three hundred yards from the wall, between two shattered dart-guns, their dead crews sprawled around. His soldiers trudged past him, their backs to the city. He did not need to be told what these worn-out men were thinking. Their dejected silence was eloquent.

The silence, the sound of their feet, the creak of wheels, were one with his own mood, so that he was startled when a shouting broke out in the ranks. Men were turning to look up at the walls. Anger distorted their faces, and the deep note of anger was in their shouts. Some shook their fists. Some discharged useless arrows.

He, too, looked up. For the first time in months he saw his adversary. She stood alone on one of the gate towers. She was looking down; in his direction, it seemed. The clamour of his men faded in his ears. For him as he stood stock-still, staring, there was no army, no wreckage around him, no city; only a tiny, jaunty figure, in white blouse and flaring red trousers, against the sky.

CHAPTER SIXTEEN

TWO PENNIES A DAY

IN THE Roman camp there were a number of traders. Some were only sutlers. Others, agents of the great Roman magnates, were on the lookout for loot, which the soldiers brought to them, and above all for slaves. When, in punishment for resistance, a city was put to the sword, its surviving inhabitants were auctioned off, the proceeds being shared by the general, the imperial Treasury, and the troops. A job lot of slaves bought in the field could be retailed at enormous profits in Rome.

Traders and troops alike had been cheated of their pickings by Aurelian's clemency in Syria. For them it was a business necessity that Palmyra, their last possible source of profit, should be plundered. Moreover, the Roman financiers, who employed the traders, wanted to make sure that there would be no negotiated peace. It was not enough to disarm Palmyra. This trade rival, planted in the path of the Eastern caravans, must cease to exist. Four centuries ago, when Carthage had been Rome's rival for the sea trade, the Senate had cried, *Delenda est Carthago.* Now it was Palmyra that must be wiped out.

It was easy for the traders, talking at the campfires, to inflame the troops. What had a legionary to look forward to except loot? He was paid two pennies a day; minus compulsory savings; minus stoppages for bedding, boots, burial club and the annual unit dinner; minus the cost of his food apart from the army issue of wine, vinegar, corn, and lard. Who could live on that?

What made a man sign up for twenty terrible years which he had little chance of surviving? Not two pennies (less deductions) a day—but a dream, that he or his children would one

231

day have the price of a farm. Many a soldier suffered for a life-time so that a son whom he hardly ever saw, in some distant garrison town, might grow up to be a free farmer instead of a cursing, trudging mercenary. It was this dream, not any general, that the soldiers followed. It raged in them like fire. It deter-mined their loyalties and their revolts. It set them afire for loot, which was their only hope of achieving the dream.

The traders played on this, and on the sufferings of the army, and on the soldiers' fury that a woman was making a mock of them in front of the world. "This is your city, not your general's. You must make it pay for your hardships with plunder. You must punish it for the misery it has caused you. You must avenge the death of your comrades. You must leave this woman dead, and a burned patch where her city was, to show the world that no one can make mock of the legions."

These words burned into the men as their ordeal dragged on. After the failure of his first assault, Aurelian had an earthwork built, seven miles in circumference and set at close intervals with brick blockhouses. The soldiers who had smashed the Goths, stormed the Roman Mint, and fought at Emesa bowed their backs like slaves, in day and night shifts, building kilns, making bricks, digging, while arrow-volleys from the walls thinned their working parties. Such is the power of many human hands that the earthwork was finished in two weeks. The men toiled, and dreamed of plunder and revenge.

Zenobia gave her answer. Bedouin raids harried the Roman camp. Supply convoys were attacked in the desert. The be-siegers were themselves invisibly besieged. To their other bur-dens were added shortage of food and supplies, extra camp guards and convoy duties. They did their duty, dreaming of plunder and revenge.

They made causeways across the ditch, filling it once more with their dead to do so, and built sheds on wheels within which iron-pointed battering rams were slung. They pushed these up to the wall.

Zenobia stood on the battlements, and her men dropped fireballs on the sheds.

The Romans built more sheds and roofed them with fireproof bricks.

Tall frameworks grew up on the wall, which turned out to be jib cranes. Zenobia stood on the battlements, while hooks were lowered to overturn the sheds; and when the Roman crews came scurrying out they were shot to death from the bastions.

Aurelian set up high screens in front of the wall. The tall pine trunks, mats, and ships' cables of which these were made had been convoyed across the desert at the cost of terrific effort and hard fighting. Behind the screens the legionaries, numbed by their labours until they were mindless organisms of hatred and endurance, built a fort.

The fort had a roof of beams covered with bricks, which was raised on endless wooden screws as the walls were built beneath it. Each floor, on completion, was occupied by sharpshooters who gave the builders some protection against the archers on the walls. Three narrow, roofed galleries were built from the fort to the wall. They were called "rats," because sappers worked in them to "gnaw" at the wall. On the roof of the fort tripods were set up, on which were swivelled long beams tipped with iron claws.

By the end of July the roof was as high as the city walls, and the Roman soldiers started to pull down the battlements with the clawed beams.

Zenobia stood on the battlements. Her cranes swung out, with bunches of men hanging from the hooks. The men dropped on the roof. Some engaged the Romans hand-to-hand. Others fixed grapnels to the clawed beams. By the time the Romans had wiped out the attackers the beams had been swung aloft and the besiegers, helpless, watched them hoisted in over the city wall.

There she stood, on the battlements, the symbol of their hardships and their defeat. They darkened the air with arrows and did not touch her, and some of them were a little frightened. She was smiling, and giving orders, and her cranes, swinging out once more, dropped boulders to crush the "rats."

The Romans set up new tripods on the roof of their fort. She stood on her battlements, laughing at them. Long wooden chutes were pushed from the wall until they overhung the fort. Boulders were loaded onto them by cranes, and came thundering down the chutes to fall on the fort. The Romans flung ropes and pulled the chutes away. More were thrust out. The boulders, some of them six hundred pounds in weight, came down on the roof; and the roof caved in, and then the floors below, until the fort was only a heap of rubble within four jagged walls.

Loot and revenge. Above all, now, revenge. The more setbacks the Romans suffered the more they hurled themselves into this contest of cunning, labour, courage, and endurance, like some doomed, furious insect species. They dug tunnels and hollowed out chambers beneath the city wall. The timbers of these chambers were soaked in oil, so that when they burned the chambers would collapse, bringing down the foundations of the wall. Zenobia countermined, drove the Roman sappers from the tunnels with smoke and used her abundant water supply to flood the workings.

August came. The sun was pitiless, a blinding white glare. Aurelian was as pitiless. He ordered another general assault. He knew how much was at stake for him. His legionaries were maddened by suffering. Latent in them was the knowledge of their power. They had made him, and they could destroy him. At any time they might remember this and vent upon him the hatred that they could not satisfy upon Zenobia.

Two assault towers had been built in the camp. They were

of timber, and they were fifteen feet higher than the city walls. Inside them, safe from enemy missiles, were battering rams on the ground floors, archers and infantry on the intermediate floors. On the roofs were drawbridges which the infantry could let down onto the battlements. There were water tanks, pumps, and fire hoses in them, to defeat attack by fire. Their wheels were twelve feet in diameter and four feet thick.

The two towers faced the sector of wall Aurelian had earlier tried to breach, for some of the battlements were still in ruins, and a minor subsidence in the foundations had caused a long crack in the wall which might help storming parties.

The plan was for the towers to be moved up to the wall, just inside the bastions. The drawbridges would be lowered, this sector of the battlements would be cleared, and two legions would be able to move forward between the towers and go in over the wall. Two more legions would watch the gate to prevent a sortie against the towers. Once the legions were over the wall, victory was certain.

Behind screens, two approach-ways were built to the wall, of brick and timber. These sloped slightly, till they were near the walls, so that the towers could be levered forward under control; then more steeply so that the towers would roll for the last few yards under their own weight.

The approach-ways were guarded day and night against delaying attacks, and listening posts were manned to ensure that the enemy did not undermine the tracks with tunnels.

Aurelian knew that Zenobia must be aware of his intention. The towers had been built in full view of her troops. It was a slow job to move them forward to the launching-points. She appeared to be planning some defence, for canvas screens were set up on the walls. Some kind of building activity could be heard going on. Aurelian tried to send patrols over the walls to discover what she was up to, but she had posted extra guards, and none of the patrols got in. He was not anxious. If she came out to destroy his towers before they were launched, his legions were ready. Once the towers were launched, what could she do? Her artillery could not damage the huge structures, her cranes were not high enough to tackle them, her marksmen could not pierce their walls. He decided that she must be strengthening the wall in some way, and that would not stop his trained, battle-mad assault troops.

On the night before the assault, the towers were levered to their precise points of launching. Safety banks and buffers were thrown up. The ways were greased in front of them. Their garrisons went aboard.

At dawn the artillery began a bombardment. The soldiers at the bases of the towers pulled away the chocks and applied levers. The towers lumbered down the inclines and came to rest against the wall, each just inside a bastion. High peremptory trumpet calls, sounding the three-note call to advance, set the columns of the Third Gallican moving forward from the camp.

Aurelian's command post was well back, by the artillery lines. He saw the drawbridges of his towers go down, the flash of silver eagles as the ensigns leaped first onto the battlements, and the tiny figures of their companies pouring behind them. Their cheering came back to him, through the whistle and whirr of missiles. Nearer, the Third Gallican, with its auxiliaries, was going over the earthwork, the columns jostling forward around their standards as dense and slow as the queues going in to a show at the Circus. At their head with the eagles, mounted and scarlet-cloaked, was Probus, commander of the main assault.

On the battlements the stir of fighting spread. The faint cheering and clash of arms awoke in Aurelian a regret that he was not up there. He saw the silver eagles move out to right and left, and the red success pennants go up, until the whole sector of wall between the battlements was in Roman hands. He frowned. It had happened in a minute or two. Zenobia could

have left only rearguards up there. Why had she not defended
the sector more stubbornly?

His men on the battlements, now, were attacking the two
bastions; but here they were being firmly resisted, and con-
tained within their sector of wall. On the ground, the Third Gallican was at the foot of the wall. Aurelian could see Probus
prancing his horse to and fro, gesturing, as the ladders went up
against the wall, and ropes came snaking down from the battlements. There was confidence in him, at the ease with which the
plan was proceeding; and within the confidence, a tiny worm
of disquiet, at the apparent lack of resistance.

Through the muted crowd-roar of the advance, and the higher
hubbub of cheers and commands, a new sound came to him. It
was a vast, slow creaking. At first he could not place it, and
it made no impact on his mind.

The groan, the grinding of immense frictions, came louder to
him. A new shouting and scurrying commenced at the foot of the
wall. He glanced at the face of the wall, covered now with
the climbing horde of stormers. No enemy fire hindered them,
yet men were falling from the wall. Why? A group of tiny figures
caught his eye. They were clinging to a patch of wall and, all
together, they seemed to be moving downward. Why? But—
yes, there it was! The wall was moving.

A part of the wall was sinking downward, and the crack in
the wall, as he watched it, ran up to the top, widened in a pitch-
black yawn, branched off in a score of hairlines, and—crash!—a
section of battlement came down. Thunderous sounds came
from underground at the base of the wall, and tremors came to
him through the earth.

His men on the battlements were waving, shouting. Probus
was galloping away from the wall, signalling his columns to go
back. Patches of the wall were bulging outward, rising like
swellings on a body, breaking up into the shapes of their pushed-
out stones, and there was a great, grinding subsidence along the

crack, the whole wall sagging down, and a crash of battlements that fell and rained in jagged fragments upon the legion beneath.

The whole wall, from one bastion to the next, bulged out and came down like a cliff. Aurelian saw his two assault towers bend back like reeds, and topple, and disappear in the long, appalling crash of the wall's collapse, in the immense cloud of saffron dust that boiled up and rolled out across the plain.

The earth shook. The thunder rolled on. The dust cloud bellied across the plain, and out of it there shot an army of huge, bounding boulders, smashing through the thick of the advancing legions.

The boulders rolled to a stop, but the dust came on and enveloped Aurelian and his officers. It seemed minutes after when the dust had passed, and they were able to wipe their blinded eyes and clear their choking throats. Aurelian saw the city. He saw that although the sector of wall had fallen, the two flanking bastions still stood, each looking down on a ragged fringe of wall. He knew then that Zenobia had done this deliberately.

But why? She had smashed his towers. They lay prostrate, askew, half buried in the immense mound of rubble that had spilled out over the plain. She had wiped out his storm troops; no stir of life showed beneath the rubble, of all the men who had been trapped.

But she had opened her city to him. She must know that he had more men, enough to carry through the assault. Even now Probus—good Probus, brave, indestructible old bear—was riding to and fro, rallying the survivors of the Third Gallican, forming them up to go in through the gap, signalling—there were the pennants—for reserves.

Aurelian gave orders for another legion to move up behind the Third Gallican. The tiny scarlet splash of Probus's cloak was bobbing forward. The columns were swarming forward over the rubble mound.

Aurelian, far enough back to see what Probus could not see, realized, as the last of the dust-haze lifted, why Zenobia had opened her wall.

He saw her trap. He knew what she had been building behind those screens.

Behind the fallen wall she had built a new wall. It was only half the height of the main wall, and it was roughly built of demolished buildings; but it went back in a deep loop, so that troops attacking it would come under fire from all sides; and Aurelian knew that it would be packed with artillery.

Probus's horse was stepping through the rubble. Scattered alongside were the leading files of infantry. The mound and the plain behind were covered with black clusters of advancing troops. They were moving, in crowds, into the jaws that the city had opened to engulf them.

The volleys from the wall began. Now that the shock of surprise was over, Aurelian had no time to feel pity for his men. There was Probus, riding forward into a blizzard of missiles, and there were his men, swarming forward, cheering, dying. Aurelian looked beyond the butchery, at tomorrow. This, for the time being, was the end. His men were spent. He had sent to Europe for reinforcements, in spite of the peril this entailed, but they would be slow in coming. It would take time to bring more materials across the desert.

And would he be able to keep his men in hand till he was ready for another major effort? What else had she in store, this astonishing woman who had been bold and ingenious enough to topple her wall on his men?

His soldiers were under bombardment from the wall, on all sides, and the archers in the bastions were firing into their rear. The litter of dead thickened on the ground. At last the trumpets uttered the jaunty signal of defeat. The survivors ebbed back. Last of them, on a horse which picked its way slowly and disdainfully over the rubble, looking back over his shoulder, scarlet cloak fluttering, was Probus.

*

After this, Zenobia came to the wall every day and spoke to the Roman soldiers. They howled at her and showered more arrows. She seemed invulnerable, and the superstitious dread of her grew among them.

She did not taunt them. She told them to go home. Had they not seen for themselves that they would never take her city? There were no riches to be had here, only graves. Why should they die for their commander's quarrel? Let them go home to their wives and children, and live to fight again in other places.

Her words were well-chosen. The legionaries kept up the siege, but for the time being their offensive spirit was broken. Their hatred of her was greater than ever. Indeed, it seemed to them that they lived in a nightmare from which only her death could deliver them. Yet their hatred, an unstable compound of many emotions, might be transformed, in a flash, into a stampede of defeatism. They might easily take their revenge, salvage their vanity, upon the body of their own emperor.

Aurelian understood this, and one day he came to answer her. Hostilities had ceased, and he mounted the rubble of the collapsed wall without interference. When he reached the top he saw her, on her new wall, not far away and at an equal height with him. Behind him, Scrofa and Probus were still climbing through the rubble. At his right hand was his shield-bearer, Maxin. The boy seemed unaware either of Zenobia's presence or of his duty to protect Aurelian. He was leaning on the shield, gazing into the distance.

Facing her, Aurelian experienced a curious, almost exultant sense of kinship. She had withstood him, giving blow for blow. But the fear that was growing in him was not of her; it was of

his own men. That superficial thing, the rough, warm comrade-
ship of soldiers, no longer united him with them. He walked
alone in their midst, seeing them as tomorrow's enemies. He
could feel close to no one in his camp. Even Probus and the staff
officers must be thinking of themselves as possible successors.
Aurelian was a self-sufficient man. No other situation but this
could have produced the emotion that he felt: loneliness. He
did not recognize loneliness in his thoughts, but it manifested
itself in a deadness of spirit.

Loneliness made him look at her with a new recognition. He
was alone here. Who was close to him except her, his enemy?
Who else was equal to him in spirit? He despised, as every
leader does at such times, the weakness that made his men sullen
in adversity. He felt remote from them, and the nearer to her.
He knew that she must also be facing the danger of mutiny.
There were fainthearts and traitors enough around her. She, too,
must feel alone, threatened by those she was leading. He and
she had wrestled, and displayed the same qualities. They were in
the same situation now. He felt a fascinated desire to strive on,
testing the limits of her capacities; but he could not hate her.
On the one hand, the obsession to master her; on the other, this
strange kinship, this admiration; the opposed feelings leaped up
in him, blended like the colours in a flame.

She looked fresh, youthful, commanding, as she spoke to his
men. He waited for her to pause, so that he could answer, but
she saw him and called, "Hallo, there, Aurelian! Have you come
for some advice? You need it, for you have been ill-advised so
far. Stay and listen. I promise you will not be harmed."

"Others have listened too long to you. You promised your
people an empire. You have lost the lands they possessed. Will
you throw away their lives as well?"

"Who has thrown away more lives, you or I? Roman soldiers,
look at your dead heaped beneath my walls."

"Men of Palmyra! Three months ago this woman called herself queen of the East. What is she now?"

"Too much for you, Aurelian. When are you going to attack again?" There was laughter from the men on the battlements. "What is the matter? Why don't you attack? Does something make you hesitate?"

"We have reinforcements coming, and more after them, and more again if need be. You have only yourselves. We have the world behind us. Rome is the world. A handful cannot win against the world. Surrender now, before it is too late."

"Go home, before it is too late. You, Aurelian—how long dare you stay here? You are not loved in Rome. If you stay away much longer, they will find another emperor."

"They will see me soon enough, and you will be with me, Zenobia, at the end of a cord."

A shout from Scrofa attracted Aurelian's attention. He saw Zenobia looking to her left. An archer on the bastion was drawing his bow. Aurelian glanced at Maxin, expecting him to draw close with the protecting shield; but the boy did not budge. In the second before the archer released his shaft, Aurelian stood his ground. If he leaped down to safety, or ran to wrench the shield from Maxin, the enemy soldiers would yell derision. He saw Scrofa knock Maxin sprawling and seize the shield. The arrow was coming. He turned, but not quickly enough to avoid it. The impact against his left shoulder spun him half round. Scrofa, too late, was in front of him with the shield.

Aurelian put his hand on Scrofa's shoulder and moved him aside. He stepped forward. The shaft protruded from his left shoulder. "Is this your promised truce, Zenobia?"

She was giving orders to her officers. She turned to him. "Here is the man who did it."

A moment later a body was flung over the battlements. She called, "And your shield-bearer, Aurelian? What will you do with him?"

Maxin had climbed to his feet. Probus was standing behind him with drawn sword.

Aurelian turned on his heels and made his way down through the rubble. When he reached the ground he sat on a slab of stone and let Scrofa take hold of the arrow. Maxin, guarded by Probus, waited negligently. Aurelian said, "Bring him here."

He sat with lowered head, ignoring the boy in front of him, while Scrofa pulled the shaft from his shoulder. He uttered no sound. Lumps of muscle gathered behind his jaws and the sweat shone on his forehead. When the bandage was knotted he expelled a long, harsh breath and raised his head wearily. He looked into Maxin's eyes. They were as blank as shutters. He said, "You little fool."

Probus spoke. "Let me kill him. Or do you want it done by law?"

Aurelian shook his head. He addressed Maxin. "You did not even have the courage to kill me yourself. You are no soldier. You live with the slaves and hobnob with them. That is all you are, a slave. Why should I give you a soldier's punishment? Be a slave if that is what you want, and shovel muck, and live in shame. Take him to the stables."

He sat stiff-backed until Maxin had gone, then he relaxed. Probus, puzzled and compassionate, was close by him; yet he sat, with lowered head and sagging shoulders, a man utterly alone. He looked up, and in his face there was a weariness that no one had ever seen there before. He said to Probus, "I had thought to adopt him as my son."

*

He remained in his tent for the rest of that day and all the next day. He had slept soundly through the second night, when he was awakened by voices in dispute. His tent was in shadow, but a dazzling stripe of morning sunlight was unrolling through the doorway. He recognized the voices of two of his staff officers, and heard Lucipor answering. "If you were Jupiter the Best himself, I wouldn't let you wake my master up."

He raised himself awkwardly from the bed. The stiffness of his wounded shoulder, within the constricting bandage, took him by surprise. He was unsteady on his feet for a few moments, but the fever and pain of the previous two days were gone. He rinsed his face, picked up his sword belt, and went out.

The sunlight made him dizzy again. It took him a moment to see and hear clearly. The first voice that came through to him was Lucipor's. "You shouldn't be up, master. Not in your state. And cover your head up!"

He saw two officers snapping up in salute and uttering simultaneous barks of "Sir!" Behind them, stiffly at attention, was the centurion Scrofa. One of the officers pointed. "Sir."

Aurelian's gaze followed the officer's moving finger. The camp was a desolation bathed in white sunlight. The earth was furrowed by tracks, pocked with craters, scarred with fire-blackened patches, untidy with tree stumps, burst sandbags, dumps of bricks and timber, the charred wrecks of siege engines, the ruins of forts, galleries ripped open, the disused roads petering into the ravine, the vast mound of the collapsed wall and around it a litter of unburied dead. Across this field of defeat crowds of men were hurrying, all in one direction—away from the city wall that rose, battered but unconquered, to mock them.

The officer was speaking, but Aurelian was not listening. His senses were trying to take in what he saw. On the wall, flashes played. They were splashes of sunlight, concentrated, too dazzling for the sight to bear, and they cut to and fro in front of Aurelian's eyes, hurting him, smiting his mind numb.

Scrofa said, "Sir, she has turned the sun against us."

As the flashes of light moved on the wall, beams played over the ground in the Roman camp. Aurelian saw tents burning.

The men hurrying back were carrying their gear, and some were pulling back the siege engines.

Aurelian's thoughts clicked into functioning shape. He said, "Reflectors."

"Yes, sir." It was Scrofa. "I saw them at sunrise, when I came out for the morning prayer." Scrofa, as first centurion of the Third Gallican, was its senior priest in the worship of Mithras, God of Light. "Soon as the sun was up a bit, I guessed what they were, and I called out the duty officer."

The duty officer said, "I've ordered all the men to pull back out of range."

Aurelian nodded. The reflectors, he knew, must be sheets of polished metal mounted on wooden frames so that they would swivel. He counted ten of them. The splashes of light which they cast darted over the ground like sunbeams thrown by a child's mirror. Tents burst into flames under their focused rays. Wicker screens caught fire. The woodwork of the artillery scorched and charred, and the elastic cords snapped. Men screamed as the shafts of heat shrivelled their skins. Sentries came slithering down from the earthwork to shelter in the dead ground behind it, or vanished into the forts.

Three months of siege, and here was his army, hurrying away from the city walls, like an army in flight! Back! Back! The voices and the trumpets clamoured. Back, five hundred, eight hundred, a thousand yards, out of range of those deadly rays! They were setting up their tents again, wheeling the dart-guns into line again, re-forming their circle around Palmyra.

They were safe now, but they were helpless. While those reflectors were up there, they dared not approach the city. They had no means of dealing with the reflectors; no material to make similar weapons.

Scrofa stood to attention in front of Aurelian. He was clad in shining brass corslet and crested helmet, in defiance of the enemy, although his men, the third of his legion that survived, slouched about half naked, gaunt, sun-blackened, kerchiefs on their necks. His short white cloak, scrubbed and sun bleached, flaunted from his shoulder. His medals hung on his chest. But inside the breastplate he was a skeleton, dried by the sun to that leanness which makes a man look a foot taller, his legs long and hairy like those of some giant spider, his face roasted like a chestnut, his lips black and broken by blood-raw cracks.

He looked at Aurelian, tall as himself, gaunt as himself, twin to himself. He looked straight into Aurelian's fever-sunken eyes; his own eyes, the eyes of a sergeant-major, unchanged by all he had seen in these last three months. "Sir!" His body was rigid and respectful; his face was impassive, but his eyes were cruel with the scrutiny of a whole army waiting to judge its commander. "Sir—what now?"

CHAPTER SEVENTEEN

WHAT NOW?

THE historian Flavius Vopiscus has recorded a letter which Aurelian sent to the Roman Senate at this time.

The Roman people speak with contempt of the war which I am waging against a woman. They are ignorant of both the character and power of Zenobia. It is impossible to enumerate her warlike preparations, of stones, arrows and every kind of missile weapon. Every part of the wall is provided with two or three dart-guns, and her engines hurl artificial fire at us. The fear of punishment has endowed her with a desperate courage. Yet still I trust in the guardian deities of Rome, who have always watched over me.

He was driven to justify himself in this way because he had heard from his wife that his enemies in Rome were busy again, seeking to discredit him because of his failure to win a quick victory. It had not needed Zenobia to remind him that he dared not stay away much longer, either from Rome or from the threatened western frontiers.

On the other hand, he dared not admit defeat. Weighing up the dangers, he decided that the wrath of his army was to be less feared than a continuance of the war. In defiance of the legions he made a last attempt to secure peace on reasonable terms. Vopiscus records this letter, too, and Zenobia's reply.

From Aurelian, Emperor of the Roman World and Recoverer of the East, to Zenobia. You should have done of your own free will what I now command. I bid you surrender, and I promise that your lives shall be spared. You, Zenobia, together with your children, shall go free, but you shall dwell wherever I, acting in accord with the wish of the most noble Senate, shall instruct. You shall hand over to the Roman Treasury your jewels, your gold, your silks, your horses and camels. As to the people of Palmyra, they shall suffer no penalty. Their property and their civil rights shall be guaranteed.

From Zenobia, Queen of the East, to Aurelian. What you want in war must be gained by valour alone. You demand my surrender. Do you not know that my ancestress Cleopatra preferred to die as a queen rather than to live in defeat, with whatever honours? The Bedouin are harassing your army. The Arabs of the south will rise in our support. Even now, an army is marching from Persia to my relief. When it arrives you will sing a less arrogant tune. You speak as a victor. Why not recognize your true position and depart?

Zenobia's letter put strength into Aurelian, for it showed him that there was no alternative but to finish her off. It also showed him, unexpectedly, how he might do so.

The letter had been handed over, beneath a flag of truce, by Worod. Throughout the siege no messages had been received from him. Perhaps he had been too closely watched. However, he must have been left alone with the letter for a few moments before it was sealed, for at the foot of it were six words scrawled in his handwriting.

These six words were the key that enabled Aurelian to defeat Palmyra.

CHAPTER EIGHTEEN

AT BAY

LESS than a month later a crowd gathered outside the gates of Zenobia's palace to demand that the city should surrender.

It was neither a large nor a menacing crowd, milling and babbling among the pillars of the Great Avenue. It came from the alleys of the poor; mothers, gowned to the mouth in white, holding up their potbellied babies as if they hoped that someone might see and pity; peasants, coppery skeletons in loincloths; small boys with big, mournful eyes and flies crawling on their faces; disabled soldiers; and an unsightly contingent from the army of beggars.

Three weeks ago the city's wells had gone dry. It had happened suddenly, mysteriously, like an intervention of the gods.

The population had suffered enough already. The troops had the intoxicant of action, the joy of successful defiance to sustain them; but for the civilians the siege had been a time of hunger, of cowering in their houses, of leaden-footed time, of fear always present, fed by ignorance, by rumour, by the distant roar of battle, by the glare of fireballs in the night, by huge stones falling from the sky.

The soldiers had fought magnificently. The knights, sons of the great merchant families, were Roman in their culture, but they despised Rome. As merchants, they were tired of being the middlemen when they might have all the profits of the East. Zenobia's magnetism and her successful defence had inspired them.

But when the wells went dry the confidence of the soldiers vanished as quickly as the water. For want of water, the cattle died and hunger came to aid thirst. A rumour spread that Aurelian had offered a lenient peace, and that Zenobia had refused. For the moment she had kept her soldiers at their posts by promising that help was on the way; but the people were in a panic, and now a thousand of them cried for peace outside the palace.

The gates swung open. The crowd rushed forward. Its shouts were eager, as if it expected the beautiful Zenobia to come out with food and water and news of peace. Instead, the palace guard rode out, a column of horsemen in two ranks, gorgeous in yellow and scarlet, with flashing silver accoutrements. At their head was Prince Wahab.

The crowd stopped running. It was a wondering crowd now, sight-seeing, admiring the big, sleek horses and big, well-fed guardsmen. Wahab's sword rasped from its scabbard and flashed above his head. The crowd was fascinated. Wahab's horse broke into a trot, and the two ranks of the guard fanned out with raised swords.

The horsemen cried *"Ay-aaah!"* and rode into the crowd, their swords slashing. The crowd broke. Screaming, they dodged among the pillars, colliding, trampling, while the guard reined and pranced their horses for the kill. Wahab rode in ecstasy. There was no more crowd in front of him, only the expanse of the avenue bathed in sunlight, a few figures running towards the colonnade on the far side, and behind him, scattered on the pavements, bundles of rags, of which some stirred. The battle cry of the guard maddened him. *"Ay-aaah! Ay-aaah!"*

This was marvellous. It was escape from the nursery, from his mother's arms. His horse's flanks were hot, sweaty, and resilient between his knees. He screamed *"Ay-aaah!"*

He was a man, a hunter. A few of the two-legged animals were still running. He galloped after them. He drew up to a fugitive, saw the head thrown back, the arms pistoning up and down with clenched fists, glimpsed the face all ghastly with fear, and struck. Oh, the excitement of that scream! The bright spurt of blood! The shock of bone's resistance to his sword! He was a man. This was better than lying on cushions in the palace, playing with soft girls, saying, "Yes, Mother" and "No, Mother." Every body that fell beneath his sword was a revenge against his life. "*Ay-aaah!*"

In front of him a fugitive turned to face him, mad eyes glaring out of a skull, chest heaving with the agony of breath. The man's arms were limp at his sides. He glared, beyond fear, and waited for the sword. He gasped out the words: "Brave one— why don't you—fight—the Romans?"

Wahab could hardly see the man for anger. His blow went wild and the man lurched away. "Mother's boy!"

Wahab scuffled his horse round and struck again. The man went down on all fours, blood gushing from an almost severed arm. "Commander of the guard—kills children—never see him on the wall."

Wahab rode his horse forward. With bit and spurs he set it trampling on the man. The voice raved, died into throat noises, silence. There was only a still, soft heap beneath the hoofs. Wahab was panting and could not see for tears. He kept his horse high-stepping on the body, shaking its mane and snorting at the smell of blood. A hand fell on his bridle. It was his adjutant. He awoke.

The men had formed up again, waiting. Their eyes were blank, but Wahab imagined he saw derision there. They had heard the man. He wanted them all to die, so that no one should be alive who had heard those words. He wanted to— Hysteria shook him. He did not know what he wanted to do, only to wipe out those words, to be a man like all the others.

They were waiting to go back into the palace. Hysteria became a hot resolve. He would show them. They did not know him. *She* did not know him. He rode to the head of the column and called, "Right wheel—forward!"

He led them away from the palace. He did not know where he was going. He only wanted to ride, towards the walls, to be seen by the people going towards the walls.

There were few in the streets to see him. This was a city fainting with hunger. The streets were empty and silent. Many houses were in ruins. Wahab wished that more people could see him. His horse was a glossy blood bay. He wore the uniform his mother had designed: a scarlet tunic fitting close at the waist, with its skirt split to the calf, loose yellow silk trousers, and a golden helmet studded with rubies, with belt and scabbard to match. He rode straight-backed, knowing he was handsome. He was taking his men to the wall. She would not let him fight, and he was laughed at for it. Now he would fight. Those men behind him would die, and what they had heard would die with them. There were few to see him, but he would make the city talk of him.

He rode towards the south gate. It was all waste ground here, bumpy, cratered, befouled. There had been crowded alleys here, and square white mansions thrusting up among them. That was in the vague dream-time, eternities ago, called peace. Soldiers went to and fro on military errands, and he was furious when they glanced at him without interest. The huge catapults stood in rows, and their crews lay around them, and some of them laughed as he rode past. He was the queen's son, an officer, and they laughed at him. Hysteria drove him on.

Banks of rubble were piled against the south gate, and balks of timber were wedged up against it, but there was a smaller gate let into it which could still be opened. Sentries kept watch on the wall. Beneath, the guard battalion sprawled at ease, dirty, bearded, swarthy men crowded wherever there was shade. They were glancing his way, and some were indifferent and some laughed.

What right had they to laugh? Why did they not salute him? He was the soldier, in his scarlet and yellow, not these grimy ruffians. He was borne on a torrent of anger, dizzy, obsessed by the need to shock all these people into taking notice of him.

The gate commander strode towards him, a spare, tired man in a Roman tunic, wearing a Roman fringe of beard. His face was weary, and in a tired, impatient voice he said, "What does your Highness want?"

"Don't your men stand up when their prince rides past?"

"Your Highness, they haven't eaten today. Let them keep their energy for a Roman attack. Why has your Highness come here?"

Wahab felt like a small boy facing a stern tutor. It always turned out like this when he tried to assert himself. He was looking at the gate. He clutched the reins tightly but he could not stop his hands from quivering. He was sure the officer could see. He clenched his teeth to control himself. A thought glimmered in his mind, one coherent idea in a chaos of anger. "Open the gate."

The officer did not even gratify him by looking surprised. "What for?"

"Don't ask questions." He was lost in a stormy night of anger. Only one idea was articulate in him: he must go through the gate. "Do as I tell you."

"Have you orders from the queen?"

"Do as I tell you." He heard his own voice rise to a screech and hated it. "I am her son."

A small smile turned down the corners of the officer's mouth. It was the kind of grown-up smile that maddens a wilful child. Wahab screamed, "Open, I tell you!"

The officer's voice was patronizing. "Now, your Highness, what do you want to go out there for? You might get hurt. You might even get hurt if you stay here, and I wouldn't like to face your mother if that happened."

"Open the gate!"

"Go back to the palace, your Highness. There's plenty of

room in the courtyard to drill your soldiers." The slightest emphasis on the last word, the slightest smile, made it a blade in Wahab's breast.

"Open the gate. I'll show you how to fight. Look at you all, lying around. No wonder nothing happens." The words poured out of him, his voice shrill, with the sound of tears in it. "I'll go out there and fight the Romans. I'll call for Aurelian. I'll show him what the son of Odenathus can do. That is who I am—do you hear?—the son of Odenathus. I shall be king, and I shall kill you. Do you hear? How dare you stand there with that grin on your face? I shall kill you, kill you!"

"Your Highness, if you want the gate opened, go back and ask the queen."

Wahab was trembling. He turned in his saddle and called to his men. "Forward! Open the gate!"

The officer, in a conversational voice, said, "At ease, men."

The horsemen stood fast. Wahab cried, "Forward, I say!"

They did not stir. It was the last humiliation. He screamed, "I'll have you all flogged for this! I'll have you hanged, every one of you!"

From the men sprawling at the roadside came a soft rumbling of laughter. Wahab whipped out his sword. "You, too," he shouted at the officer. "I'll kill you."

His sword came down. The officer, without even moving his feet, snaked his body away from the blow and seized Wahab's wrist. His grip hurt Wahab, but it was not so painful as the sight of his smile. Under the iron pressure, Wahab's fingers parted and his sword fell. The officer called to Wahab's adjutant. "Mussad, take the young gentleman home."

Mussad rode alongside and took Wahab's reins. Wahab sat limp while the infantry officer slipped his sword back into its scabbard. His madness had burst and now he was weak, chilled inside, oppressed by grief and shame.

He sat his horse while Mussad led him home, and the column

trotted behind. He did not care what they thought, or what the soldiers at the roadside thought, or the people in the streets who turned to look. He wept for shame, shamelessly as a child.

*

Zenobia had been watching from her palace window when her son charged the crowd. She said, "Wasn't he splendid? I wonder where he's off to now? For a ride through the town, I expect. It will cheer the people up."

Longinus remained silent. Worod, who was also at the window, said, "His Highness did not cheer them"—he indicated the corpses—"up very much."

Zenobia's voice was scornful. "A few ruffians!"

"The people, my lady." Such boldness, from Worod, **was** new. No one is more impudent than the weakling who at last thinks he has the upper hand. Worod, as a matter of fact, had organized the demonstration himself; just as he had let it leak out in the city that Zenobia had refused a fair peace offer. He was a timid and treacherous man. He was quite complacent about his character. Why should he not be? He wanted a quiet life, no crises, no wars. He had worked for the Romans because they stood for "no change." Now, in spite of his efforts, war had come. If it went on, everyone would be wiped out. He would be wiped out. This was not to be countenanced, so he had made his bid to end it.

Three weeks ago he had smuggled out to Aurelian the message that had caused the wells to dry up.

The Romans, of course, had long known the number and capacity of the wells in the city. It was only a few years ago, however, that Rufinus, with the complicity of Worod, had sent a surveyor who had discovered that all the five wells in the city, which ran in an irregular line from south to north, were fed by the same underground stream. This stream rose in the hills to the south, and fed the Spring of Efca, just outside the walls, before it entered the city. That was why Zenobia had been compelled to leave the spring unpoisoned.

The best of systems have their dark corners of inefficiency. Rufinus must certainly have sent a report to Rome; but it must have lodged in some bureaucrat's dusty document-chest. When months of siege went by without any move by the Romans against the water supply, Worod guessed that the report could never have reached army headquarters. He also guessed that Rufinus would most likely have kept a copy of it in his own archives. With only a few seconds in which to add his own message to Zenobia's letter, Worod had scribbled a few words directing Aurelian's attention towards those archives.

The hint had been acted on. Aurelian had dug tunnels, dammed the underground stream, and cut off Palmyra's water supply. The city was dying of thirst. Worod gazed on its suffering with the smug satisfaction of a man who is in no doubt of his own rectitude. He glowed with virtue. The city must surely surrender soon. It would be saved from slaughter. *He* would be saved from slaughter. And so, for the first time in his career, he spoke boldly to Zenobia. "Lady Zenobia, swords can silence a few, but not all. For if you kill all, who will keep out the Romans? And believe me, it will not wet the throats of the thirsty to see your son riding through the streets in his fine new uniform."

"My people are loyal. You must not be misled by a few cowards."

"Your people, my lady, would sell you, your son, and your city for a cup of water and a crust of bread."

"That is a foul thing to say. My people love me. My soldiers still fight for me."

"Yes, because you have promised them that help is on the way."

"And so it is!"

"Is it? From where? You sent to Persia. What did their king answer? The woman who would not have his son could not have his army. You sent to Armenia. Forgive me for being coarse, my lady, but the Armenians will fight when roses grow out of my backside. You counted on Aurelian's enemies in the West. They have not stirred, though he has taken even more men from Europe. The Bedouin once helped you. Where are they now? Aurelian wiped out one of their tribes, and sent gold to all the rest, and told them to choose between the sword, if they opposed him, and gold, if they helped him. Now they are bringing his supplies across the desert for him. So much for your promised help, Lady Zenobia, and when your men find out they will not be so loyal, I promise you."

"Speak for yourself, Worod. They are men. You always were a wretched little coward."

"Say 'realist,' my lady. That is a better word. The choice is between giving in sensibly, now, and saving our lives—and waiting till the storming parties come over the wall, to cut all our throats."

"If it comes to that, let them cut our throats. I am Zenobia, and I will not surrender. But don't worry about your poor throat, Worod. Time is on our side and, if we hold out, something will happen to rid us of the Romans. What do you say, Longinus?"

"For once I am with Worod."

Zenobia sat down, slumped deep in her chair, elbows on its arms, fingers laced across her breast. Her head was lowered, her eyes agleam with thought, while their gaze remained fixed in contempt upon the two men. She was like a woman brooding before a love-quarrel, calm yet filled with stirring power, passive yet on the verge of some proud, destructive act. "You are both the same. Oh, you men, you feeble, frightened creatures! The Persians, the Armenians, the Bedouin, these famous barbarians in the West, I have given them all their chance—I, a woman. And they, all these warriors, these men with spines of straw, they throw the chance away. They desert me. And now you desert me, too."

"You are being silly and self-pitying," Longinus said. "Of course, I'm against this war. I want it to end. I've never said otherwise. But while it's on I'll stand by you. Who told you about the reflectors, which Archimedes invented five hundred years ago, and the cranes, and worked out the calculations to make the wall fall down?"

"I don't want boasts," she said bitterly. "I want help. Quickly. Find water. Make it rain. Invent new engines. Do something." She thumped the arm of her chair with a small clenched fist. "Do something, do something, do something!"

Worod had gone to the door and entered into consultation with a servant. Now he turned to Zenobia, and he smiled with relish, as if he had found just the surprise to produce at this moment. "Lady, his Highness is here. I do not think you would like him to be kept waiting."

He beckoned, and the adjutant Mussad came in, propelling Wahab gently by the shoulder. The boy shuffled apathetically, as if he would not have moved without the older man to steer him. Worod sank down in a low bow which he contrived to invest with an air of gloating. Zenobia rose. Her "Darling!" was eager and surprised. Wahab stood slackly in the centre of the room, flushed and tear-smudged, his helmet askew, looking like a small boy dressed up to play soldiers who has fallen down and hurt himself. Zenobia started forward with another "Darling?" this time interrogative and faintly dismayed.

Worod closed the door behind Mussad. Zenobia said, "What is it, darling? Have you fallen from your horse? Are you hurt?"

She tried to take her son's two hands in hers. Wahab pulled his hands away. His face puckered sulkily. He muttered, "Oh, leave me alone." He sniffled, then perked his face up. "They wouldn't do what I told them. The officer at the gate laughed at me. And my men wouldn't do what I told them. I want them flogged."

"Lady"—Worod's voice was sleek—"his Highness only wanted the south gate opened, that was all. He only wanted to ride out with the guard and attack the Roman camp."

Wahab lifted his tear-streaked face, in a pathetic attempt at defiance. "My father would have done it."

Zenobia uttered a little "Oh!" Longinus laid a hand on Wahab's shoulder. "Your father would have had more sense. But you showed a good spirit, boy."

Wahab twisted away, rejecting with a new blush of anger the adult gesture of condescension. Zenobia clutched her hands at her breast. "But this is impossible! Wahab, my pet, it isn't true, is it?"

Wahab glowered at her in silence.

"Wahab, little lotus, my darling, who put this mad idea into your head? Tell me. You couldn't have thought of it yourself. Was it Mussad? Was it Zabda? I'll have the skin pulled off him with pincers, whoever he is."

Wahab muttered, "It was my idea. Is that so strange?"

"What made you think of it? Don't you know it upsets me to think of you in danger? You mustn't upset your mother, little falcon. She has so much to worry about already. You must stay at the palace, and guard her, and drive bad people away, as you did today. You were wonderful, darling. I was so proud of you."

Wahab lifted his head and shouted, "What sort of fool do you think I am? You want me to play with toy soldiers in the palace. You think I'll be satisfied to stick my sword in blind beggars. You're only laughing at me. And *he's* laughing at me"— a toss of the chin at Longinus—"and *he's*"—this time at Worod—"laughing at me. Everyone laughs at me, and it's all your fault."

"But, little one—"

"You see—" The boy's voice was desperate. " 'Little one!' "

"Of course, of course." She was smiling, soothing. "You're not a little one. You're a man. You're an officer. You're captain of the royal guard."

"Yes." His voice, hoarse with puberty, cracked suddenly. "And they won't do what I tell them. And I don't blame them either. Captain of the guard! You had me in this room for days, with all your women kneeling round me, stitching and pinning and trying on materials, the red and the blue, and try it a little lower, and let's see how the black and silver go together. You dress me up like a dancing girl, and all the guard in the same colours, and then you wonder why they laugh at me."

It was true, Worod thought. At the height of the siege she had gone from a staff conference to a dressmaking session; from the battlements to her daughter's bedroom; just as in the past three minutes she had changed from fierce autocrat to fluttering mother.

"You don't think of me." The boy's voice raved on, husky and broken by squeaks. "You want me out of the way, playing with toys like a child, while you go to the walls and show off."

"Darling, you mustn't say things like that. Don't you know how you hurt me?"

"It's true. You want all the cheers for yourself."

"Wahab, my precious, everything I do is for you. How can you say I don't think of you? I've gone through so much for you. I want to give you kingdoms. I want to give you everything. It is for you that I fight on the wall."

"No, it isn't. It's for yourself. You go because you love it. Philomene shows off with new dresses. You show off with swords, and chariots, and battles, and telling the generals what to do. You're no different from her. It's only yourself you think of. You don't want kingdoms for me, you want them for yourself. Other women have husbands, but you like to make men run about doing what you tell them, and the more countries you rule over the more men you can see doing it."

"Oh!" Zenobia clapped her hand to her mouth. "You hear him? Longinus, do you hear how my own child speaks to me?"

"I didn't know he was so intelligent. The boy has seen through you, Zenobia. Yes, you love him. You love him too much. That's why he's too soft inside to be the man he'd like to be. But you have a lover to whom you are just as devoted. Your lover's name is power. You've lived without a man since your husband died because you've had power to embrace. A man seeks power for its fruits, rationally. You woo power as a woman, sensually. And, like a woman, you will pursue your lover, insensately, to destruction."

It was Zenobia's turn to flush. "Be quiet! How dare you talk like that in front of my boy?" She held out her hand. "Wahab, precious, come with me. We'll find Julia, and we'll all have lunch together, shall we? All on our own, as we used to, yes?"

"I don't want any lunch. I'm going."

"Wahab, where—?"

"I'm going! Isn't that enough?" Wahab's voice rose to a shout again. "It's none of your business where I go, and leave me alone, and don't run after me. I hate you, and I'm sick of being pawed about, and you can't even fight the Romans!"

He ran out of the room.

Neither Longinus nor Worod dared break the silence. Zenobia stood in the centre of the room, her hands still clasped, her eyes thunderstruck.

The two men waited till the stormy violence of her breathing had diminished. Worod coughed. Zenobia turned to him. Her eyes were vague for a moment, then the lights grew sharp in them again. She said, in a voice that was quiet, melodious, and full of decision, "We are going to beat the Romans."

She began to walk up and down, looking at the floor. Her arms were folded now across her breast. "He will see what his mother can do." Her voice remained calm, musical.

Her pacing continued. "The Romans are worn out. They

could not face another battle. If the Persians come, they are finished."

Worod said, "My lady, the Persians will not come."

She looked up at him, triumph in her eyes. "They will come."

"Not unless you agree—" Worod paused, his mouth slack with astonishment. "You mean that you will marry their prince?"

"Why not, if it means victory? I would do more than that for my children."

"Once you were afraid to let the Persians come here."

"One thing at a time. If I beat Aurelian, will anyone else in the world be too much for me?" She laughed. "I shall tame that Persian fop, don't you worry!"

Worod stroked his chin. His eyes shifted about the room. He was defeated by this new situation. Playing for time, he said, "We should have to smuggle another messenger out." It occurred to him that an envoy sufficiently bribed might ensure the failure of the mission. "It will need a good man. Shall I find someone?"

"Yes. Wait—" Zenobia paused at the window and gazed across the city. "I can't take chances. What if the messenger didn't get there? What could I do but wait, and eat my heart out, and wonder what had happened? What if he didn't put my message well enough? What if the need arose to plead, to argue? Could a messenger do that? Could a messenger remind them what Zenobia looks like?" She turned to face the two men. "I will go myself."

CHAPTER NINETEEN

THE FOURTH MEETING

IT WAS three hours after midnight when the camp orderly officer was called from his bed. A woman had been brought in by one of the patrols. She was in the outer compartment of the duty tent with two men of the patrol and the officer of their cohort.

The dim light of the oil lamp that lit the tent, a tiny clay saucer with a spout from which the flame issued, had scarcely been sufficient for him to tell the time from the waterclock. It warred feebly with the shadows and failed to reach the woman. The orderly officer peered at her with sore, still unfocused eyes, while he listened to the patrol's report. He had an impression of large, vaguely lit eyes, a small white face, dishevelled auburn hair. She seemed familiar, but he could not place her, and he felt it beneath his dignity to step nearer. She was young, that much he could see; and she stood with an undaunted lift of the chin, in a soiled, torn robe of green linen.

The patrol, a dozen archers with a signal trumpeter, commanded by a decurion of the Tenth, had been watching the city from a post dug in the mound of the collapsed wall; a trench and breastwork occupied as an observation point at nights, when the reflectors could not operate. In the darkness, the patrol had heard a shout from the top of the wall—they were facing the centre of Zenobia's loop of makeshift wall. A flare had been thrown down from the wall, then another. The balls of light had fallen to the ground, giving off trails of white smoke and an intermittent glare. In the flickering light, as the shouting on the wall had spread, they had seen a woman slide down a rope, drop to the ground at the foot of the wall—and run towards the Roman lines. There had been more flares, more shouts from the walls, a whisper of arrows riddling the darkness, but she had stumbled to safety.

"You are wasting time. Take me to Probus."

Something peremptory in her tone penetrated the officer's sleepy mind. "Who are you? What brings you here?"

"Take me to Probus. I will tell him."

"Have you information? You can tell me."

"Don't waste time. You'll be sorry if you do." The officer stepped closer and looked into her face.

A few minutes later he ushered her into the *praetorium*. Probus glanced up from the map over which he and Aurelian were hunched. He straightened his back. "Philomene!"

Her torn robe scarcely hung together. Through its rents she was all dirt, bruises, bloody scratched patches: for the two men of the patrol who had run out to bring her in had dragged her over the rubble like a sack; but her pose was pert, cool, provocative, as if she were standing in the doorway of a banquet where a dozen dandies awaited her. "Hallo, my old woolly bear. Are you glad to see me back?"

Another pair of eyes glittered at her across the tent. She returned their stare. "Greetings, Caesar. Don't cut my head off yet. I've news for you."

This time her words aroused Probus. He strode towards her, a grin creasing his broad face. "By all the gods! Is this a dream?"

She arched her back voluptuously against his encircling arm. "Do I feel like a dream? Oh, you are glad to see me back. I can tell it." Aurelian, stern and silent, was watching her from the shadows, but she ignored him. "I've missed you so much, woolly bear. Every day since you sent me away I've craved for you. You don't know what it's like being without someone you want. I know you, my big bear. You've never wanted anyone like that. It's like a charcoal fire inside me, day and night." She flexed her back against his arms, taking in happiness through her muscles; utterly at home and unafraid, as if she had never been away from him. "I've been playing up to Zenobia, and telling her how to beat the Romans, and how much I hate that swine Probus, and it was all like a silly dream, because all the time I was thinking, 'How can I get back to him? When can I get back to him?' "

"Probus." Aurelian's voice was harsh. "Get her out of here. We've work to do. We'll talk about her later."

"Wait a moment." Her voice was light and insolent. "Caesar, this is for you, too. I have news that cannot wait. You see, Aurelian, I know you are a man of your word. I know that if you said it was death for me to come back, you meant it. And I knew that I would have to do something big, something really big for you, to be able to come back. I've prepared for a long time. I've gone to the wall every night, and made friends with the sentries, taken them food and wine. You know, the patriotic whore coming to comfort our brave men. Till they got used to seeing me. Tonight my chance came. I went to the wall with a bottle of drugged wine and twenty feet of silk cord round my waist. I put them to sleep all right, the men I went to see, but while I was climbing down the others saw me, and that's when the trouble started. Still, I got here, and I've brought you my peace-offering. Aurelian, you're a hard man but you're not ungenerous, and I'm not going to bargain with you. Here it is— Zenobia has escaped."

He was across the room in three strides, towering over her. "When?"

"She started at midnight. I had to stay with her till she left or I would have warned you in advance." She looked from one man to the other. Probus's Asiatic eyes were gleaming with admiration. Aurelian's eyes were like those of a tiger crouching for the spring. "She is going to Persia. The king has promised her an army if she will marry one of his sons. She has gone in person to accept these terms. She says it will be worth any sacrifice to come upon you with a fresh army, Aurelian."

He gripped her arm. "How did she leave? Where is she making for?"

"I don't know where she's going. She slipped out through the postern of the north gate. She had only one man with her, a *daleel,* a caravan guide. She was dressed like a man, in black Bedouin robes, with a veil and a headcloth, and they were going to crawl over your earthwork in the dark, between the sentry posts. I had to wait with Longinus an hour after she'd gone, and there was no sound from your sentries, so she must have got through."

Aurelian turned to the orderly officer. "I want two troops of Imperial Horse on parade, one to move off in five minutes, in patrol order, the other to start in one hour, with enough re-mounts, food, and water to re-equip the first." He turned back to Philomene. His gaze dwelt on her for a moment. There was a curious darkness in it. "A fine friend you are to Zenobia!"

"Why?" Her eyes were clear and bold. "I'm not in love with *her.*"

He was silent for another moment. Then, "Which way did she head? You must know something."

"She had twelve miles to go on foot. I know that. To the oasis of el Habid. The *daleel* has kinsmen there, and he was going to get racing camels from them, to take him and Zenobia to the Persian frontier."

"That means they've got to reach the Euphrates. Where about on the river?"

"I don't know. All she said was 'This time tomorrow night I'll be on the other side.'"

"Twenty-four hours. And four hours of that on foot. There's only one point on the river she could reach in twenty hours, even on a racing camel."

Probus said, "Sura. It's less than a hundred miles. There are boats there, and a Persian frontier post. But she'll be hard to catch. A racing camel goes half as fast again as a horse."

"She's on foot as far as the oasis. If we don't catch her up, we'll be close behind her. Once she's in sight we may be able to ride her down at the gallop. Two dozen horses ought to be able to ride two camels to death. I'll take the first troop myself. If we do kill some of our horses, the second troop will catch us up with replacements. Probus, you'll be in command of the camp while I'm away."

"What about me?" Philomene was holding Probus's arm, from underneath, like a child. Her face was serene. "Am I forgiven?"

Aurelian paused in the doorway. "Do you know," he said, "we have a good friend in the city. An influential man. He must have known what you knew, and he could not get the information out to me. You're a remarkable girl."

The tent flap fell. A moment later Philomene heard him riding away.

*

There were a few Bedouin families in the black tents at el Habid. They were ready enough with their information, and Aurelian spared them, but he slaughtered their camels as a punishment, and to prevent a rider from setting out to warn Zenobia. She had left a few minutes before his arrival.

The stars were uncertain spots of light pricking the thick darkness; the hills, a curving range which marked his way to the Euphrates, were a vague, thicker blackness on his left. By hills and stars he fixed his course.

There was no reason to suppose that Zenobia would be travelling fast. She would not expect pursuit. The Roman Camel Corps, the only unit that might have intercepted her, was at present operating only on the far side of Palmyra, on the Roman lines of communication. Aurelian set a steady pace to reduce the risk of passing her in the darkness, and ordered silence so that she should not hear his approach.

The warm darkness enclosed him. No sound claimed his attention except the soft rumble of hoofs on clay. He rode towards the moment of climax, through a thick darkness, and he was free from thought or feeling. All of him was in his eyes, watching the darkness rather than trying to penetrate it, patiently measuring its slow graining with light as the hills on his left emerged as shapes of shadow, then slowly took on sharper outline until they were stamped dramatically against a hollow clarity of dawn.

Hoofbeats measured another hour away. The hills curved gently to the north, low, ribbed, burying their brown, rounded spurs in the flat desert floor on which he rode. Grey dawn turned to sun-flushed apple green and to pale summer blue, a vast vault over the earth in which the light became golden. There was no one in sight. Aurelian kept his course. If she turned north or south she would only prolong her journey. North was unlikely, for camels made poor going in the hills. South he would see her, on the flat bare plain.

His reckoning was confirmed when he came to sand and saw camel tracks. They were shallow dents in the sand, not the sharp deep stabs of fresh prints; but they might still be recent, for he saw how quickly the sand trickled back into them. He was approaching an angular protrusion of the sandstone wall, beyond which the line of hills could no longer be seen. Here the range turned sharply away to the north. The line of tracks vanished at the corner: obviously Zenobia had turned it and was keeping close to the foot of the hills.

The sandstone was cliff-steep here, dark red, eroded. The corner presented a silhouette like the rusted edge of a sword against the sky. He peered round it, keeping his men well back. He saw his quarry. Far ahead, two tiny shapes crawled at the foot of the hills.

He sat down, back to the cliff, knees drawn up. His men were watching him with puzzled, impatient frowns. They expected an immediate pursuit. He glanced up, and told them to water their horses. It might be their last chance today, he said. They must make soft balls of meal mixed with water, which they could feed to their beasts on the march. The Arab horses they were riding, incomparable in these conditions, could keep going on no more than this all day, had been known to do so for three days. He leaned his head back, shut his eyes, and calculated. She was five miles ahead, he estimated. She must have gone fast in the cool night; but now, in the day's heat, she was jog-trotting along at the march pace of four miles an hour which would bring her to the Euphrates by nightfall. If he revealed himself now, and chased her, she would pull away from him, with a safe lead, and he would lose her. Her camel was faster than any horse over a long distance, its speed based on endurance rather than fleetness. It could keep going fast enough and long enough to do ninety miles in a day, whereas fifty for a horse, in these conditions, was heroic. His only chance was to come up close to her, undetected, and ride her down in a short sprint.

She had time in hand. She did not know she was followed. He guessed that she would rest, at some time in the noon heat. She would rest if she remained unsuspecting. Then he could come upon her.

He began to stalk her. All day his troop of horsemen threaded close to the foot of the hills, barely keeping their quarry in sight, using the cover of ravines, outcrops, spilled boulders. The sun, overhead, poured down white light and drank up the strength of all living things. The horses walked in the midday glare with patient, dainty step, their riders slumped on their backs. Aurelian, his mind heat-stunned, could feel the one thought that lived in these heat-stunned men; the question, *Why don't we catch her up? why don't we chase? why the torture of this slow ride?* He kept her in sight, kept his men in cover, took care not to gain on her, and suffered the snail's-passage of the hours.

His reward came three hours after noon. He rounded a
knuckle of rock and saw, in the distance, two camels tethered
close to another outcrop. This was the hour of the worst heat.
She and her companion must have chosen it for their rest, and
gone into the shade.

What now? She had thirty miles to go, and a spur of hills to
cross, whose steep, sloping gullies would be bad going for
camels; but she had plenty of time; she could afford an hour's
rest. He, too, had plenty of time, then. He must not hurry. He
must approach her as stealthily and quietly as a beast wriggling
on its belly for the last pounce.

He went forward on foot, leading his horse. He sidled along
the rock wall, drew back into ravines, waited behind boulders,
watching the outcrop behind which she was resting for signs of
a lookout. He could see none. Perhaps she and the *daleel,* sure
of their safety, were both asleep? The pad of hoofs, the whirr of
horses' breath, sounded loud to him. Sometimes a stone scut-
tered away from a man's foot and the whole troop halted, for a
long minute, still as the rocks around them. The horses were a
nuisance. He had to take them in case it became necessary to
mount at once and pursue. But when they came within scent of
the camels, they would inevitably become restless and noisy.
Even the best-trained of them frantically hated their desert
rivals.

He gained the cover of a broad buttress of hillside and was
able to move a little faster. The flank of the hill brought him to
within a thousand paces of the tethered camels before it turned
in again. There was no more cover now. He had to creep—or
dash—across the intervening space. He chose to dash. After all,
perhaps she was sleeping.

The troop mounted quietly. He rode out into the open. At
once he heard a woman's cry; and for the first time he saw the
bob of a head behind the rock. He had underestimated her. She
and the *daleel* must have taken it in turns to sleep and watch.

Their two black-gowned figures emerged from the rocks, running to the camels. He lashed his horse to a gallop and felt it start away beneath him.

Zenobia and the *daleel* were up and away, with a thousand paces' start. Aurelian crouched over his horse's neck. He was not aware of the wind roaring in his ears, or of his horse's hoofbeats drumming through his body. He was marksman and missile in one; the eyes focused on the target, with nothing but purpose behind them; the body insentient, destined in its swift course, thought left behind.

The Romans gained, but not fast enough. They could not keep their present pace for long. They raced beneath the brown, sleeping hills like a pack of jockeys at the Circus, amid an oddly dead thudding of hoofs that accentuated the silence around them. The bunched, sleek beasts, gleaming with sweat, seemed to fly over the ground. The two camels, by comparison, looked ugly and comical, slow in their long-legged stride; yet they kept ahead.

The sun was low in the western sky, the light losing its glare. The gap between pursuers and quarry was halved, but Aurelian felt no exultation. He heard the thump of his horse's labouring heart. He sensed the diminishing drive in the flying hoofs. The long crooked legs of those cursed camels ahead loped on, steadily, unhurriedly, like mechanisms incapable of tiring.

The gap began to widen once more. Aurelian made his decisions. An attempt had failed. It was no use killing the horses now. The hills were ten miles ahead, between Zenobia and the river. Let the hills be his allies. He slowed the pace, so that the horses could be refreshed with soaked meal balls and could recover their wind. Without alarm he watched Zenobia and her companion draw away, dwindling into the distance until they were insect-size again. He had panicked her into headlong flight. Camels could keep going all day—but not at racing speed. And the hills were in front of her. He followed steadily, through the last hours of the day.

The hills drew nearer. They were his last chance. He saw the camels passing among a litter of boulders, climbing a stony gully. He increased the pace and the noble ungrudging horses responded. They picked their way swiftly and nimbly up the steepening track, gaining constantly. The camels laboured to keep up their speed, but the gradient had broken the rhythm of their movement. Their progress was like an unskilled lurching on stilts. After the excessive effort that had been forced on them, their reserves of strength must be almost gone, and this climb, with its broken, unfamiliar rhythm, would rapidly exhaust them.

The air was cool with the nearness of evening and of water. The scent of water revived the horses. Their riders, transformed by the day's ride into sacks of jolting, agonized muscle, were roused by hope to become men again. The camels appeared on one false crest after another and vanished into the dip beyond. Each time they reappeared they were nearer, more distinctly outlined against the pearly light of evening. The slower they went the faster and more frantic the strutting of their legs seemed. Their heads, instead of drooping in fatigue as horses' would, were piteously uplifted on the ends of their long necks. The hills had beaten them.

The downhill path was no easier for them. The Romans came to the last crest and saw the river, a gleaming yellow serpent in the fading light, bordered by green fields. Away to the north the houses of Sura clustered. Boats, like black splinters, moved on the river or were drawn up on the banks. Aurelian could see Zenobia and the *daleel* lashing their camels with sticks, but the beasts had slowed down to a timorous, stumbling trot, fearful of falling. The smell of the kill seemed to have given the horses, as well as their riders, new strength. The Romans poured over the crest, in a last yelling pursuit.

One of the camels stumbled, and did not rise. The *daleel*, its rider, dispatched it with his sword, then sat on its neck with bowed head, waiting, in his turn, for the death-stroke, and the last Roman soldier galloping past gave it to him.

Aurelian rammed his heels into his horse's belly and broke away from the troop, drawing up behind Zenobia's lone camel. She was not far ahead, but it was becoming hard to see her in the failing light.

The road was bordered by dusty palms. Irrigation ditches gleamed in the fields on both sides. Peasants scattered from the road as the torrent of riders thundered upon them out of the mauve twilight. The road opened out onto a foreshore. A stretch of rushes, black in the dusk, went down into the water. A flat-bottomed boat was moored among the rushes. The five half-naked peasants who had been loading it with rice sacks stopped in a tableau of fear and astonishment.

Zenobia slipped down from her camel. The animal went off in a relieved, drunken lope, into the shadows. Zenobia ran down to the water's edge, splashing and stumbling among the rushes, towards the boat.

Aurelian rode past her into the Euphrates. His horse, refreshed by the river up to its hocks, whirled round in a churning of water. He was in her path and she stopped. He said, "No boating party this time, Zenobia. And no swimming, either."

He was a proud, upright silhouette in the twilight. Like his horse, he seemed miraculously refreshed. Zenobia, veiled, in her black robe, was a figure of defeat. He watched her, this woman whom he had thought incapable of surrender: for a plunge into the water, a scamper into the dusk, a cry for help to the Persian frontier guards who stood on the far bank, for some ingenious ruse, at least for some answer of mockery or defiance. But she was inert and without will, a bundle of black that might slump down into the reeds at any moment.

He saw now that she was utterly exhausted by the day's ride. It had been punishment enough on the horses. On the camels it must have been torture. This small slender woman had matched him in endurance; now she was spent.

She lifted her head. The movement was slow and full of agony. Her eyes were large with dolour over the veil. Her hand came up as if it were a great weight, and numbed fingers undid the veil. The upper half of her face was thick with dust, accentuating the dark hollows from which her eyes stared. Her cheeks, revealed, were sunken, all their sensual fullness gone in a day. Her hand, when it had undone the veil, fell to her side.

His horsemen had ridden past him into the water, forming a circle. There were many peasants in the fields. On the far bank Persian soldiers were watching, recognizable by their jerkins, puttees to the thighs, helmets with chinpieces, ram's-horn bows and small round shields. It was unlikely that the Persians were interested. To them, this must appear the arrest of some peccant Bedouin by a Roman patrol. Aurelian, however, was taking no chances. His men sat their horses in a stern, looming circle, and Zenobia, small as a child in their midst, turned a stricken face up to them.

Aurelian said, "You had better go ashore."

Her lips parted but she could not summon her voice. Only her eyes, a trapped animal's, spoke. Now that the moment had come, Aurelian could not believe in it. Nor could he take in what his eyes saw: the inexhaustible Zenobia exhausted; the indomitable Zenobia broken. He felt no satisfaction. There was only a numbness, and an ache of wonderment mingled with the ache of his muscles.

She stumbled to the shore, and the circle of horsemen became two lines riding quietly, one on each side of her. Aurelian rode close behind her.

He watched in silence from horseback while a soldier tied her hands in front of her. He called to the soldier, "Give me that."

When he had taken the cord from the soldier, he said to Zenobia, "This is what I promised you."

There was not even recognition in the eyes with which she looked up at him.

He called to the troop. "Mount up. We'll get away from here. We're too near the Persians. We'll ride back to meet the relief troop, and if we don't find them by dark we'll lie up in the hills."

Dusk became clear darkness. The moon's pallor became a radiance. The white moonlight glimmered on the river and the silent fields and made black silhouettes of the roads and the trees and the line of horsemen. The horses walked slowly, and their necks drooped.

Aurelian rode at the head of his men, leading Zenobia at the end of her cord. She trudged with her body leaning forward, her head bowed. Aurelian was still numb. This was the moment; the end of a great trial, the symbolical humiliation of his adversary; and he was numb. He knew nothing but the pain of his muscles, the fatigue that weighed on his eyelids. It was not only the last twenty-four hours that crushed down on him now; it was the last three months, the whole herculean campaign. For all he felt, he might have been Zenobia's companion in defeat.

The horses plodded as if in sleep. The soldiers sat them like sleepers. Aurelian glanced back. Zenobia, lurching behind him, lifted her face. This lift of the head was the utmost defiance she could muster; there was no defiance in her moon-blanched face.

He rode on, numbed, dreaming yet fighting off sleep. There was a jerk on the cord. She had fallen. He stopped his horse. She tottered to her feet, gave him another of her woeful, defiant looks and began to drag her feet forward once more.

He looked back two minutes later. Her head was lolling to one side. There was a weaving, drunken lurch in her walk. He rode on. This was the tradition, the punishment, the breaking of a reputation. When she fell, he rode on, dragging her vanquished body through the dust. He rode on for ten paces; then he stopped. She lay in a heap. Her head lifted, and fell again. His soldiers were watching. Their eyes were implacable. If he let them, they would violate her, befoul her, hack her, trample her. She was the hated one. They were watching Aurelian, too.

She raised herself on her hands, and collapsed. She got up on her feet, swayed, and fell. The next time, she remained on her feet. She looked at Aurelian. There was an infinitude of pain in her eyes, but no appeal. She began to stagger forward.

When he had ridden on for a few seconds, he reined back. She shuffled alongside, black-clad, bowed, tiny. He leaned down, lifted her from the ground and set her on his horse in front of him. He touched his horse into movement again. He did not look back at his men.

CHAPTER TWENTY

THE ACCOMPLICES

FOR the ceremony of victory, Aurelian sat in his chair on an earth platform facing the south gate of Palmyra. Picked detachments of troops were paraded before him, in two blocks between which an avenue led to the gate. At his feet were his twelve lictors, his brass band with its big, coiled trumpets, and the massed eagles of the legions. Facing inward in two ranks, keeping open a space in front of him, were his guard of honour, the medal winners of the campaign. The nearest of them, on Aurelian's right, was Scrofa, whose fierce oaken face was uplifted in profile. Behind the guard of honour was a crowd of spectators, civil and army officers.

Aurelian sat upright, the bandage on his shoulder concealed by his armour. His face was hard and sombre. Victory had come quietly. When Palmyra had seen its queen a prisoner it had surrendered without fuss. Aurelian's soldiers, massed in front of him, were jubilant, refreshed by rest, their war over. He had not rested yet. His body was tired and his spirit was cold. His isolation from all other men was complete. His war was not over. It never would be over while he lived. For the man with a throne to defend, all mankind were possible enemies. He had overcome one threat, but another now faced him, from the Roman army, destroyer of emperors. The soldiers wanted their price, the looting and wiping-out of Palmyra, and of this he was determined to cheat them. They wanted, obsessively, the death of Zenobia. About this, too, he had his own ideas.

The music of the *bucinae* ceased. Distant trumpets sounded a shrill call. A forest of tall banners came moving out of the city gates. Small in front of them, a group of men walked, their slow step obedient to the fanfares. They approached, between the ranks of Roman soldiers, and Aurelian recognized Worod at their head carrying the keys of Palmyra on a silken cushion. Behind Worod, in senatorial togas, were the members of the puppet government he had set up. Chained prisoners came next, and the two children of Zenobia holding hands, and then a long procession stretching all the way back to the gate, the treasure of Palmyra.

Worod reached the foot of the platform, bowed, and placed the keys on the ground. He and his colleagues moved aside. The banners came forward, to fall in rows like scythed corn at Aurelian's feet. Aurelian took no notice of the tumbling banners. His legions, too, ignored banners, prisoners, and treasure. They were stirring in a ripple of hatred that defied discipline, and a growling murmur arose from them. In a break in the procession, alone except for two guards, Zenobia walked. The army, a hungry menagerie, watched her and growled.

She wore a simple white robe, girdled at the waist. She walked like a penitent or, for she looked so small between the tall soldiers, like a child going to punishment. Aurelian was surprised at the humility of her bearing. He had expected a proud step, a disdainful face. She approached, and a moment of decision came nearer for Aurelian, for he did not want to kill her. It was not clear in his thoughts why this was so. If he had to, he assumed that he would sacrifice her. It would take more than a woman to soften his iron insensibility. If he ever had to face the necessity of his own death he would do so bleakly and without distress, and in the same spirit he would order hers. Yet the mystery remained. He did not want to kill her.

Her guards drew her aside. There was time yet. Aurelian had a prior task to accomplish, the saving of Palmyra. The trumpets had fallen silent. There was no sound but the creak of treasure wagons, the thud and crash as slaves built up the heaps of spoil. A stack of bar gold grew as high as a house. Statues of precious metal were set up in long ranks until they were like another regiment of soldiers. Wool dyed in costly purple was piled in heaps that would fill warehouses. Ivory, ointments, spices, salt, jars of olive oil and rare perfumes, pyramids of silk in many colours, filled the space in front of the emperor until it was like a market-place.

All this was as Aurelian had ordered. A good commander is always a good showman. He was dazzling his soldiers with wealth. He was lulling them with the slow, apparently endless passage of the procession, making them feel that all the treasure in the world was being laid out before them. Gold coin from the treasury of Palmyra was being stacked, and the sacks were emptied in a continuous cascade onto one great heap. He wanted his soldiers to see the dazzle of the coin and to hear its tinkling music.

In this way he hoped to sate them without the need for pillage, to turn their gaze away from the city and from Zenobia. Behind the treasure came the slaves. The richest city in the East owned a multitude of slaves, and Aurelian had taken them all. He wanted to create the illusion among his soldiers that this captive army paraded before their eyes was in itself a whole population. Last night he had cut short Worod's protest with the answer, "I am being merciful. Send out your wealth and I will not send my troops in. Give me your slaves and I will spare your citizens."

Perhaps his plan was working. Zenobia stood at one side, small and unregarded, while the growl of the troops had changed to a bees' mumble of cupidity. She was looking around her with a calm, spectator's gaze. She had no eyes for Zabda and his fellow officers in their fetters nor for Longinus, who was with them, a fat, dejected little man among the defiant soldiers. Her glance rested for a moment on Philomene, who was with

Probus among the onlookers. Philomene clung to her lover's arm, flaunting him, and she grinned insolently at her former mistress as if she expected spittle in her face. Zenobia's glance moved on, without interest, seeking until she found her children. They were opposite her. Wahab's shivering was plain to see. His eyes were big with fear and he looked as if he were about to be sick. His sister clutched his hand, but protectively, like a little mother, and she was looking up at him with a brave, childish smile.

Aurelian was looking from the children to their mother. He sensed that for Zenobia nothing existed but her children. The sight of them had struck her into a yearning stillness. He tried to read what he saw in her hungry, dreaming face.

All through their strange, long ride back across the desert he had been aware of his men watching him from behind, and he had not spoken with her except to utter occasional curt commands. He had been preoccupied with his own thoughts and she, too, must have been debating inwardly what to do next. Yet something powerful had flowed between them: a contentment in each other's presence; a sense of destiny accomplished that had nothing to do with victory or defeat; and, for Aurelian at least, a feeling that could only be defined as the absence of accustomed solitude, as of a weight lifted.

He felt it again today; all the more so because of the rift in spirit between him and his assembled troops. Solitary as a statue against the sky, he looked down at her, and wondered how to avoid killing her. If he had to do so, the earth would again become an empty place.

The procession was over. The noises had died away. Army and captives were a vast, quiet crowd, waiting for Aurelian. His time for thought had expired. He feared, at this moment of action, that the worst obstacle to his saving Zenobia would be Zenobia herself. Let her be dramatic, defiant, proud, as he expected her to be, and she would touch off a fury among the legions that might sweep both him and her away. He said, "Stand forward."

Silence lay upon the parade. She came to the foot of his platform. She cast one more glance at her children, a long, fascinated look; then she faced him and sank to the ground in a bow.

"Zenobia Septimia, known to your people as Bath-Zabbai, widow to Odenathus?"

She inclined her head in a meek affirmative.

"You are here to answer for rebellion against Rome, for a betrayal of the obligations that your husband, a brave soldier, bequeathed you. These charges are already proved by events. Do you admit them?"

Again she bowed her head. He was puzzled. He had expected arrogance. Instead, she stood like some submissive wife of ancient times, a Lucretia shamed before her husband. "Then rise and hear my judgement."

She rose. Her face was contrite, but in her eyes, for him alone to see, were teasing spots of light, challenging him to understand. He frowned, intent upon her, for one false word would be fatal. He made his voice harsh and strong for the soldiers to hear. "Zenobia, you have broken a trust laid upon you. You have defied the imperial authority. You have imperilled the security of the frontiers. For your own ambition alone, you have caused the death of many Roman soldiers and the ruin of your own people. For these crimes there is only one punishment—death. The manner of death, prescribed by custom, is scourging in front of the legions and beheading by the sword. Before I pass sentence, have you anything to say?"

The next move was hers. She looked up at him with large eyes. "My lord, I am guilty."

There was a stir among the spectators. They, too, Palmyrenes and Romans, must have expected a theatrical defiance. Baffled, he stared at her. Then she spoke again. "My lord, before you decree my punishment, I wish to make a statement, in the presence of your soldiers, and of my people, and of the whole world. For, whatever befalls me, it is my duty to make amends. My crime is known. I wish the world also to know that I was guilty of folly, in challenging sacred and invincible Rome. I wish to warn all others who harbour wicked ambitions, to desist before they destroy themselves and their subjects. Perhaps these words of mine—my last, for all I know—may thus be of service to the Empire." Humble, yet bold, she looked up at him. The challenge was clear now in her eyes. She raised her voice. "I was beaten because Rome is invincible. Rome may not be challenged. The gods have decreed that Rome shall rule the world, and the gods fight with Rome. I say to the world that Rome's strength, Rome's generals, and Rome's soldiers are superior to all others, and that my deserved downfall is due to their skill and valour."

Aurelian's puzzlement deepened. Did she imagine that this pretty little speech was enough to appease the blood lust of his troops? He glanced at the nearest man, Scrofa. The centurion's face was carven, impassive, but his eyes were fixed on Zenobia with a snakelike, merciless glitter.

She was speaking again. "Yet one thing I must add, my lord, if I am to speak the truth. The guilt was not mine."

"Whose was it then?" Aurelian was leaning forward in his chair trying to read her intentions in her eyes.

She raised her head, and pointed. Her posture had become imperious, at last that of the woman he had known. "These men, my lord." She was pointing at the chained prisoners. "The men who led my army. They wanted war. They hated Rome. How could I, a woman, young and weak, withstand them? Lord Aurelian, I am only a woman, vain, foolish. My faults are those of a woman. Since my husband died I have been alone. I have not known how to rule. Weak, as a woman is, I have let others rule through me. I have let my counsellors mislead me. I have been used to further their crimes."

Even Aurelian was thunderstruck. He could only lead her on. "They are rebels who have broken their military oath. Do not fear, Zenobia, they will die."

"But this one—" For an instant Aurelian could not believe what he saw. She was pointing at Longinus. A twitch of utter astonishment distorted the philosopher's face. She repeated in a clear, musical voice, "But this one, my lord? He was my master. He was my appointed guide. I was a simple girl when he came to me. I knew nothing but what he put into my mind. My deeds were his, and it is he who should pay."

Longinus was calm again, but staring at her. Her eyes looked up into Aurelian's, candid yet with a woman's slyness behind them, serious yet with a secret smile in their depths. "How could I say 'no,' my lord, when this man said 'yes'? How could I say 'peace' when he said 'war'?"

"Are you suggesting that he is responsible for your policies?"

She turned towards her children, and in this moment Aurelian understood her. She smiled at them. Her smile was a mother's, reassuring, promising safety. Julia, still squeezing her brother's hand, smiled back. Wahab's face was desolate, imploring, as if he wanted to run to his mother. She faced Aurelian again, calm, conscience-clear. "Yes, that is what I am saying, my lord. It is not out of fear that I plead. There are other things in my mind, and I think you know them. I plead for my life so that I may serve Rome and make up for what I have done in the past. I plead as the widow of a man who served Rome well. I plead as the mother of two dear children who need me. I plead for a chance to acknowledge you, Aurelian, Caesar, as my true master. When I turned onto a false road, another was emperor. You I wish only to serve. I have much to offer you. Look at me, my lord, and ask yourself if you want the world to believe that a woman, and so young, could have brought Rome to such a crisis? Is it not more plausible, less offensive to the majesty of Rome, that the mind which conceived so formidable a challenge was the mind of a man, one famous throughout the world for his learning and ingenuity? Think of the reflectors, and the cranes, and the casting down of my city wall. Whose mind do you think those came from, mine or his?"

She broke off, and cast at Longinus an extraordinary look, in which entreaty and brazen defiance were mingled. He stared at her for some moments; then he said hoarsely, "Those inventions were mine, Caesar."

"You see!" She turned her back on Longinus. "Would it be so hard for your Senate"—was there the slightest signalling lift of eyelashes?—"and your soldiers to see their real adversary in this brilliant, ambitious scholar? Would it not vindicate the honour of Roman arms?"

She burned with a dazzling purity, the purity of a woman's egoism, so complete, so confident that it was itself an innocence. Aurelian was fascinated by the candour in her eyes. "Longinus, what have you to say?"

It was to Zenobia that the philosopher spoke, smiling. "My lady, you hired me to complete your education. You have completed mine."

Aurelian felt a touch of regret at the weary dignity of this fat little man. But the choice called for no hesitation, between *her* and a grubby old windbag. She had shown him how to save her. He saw no wrong in her action. It was a monarch's prerogative to sacrifice soldiers; and to Aurelian, a bookworm was of less use to the world than a trained legionary. He rose. "Then let the criminal die. At dawn tomorrow, before my army, the generals who broke my oath will die by the sword, and their instigator, Longinus, by the scourge."

Longinus heard the sentence with composure. Zabda perked up his beard, jaunty and defiant. Zenobia was smiling at her children.

A murmur among the legions grew into a roar. The massed cohorts rippled like cornfields in a storm. Out of the tumult broke shouts of protest and anger. Aurelian raised his hand and shouted into the din, "Soldiers!"

Crisis came. The most disciplined soldier in the army broke ranks to deliver the army's challenge. Scrofa, in his medals and valour bracelets, stepped forward. Fury ripped in his voice. "Kill her! Kill the sow!"

Aurelian could not make himself heard. Scrofa's face glared up at him, and he heard the centurion's snarl, "She's ours, Caesar! Give her to us!"

"Men!" It was no use against this uproar. Five more seconds and those wavering ranks would burst into a mob, rushing upon him. He flung out an arm. All the strength in him drove up through lungs and throat. "THIS—GOLD—IS—YOURS!"

The roar diminished a little. Scrofa was silent, fangs bared. Farther away, men were still shouting.

Aurelian repeated, in a voice less prodigious but sharp as steel against the noise, "This gold is yours!"

He was pointing at the mound of gold coins. He waited. The noise died down.

"Soldiers—silence!" The silence was complete.

"It is the custom to divide the spoils of war, a third to the Treasury, a third to the emperor, a third to the army. This gold you see is for you only. It will be shared among you tonight. The rest of the spoil will be sold, and you will receive your shares in the normal manner." He cut short a timid beginning of applause with a whiplashed, "Silence! Your emperor is speaking."

He let them feel the silence, weighted with his authority, before he resumed. He noticed Scrofa beneath him, rigid but still as menacing as a crouched beast. "This gold is yours, from this moment. I shall not let the paymasters lay hands on it. Your own comrades will guard it and share it out among you. And the man I place in charge of it, who will appoint guards and set up a committee, is a soldier you all know, a soldier you trust, a soldier whose valour I have rewarded today." He beckoned. "Up here, Scrofa!"

This time he let the cheers burst out. One moment Scrofa was a tensed enemy, the next moment he was on the platform, at Aurelian's side, swelled up with a soldier's servile conceit, enjoying one of his life's great moments. Aurelian raised a hand to stop the cheers. "Lads!" Now his voice had warmth in it. "We'll sell the slaves, too. One thing we will not do, though I've heard of a few fools who want to. We're not going to burn this place down. Oh, I know we'd all feel better if we did. We've suffered here. We've buried good comrades here. We've all got our wounds. But who'd kill a cow when it gives good milk?" He listened approvingly to the surge of laughter. "And I tell you, men, we're going to milk this place for years to come." More cheers.

"As for this one"—he pointed at Zenobia, and his voice became casual—"I wouldn't like people to say that she was the one who'd led us such a dance. Would you? I can imagine some of the songs the other legions would make up about us. We'd never live it down. And what she says is true, after all. She was loyal enough when her husband was alive. And a good man he was, too. No!" His voice rose as he indicated Longinus. "We shall never let it be said that a woman defied us. This is the one! This is the scoundrel! He's the one who got hold of her when her husband died. He gave all the orders. Worse still, he hid behind her back. But we've dragged him out. Haven't we? He's one of the clever ones. The speechifiers. The book readers. You know them, don't you? The cause of all the world's troubles. But he wasn't clever enough for us. Not for Roman soldiers! We've got him, and we'll make him pay. Tomorrow morning, men! You'll see! I know it'll be worth watching."

Satisfied, he watched the stir and jostle in the ranks. Indiscipline did not worry him at this moment, as long as it was the indiscipline of men relaxing. "Soldiers! You're going to have a feast tonight." A fresh murmur of applause. He let it grow. "I've

got a good ration together for you. You're finished with short
commons. I'm turning over to you all the wine in the palace
cellars. And the wenches of Palmyra will serve it to you." He
paused, enjoying the warm, tamed roar of his men. "I see you've
all heard about them. You won't find prettier girls, or more art-
ful, between here and Hadrian's Wall. You'll all sleep late tomorrow morning except for duty men. And I'll tell you what,
we'll put the execution off till midday so as not to spoil your
sleep. And now, my last word, comrades. Thank you for all
you've done in this campaign. You've been the best soldiers a
man could wish for. I'll see that the whole Empire knows what
you've done. For the rest of your lives you'll be proud to say
that you were in the desert with Old Hand-on-Hilt. And remember this. You won't be any more proud than he is of you."
He turned to Scrofa. "Centurion! Dismiss the parade!"

Scrofa was rigid and aquiver with pride, a ferocious spectacle of obedience. His lips rolled back. His chest swelled and
his face darkened. His right arm shot up in salute, and from
him there burst a roar that surpassed Aurelian's. "Legions—
HAIL CAESAR! CAESAR HAIL!"

A host of arms went up. Amid the roar of response Zenobia,
unnoticed, went to meet her children. Aurelian saw them directly beneath him. She had an arm round Julia's shoulder,
holding her daughter to her side. Wahab was sobbing with
relief against her. With her free hand she stroked his hair, pressing his head to her bosom, accepting her son's surrender.

The legions thundered, "CAESAR HAIL! . . . HAIL! . . .
HAIL!"

*

Longinus lay on a paillasse in the corner of his cell. Through
the brick wall he could hear a distant roar of festivity. It must
be far into the night. There were no windows, and the flickering
oil lamp gave no clue to the passage of the hours.

Footsteps and voices sounded in the corridor. He refilled his cup from the flagon of wine at his side. The footsteps stopped outside his door. Bolts screamed and the door opened. There was a glimpse of soldiers. Zenobia came in.

Longinus sat up as the door closed behind her. "I did not expect this."

She stayed in the shadows, not speaking.

He said, "I shan't get up. I feel sick and cold, and I'm rather tired."

She said in a low voice, "I have come to ask your pardon."

He looked her up and down, curiously but without rancour. "Tell me, has he set you free?"

"I am in protective custody, with the children. But he let me come to see you." The appeal came into her voice again. "Longinus, dear friend, he will pardon you. I am sure he will, at the last moment. I only said what I did because I was sure he would not kill you. You're not angry with me, are you?"

He did not answer.

She said, "I do want you to understand."

He uttered a brief laugh. "When a woman does a thing like this to a man she always wants him to understand."

"It was for the children."

"Perhaps." He touched the flagon. "Did you send this wine? It is a great comfort."

"No. You are mocking me."

"I am not mocking you. I am surprised, and a little moved, that you should come to make excuses."

Her voice hardened. "I am not making excuses. Listen, Longinus. You taught me to think clearly. You taught me to keep an aim in view and not abandon it for sentiment. You taught me to be a realist. Very well, that is what I am. What I did today I did for my children. If he kills me, he will kill them, or they will not long survive me, for they would be my successors and my possible avengers. I have sacrificed armies for

my children and I have thrown away my kingdom for them.
Why should I hesitate to sacrifice your life for them? Yes, and
my honour, too?"

Longinus smiled. "That is a mixture of truth and self-deception. But I am not going to lecture you about it. When I see
where all our improving discussions have led I do not relish any
more. I would like to sleep. I am terribly tired."

She lingered.

He said, "What do you want? A kiss on the brow? My bless-
ing? A touching farewell? I am sorry. I am not generous enough.
Please go."

She turned away. He watched her, then said, "Zenobia—"

She looked back from the door.

"There is no blame. We think we are the masters of our ambitions, but we are their slaves." He turned to the wall. He
heard the door creak behind her and the bolts slide home.

He lay for a long time listening to the distant noises of celebration. Fear kept him awake, but he was fuddled, half sub-
merged in sleep. He had no idea how much later it was when
he became aware that the door had opened again, and he turned
over, to see Aurelian in the room.

He wiped his eyes and sat up laboriously. "This is a mem-
orable night. It is a pity I shan't live to boast of it."

"Old man, I am sorry about all this."

"More apologies. I did not know the consciences of monarchs
slept so lightly. Thank you for the wine, Aurelian."

"Shall I send another flagon? It's good stuff."

"You tempt me. I envy those who die drunk. But I'd better
not. I have my reputation to think of."

"Food?"

"No, thank you, my stomach is too upset. On the threshold
of death, my main concern is a bellyache. If I had time I would
write an essay on this."

Aurelian began to pace the cell slowly, hands behind his back.

He did not look at Longinus. "Why didn't you speak out for yourself today?"

"Why should you care? I made your task easier, didn't I?"

Aurelian took a pace or two. He looked up sharply. "Yes, you did."

"It would have been too demeaning, Caesar. Truly, for all of us."

Aurelian nodded, pondering. Then, "But I should have thought, out of sheer anger—"

"Caesar, I have always taught myself to look at life with detachment, to be surprised or angered at nothing. Today was my test." He smiled. "Besides, you know the truth. She fascinates us both."

Aurelian lifted his head angrily.

"Yes." The old man forestalled him. "You, too. Oh, we aren't boys. We're not lovesick for her. We could both live very well without her. But we cannot take our eyes from her. I would rather die than put an end to such a performance."

Aurelian stood with arms clasped across his chest, absorbing this. "I sat there today. I looked at her and at you. You are a good man. She was the guilty one. She was betraying you." He looked down at Longinus, eyebrows hunched in perplexity. "I did not give you a thought. I sat there and stared at her. And do you know, I admired her for what she was doing."

Longinus laughed. "All the same, you said some unkind things about me."

"There was nothing personal. That is the way one talks to a crowd."

Longinus lay back. "It is odd that I should feel aggrieved about it. I suppose I still cannot believe that I shall not exist at this time tomorrow. You, I should imagine, never think about death, being a soldier?"

"No. What is there to think about it?"

"I don't know. Certainly there is nothing new to say about it.

I am only discovering what everyone discovers. Life is such a painful business that we ought to look forward to our release from it. Yet, when the time comes, there is such a bitter regret at going. There are so many little pleasures." He sighed. "Yes, it is the little pleasures I regret. Caesar, do you know what we are doing here? We are whiling away a little time in the antechamber to death, that is all. Nothing matters except to spend this little time agreeably and without harm to others. All else is to no purpose."

"While we are here, the world is ours. We've got to keep it in good order. When we go, others will take charge. Men are fools, and beasts, and someone has to show them this. That's my job. Order, discipline, keeping the world tidy and fit to live in. The Empire."

Longinus shook his head. "My poor friend! My poor man of action who is only a dreamer! Your empire is dying like any mortal man. You will not save it, nor a thousand like you. Death is a disease that you can retard but not cure. Your work will perish, and your memory will perish. Death will defeat you. If you had been born at a time when a new life was coming to birth, or to maturity, you would be remembered for a while, and called hero. So with Julius Caesar. But you, who are no less than he, are fated to spend your genius in a vain wrestle with death, and you will fail and be forgotten."

"Have I asked to be remembered?"

"No, you do not live for acclaim. Duty is your master. It is enough for you to obey your mission and die. In any case, did I say there was any merit in being remembered? Happy the man who is never known. What use was fame to stabbed Caesar? In my last hours, Aurelian, I shall not sing of arms and the man, but of life and its little pleasures. To value them is virtue, to despise them is vice. Alas, that is the tragedy of the Empire. We say it is sick, corrupt, degenerate. Why? Because it wants to rest from the struggle, and to enjoy life. We say that the

Romans are soft. Why? Because they do not want to fight. Good luck to them. The golden age will come when all the race are cowards. But the law of life is against them, poor wretches. All the hungry of the world smell their prosperity, smell their softness, and swarm in to tear them to pieces. And these hungry ones have in their loins new empires, which one day will reach the end of their roads, and grow contented and peaceful and soft, and be torn to pieces in their turn. Good sense comes with old age, Aurelian, when it is too late to make use of it. Corrupt our way may be, but it is comfortable, and rich in the things I value: art, learning, and the secrets of good living. Perhaps, after all, it is time for me to die, for I would not like to outlive all this."

Aurelian's face was sombre in the lamplight. "Old man, I am glad I am not a thinker."

Longinus settled back and pulled the blanket up to his chin. "Aurelian, might I ask a favour? One only? Could it not be an easier death, tomorrow? A cup of hemlock, say?"

"I am sorry. We have to give the troops a show. That is the whole point of it."

"A pity. Give me a couple more blankets, then, to stop my teeth from chattering."

"I'll have them sent in."

"My body is not so brave as my words, you see. I expect I shall make a good show of it when I walk there tomorrow, consoling my heartbroken friends, and so on. But I prophesy that when the lash falls on my back I shall yell lustily enough. Well, why not? I came into the world yelling." He sighed. "Good night, Aurelian."

CHAPTER TWENTY-ONE

WHOSE TRIUMPH?

AURELIAN'S triumphal procession through Rome was held on a mild, sunny day in October.

People had been pouring in for a week, from the countryside and from all the towns of Italy. This was to be the greatest triumph ever seen in Rome. There were to be two weeks of carnival, with free feasts, wine for all, thousands of prizes, races, plays, gladiator fights, wild beast hunts, and a naval battle in the flooded Circus Maximus.

The city was an immense grandstand. The crowds covered it like a crust. The hillsides were black with them. They packed the two Circuses, through both of which the procession would pass. They besieged the route, at street level, on the steps of public buildings, in windows, on roofs, and on scaffolding specially set up.

It was a day of wonders for the mob. They shouted at everything. They shouted at false alarms before the procession came in sight. They shouted at the police cordon that held the ribbon of roadway clear. They shouted at the messengers who, from time to time, galloped officiously along the route.

When they saw the white-gowned senators and magistrates who had gone to greet the emperor in the Field of Mars and who now led the parade, a million shouts swelled into a single yell that pierced the sky.

There were *aah*'s and *ooh*'s, screams and cheers, for the massed trumpeters who followed.

A babble of excitement travelled through the streets as the next section came in sight: the ambassadors of friendly and vassal nations, a many-coloured pageant of strange costumes and strange skins. Cheers for the representatives of fifty-six conquered cities, each carrying a gold crown, each announced by a placard. Cheers for the banners of defeated Palmyra. Cheers for the pictures of battle, victory, and divine aid painted on huge canvases carried on bamboo frames. Cheers for the martial tableaux, mounted on wheeled floats, with their real soldiers, real sword-fights, with real, wounded captives bleeding into the roadway, and real naked girls in symbolic poses. Cheers for the spoils of war, a rumble of wagons going by for hour upon hour, the longest section of the procession, endless, it seemed, dazzling the crowds with wealth and colour and beauty, hypnotizing them with its unending passage. Past the Pantheon, past the Baths of Agrippa, along the Tiber's bank, through the Circus Maximus, along the esplanade between the Palatine and the Caelian, north to the Forum and the Capitol Hill, endlessly the wagons passed and the cheers surged.

Along the route the noise would subside to a dull hubbub of exchanged gossip as the white oxen for sacrifice lowed past, with gilded horns and silk-clad flanks, led by the priests, followed by boy and girl acolytes carrying the instruments and vessels of sacrifice. It would grow in volume as another military band came past, then burst out in unprecedented fury as the crowd glimpsed the wonder of all today's wonders—the captive Zenobia.

The roadway around her was empty. She walked, small and meek as a lamb, with a slave woman at her side. Behind her, a young groom led her horse, and it was shouted in the crowd that this groom was the Goth prince, Maxin, who had fallen from the emperor's favour.

As each section of the crowd saw her, not only did the thunder of triumph burst from it, but there was a stir of surprise: for she, whose presence today was supposed to be a public humiliation, was dressed like an empress—a Roman empress.

She wore a long robe of gold brocade, with short, fan-shaped sleeves in the Dalmatian fashion of the day. A golden train, hanging from her right shoulder, was gathered up by the slave who walked with her. On her braided hair was a golden tiara inset with pearls and emeralds. An immense necklace hung down to her knees, of six rows of pearls, the biggest of which seemed to the gaping crowds as big as grapes. Her forearms were loaded with pearl and emerald bracelets.

In accordance with custom, she was fettered; but the bands on her wrists were of gold and the chain between them, long enough to leave free movement for her hands, was so lightly wrought in gold that her fetters were no more than an additional ornament.

The roar of the crowd, moving with her, was the heart of the procession. It made all that followed—and the emperor himself was farther back in the parade—seem of lesser importance. She walked sedately, ignoring the noise, looking at the crowds as if she were a strolling sight-seer.

Sometimes, amid the blank idiot howl of the crowds, she heard screams of hatred. Sometimes she heard the snarled derision that the weak fling at the vanquished when it is safe to do so. Sometimes she heard obscene remarks, the hungry cries of poor men for her beauty.

She ignored them. They did not matter. It was Aurelian who mattered. And her attire was the proof that she need not fear him. She had seen little of him in the month's journey from the East, but yesterday, when they had spoken, he had promised to spare her children the ordeal of this procession and he had given her permission—how she had taken advantage of it!—to dress as she wished.

She had forgotten her lost throne, as a woman forgets last year's fashion. She had forgotten Palmyra. There had been a riot in the defeated city—a small affair, mysteriously provoked, but enough to force Aurelian, who knew the limits of his power, to let his furious legions have their head. Now Palmyra, that great and lovely city, was as Rome wanted it: a burned patch on the desert, a few broken columns and jagged walls and ten thousand skeletons picked clean by the vultures. Zenobia had forgotten Palmyra. She thought about herself, and about Aurelian.

She saw the rich at their windows. Conscious of her beauty, the audacity of her attire, the wealth of her adornment, she enjoyed the envy of the women, their heads together in malicious consultation, she enjoyed the appreciative faces of the men. That promised well for the future.

As for the crowd—

She had been gazing, deeply impressed, at the Colosseum on her right, a curve of brownstone wall so lofty that it cut out half the sky. Its parapet, a hundred and sixty feet above, was fringed with spectators. Its galleried arches were packed. At its base swarmed the people of the slum that lay beyond it, the foul Suburra. They were yelping like angry dogs.

She took a bag from her slave, dipped into it and flung out her hand. Gold coins, glittering in the sunlight, scattered over the heads of the cordon and fell among the crowd. Where they fell, there was a canine scramble, a clamour of eagerness and greed.

Now to her left she flung a handful of coins, and to her right, and to her left again; and as she walked, the crowd fought for her money and cried out for it.

The news babbled ahead of her that there was gold to be had from Zenobia, and there was no more hostility or insult in the shouting that welcomed her, only delight, and greed, and entreaty.

The Roman crowd pressed against the cordon, a multitude of beggars stretching out their hands. Zenobia was the queen, they the suppliants, clawing and jostling at each other to be

where she might look. They cheered, hoping to please her. They
yelled her name.

She walked serenely, scattering her gold like a sower, and she
heard the crowd calling, "Zenobia! . . . Zenobia! . . . Zenobia!"

*

Aurelian, who headed the second part of the procession, could
hear the roar that greeted Zenobia, for he was not far behind,
and he could see the gold coins showering into the crowd. He
could hear them shouting her name. He was not angry against
her. He hated the sight and smell of the Roman crowd, this
multitude of puny, ugly wastrels to secure whose ease good
soldiers died and nations were desolated. He and she, victor and
captive alike, were undergoing the same ordeal, and today's
performance was no less than he expected of her.

He was tired. There was no rest for him in Rome. Sacrifices,
ceremonies, banquets, the dreary round lay ahead of him. But
even if he were to rest, his weariness would not leave him, for
it was a weariness of purpose, a part of himself.

There was no pleasure for him in this triumph. In ancient
times a triumph had been a religious ceremony, a military parade. This was only a show, in which he was no more than an
exhibit. In front of him were the lute-players and the dancers.
Theirs was supposed to be a celebration of triumph; but the men
were clowns, wielding gross, phallic toys, and the girls whirled
lewdly, in flimsy veils of gauze. It was all a show, for a lusting,
screaming crowd. Behind him marched the so-called knights of
Rome, those heroes of the business world who for all their
armour had never been to war; and behind them, carrying banners, were the workers' guilds, who never worked as long as
there were free bread and circuses. It was all a show. The captives marched, a procession miles long behind him, proud Goth
women who had fought at the side of their menfolk, Arabs still

haughty in their bondage, splendid Germans, people who loved, as he did, freedom and clean air and broad plains and healthy labour. And he had brought them here to choke in the stink of Rome, to be howled at by their inferiors, to slave for idlers, to make a show of which he, too, was part, a captive like them.

It was all a show, the eight hundred pairs of gladiators who would slaughter each other in the coming week, the forty elephants, the menagerie of tigers, bears, crocodiles, pythons, and giant apes, the two hundred human freaks. Man of power—master of the world—this was his true station, an exhibit in the menagerie, a freak among freaks. Even his soldiers, released from all discipline for the day, were soldiers no longer, but a tipsy rabble reeling along with laurel-crowned spears at the tail of the procession.

It was all a show. His gold and ivory chariot was drawn by four stags, an equipage captured from the Goths and used today as a novelty for the crowd. He was dressed as the god Jupiter. He had to stand in a stiff, stupid pose, holding a laurel bough with the reins in his right hand and an eagle-headed sceptre of ivory in his left. He had a laurel wreath on his head, and Lucipor stood behind him, holding over him another wreath fashioned in gold. It was not the conqueror the crowd cheered, but the show, and the giver of the show, and the giver of gifts.

Nor did they always cheer. When he passed the grandstands and the windows where the people of fashion sat, he saw them silent, their hatred unconcealed, or bowing with a servility that was also a mockery. His own drunken soldiers were bawling obscene songs about him. Amid the bought cheers of the poor, he heard the impudent jokes, the derision, the king-baiting of the poor. They called him Old Gloomy-Face because he did not smile and wave. They screamed crude insults because he did not keep a bevy of mistresses. He heard, at one street corner, a song in which Maxin was called his sweetheart. They held up the gold coins Zenobia had thrown them and called, "Where's

yours, Aurelian? . . . Come on, don't be mean!" One white-faced
runt stuck his face under the arm of a policeman and shouted,
"Look at the hero! He beats a poor little woman like her, and
then he calls it a triumph!"

Stony and full of hate, he rode in his bitter triumph. Ahead
of him, where his captive walked, he heard the roar—roar—roar
—of the crowd, and he heard the cry, "Zenobia! . . . Zenobia! . . .
Zenobia!"

*

Zenobia sat on the balcony of the villa that Aurelian had prepared for her. Rome was a darkness spotted with firefly torch-
lights. A soft roar of celebration mounted towards her.

Many currents of feeling flowed in her, and their conflict
produced a strange, murmurous excitement in her blood. There
was the elation, chilled with fear, at starting a new life. There
was the deep underflow of melancholy that she had lost all.
There was the strengthening warmth of her children's presence.
There was apprehension of unknown things to come. There
were gusts of confidence, and when she thought of her success
today, these filled her with a delighted tension. She had not lost
any of her old capacities. That was the important thing. Whatever she had lost, she had done much in the past and she had
the power to do much in the future.

She was sure of one thing: that she was safe for the present.
She had known it this evening when a chariot had brought her
to this rich, gardened villa in the suburbs. She had known it
when her children, safe and sound, had embraced her at the
gate. She had known it when she entered her own room, to find
that Aurelian had installed there her own bed from Palmyra,
her own wardrobe, her own carpets, and her own favourite
statue of Psyche. She had known it when the groom, that strange,
silent Maxin, had led her through the stables, where her own
white Arab kept company with half a dozen other blood horses.

She was safe, she was her old self, and if the future was dark, its darkness tingled with opportunity. In a simple wine-red robe, with her hair loose upon her shoulders, she sat with her chin cupped in her hands, looking out over Rome. She was in her own house, and her children were safely in bed.

The soft beat of hoofs approached in the darkness. She heard the watchman's challenge and the squeak of opening gates. The horseman came up the avenue of cypresses and dismounted at the door.

She had been half expecting him. She met him in the reception room. She took both his hands in greeting, and looked at his weary face. He was in military cloak and tunic, his helmet under his arm. He was thinner after the campaign, and this made him appear taller. His deeply lined forehead seemed more prominent, because of his pinched cheeks. His hair and his fringe of beard were iron-grey. His keen sunken eyes were cold with lack of illusion.

He gave his cloak and helmet to the butler, and said, "I came to make sure that everything was in order here."

She said to the butler, "Leave those in the anteroom, then see that we are not disturbed." She turned to Aurelian. "Everything is admirable. Thank you a thousand times, for my children and myself."

He stood dogged and frowning, in the centre of the floor's mosaic pattern. "There's nothing you need?"

She smiled. "Nothing."

"I thought I would make sure."

"So you said." She laughed. "Aurelian, it is years since you were so stiff with me. You are not frightened of me now?"

"Frightened?" His face cleared, and he added his laughter to hers. "That's a fine thing to ask me after all that's happened between us."

"Please sit down. You look so tired. It was good of you to

come tonight. I know how busy you must be. Isn't there a feast at the Temple of Jupiter?"

He nodded. "Official reception by the Senate. I came away from there."

"Because of me? I'm so sorry."

He had seated himself on the couch. He lifted his head in a tired, abrupt movement. "I was glad to get away." He took the cup of wine that she had poured for him. "Thank you. It's quiet here, isn't it? You should see the palace. A thousand people waiting to see the emperor. Deputations. Invitations. Documents. A dozen official functions every day. The games, the races, the theatre, banquets. I'll get no rest there. By Hercules! When I think of the frontier—the cold, clean air, the plains as far as you can see, the smell of pine forests—I want to mount up and go off tonight. I'm sick of this place already."

She drew a small chair up and sat down to face him, hands in her lap. "After your triumph?" She was teasing again.

"Triumph? You saw it. I should think you enjoyed it more than I did."

"Were you angry at that?"

"No. On the contrary." He lay back and uttered a harsh, luxurious sigh. "Do you mind? I've wanted to do this for hours."

"Please make yourself comfortable."

"Zenobia, don't you want to know what is going to become of you? You have never even asked."

"I trust you."

He lay quiet for a few moments. "You will have nothing to fear." Another pause. "And you? What do you want to do?"

"To rest, that is all, for a while. To let the picture of life take shape again. I do not think beyond that. Do you know, it is pleasant just now not to bear a load any more, to be alone in my house with my children. Aren't there times when you, too, would like to set aside the burden?"

"I would like to, many a time. But I can't. There's too much work to be done."

"Oh, your work! Your sacred mission! You will never succeed in it. Do you really believe you can? Think of that crowd we saw today. Why wear yourself out for nothing?"

"It's my job."

"Aurelian, you can beat the enemies of Rome. But if you try to make a new Rome, you will have Rome for your enemy, and you cannot beat Rome."

"Perhaps. I don't delude myself. That old man—the one we did away with—Longinus—he gave me a thing or two to think about."

"Yet you go on?"

"Yes."

"Why?"

"What else is there for a man to do?"

"But what satisfaction do you get from it?"

"The satisfaction of going on."

"Until you are killed?"

"Just so."

She sighed. "My poor friend!"

In the ensuing silence she watched his eyelids droop. He yawned and squirmed to stretch the muscles of his back. "I shall fall asleep if I don't go soon."

"Why not? It would do you good to stay here and sleep for a while."

He raised himself and looked at her keenly.

She said, "You can trust me, you know. You are safe here. You have no enemies in this house."

He smiled. "I was not frightened of that." He rubbed the back of his neck. "I've got to be up by sunrise."

"I will wake you in time."

He swung his feet off the couch and set them on the floor. "Do you know why your offer attracted me? It wasn't the idea of sleeping. I can do without that. It was the thought of being away from them all, where none of them could find me."

"Then stay. None of them will find you here."

He sat with his shoulders hunched, deciding. "Very well. I'm grateful. Will you have me called in two hours?" He stretched himself out on the couch. "There's no need for you to stay up. But I'd like to come and see you again."

She rose, and came to the side of his couch. "I want you to come here whenever you are tired, Aurelian. Let this be the house where you can rest, and find some peace, and shut out all enemies and problems. You will always find friendship here. I have waited a long time to be near you. Perhaps you, too, find a need answered when we are together. And if it is ever counsel you want, who is more likely to advise you well than I? After all, I am the only opponent you have never beaten."

He grinned. "Who walked captive in whose triumph today? I beat you, Zenobia."

"Never! Treachery beat me!"

They looked at each other and joined once more in laughter.

She said, "Now you must sleep. I shall call you myself, and we shall breakfast together." She turned away, to let him settle down, and moved about the room, quietly arranging things. When she heard from his deep, slow breathing that he was asleep, she came back to his side. She stood over him for some time, looking down at him. At last she went into the anteroom.

She carried a small table from a corner of the room into the centre of the floor, where he might see it through the doorway when he awoke. With brisk, stealthy movements she brought wine, fruit, vessels, cutlery, and napkins and set them out on the table. She arranged flowers. She did not touch the slave gong. She needed no help tonight.

She went to a mirror and shook her hair out, drawing it back and tying it with a ribbon that matched her gown. She wet her lips with her tongue, and touched her eyelashes with her fingertips. She heard a sound from the outer door, which was behind her. In the mirror she saw the door open slightly. She kept still and watched. The door opened wider. Someone slipped in. She would have turned and spoken sharply, but for the stealth with which the intruder pressed himself against the wall. He moved along the wall. It was the Goth boy, Maxin. The open door still hid her from his view.

He was dirty from his work. He kept one hand in the breast of his soiled tunic. He cast a sharp, reconnoitring look round the room. She saw his gaze rest on Aurelian's cloak and helmet, then on the doorway through which the sleeping Aurelian could be seen. He stepped away from the wall, and saw Zenobia across the room.

She had thought, for a second, that he had come to see her, or perhaps to beg a second chance from his old master. Now, as she saw him, tense with ferocity, she knew why he had come. She turned, and moved casually across the room, hoping that he would not notice the slave gong against the wall. "Maxin, what are you doing here?"

She spoke softly. For some reason which she could not fathom she did not want to wake Aurelian. She was strangely fascinated by the boy's stare.

He was breathing heavily, watching her with doubt in his eyes. "You speak softly." His grin was wolfish. "You do not want to wake him. You know why I am here." The hand at his breast moved, and she saw the gleam of steel.

She stared at him, fearful, curious. "You would kill him? You really would?"

"Why not?" His voice was as low and distinct as her own. "It is time."

He took two silent cat's-paces towards the inner door. "You would do it now? In front of me?"

Again the fanged grin. "Why not? He is your enemy." He was trying to read her face. "You have wished his death."

She did not move. He glanced over his shoulder, to make sure that Aurelian was still asleep. He spoke in a soft, intense voice. "You are afraid I will leave you to be punished for his death. You can come with me. We will take horses. In the open country no one will catch me."

His eyes glittered at her silence. "What do you fear? Are you afraid to come to my people? You think they are savages who will eat you? We are no savages. Yes, there is a fury when we attack, because we have suffered much. But after that— Listen to me. They tell you we burn cities to the ground when we cross the frontier. That is a lie. We have no books, no works of art, no buildings, but when they fall into our hands we cherish them. One day we will have these things, and we will do better with them than the Romans have done. Do you know what we do when we capture a Roman soldier—one of those soldiers who sell us for slaves or make us fight in their arenas? We offer him freedom, land, and the right to a wife if he will join us. Our women are equals and sit in the councils of the tribe. You will be honoured by my people. With them, you will fight on against Rome. Perhaps one day you will be a queen again. That is what you want."

She could not take her eyes from his face, so much did his intensity dominate her. She murmured, "My children—"

"We cannot take them. What of it? You have courage. Many times our women have sacrificed their children for the sake of the tribe."

She shook her head dumbly.

He held her for another moment with his stare, then he trod silently towards the inner door. Her hand went to the gong. She said, still softly, "Stop!"

He paused. He watched her like an animal about to pounce. She said, "Why have you not done this before?"

"I have waited. I wanted to learn."

"To learn what?"

"All that the Romans know. When my people know these things, Rome will die."

There was murder in his eyes. While he talked, she could see him measuring the distance between them, for a leap. She said, "No, I would strike the gong before you killed me. Aurelian would wake. Servants would come. Aurelian would live, and you would die. The knowledge you have gained would not reach your people. Now go away."

The doubt had come back into his face. "You still speak softly. Why don't you rouse him?"

"Never mind that. Pay heed to me now. My horse is the best in the stables. Take him and go away, tonight."

She saw the conflict behind his eyes. "Go," she insisted. "Do not waste time. He may wake at any moment. Your people need you. You can reach the frontier. You are brave and cunning enough to do anything. Go, now, this minute."

He looked once more at Aurelian, then at her. His shoulders relaxed. He said, his voice still grim but infused with pleading, "He killed my father."

"Rome killed your father. Rome would have killed your father even if there had been no Aurelian."

She came swiftly to his side, laid her hand on his arm and pressed him towards the outer door. He did not resist. "Do not kill Aurelian. Go, and come back with your horsemen, and one day you will kill Rome."

CHAPTER TWENTY-TWO

CONVERSATION ON A SPRING
MORNING: AN EPILOGUE

"DO YOU know," Probus said. "He was my best friend, but he never spoke to me about her."

Philomene nestled her face against his arm. "I could never get her to talk about him."

They were leaning side by side on the marble balcony of a platform that looked down on Rome from the eastern flank of the Aventine Hill. A statue, high on its pedestal behind them, gazed with blank, carved eyes at the panorama.

"I never knew a pair as discreet as those two," Probus said. "I wonder what did happen between them."

Philomene giggled. "Well, he was always visiting her house. And, after all, she is good-looking, in her way. Even a cold fish like him— Oh, I don't know. I really don't know."

Philomene was flushed and fresh and happy. She had a new dress and a sensational new hair style. The day was sweet and cool. Rome was a floor of red roofs and white walls at her feet, broken by tenement blocks of russet brick and hillsides terraced with greenery and tiers of buildings. Beyond was the chequered plain of the campagna, mist-hung and enclosed by a far, blue rim of hills.

This was her playground and her property, for Probus, her man, brave at her side in purple cloak, was emperor. Aurelian, whose statue stood behind her, was six months dead.

*

Aurelian had lived for only two years after his triumph. In that time he had done his best to "bring virtue back to Rome."

Backed by his troops, he had imposed a discipline as severe as that of his camps, and he had decreed a series of reforms.

He called in the old money and issued a new, stable currency.

He controlled the price of bread, and increased the free ration by an ounce, paying for it with new taxes in the East.

He launched a programme of public works, of which at the time of his death the deepening of the Tiber, the strengthening of its embankment, the city wall, and a new barracks in the Field of Agrippa were completed, and a new Forum at Ostia begun.

He had not been afraid to make war on all those interests which stood in the way of his "new Rome."

He made enemies of the Civil Service by the terrible punishments he meted out to corrupt officials.

He aroused the speculators against him by his severity to swindlers and profiteers.

He outraged the young men of fashion by banning a number of excessive luxuries and effeminate styles of men's clothing.

He antagonized the priests of all the established cults by building a magnificent Temple of the Sun in gratitude for his victories, which he decreed to be the supreme temple of Rome, for he wished to unify all the nations of the Empire with one universal religion and to combat with it the growing menace of Christianity.

Finally, he introduced a measure which was a declaration of war against all the dominant classes in Rome: the abolition of debts. For centuries an immense system of debt, going down through every class to the poorest hovels, had been the classic means by which a few Romans ordered the lives of the many who were in their power. Aurelian, who saw a new start for everybody as the foundation of a healthier economic life, was thus attacking with a single decree the heart of the political system; and, to set an example, he had the records of all debts to the state publicly burned in the Forum.

No one can make enemies so numerous and so powerful unless he has allies. Aurelian's troops could secure him against revolt, but not against conspiracy. The people? They cheered him for his gifts, but they were too rotten in their idleness to sustain him. He knew that there was no hope in them, and his policy was merely to keep them quiet with more and more bribes.

One project of his which died with him seems at first glance to be no more than this, a bribe to the mob. It was to institute a free daily ration of wine in Rome.

In fact, it was far more profound than this. It was his bid to plant new roots, truly new roots for Rome. He intended to turn thousands of square miles of neglected land in northern Italy over to vine culture. He intended to free thousands of slaves of barbarian origin and settle them on this land, as the beginning of a new human stock, the only human stock in which he saw any hope, which would provide Rome with the free farmers and the citizen-soldiers on whom a stable system could be based.

It was inevitable that he should die before he could carry out this plan. All-powerful though he seemed, he was alone and helpless in the face of all that he had roused against him, the will to death of a whole epoch.

While he was touring the camps in Asia Minor, his secretary Eros forged a document in Aurelian's name in which a number of officers, of whose secret vices and offences the secretary had become cognizant, were named as due for arrest and execution. Eros showed this to the officers who, that night, went to Aurelian's tent and killed him.

They, and Eros, were immediately hacked to death by the infuriated troops.

So simply did the times carry out their sentence upon the man who had challenged them.

No chain of conspiracy was ever laid bare between Rome and the embittered secretary. But it was remarked by those present in the house of Manlius Statianus, when the news of Aurelian's death arrived, that the now aged magnate showed no surprise.

*

"And you," Philomene said, "you will go the same way as he did, and I know you will."

Probus squeezed her round the waist, "I'll have a good time first, lass. I promise you that."

"Darling!" Philomene gripped his arm and turned a wheedling face up at him. "Why go away at all? Why don't you stay here with me? What's the use of all this silly fighting?"

"You wouldn't call it silly if you were on the frontiers, my sweet one. The savages are coming at us from all sides. You'd think there'd been no Aurelian at all. As soon as we stop them in one place they burst through at three others. One day there'll be too many of them, and too few of us, and our few will be in the wrong places, and then—"

"Oh, you're such a gloomy old thing! Look!" The city was a series of views framed between the flat-topped pines on the hillside. The straight ribbon of the Appian Way was alive with southbound traffic. Nearer, the Ostia road, which tonight would be jammed with wagons from the docks, was dotted with pedestrians on their way to the municipal swimming pool. It was one of those golden spring mornings when everything seems to sparkle and even the daily round of life goes past like a ballet. "Isn't it nice? Everything the same as it always was? You talk as if the end of the world was coming. You'd feel better if you spent more time here. Nobody in Rome worries. The shows are crowded, the shops are crowded, there've never been so many parties, everyone's talking about whether to go to Capri or the lakes this summer. Statianus says we're entering a new age of prosperity. The frontier's a long way off, darling. Stay here; everything's lovely here."

He did not answer. They leaned contentedly on the balustrade, taking in the peace of a spring morning. Philomene said, "She's the one who came out of the whole business best."

"Zenobia?"

"Yes. Every time I go to see her I marvel. You know, they call her the queen of Rome. There she is, with a private fortune, thanks to Aurelian, and a nice house at Tivoli. She's the most popular hostess in Rome. Whatever she wears becomes the fashion. There's hardly a man who matters who doesn't go and consult her about his affairs. She holds court as if she was still in Palmyra. She made up her mind to marry Julia into the best family in Rome, and she did. She made up her mind to article Wahab to the best lawyer in Rome, and she did. Those children are still the centre of everything for her, and do you know?—she put as much cunning and effort into getting them settled as she ever did into her wars. And I'm sure she got just as much satisfaction out of succeeding as she ever did out of a victory. I'm sure she's happy. I look at her sometimes to see if she is dreaming of the old days, if there's any discontent in her face. But she looks as calm and proud as ever. After all, when you come to think of it, she's got everything that she had before, only in a smaller size. That's the best of being a woman, darling. You'll turn the world upside down for what you want, but it could as well be a string of beads as a kingdom."

She turned around, leaning the small of her back on the balustrade, and in a mocking declamatory voice she read aloud the inscription at the base of the statue. "To the Emperor and Caesar—Lucius Domitius Aurelianus—Pious, Happy, and Unconquered—Augustus and Chief Pontiff—Named Gothicus, Germanicus, Parthicus and Carpicus—Tribune of the People—Five Times Consul—Thrice Hailed as Imperator—Proconsul—Father of His Country—Restorer of the World—A Most Brave and Victorious Leader—Prefect of the City—Faithful to the Divine Will and Majesty." She pulled a face at the statue. "A lot of good it has done you, Aurelian! You have an epitaph. She has all the best people to dinner. When will you men learn sense?"

AUTHOR'S NOTE

THE historical facts on which this novel are based may be found, in barest outline, in Chapter Eleven of Gibbon's *The Decline and Fall of the Roman Empire*. The story of Zenobia and Aurelian abounds in incidents so highly coloured that no writer would dare to invent them—for instance, the use of the giants at Emesa, the impersonation of Aurelian at Daphne, and the capture of Zenobia, which, although Aurelian did not accompany the pursuing squadron, did in fact take place when she had reached the bank of the Euphrates and was running to a boat. All these are mentioned in Gibbon or in my other main sources of this novel, which I list below. The suspicion that Zenobia instigated the murder of her husband, which Gibbon dismisses with the footnote "some unjust suspicions have been cast on Zenobia," is considered credible by Février. Pollio hints at it; but the fact that he, a Roman, does not dare to assert it outright may perhaps be evidence to support me in rejecting it.

Pollio quotes a remarkable letter that Aurelian sent to the Senate after he had defeated Zenobia. The vigour with which it is written surely reveals a considerable personal feeling for her. "I have heard, Conscript Fathers, that men are reproaching me for having performed an unmanly deed in leading Zenobia in triumph. But in truth those very persons who find fault with me would praise me in abundance did they know what manner of woman she is, how wise in counsels, how steadfast in plans, how firm towards the soldiers, how generous when necessity calls and how stern when discipline demands. I might even say that it was her doing that Odenathus defeated the

313

Persians. . . . Nor would I have spared her life had I not known that she did a great service to the Roman state when she preserved the Imperial power for herself or for her children. Therefore let those whom nothing pleases keep the venom of their tongues to themselves."

Augustan Histories (Flavius Vopiscus on Aurelian and Trebellius Pollio on Zenobia.) Vol. 3. Loeb. 1924.

Cambridge Ancient History, Vol. 12.

Eusebius, *Ecclesiastical History*. London, 1927.

Février, J. G., *Essai sur l'Histoire Politique et Economique de Palmyre.*

Homo, L., *Essai sur le Règne de l'Empereur Aurélien.* Paris, 1904.

Rostovtsev, M. L., *A History of the Ancient World* (Vol. 2). Oxford, 1926.

Starcky, J., *Palmyre.* Paris, 1941.

Zosimus, *The History of Count Zosimus.* London, 1814.

The only major characters in my story who are not historical figures are Maxin and Philomène. Such small embellishments as I have added to historical fact do not affect the main course of my story.

A. B.